Glor...
Beco...

Quade Wylde listen... felt the furious pounding of blood in his brain. He had spent two years getting her off his mind, two years burying himself in the wilderness, going where no man had dared. He tried to forget her. Nothing had worked. All the months, all the miles had brought him circling back to this place where it had all begun, to her . . .

ANDREA PARNELL
WILD GLORY

POPULAR LIBRARY

An Imprint of Warner Books, Inc.

A Warner Communications Company

POPULAR LIBRARY EDITION

Popular Library® and the fanciful P design are registered trademarks
of Warner Books, Inc.

Cover illustration by Tom Galasinski

Popular Library books are published by
Warner Books, Inc.
666 Fifth Avenue
New York, N.Y. 10103

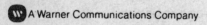 A Warner Communications Company

Printed in the United States of America

First Printing: April, 1990

10 9 8 7 6 5 4 3 2 1

This book is dedicated to Adele Leone
in appreciation of her friendship and support
and her belief in me.

CHAPTER

1

Massachusetts, 1690

Glory's wet footprints stayed a fleeting moment on the warm stones. The pace of her breathing quickened, half from excitement, half from fear. She was too far away from home, miles farther than she had permission to go. She had just crossed the river that was the unspoken boundary between her people and the remaining Indians near the township of Sealy Grove, Massachusetts. Skirts held high and blue eyes nervously alert, she scuttled into the gnarled brush at the base of a rocky hill.

Women in town whispered grim stories of the horrors captured females suffered at the hands of savages. Those tales came all too easily to Glory's mind as she crept through the wood. For a moment, when the hem of her linsey-woolsey petticoat snagged on a thorny bush, she hesitated and toyed with the thought of turning back, but the irreverent curiosity and daring that set Glory Warren so apart from other Puritan

1

girls took a firmer hold and wrestled her fears aside. Guided by a quiet inner voice that spoke more firmly than dread or danger, Glory, one hand clenched over her furiously pounding heart so that the weight might steady it, pressed on.

With the grace of a mountain cat, the lissome girl climbed from rock to rock. She gave no thought to the fact that she was indeed behaving more like an animal stalking prey than a girl tottering on the verge of womanhood. Given a choice she might have chosen the life of a wild feline over the fate given her. As many in Sealy Grove had pointed out, Glory Warren, tomboyish and with an appetite for excitement, hardly fit the mold of a Puritan maid. Much of the credit, or blame, could be laid on her late father. He had not viewed meekness as desirable in a woman.

"Speak up, girl," he would say to the sprightly youngster if ever she hung her head. "Stand your ground."

A rowdy Englishman who had fallen in love with a Puritan woman, Noble Warren had found it hard to yield to Puritan ideals. He indulged his young daughter with license to think and to question what life required of her. Perhaps his failing was that he lacked the vision to predict how an early taste of freedom might handicap such a girl when she no longer lived within the sturdy ring of his protection.

Glory's mind spun to thoughts of her father as she gained the top of the bluff and paused catlike to confirm that the ripple of noise she heard was that of human voices. The sounds were soft and rhythmic, like water lapping on stone. Just for a moment, Glory found herself swaying and stepping to the tempo of the haunting chant. When she was a small lass her father had taught her an Indian dance. Once she had been soundly scolded by one of the church elders for performing her dance on the meetinghouse grounds.

Glory smiled at the memory. Sometimes when she was

completely alone she still practiced the shuffling steps and turns. Now, however, was not a time for dancing. Now was the time to practice moving as soundlessly as a shadow. That too she had learned from her trapper father, as well as how to sit so quiet and still that woodland animals took no notice of her presence.

" 'Tis a gift, daughter, to gain their trust when 'tis given to few," Noble Warren had told her. "Do not abuse it and you will always have a friend at hand."

Her father's praise had encouraged Glory to hone her skills until in time she made pets of creatures who fled before any other. Deep in her mind was a secret belief the chanting savages would be no different should she encounter them. As for Noble Warren, she reasoned to her nagging conscience, were he still alive he might have led the way on this merry adventure.

Perhaps she was out of practice. A few pebbles rattled unexpectedly beneath her feet. Glory halted and held the warm cloud of her breath tight within her lungs. By a quick count she saw below a dozen braves, mostly old and wizened men, sitting in a rough circle on the sandy soil at the foot of the bluff. The oldest among them chanted and thumped the ground with carved and feather-laden sticks as others sharpened the blades of their hunting weapons. The clack of metal striking stone mixed and rose with the muffled voices.

Assured she had not alerted them, Glory freed her breath and noiselessly hoisted herself to the highest point of the rocky prominence. To her left stretched the new lodges of the small band. To her right lay shallows in the river where women sloshed water into clay jugs. Her nerves tingled beneath a coating of excitement and wonder that the Indians could not hear her every breath and heartbeat.

The sudden shrill shout of a rambunctious child splashing

water on his playmates tightened her nerves even more. Cautiously, she scrunched down as the added noise of women's laughter joined the excited screeches of the children in an eerie echo up the walls of the bluff.

She knew who they were—the Narraganset, a once mighty tribe nearly decimated sixteen years before in King Phillip's War, a bloody struggle which had also claimed the lives of almost a thousand colonists. Now a pitiful remnant of the Indian nation that once ruled these woods had banded together to reform the tribe. She wondered if they knew that the men in Sealy Grove already spoke gravely of the threat to the town. Burrell Collier, often vocal where Indians were concerned, had proposed that all able-bodied men make ready to smite these last of the Narraganset.

But what need for fighting if the Indians proved peaceful rather than warlike? In a moment she would know for herself which they were, these people who had once fought so ferociously to retain their lands, who had slaughtered and been slaughtered in years past.

With a flick of her fingers Glory tossed one tumbling black braid over her shoulder and edged out a bit more for a better view. Her white kerchief and cap, her shoes, and the basket of herbs she had been sent to gather were tied to the saddle of the mare tethered and grazing across the river. If Paddy, her pet crow, had minded, he would be perched in the branch of a tree near the mare, waiting for the return of his mistress.

It would not do to have Paddy here with his mischief and cawing. The crow was as talkative as the goodmen of Sealy Grove and she sometimes wondered if the bird did not know just as much. For several weeks the men had argued about the Narraganset. When she could she listened, but as far as she could tell no one from either side had actually seen the camp. She would be the first.

An insect buzzed around the bared shell of her ear. Glory reflexively swiped at it before realizing the move might be seen from below. When the pesky biting thing came back she acted more wisely, merely grimacing silently and covering her face until the bug relented and flew away. When she slid her fingers from her face and peered down once more, the women and children had grown quiet and the old men had ceased their chanting. The feathered heads bobbed slowly as the old braves mumbled among themselves. Glory shook hers ever so slowly. It was no wonder they had been defeated if a mere girl could slip upon them as easily as she had.

A sudden thought took away her disdain as she made ready to leave. Had she not counted twelve men at first glance? Now only ten sat in the circle. Lips drawn tightly together, she puzzled over the matter for a moment, then ignoring the inner voice that warned she was wrong, concluded she had misjudged on the first look. Her nerves had been more on edge then, a handful might have looked like a hundred. The problem was forgotten as she watched one brave, already round-shouldered with age, bend forward and draw lines in the dust. Her eyes strained to see the shape dexterously rendered by the aged hand. A religious symbol, she thought, the sign of one of their gods, one whose magic had failed to protect the people who believed in it.

Momentarily Glory's disappointment at being unable to make out clearly the swirl of lines turned to satisfaction that she had nevertheless accomplished what she'd come for. A slight but contented smile softened the firm line of her mouth. She had seen enough. The once-fierce Narraganset looked harmless, the braves mostly aging men, the children few, their weapons readied for hunting and not for war. The number of lodges indicated less than two dozen families and hardly enough young braves among them to constitute danger to Sealy Grove.

Unfortunately, she could not report her conclusions to anyone, so neither the Indians nor the townspeople would be better off for her having come. She dared not reveal to even her closest friend Sarah—the daughter of Burrell Collier—that she had crossed the river and spied on the Indians.

Glory's heart skipped a beat at the thought of the trouble she would be in should her mother learn of this breach of trust. Apprehension over that possibility chewed at the edges of her heart. What a shame trouble came in so many forms. She would have a batch of it for sure if she was late reaching home. Abruptly conscious she had tarried longer than intended, Glory sought to establish the hour. With all the caution of a wary woodsman she glanced about. From the fall of the shadows she determined that noon was but a few minutes away. She might just reach home at the appointed time if she hurried. Slithering back from the edge of the overhang, she prepared to spin about and start down the incline.

But she stopped short and glanced hurriedly back. Had one of the braves looked her way? Instinctively she peered in every direction, confirming that the escape route remained clear. Still, she felt a sudden prickling at the back of her neck and was overcome with a peculiar feeling that something was wrong. Though worried, her haste to leave did not prevent continued caution. Without so much as the patter of one bare foot she shimmied to the ground, surreptitiously eyed the path she had taken up, then started down it, taking care to remain behind a cover of brush until she reached the river.

Daring to breathe a loud sigh of relief, Glory held her dusty skirts up to her knees and stepped onto a rock at the water's edge. Though it was a sunny day in early spring the river was still wintry cold and she wished to cross as quickly as she could. She lowered her gaze to follow the staggered path of stones which made fording possible though the water was fairly deep at that spot.

"Mercy of God!" she cried, halting sharply on the second stone. A chill of fear ran the length of her as she stared into the deep, flowing river. From the clear, cold depths two pairs of black eyes set in distorted, dark-skinned faces stared back at her.

Glory's scream split the still air and sent a startled covey of quail bursting out of a nearby bush. Her heart pounded like an explosion of cannon fire against the walls of her chest. The skirt she had so carefully kept dry on her first crossing fell from her hands and dipped into the water.

Her thoughts raced. Had an attack begun? Had the Indians been caught on the wrong side of the river, been killed, and their bodies thrown in? She shivered anew as the bodies drifted nearer the rock, the current waving lifeless arms and legs not yet grown stiff. Glory whimpered as a bolt of dread shot through her girlish frame. Whoever had done this might still be near. Caught between them and the Indians she might be in as much danger as those who had recently lost their lives.

Using all the courage that remained within her, Glory gathered her wits, intent on dashing to the far bank and escaping. But no matter how hard she tried to move, her unwilling feet would not obey the command to hop to the next stone. Time seemed brought to a chilling halt by her fear, though in truth only a few seconds had passed since she spotted the braves beneath the water.

"Dead men," she mumbled, hoping the sound of her voice would calm her. "Dead men cannot hurt me." Her voice would have calmed no one; it had the sound of breaking glass. Her dry but terror-ridden eyes darted from bank to bank. No path but this one would lead her clear, this one that led past those bodies pitching beneath the blue-green waters.

Moaning her distress, she tried recalling that she had seen dead men before. Whatever reassurance she might have mustered in that way was lost in the rupturing sound of her own scream as hands shot from the water and snared her ankles. Fear, burning like a gush of hot oil in her veins jolted life back into frozen muscles, goading her to attempt to wrench free of the snaring hands. She succeeded in kicking one leg loose, but with the sudden move on the slick rocks her balance failed. Thrashing her arms and shouting for help, Glory plunged headlong into the cold river water.

The two braves who hauled her out were anything but dead. They effortlessly lifted the slight girl to their shoulders, though not before she had swallowed many mouthfuls of icy water and exhausted herself trying to break free. On the bank one brave clamped her ankles tight while the other grasped her outstretched arms.

Too frightened to open her eyes, Glory faced the thousand dreadful thoughts that poured into her mind. If she did not break loose, at least some of them would become realities. Pleading, screaming useless threats, she twisted and pulled against the iron grip of the braves until the effort left her drained and gasping for breath. Her lips were blue with cold, but when she could breathe freely she bit them until they were white as her blanched cheeks. Even the least horrible thing she had heard of what Indians did to captives was too ghastly to bear.

Moaning helplessly, Glory anticipated being scalped alive then slowly killed, or tortured and kept as a slave, or sold to a renegade Frenchman who would haul her up to Canada for some dread purpose.

"Free me!" Having regained a little of her strength, Glory shouted and twisted violently until the Indian who held her arms grabbed her hair and jerked back so hard her eyes sprang open. The pain was enough to quiet her struggles for good, but if it had not been, the reaction of the Indians, upon looking her in the face, would have served as well. The brave who held her hair stiffened and gave a cry of alarm. The other spoke rapidly, staring first at her face then at his companion. By the grim set of their mouths, neither was pleased with what he saw.

An argument broke out between the two. For a time Glory feared she would have her limbs ripped off as each pulled in a different direction. Finally one gave in to the other. He hastily tied a leather thong about her bruised ankles. The other bound her hands. A moment later she lay draped like a sack of corn across the stoutest one's shoulder, bouncing roughly as he carried her in the direction of the camp.

An arrow killed quietly. Crouched behind a cover of bushes, Quade Wylde reminded himself of that as he shifted his weight from one cramping leg to the other. The steel-eyed Indian hidden in the brush a few feet beyond hadn't moved a muscle in close to an hour, hadn't breathed as far as the trapper could tell.

Quade willed away the knotting pain in his calves. Sweat flowed in a tickling stream from brow to cheeks despite the cool air. The Indian, who seemed immune to discomfort, sat like a carved rock. Quade cursed himself for the challenge he had issued the old warrior. It wasn't the fact he had to beat the red man with his own weapon that bothered him; it was the long wait for the right shot.

Ahead and almost hidden by a full growth of new spring leaves, his quarry stirred and tested the wind for reassurance no danger lay ahead. Quade hoped the smell of his sweat had not overcome the animal scent smeared on his skin. The moment of truth came as the sound of cautious footsteps revealed the movement of the quarry toward him. Giving no more thought to discomfort, Quade pulled taut the slack string of his bow and felt the weight of the arrow poised for a silent and deadly flight.

A few more steps, he counted them with the thump of his pulse, and the range would be right to send the missile directly through the heart. Quade held his breath so the action of his lungs would not interfere with his aim. He still preferred his musket, he decided, even if it did blast a hole a moose could run through and announce his presence to every Indian and animal for a mile around.

Damnation, he muttered inside his head. The wrong one. He had misjudged. The other one, the one he wanted, would be moving off at an angle, probably circling behind him right now. Disappointed but determined, Quade corrected his aim and started to ease the grip that held the arrow fast in the bow. Maybe he could get this one and then the other. That ought to show the Indian what he was up against.

The instant came to free the arrow, but a sudden skittishness in his quarry caused Quade to instinctively tighten his fingers. The cause of the alarm, a fawn with the spots barely faded from his back, trotted up to the doe's side and nudged his nose beneath her belly. The nervous doe relaxed and returned to feeding on the tender leaves of a sapling. A few minutes later, as both deer ambled past, Quade's unused arrow rested in the quiver on his back.

Not far away he heard the crackle of brush and the heavy thud that indicated the Indian's arrow, unlike his, had found a mark.

"Fires of hell!" He rose and shook each leg in turn to

restore the faltering circulation. The deer would have been his first big kill with the bow and would have proved his worth to Tomanick. The hide would have provided the new shirt the women in the village had promised to sew for him. Prepared for a ribbing from the Narraganset sachem who had bested him in the hunt, and not for the first time, Quade hurried through the undergrowth to where Tomanick had already begun preparations for skinning a big buck.

Tomanick lifted jet black eyes to Quade, but instead of the expected boast gave a nod of approval that the trapper had held his shot.

"You take to our ways quickly, my friend," he said. Tomanick knew with pride the growing skill of this white man with the bow. He himself had taught Quade Wylde to use the red man's weapon. It pleased him to see his friend also use the red man's thinking. He pulled his arrow from the buck's flesh. "To kill the doe now is to lose next year's meat."

"Tell that to an empty belly." Quade slipped the straps of the quiver from his shoulder and dropped it to the ground. Two more Narraganset braves appeared, moving without sound through the heavy brush and the litter of dry twigs on the forest floor. The pair joined in the skinning and in a matter of minutes had the hide off and the carcass strung up for butchering. Tomanick promised the hide to the braves and left them to complete the work as he and Quade walked to a small stream.

"A Narraganset never goes hungry." Tomanick knelt at the water's edge and washed the smears of blood from his hands.

Quade shrugged. "I prefer hunger to some of what you call food." He was glad one of them had made a kill. Despite years spent living in the wild he hadn't developed a taste for what the Indians often substituted for meat. Roots or leaves or even insects that the Indians found edible still turned his stomach. *Nookick*, the ground, parched corn that could sustain a man with just a few bites a day, he could tolerate well enough, but if he had a weakness as a woodsman, it was his craving for cooking better than his own.

"The white man is too choosy." Tomanick rinsed his knife and wiped the blade dry. "That will be his downfall. When what he likes is gone from the land he will go away. Then my people will take back what is theirs."

Quade opened his mouth to correct the sachem but changed his mind and kept quiet. From experience he knew the warrior would not accept his words. Being too choosy would not be the white man's downfall; it would be his path to success. The settlers and soldiers who had nearly destroyed the Narraganset tribe would not stop pushing into the forest and chopping down trees to make new fields. They wouldn't stop killing Indians they couldn't convert and they wouldn't go away. Trappers like him wouldn't stop coming and taking the beaver and fox, and most of them wouldn't worry about whether or not an animal had young before they killed it.

Tomanick, however, needed his dream that the Narraganset would someday reclaim the lands that had once been theirs. He was happier believing his people would again become a large and mighty nation. If the fact that only a handful of his tribe had survived the carnage of King Phillip's War could not sway him, Quade knew nothing he said would either.

"We will eat well tonight," Tomanick remarked as the signal came that meat was ready to be taken to the village for cooking.

Quade nodded and fell in line with the braves as they led the way to the bend in the river where Tomanick's people made camp. The choice of the site was another matter on which he and the Indian disagreed. Sealy Grove was only a dozen miles away and as in every settlement, some men there would believe it their duty to rid the world of savages. He doubted if the small band of Narraganset would be left undisturbed for long.

Before the hunters reached the village the sound of a commotion within it reached them. Quade considered that those left behind might have come under attack, but as he drew nearer it was evident that only one English voice was responsible for all the disturbance. Women, children, and braves stood gathered in bewilderment around a black-haired Puritan girl who, though tied at wrists and ankles, demanded in no uncertain terms they set her free. What astonished Quade most was that the lot of them, even the worthy braves, seemed in awe of the girl.

Glory Warren's eyes fell on the group approaching the village and she knew a moment of hope. One among them wore a lush black beard and was assuredly not an Indian.

"You there," she cried to the man who towered a head above the savages. Heaving for breath, she raised her hands to show the bonds. "Tell them to set me free."

"And why should I do that?" The trapper, garbed as the savages in fringed buckskins, though devoid of feathers, parted a path through those clustered around the girl. She was a sight to behold—chin held high, arms uplifted, a woman-child who faced the Indians with bold impudence rather than trembling and cowering before them.

Her beauty stole his breath and for a time he stood and stared, recalling the long space of time since he had seen or held a woman of his own kind. Aware he might have this one if he so chose, he allowed his senses to play out what he might do with so lovely a female. A stab of regret pained him, a pointed reminder that he was not totally uncivilized, decidedly not enough to bend an unwilling woman to his will.

The trace of a smile on his lips mocked the adjustment of his thoughts. The girl bore his lengthy perusal with surprising patience or else needed time to consider a reply to his crusty remark. Still uncertain of what was best done with her, he made no haste to pull his eyes away. She was worthy of a long look.

Ebony hair as dark as any savage's hung to her waist in loose, luxuriant braids. The cords that had held the ends secure had been lost. Here and there a strand had worked free and lay in a damp abandon of curls against her neck and shoulders. As he observed the twists and turns of black silk he had the urge to free the whole of it and see how the dark masses would shine in the afternoon light.

Her skin was as tempting. She was no milk white English maid who looked as if she had grown without the benefit of the sun. Some Spaniard had cut a notch in the family tree and the subtle proof of it glowed in the honey and cream color of the girl's skin. A steady glance at the fine-boned face revealed what it was about her that had the village mesmerized. Black-lashed eyes of an oddly crystalline blue sparkled as if they emitted a mystic light of their own. He had the strange feeling, as he suspected the Indians did, that if he looked into them long enough he might be set afire.

Glory's patience gave way as she waited for the man to come to his senses. She found her tongue. "Because you are English and because you ought to," she snapped, angry to find the Englishman as impossible to deal with as the Indians. She had not been mistreated other than being hauled to the village and put on public view. She'd concluded she was not to be scalped or tortured and that the Indians were as alarmed at having her among them as she was to be there, but not a single one could or would speak to her in words she could understand. For an hour they had stood and stared at each other. She'd had enough of it.

Quade laughed at this second display of spunk, though he detected in the tremble felt when he caught hold of her bound hands that it might soon run out. Still chuckling, he pulled a broad-bladed knife from a leather scabbard strapped to his side. The steel blade gleamed a threat as he tested the tip with his fingers.

"I am not so English as you think and I do little I ought to." His dark eyes met the angry heat of hers for a moment, then he turned aside to speak to Tomanick and those on his council. Receiving a nod of approval he wheeled back to the girl. "What's in it for me if I cut you free?" he taunted.

"Cut me loose and find out," she returned, shooting a challenging glance at the trapper.

Quade laughed. She was as feisty as a badger. What Puritan household had fostered one such as this?

The girl hardly flinched when he raised the knife and sliced the tight leather thongs. As he knelt to cut through those binding her ankles she stood quietly and rubbed her wrists. The sodden hem of her skirts brushed his hands. He pushed it aside and uncovered the slim ankles above a dainty pair of bare feet. Her skin beneath his fingers was like cool, smooth satin. Intrigued by the sensual feel of it, he obligingly massaged the reddened flesh where the thongs had been, well aware his fingers lingered longer than required.

"Don't try to run," he warned without looking up. "They will catch you."

"I won't run."

Glory shuddered at the feel of his warm fingertips against her skin. At sixteen she was unaccustomed to a man's touch.

The Indians, when they caught her, had bound her with a methodical and impersonal quickness. She had thought only of escape as their hands moved on her limbs. Immediately she was aware of a difference in the way the trapper's hands felt, though only vaguely aware the difference might constitute an entirely new danger.

Quade stood, taking another long, slow look at the girl. Rose pink lips were slightly parted, the cheeks flushed, the slender fingers laced together prayerlike. The simple dress of deep gray kersey, rather than minimizing, served to emphasize her beauty. And those curious blue eyes would always set her apart. She was younger than he had first observed, more child than woman, but the wet clothing defining the pleasing contours of her body revealed that it would not be long until she was as much a woman as any man had ever seen.

Glory forced herself to think logically. This man, though white, could be friend or foe. She had agreed she would not run but mentally measured the distance along the narrow footpath to the river crossing. She was quick on her feet and had always been capable of outrunning every lad in Sealy Grove. A comparative look at the lean-limbed savages soon brought her to the conclusion that she would not have the same advantage against them. Little choice was left to her but to stay at the trapper's side and try to win his assistance.

"You have got yourself in quite a fix." Quade made his voice deliberately gruff. The girl needed a lesson if she was prone to ramble alone where she had no business.

"Aye," she agreed meekly, though the look on her face showed far more mettle.

Quade smiled. He had heard enough from the braves who captured her to discern they had taken the Puritan girl by mistake. One of them had spotted her on the bluff overlooking the camp and, seeing her black braids, believed her a runaway Indian servant from the town. Ever mindful that her presence might be a trick, two braves had waited at the river until they were sure she was alone, hiding beneath the surface when she drew near. Only after they had her in hand and saw her brilliant blue eyes had they realized their error. At that point they were afraid to let her go for fear she would immediately send men from Sealy Grove to punish them.

"I meant no harm," she said, her voice a breathless rush, at last revealing a trace of alarm over her predicament. "I only wanted to see these Narraganset. Please." She lifted the startling eyes to him. "I must get home."

The trapper wrinkled his brows together and spoke brusquely. He believed she had no idea what she had unleashed. "To send your father and others back to slaughter a people who want only to live and hunt in peace?"

He stared menacingly down at her. He was a good foot taller, his dark hair long and thick beneath a fur cap. His eyes were a deep brown and he looked as untamed as one of the Indians. Glory shuddered but kept her eyes locked with his. Somewhere deep in the folds of her mind she uncovered a memory of having seen the man before. The recollection was dim and she had no inkling whether her mind was playing a trick or if they had actually crossed paths.

"No." In her desperation to win him to her present cause she clutched his shirtfront. "I would not. My father is dead. There is only my mother and myself and I pray she will never know I came here."

Quade sighed heavily and felt his worries tumble away. He believed the girl, swayed partly by the pleasure of being near her when he had not seen a white woman for months. There was also the truth he saw in her face. The latter he decided to put his trust in. A man who lived by his wits as did Quade Wylde depended on the ability to judge a face. As a trapper, almost every face he saw was that of a stranger. His life often depended on an instant assessment of character.

The girl, reading his expression, released her hold on his garment. Again Quade turned aside to confer with the Indians in their language. Those who had remained to listen to the exchange between trapper and captive now left to go about their business, satisfied a trusted friend would find a solution to their plight.

"They thought you an Indian, a runaway who wanted to join them." To emphasize his explanation, Quade lifted the long braids from her shoulders. "From a distance this hair would fool anyone," he said. The dark, damp braids, half-loosened, curled around his hands. He was not conscious that he wove his fingers into the soft, flowing tresses as he talked.

Glory's eyes widened. She was aware her appearance differed from that of other girls in the settlement. Her skin kept a sun-burnished hue no matter how hard she scrubbed when she bathed; she had been teased about her eyes and often wished they were gray-blue or hazel like those of most living in Sealy Grove. To be mistaken for an Indian by Indians was, nevertheless, disconcerting.

She took a step back from the tall trapper, pulling her hair free of his large hands. As she did a small shiver ran over her flesh. Until now she had been too worried to realize she was both cold and wet; suddenly she was acutely conscious of the chill. She crossed her arms over her chest to ward it off.

The chill, however, did not dull her spirit, and she huffed her opinion of his story. "When they knew I was not Indian they might have let me go." The present danger having lessened, Glory had in mind the trouble she was yet to encounter at home.

"As I said before, you have got yourself in a quite a fix." He closed the short distance between them, giving her no room to break and run. Though he believed the girl sincere, he could not be certain what others would do when they heard her story. "How can the Narraganset be sure you will not bring harm?"

Her eyes widened and the brightness of them magnified. "I give my word, my pledge. I will tell no one."

"Your word?" Even if she meant what she said she might forget the promise when asked to account for her time.

"My word is good. I do not lie." She trembled and began rubbing her arms for warmth.

He leered down at her, the set of his mouth stern, the white teeth flashing against the black of his beard. "And if your mother asks where you have been, what will you say?"

The little confidence she held faded and she feared she had not swayed him her way at all.

"I would tell her . . ." She saw her predicament and deliberated a moment. Apparently the Indians trusted this man. If she could convince him there would be no retaliation for her capture he would undoubtedly convince the Narraganset to let her go. Her voice broke, then gained strength. "I—I would say I fell in the river, which is true if not all the truth."

Quade looked over his shoulder at Tomanick who squatted at the front of one of the lodges. Glory prayed the words traded were in her favor and that soon she would be allowed to leave. Meanwhile, she deemed it wise to stay put when the trapper walked off. She stood quietly and kept her eyes on the ground until he returned shortly, carrying a crudely woven blanket which he draped over her shoulders.

"I'll take you home," he said, and for the first time she heard a trace of tenderness in his voice.

Glory pulled the blanket loosely around her as the trapper led her away from the village. She walked at his side only a moment before her bright eyes turned dark with a new concern. She could foresee her mother accepting the tale of falling in the river. But her mother was no simpleton. Glory could not imagine how she would explain the trapper's presence to Maudie Lair Warren.

She stopped and faced him. "If you will escort me to the river I can go the rest of the way alone," she said firmly.

"No," Quade responded just as firmly and touched his palm to her back to start her moving again. "I'll see you to your home."

Glory drew in a deep breath then expelled it slowly. "You want to be sure I keep my word."

The trapper nodded. "Perhaps. Or perhaps I have a yearning for a meal from an English kitchen."

Taken aback, Glory realized she had been thinking only of her predicament and of herself. She did owe this stranger a debt of gratitude now that he had persuaded the Indians to let her go.

She swallowed hard. "My apologies," she said, as they walked toward the river. "It was not my intent to be thoughtless or rude. I owe you much—my freedom, perhaps my life. You are welcome in our house and at our table."

Quade nodded. He liked this girl. Any other in her circumstances might have given way to quivering hysterics. Of course, he considered, a girl of that disposition would not have come out spying on a camp of Indians.

Before they were a great distance from the lodges Glory stopped a second time without warning. Quade came close to treading on her heels as he pulled up short behind her.

"Is something wrong?" he asked, suspecting she had injured a foot on the sharp stones or briars.

She pointed to the Indians, many of whom stood in a group watching the pair walk away. "Tell them . . . tell them I am grateful they let me go," she insisted.

Quade relayed her message and got a lively reaction, much waving of arms, and then a shout from Tomanick. "They have given you a name," he told her.

"A name? Why?"

"You seem to have made a strong impression. I half think they would have liked you to be Indian."

Glory shuddered. She found the Narraganset interesting but their way of life hardly measured up to the comfortable existence she knew with her mother on the Warren farm. Nor had she any plans to cross the river on more clandestine missions.

Quade scratched his beard and watched her face as if following her quick thoughts. "Had I had not been among them you might be getting used to their name for you."

Her curiosity, having been suppressed for several hours, began to make itself known again. "What is the name?" she asked.

"Firefly." He laughed and spun her about as they reached the riverbank. The girlish expression had given way to a woman's look; his body responded in kind. "A name well chosen," he said. "I see the reasoning. 'Tis a legend among them that fireflies are the spirits of their dead. When they are pleased, they visit the earth at dusk." His large hands rested on her blanketed shoulders, and his thumbs splayed over her collarbones. His mind fought to forget he was a civilized man. His voice took on a husky tone. "The same light is in your eyes, the glow of fireflies at twilight."

Glory smiled. The story pleased her. She liked the trapper. At least she thought she did. He was pleasant and lighthearted, not at all like the somber goodmen in Sealy Grove. She couldn't see much of his face to say if it was comely or not. It was mostly covered by the heavy beard. His voice and carriage were that of a young man. She could not quite pin-point what there was about him that made her fidgety. Her experience had proved him fair in his dealings. What she did know was that when he looked directly into her eyes as he was doing now, she felt a curious tingling even stronger than that she had felt when she feared being discovered by the Narraganset.

"Did they give you a name too?" Glory broke the contact between them and hopped to the first rock at the fording spot, making certain this time no braves lurked beneath the water.

Quade sighed as she ambled away. "They call me friend."

"And so do I." Glory tossed the words over her shoulder as she hopped lithely from rock to rock. Quade followed a pace behind, his eyes set on the sway of her hips as she moved ahead of him. When she stepped on a corner of the blanket and tottered he was there to catch her in his arms.

"One dousing a day is enough," he said as he swept her up and delivered her to the far bank.

Glory had enough of the child in her to think of being car-ried in a man's arms as merely a convenience for crossing the river. Quade had nothing of the child about him and soon re-alized he had made a mistake. She was pretty and warm and in his arms felt more woman than girl. He wondered if some farm boy had already stolen kisses from her or if her lips were untouched and he might by chance be the first to taste them.

"My horse is there." She indicated a clearing where a bay mare stood hobbled and grazing. Overhead a blue-black crow cawed and circled then swooped to light on the girl's shoulder. "Ha!" she cried as the bird affectionately rubbed its head against her chin. "Happy to see Glory Warren, are you?"

"Glory Warren?" Quade roughly swung the girl to her

feet and stepped back, deliberately putting distance between them. "Of what family?" he asked.

"My father was Noble Warren, once a trapper like yourself," she said, plopping down on a rock to slip on her hose and shoes. "As fine a man as ever lived," she went on.

"That I know well," the trapper said, thanking fate he had not done what had been on his mind. Noble Warren had once taken an orphan boy under his wing and taught him the skills of trapping and the ways of survival in the woods. He owed not only his livelihood but on many counts his life to this girl's father.

"You knew him?"

"As well as I have known any man. You might have heard him speak of Quade Wylde. Two years we worked hand in hand. Goody Warren I know too. And you, if you are the same black-haired child who played at her knee." He could hardly believe the little mite with flashing eyes had grown into such a beauty. But he did not tell her that. "Is your mother well?" he asked instead.

"Aye," Glory smiled. Quade Wylde was a name she knew and had often heard her father mention with affection. But the Quade Wylde she remembered had been but a youth, not this imposing, bearded man. She recalled vividly a long-ago ride on shoulders not nearly so broad as those she now looked on. Nonetheless it pleased her that this same Quade Wylde was the one who had intervened with the Indians and effected her rescue.

She was also pleased that she would not have to stretch the truth too far in bringing a stranger home for supper. Her mother would be happy to extend hospitality to Quade Wylde.

What she could not understand was why, when she suggested he swing up behind the saddle and ride with her, the trapper chose to walk.

CHAPTER
2

"So you have had your first swim of the season." As Maudie Lair Warren had surmised between worries, her daughter returned home little worse for the wear, if somewhat bedraggled and long overdue.

"Not by choice, Mother," Glory offered. "Was an act of fate that got me soaked. I would have picked a warmer day for a dunking." She pulled the bay mare to a stop and hurriedly slid to the ground. Before her mother had a chance to bombard her with questions, Glory reeled about and pointed to the break in the tree line where she had purposely kicked her mount into a trot, leaving the trapper to follow at his slower pace. "See who I have brought home. 'Tis Quade Wylde come to share our supper."

Maudie Lair shielded her eyes against the sun and peered at the approaching form. She knew the walk, the confident, easy gait of her husband's young protégé. Soon the trapper grew near enough that his face, too, was discernible. She lifted her hand in salute. Quade responded with a like gesture.

At the same time a quiet smile of understanding appeared on Maudie Lair's face; Glory's deft change of topic had not passed by her mother unnoticed.

Maudie Lair glanced up to see Glory's somewhat anxious face relax into a smile. Her daughter must have guessed she would not press for explanations under these circumstances. And she was right. It was enough to know whatever mishap had befallen the girl had done no lasting harm. She was accustomed to Glory's youthful antics, and indulged them, disregarding the mothers who warned she would rue her leniency with the girl. She did not see how that could be. More often than not she was gladdened by Glory's energetic and imaginative capers and looked with sadness on the time she would need to restrict her frolicsome ways to the proper acts expected of a young woman.

That time was not yet upon her. At present Glory looked like an untidy child fresh out of a mud hole. Perhaps she was due a reminder of her age, but as the words came to the tip of her tongue Maudie Lair changed her mind and again postponed curbing Glory's exuberance. Life in Sealy Grove was solemn at the best of times. Since the death of her father five years before, Glory was the only source of joy in her mother's life. Maudie Lair could not find it in her heart to quell the lively nature God had given her daughter.

The trapper drew near, a smile beaming from his face. With animal quickness he slung the rolled pack from his back and spread his arms wide.

"Welcome, Quade Wylde." Maudie Lair hugged the young man as best she could within the tight enclosure of his strong arms. His manner and the buckskin garb of a woodsman reminded Maudie Lair of her beloved Noble. How many times she had stood in the same place and waited for Noble to appear on the winding footpath following a hunt. When tears threatened to flood from her eyes she willed them away and brought out a fond smile for Quade. "You have been too long absent from our home," she told him.

"That I have," Quade agreed as, still locked within Maudie Lair's embrace, he surveyed the Warren house. It was as he remembered and a welcome sight after more than three years in the wilderness. A four-gabled roof topped the stout structure. At the juncture of the second story an overhang extended over the squared bottom floor. Windows with panes latticed in diamond shapes sat symmetrically in each unpainted side wall. Heavy wood shutters and a sturdy set of brass-banded doors protected the first floor from entry by any but invited visitors.

The garden was neat, the shrubs trimmed. Lining the entrance walk were the broad-fanned blades of rows of irises, regal blooms of purple, yellow, and pure white perched on tall green stems.

An air of peaceful domesticity hung in a pleasant cloud all around. Here a man need not constantly look over his shoulder or measure every sound for the danger it might signal. Here a man might sit by his fire and light a pipe and close his eyes in contentment. Briefly the smile left his face as the unexpected range of his thoughts perplexed him. He had been sure he had no need of such comforts as the Warren farm afforded a man; a desire for adventure and a life unrestricted by the bothersome rules of his fellow men fueled his blood. He was surprised that the prospect of a hot bath, a soft bed, and the company of dear friends sat so agreeably in his mind.

When the hugging was done and each needed a breath of air, Maudie Lair paced back but left her hands braced against the young man's chest. Once she had thought of this lad as she might a son. It was good to know the feeling had not changed for either of them.

"After so long I thought you had forgotten the way here," she gently chided. "What brings you to us now?"

"A promise and the push of my conscience," he replied, wrapping her weathered hands with larger, callused ones. In the mother's gentle face lingered faint traces of the beauty she had bestowed on the girl. She was a small woman, her skin lined by the passage of twoscore and seven years. Streaks of gray lightened once-dark hair. Her eyes were a faded blue, but had a luminous quality which must have once been as enchanting as the girl's.

Glory had been born to Noble and Maudie Lair Warren late in life and long after they had given up hope of having a child. That Quade knew from spending long nights around a campfire with his friend and hearing of the happiness wife and daughter had brought Noble. The love expressed had awed Quade, for it had been heartfelt and not simply the outgrowth of duty such as a man generally felt for spouse and children.

Only one other married pair Quade knew had felt as warmly toward one another; his parents had been as affectionately stricken. Orphaned and indentured by his twelfth birthday, however, Quade had long been without family bonds and wanted no part of them again.

Friendship had proved another matter for the young trapper. When Noble Warren had come across a runaway cooper's servant in the woods he had not even considered dragging the boy back to his master. Noble had proven a true friend and had believed a hapless boy's story of having been indentured against his will. He had pleaded with Quade to come and live with his family.

Quade refused and Noble accepted the young man's stand without question. Rather than lecturing or warning a very green would-be trapper away from the wilderness, Noble taught the youth all he needed to know to survive. When Quade lived through that first winter alone, Noble Warren rejoiced in the accomplishment along with him.

" 'Tis your life, son, to make and use as you will. Make it good, make it full. That's all a man owes anyone.''

Quade recalled the words of advice from Noble. Noble had given his love and shared his wisdom with a boy he hardly knew. He asked nothing in return except that Quade keep an eye out for his family should any misfortune ever befall him. The request had come the last season they spent together and had been spoken over a smoldering fire following a brush with death. Had that encounter been an omen? Quade wondered.

He and Noble had hidden a store of "made" beaver, prime pelts. On returning at sundown they had come upon three Indians packing the furs onto a sled. A fight broke out over who the furs belonged to. Outnumbered, somehow he and Noble had rousted the Indians, though he still wore a jagged scar on one shoulder and Noble had been left unconscious for a time.

That night as he bandaged Noble Warren's head they counted their blessings and their pelts and Noble had made him pledge to look after wife and child. Neither man had guessed Noble would-not live another year, nor that through a strange crook of fate, a fever, not a savage's ax or arrow, would take the robust Noble Warren.

Quade supposed if he had ever loved anyone since his mother and father, it was Noble Warren. As he stood face-to-face with Maudie Lair and Glory he renewed the pledge he had made nearly six years ago.

"I swore were he ever taken I would see you and the girl through any trouble that came upon you. I have been remiss in making good on my word." His eyes swept over the two of them. Maudie Lair noted the tenderness in the gaze as it passed over her daughter.

"You have no need for reproach," she assured him. "Had we been in need I would have sent for you. As it is Glory and I have seen no trouble and have all we desire. The house is solid, the farm prospers, we are in good health."

As Glory hung back and listened, her interest in the trapper grew keener. Remembered tidbits of earlier visits floated into her mind, though they were colored with the distractions of childhood. She recalled her happiness over a patient youth who bounced her on his knee and indulged her in games he must have found trying at his age. She had sought him out then, longed for his infrequent visits. The last had been when she was scarcely ten, for her father's burial.

A small and unnoticed sigh slipped from her lips. She regretted there was so little else of Quade Wylde to call from her treasure chest of memories. In earlier years when he visited her parents she must have often been tucked away in her cradle or crib. Tonight that would not be the case. She hoped he had news from other parts. Had he been to Boston or other of the colonies? Hardly anything of interest happened in Sealy Grove. She hoped her mother had finished the churning and started supper early and there would not be a long wait before the three of them sat around the plank table in the kitchen for a long evening of talk and reminiscences.

"I'll put the horse away, Mother." Glory unhooked from the saddle straps the basket brimming with green leaves and stalks of cowslip, boneset, birthwort, and the other herbs she had searched out. She passed the basket to her mother and clucked the horse to a slow walk toward the barn.

Since the mare needed no guidance, Glory twisted her neck for a backward look at Quade as she rode away. She much preferred staying so that she would miss nothing of the present conversation, but two factors dictated that she not put off unsaddling and feeding the mare. The first was a wish that her mother would become so distracted by the unexpected return of a friend that she would forget to ask how a harmless fall in the river had made her daughter excessively late.

The second factor was Glory's love of the mare, and all animals for that matter. Until the horse had been given a rubdown and a measure of grain she could not think of her own comfort or whims.

Quade refused to enter the house until he had bathed, though if he smelled Glory had not noticed it. Even though it meant a longer wait for supper, she willingly helped carry kettles of steaming water from the kitchen to fill the round wooden washtub in the barn. She enjoyed frequent soaks in a tub and was glad she and her mother could offer such a comfort to a guest. When the last kettle of hot water was poured, Glory tested the temperature while Quade sat on a barrel untying the laces that held his leggings secure.

"Mother sent the pine soap and Father's strop and razor." Glory gestured to the shaving implements and a moss-colored cake of soap lying on the folded linen bath sheet she had draped across a keg.

Quade tilted his head in acknowledgment. His leggings were loose but he held off removing any of his clothing until the girl finished what she was about. He did not wish to offend her by being overly bold, though he knew it customary in many households for the women to see to the bodily comfort of a guest.

He smiled to himself and made a note that should he ever have a wife or daughter they would not attend *too* closely to the needs of another, whether friend or stranger. As for him, he was content to sit and watch Glory as she made a ceremony of crushing an aromatic mixture of dried herbs into the bath-water. A pungent and refreshing scent rose up in the wisps of steam.

"Will soothe your muscles," she said as she brushed the last shreds of it from her hands. Nothing else was left to do and her own tub waited in the kitchen. She could not imagine why instead of leaving Quade in privacy for his bath she toyed with the hem of her apron and awkwardly searched her mind for something to say.

Lest she look foolish standing idle, Glory smoothed a min-iscule wrinkle from the towel, then repositioned the soap and razor. Her mother was noted for her skills in both soap making and medicine brewing. Glory debated telling Quade of the exceptional quality of the fragrant soap she had set out for him, but held back. Such a comment sounded trite even to her. What did a trapper care about soaps when most of the time his bath was a splash of water from a stream?

In the glow of afternoon light streaming through the open barn doors Glory looked as fresh and pretty as the first flowers of spring. He wondered if it was his inexperience with chil-dren that had left him so unprepared for what Noble's young daughter had become. Could this lovely girl who made a man's breath hang in his throat be the same sunny-faced child he had once jiggled on his knee?

Smiling, he thanked the heavens she was still much a child at sixteen. Most girls did not wed until past nineteen or twenty. Just briefly he considered that if she were older and her mother prepared to give her to a husband, he could be tempted to give up his roving ways and become a farmer or a barrel maker and one of the goodmen of Sealy Grove.

Before he could find any enjoyment in what he enter-tained, a bitter memory lashed back and spoiled the con-templation. The pleasant image fled, like dry leaves before a surge of winter wind. Unwillingly he was swept along by the harsh wind to the time of his service in the household of the cooper Avery Fisk. The shadow of Fisk's rod seemed to hover over his back. The shrewish bark of Goodwife Fisk's voice grated in his ears; the remembered taunts of the Fisk children tightened his jaw. Such family "bliss" had sent him fleeing to the wilderness where he might be free of "loving" bonds.

His long, trail-hard body tensed. Nay. To be bound to another, though it be with satin ties, was not for him. Free he would stay. Not even for a sweet creature like Glory Warren would he change his ways. He lacked the temperament for staying home and she deserved a husband whose disposition matched her own. Annoyed by the ache of memories and the rambling thoughts that had brought them about, Quade sprang to his feet, unaware the scowl on his face would have sent a bear flying.

Glory knew she should have left minutes earlier and believed his scowl bespoke impatience at the delay of his bath. She wasted no time crossing the ground between the barn and the house nor in climbing into the wooden hip tub near the stone fireplace in the kitchen.

She completely forgot to add any of the herbal mixture to her own bathwater. On a normal evening she would have stayed at her ablutions until the water cooled unbearably or until her skin wrinkled like sun-dried apples. Tonight she washed without dawdling, then quickly fled to her room for clean clothes, and had time to help her mother finish the supper before a gentle tap sounded at the kitchen door.

Thinking that he might still be perturbed with her, Glory hesitated to rise from her stool at the fireside, hoping her mother would hasten to the door before her. When a second knock sounded Maudie Lair looked up from stirring the contents of an iron pot hung from a trammel over the banked and glowing coals.

Tansy, the black and white cat asleep on the hearth, flicked her tail and slitted a green eye to see why her mistress had not attended to the disturbance at once. The message from both was clearly given. Glory swiftly went to her duty and opened the door to invite Quade inside. At the sight of him she immediately forgot her reservations.

Her chin quivered once and dipped nearly to her chest. What the beard had obscured seized her attention. The clean-shaven face was rakishly handsome, the mouth turned in a moody, sensual curve. The nose was straight, the line of his jaw strong and firm. The dark eyes contained a glint of gold she had missed before.

Her eyes roamed unchecked. A subtle, familiar trace of the youth she recalled still remained, but the transition to manhood had wrought a noteworthy change. The look was one of quiet power, of a man who knew his strengths and weaknesses and who relied on that knowledge to stay alive. His smile was one of warmth and confidence, but it made Glory as giddy as if she had sampled the wine her mother kept in the cupboard.

Maudie Lair had lent him a shirt of sun-bleached linen which had belonged to her father. The pristine garment dispelled the savage air of the buckskin-clad trapper who had followed her to the farm. With his dark hair damp and clean, combed back and tidily bound in a queue, he needed only a fine doublet to take his place among any gathering of gentlemen.

"Will you gawk or bring Quade in?" Maudie Lair teased her astonished daughter. She did believe the girl was befuddled by the trapper; generally she was all talk and questions when a visitor came. Was Glory finally developing womanly interests in the opposite sex? If so, she could see why Quade would catch her eye. He had been a handsome lad but, unlike some whose looks peaked early, his had grown more pronounced and comely with the years.

"Please join us." Glory recovered in a moment, despite the flutter that stayed awhile longer in her stomach. She led Quade to the table where a pair of bayberry candles burned in place of the usual rushlights. Three poplar-wood trenchers had been set out on the lockram board-cloth and with each a pewter mug, two of them filled with brew from Maudie Lair's beer barrel, the other with fresh goat's milk.

The fieldstone fireplace made one end of the room. The heat was not unpleasant since the night had grown cool; the rosy light danced lively on the shiny surfaces of pottery and tinware shelved around the walls. Various kettles and pots steamed appealingly from above the firedogs. A brick oven was built into the high stone wall. From the iron-latched doors the aroma of baking bread whirled out and filled the air and made Quade's mouth water.

He breathed heavily, drawing in the appetizing scents. He had not realized his hunger and yearning for well-prepared food to be so keen. When Maudie Lair immediately set about removing a crusty brown loaf from the oven and spreading the table with half a dozen or more covered pots, she did not have to ask him twice to take a seat.

"You cannot know how I have longed for a meal such as this." He spread a napkin over the borrowed shirt, then ate heartily of the sausage and boiled meat cooked with carrots and turnips and the special spices Maudie Lair added to dishes. Most of all he savored the fresh-baked bread, sliced and spread with new-churned butter. He made room too for the apples stewed with honey, though all the while protesting he was as stuffed as a buck in a gooseberry grove.

Glory, whose appetite was usually good, picked at her food and ate only a few mouthfuls during the supper hour. She had no lack of questions and plied Quade with requests for an accounting of his travels since last he had visited the Warren farm. Several times she found herself wishing she was not ten years younger than he. Had she been older when he visited in those days, she would not have been put to bed early while her father and mother and Quade sat up and talked of fascinating things.

"I have been both north and south," he answered. "North as far as Canada where the trapping is good but the winter hard. The Bay Company is taking the whole of it there and as I lean now, I'll go back and be a Bay man this winter and next." Quade pushed his empty trencher aside and pulled the linen napkin from his chest. "Don't find it easy to stay in one place and as long as the trapping's good there's no reason to," he added. "Last year saw me a good store of furs and a sharp profit on the trade." Smiling, he accepted a refill of beer from the wooden pitcher, then savored a slow drink of the bitter brew. "With a few coins in my pocket and plenty of shot and gunpowder in my pack, I joined the Narraganset and turned south."

Quade paused to consider that was how he had differed from Noble Warren. The older man had loved the woods and the freedom of a trapper's life but when the high season ended, the call of fields ready for plowing and the lure of a loving wife and child waiting at home won out.

"The Narraganset?" Maudie Lair sat straighter in her chair and allowed her eyes a curious sweep over her daughter's expressive face. "Those recently camped across the river? You traveled from Canada with that band?"

"Aye," Quade answered, seeing Glory's cheeks pale and feeling immediate regret that he had mentioned the Indians after cautioning her so harshly to hold her tongue regarding them. "Those are the few left of the lot who fled to Canada. They have come back to be nearer the land of their fathers and with hope of rebuilding the tribe."

Maudie Lair frowned. The talk which had piqued Glory's interest in the Indians had not missed her mother either, though Maudie Lair's concern was for the trouble sure to ensue from the camp's nearness to Sealy Grove. Among the most vocal men were several incapable of leaving well enough alone. "I fear for them," she said, her face mirroring the wisdom of one who had seen much heartache and regret result from the actions of hotheaded men. "They will not find peace in this place."

"Aye," Quade agreed. " 'Tis against my advice they are here. I warned them to stay in the French lands or else go west where the name Narraganset is not hated. But Tomanick and his council believe they must return to the land of their origin if they are to become as they once were."

"Can that happen?" Glory asked.

"Nay," Quade replied, sadness showing clearly in his dark eyes. "They can never be as before. Many of those in the camp are not of pure Narraganset blood. Some young men took wives in Canada after their women were sold. For the true Narraganset the years left are few." He drew in a heavy breath and shook his head slowly as he expelled it. "They do not admit it but they have come to die in their own land. 'Tis the best they can hope for."

Glory remembered the industrious women in the camp, the laughing children, the proud braves. She could easily share the sadness Quade felt for his friends. For a short while she sat silently considering why it was that men could not find the harmony that would allow them to live side by side. The lands were vast, the game abundant. What need was there for one people to be forced out by the fear or greed of another?

Admittedly her knowledge of Indians was small, limited to the teachings in the village school and those expounded from the meetinghouse pulpit. The minister was as sure the red men were heathens as was the outspoken Burrell Collier. And if so, according to Goodman Collier, the world should be purged of them. Glory found it difficult to squash even an insect and could not fathom how God could direct one man to kill another. She wondered if it might not be better to convert the heathens than to kill them. Perhaps she would put that question to Goodman Collier if ever the opportunity presented itself.

"Will they stay at the river camp or move on?" Maudie Lair asked as she rose and moved quietly around the table gathering the trenchers, spoons, and soiled napkins.

"They will stay for the summer if they are left alone."

He rocked back in the sturdy chair and rested the pewter mug on one knee. It went without saying that he held no more hope than Maudie Lair that his friends would pass the summer undisturbed. If a young girl had been moved to cross the river and look the Indians over, how long could it be before others, less friendly, made the same journey?

"How is it you came to be with them?" Glory wondered aloud, forgetting she should be up and helping her mother store the food in the cupboard.

Quade took another long swallow of the beer, a civilized luxury he admitted to missing. Glory had turned those enchanting eyes, full of interest, on him. He could not tell if it was her admiring gaze or the potency of the beer that made him feel unusually relaxed and warm.

"I came across them in the lake country in Canada. Only

one of them to start," he amended. "A boy, the son of Tomanick. Was near thaw time. I found the lad struggling out of a chop hole in the ice. He was a scrappy lad and had gone out alone to fish but misjudged the thickness where he made his cut. I hauled him clear and helped him fight the cold. Was after that the Narraganset befriended me and helped with the setting of my snares. When they decided to move south and I could not dissuade them, I came along. As I told your mother, it's past time I looked in on the two of you." His grin was sheepish and more for her mother than her. "How long has it been since I was last here?"

"Six years at midsummer." Maudie Lair turned from latching the cupboard. Her voice fell low. "When Noble died."

Quade nodded as he recalled the day and his impatience to move on once he had made sure his friend's family was not in need. It seemed six years could not have passed so quickly and yet he was sure Maudie Lair Warren was right. Civilized people were given to keeping records, setting down dates, and breaking time into the precise, small packets that made life manageable.

A trapper marked time by seasons rather than days or months. The passage of one year or four didn't measure very differently to him. What did sting was that he had not kept his word to Noble as he should have. Thankfully Maudie Lair was a capable woman and had managed her affairs well on her own. He was just a trifle surprised she had not married again. A widow with property could do well for herself, but not, he supposed, if she was looking for a man to measure up to Noble Warren.

The soft feather mattress seemed to drift in place around Quade's hard muscles like clouds around a rock-strewn mountaintop. He slept deeply until a crow's bothersome cawing reached into his dreams and pulled him to wakefulness. He came to with a start in the comfortable surroundings, tried to bolt out of the feather bed, then gave up the attempt and fell back chuckling.

Morning light, still pale and cool, filtered through the diamond-shaped windowpanes. How long since he had slept past sunup? A year? More? How long since he had slept without being fully clothed? He liked the feel of a good airing out, he decided, as he swung his bare legs from beneath the quilts and rose. He allowed himself the luxury of a good slow stretch, an action that would have left him dangerously vulnerable were he to take time for it in a bedroom of trees. Out there he rested while awake and slept with one eye open.

His buckskin breeches hung on one of a series of pegs set around the walls at shoulder height. An airing out had done them as much good as it had done him. The leather felt soft and cool and slipped with supple ease over his slim hips. He laced his leggings with care then looked to the washstand where Glory had left a bowl of water and the shaving implements used the night before. Accustomed to a cold shave or none at all, it did not cross his mind to fetch a kettle of hot water from the kitchen before he soaped his face and dragged the sharp blade over the dark bristles on his chin.

A short while later he was fully clothed and had thrown open the sashes at the window. Glory, in a dress of darkest green, her cap forgotten and her long black hair streaming over both shoulders, was hurrying into the barn with a milk pail. The crow, Paddy, sat atop the bronze weather vane on the barn roof, intent on making sure no one within range of his brash cawing slept another minute.

Quade watched Glory until she was lost in the deep shadows within the barn. Plainly the day was under way for all but him. The least he could do was to make himself useful while he enjoyed Maudie Lair's hospitality. With a quiet step learned from years of practice he started down the flight of stairs that led to the parlor and kitchen. He'd wager there was tea brewed and waiting.

The tea was ready and a porridge sweetened with honey and raisins. Maudie Lair had cut slices of ham and picked fresh strawberries still glistening wet with morning dew. Quade found his appetite renewed. If to eat heartily was a compliment to his hostess, he surely flattered Maudie Lair Warren.

"You slept soundly?" she inquired when he had eaten his fill and Glory had joined them sitting by the fire.

Quade laughed. "If I slept as soundly in the woods I could wake up without my scalp." His dark brows lifted. "A feather bed takes all the vigilance out of a man. What I need," he went on, "is a good day's work so I deserve to sleep so well."

Maudie Lair pondered his light comment. Noble had not been a man to sit idle and neither was Quade. The quandary was that her lands were leased so there was no work he could do in the fields. She hired a man to do the chores that she and Glory could not do themselves. Little else required a man's strength or special skill. She understood, however, that Quade preferred to earn his keep while he remained with them. Nor did she wish to hurry the young man on his way; indeed, she hoped to extend his stay.

Covertly casting her glance first at her daughter, so soon to be a woman, then at Quade, a man who reminded her of her beloved Noble, Maudie Lair allowed her thoughts to roam where they would. A woman had certain premonitions which were best nurtured, if sometimes secretly so. She was wont to trust these inexplicable notions.

Her smile was as hidden as her glance. Intuitively, she

believed Quade Wylde should not make his present stay as short as the last. He was far too close to severing his last ties to society. To do so would be his loss as well as hers and Glory's. She sought a way to detain the trapper.

She was wise enough to comprehend that some dark deed in the trapper's life, an event more terrible than the beatings Fisk had given him, had broken his trust in mankind. More was the pity the boy had not shared the dark secret with Noble or any other, so that it still boiled and burned within him and there was no healing balm to soothe the pain.

Let him stay awhile longer, she thought. Let him find that which would make him the whole man he was meant to be. Quade Wylde might never fathom what was put in play around him, but she had an idea the time would come when he would be glad of it. A look came to her face that only a woman's heart could understand. Fondly, she took the trapper's hand as a mother might her son's and told him of a job her husband had left unfinished and which she would entrust to no one else.

"There is a chest Noble began and had not the time to complete," she said, smiling in her quiet way. "It was to be for Glory, a part of her dowry. The makings of it are stored in the barn loft. The tools are there also. A man who knows his way around a plane and chisel could finish it in under a week."

"I would be pleased to try." The prospect appealed to him. He was no cabinetmaker but he knew his way around woodworking tools, as much as a cooper could know in any event. It would feel good to put his hands to work Noble had begun and bring the venture to fruition.

"Glory will show you the place when her chores are finished," Maudie Lair said.

Glory took her cue and promptly rose to wash the breakfast

dishes. When they were dried and put away she added a small log to the fire so that it would not die down too much before it was time to start the noon meal. It was not Glory's nature to shirk her chores as she had unwittingly done following supper the night before.

With spirits soaring for no apparent reason, she enthusiastically tackled her other work in the house. Soon it was done and she hurried to the barnyard to feed the pigs and chickens; nor did she forget to set out a porringer of milk for Tansy and scatter a few kernels of corn for Paddy.

Slightly more than an hour later she returned to show Quade the blanket-covered chest her father had begun.

"'Tis here," she said, exposing the sundry pieces of a drawerless chest, cut but not yet smoothed and joined or fitted with a lock. "See where he set my name." She traced her fingers over the smoothly notched letters. A hint of sadness displayed itself in her face for a moment as her fingers paused on the Y of her given name. "Here he held my hand on the chisel that I might say the work was partly mine." She held one hand out before her. "Was small then," she said softly. "Would that he could see it now."

On the fifth day of his sojourn at the Warren farm Quade applied the last coats of red and blue-black paint to the completed oak and pine chest. In another day the finish would be dry enough for removal to the house. In addition to Glory's name, Noble Warren had intricately carved the three front panels with scrolls, tulips, and leaves. The work showed a fine, steady hand engaged in a labor of love.

At the last flick of his brush, Quade rocked back on his heels and surveyed his work. Had he done justice to what Noble had begun? The pieces had come together perfectly, the lid was snug, the legs even, the lock secure.

"'Tis perfection," Glory pronounced over his shoulder.

Still kneeling, Quade spun on his heels and looked at her. He would have used the same word to describe her beauty. For the five days he worked she had been often in the loft, bringing him drink or on occasion passing the time by watching him work. Some days she was a mischievous girl, chasing the cat, telling him riddles, making dolls of straw. Other days she was a winsome maid, sitting with hands folded, speaking little, her eyes touching him so forcefully that once he had sent her away lest his self-control snap and he shame them both.

"I have given it my best," he said, his critical eye searching for flaws. "Your mother will approve the work, I trust."

Maudie Lair had come to the loft but once though she had asked daily how the work went or if he lacked anything. The widow was an industrious woman and her house ran as precisely as a clock. None of the day's work was left undone nor was her table ever sparsely set. He had eaten like a king and slept like a prince. In the evenings as they sat and talked her hands had worked at stitching him a shirt of heavy wool for the coming winter.

Glory added a gift of woolen socks and mittens knitted in the same space of time. The week had been one of comfort and ease and plainly his welcome was good as long as he wished to use it. Nevertheless, he had made up his mind that before the sun sunk below the hills on the following day, he would take his leave. He feared if he stayed through another dawn he would be as tame as the once-wild crow that flew to Glory Warren on command.

"My mother will be pleased," she said, bending innocently but so closely beside him that her dark curls brushed his arm and her warm breath fanned his cheek. She smelled tantalizingly, temptingly of honeysuckle. Before his blood could quicken, Quade rose and busied himself cleaning the brushes and sealing jars of paint.

"And your intended?" he asked huskily as she moved in a kind of slow dance around the chest admiring his handiwork.

Glory gave pause and her dark brows arched in surprise.

Quade shifted his eyes to the work of packing the tools in a wooden box. "The chest is to be part of your dowry," he said. "I thought perhaps the lad was chosen."

Glory laughed. Marriage was far from her mind. She had yet to understand what drew her to the trapper as fervently as deer to the salt rocks in the forest, or to understand the strange budding feeling which brought his face to her dreams and his name to her lips without warning.

"Nay," she answered softly. "No lad is chosen."

With his pack full of goods from Maudie Lair's larder, a restless yearning in his blood, and the sweetness of Glory's goodbye kiss on his lips, Quade left the Warren farm while the noon sun sat high in a cloudless sky.

Inside the tree line he turned and took a last look at the cluster of buildings and the two women who stood beneath the maple tree in the garden. It was just as well he could not hear their voices or see the quick tears filling Glory's eyes.

"Will he be back, Mother?"

Glory brushed the wetness from her cheeks. She had become accustomed to hearing Quade's deep laugh and listening to his suppertime tales of a trapper's life. From the first day he had come she had known he would go away again, and yet as he disappeared from view she felt tempted to run after the trapper and bring him back. Her purpose she could not name, but she did know that tonight at the evening meal the table would seem empty, the kitchen too quiet.

Maudie Lair had no tears. Her lips curved with the quiet smile of a woman who knows a secret. She wrapped an arm gently around Glory's shoulders.

"Ease your mind, daughter," she said softly. "Of a surety, he will be back."

CHAPTER
3

1692

The lad William Cook—"Daft William" was one of the
kinder names the children called him—lay on his back in the
dust. His feet and legs, numb and swollen from being raised
above his head half a day, were held fast in a pillory. Around
the boy the littered ground was rank with the smell of ancient
eggs and rotted fruit with which a group of heartless urchins
had pelted him. In the long hours of his imprisonment not
one person in Sealy Grove had offered William Cook so much
as a sip of water from the nearby well.

Perhaps his penalty would have seemed just had the crime
which sent William into the stocks been of his own doing.
But those boys who had bombarded him with foul missiles
were the same ones who had sent him peeking into Mary
Prince's window as she slipped on her petticoats. Simple-
minded, William was wont to do as bidden, and when told

that Goody Prince had called him from her window, he was quick to show himself there.

To Glory Warren, walking by the stocks with her mother, it would not have mattered whether William was guilty or innocent. She could not pass him by and see his parched lips and sunburned cheeks without wanting to hasten to the well to draw up cool water and take a dipperful to the suffering boy.

"Go on without me, Mother," Glory said. "I will see to William before I visit Sarah. The poor boy looks near baked."

Maudie Lair Warren took the basket of herbs and medicines her daughter carried and nodded her consent. She too was touched by the boy's discomfort and, knowing his nature, doubted his punishment had been fairly administered. "Make him drink slowly," she advised. "And tell William tomorrow he can sup with us."

As her mother went on her way Glory turned the wooden crank that raised the bucket from the well. She took the dipper from the peg and filled it with the cool, fresh water. With the full dipper poised carefully in her hands, she walked slowly to avoid spilling any of the precious liquid before reaching the boy.

William, at seventeen a year younger than Glory, was the village orphan. A strapping big lad, his muscles somewhat made up for his lack of intellect. Since the age of fourteen he had supported himself by doing odd chores for the townspeople and by hiring out to a neighbor, Asa Douglass, who leased and farmed the Warren lands. Glory felt the ache of a lump in her throat as she approached the boy. He looked so lonely and scared lying there, like an overgrown child scolded too severely by his loved ones.

Poor William. He was lonely even when he was out of the

stocks. Though Goodman Douglass treated him fairly, he spared little affection for the boy. A pity. If she did not miss her guess it was William's desire for acceptance among the younger boys that had again brought him trouble.

William, thinking himself little better than a trapped rabbit waiting the hunter's knife, heard the sound of quiet steps and cringed. Not half an hour before while he had mercifully dozed, some heartless prankster had sneaked up and given him a painful kick in the ribs. To make matters worse Francis Stevens had run in behind that lad and poured the contents of a chamber pot over him. Offering an angry protest against any more abuse, William strained his stiff neck to see who advanced on him this time. The grimace left his face when he saw that it was Glory Warren, who had never been anything but kind.

Wrinkling her nose at the putrid smell of him, Glory nevertheless knelt and lifted his head, placing the wooden dipper at his parched lips.

"Drink slowly, William, or it will sour in your stomach and come back," she warned. "You have grown overheated here in the sun." The boy nodded obediently but gulped water as if he would never have more. "Tell me how you came to be here, and who has taken your hat?" Glory asked as she gently pulled the dipper away from William's lips since he would not heed her advice to drink slowly.

The feel of cool liquid in his dry throat tickled and William coughed several times before he could answer. When he did he confirmed her suspicions about how he had landed in the stocks.

"Francis Stevens's dog carried my hat off and none would bring it back," William said thickly. "They thought it great sport to see the dog steal it."

Glory frowned and wondered how Christian boys could

behave like savages. To take a man's hat and leave him scorching in the heat was as great a sin as any.

"They are cruel, William." Glory gave him more water to drink, her soft voice soothing him as much as the refreshing draught. A bit of the redness left his rounded face when she dampened a corner of her apron and sponged his brow and cheeks. "I'll find your hat and bring it to you," she promised as William clumsily thanked her. "You should have it to shade you if you are to stay here."

William's cracked lips formed a feeble smile. "You are good, Glory. You do not taunt me as the others do."

She smiled back, her heart wracked with pity for the boy who was so abused by those he wished to befriend. "That is because you are good yourself, William, and do not deserve their harsh treatment. My wish is that you could know when to do their bidding and when not. Would keep you out of much mischief."

Glory sighed, knowing what she wished was impossible. William was older in body, but not in mind, than the boys who plagued him. He was sure to obey any command they gave and lacked the forethought to see the dire consequences for himself. Next week would find him again in the stocks or with stripes on his back in answer to more guileful ploys by the village boys.

Glory stood and shook the dust from her skirt. William's plight rankled. How was it the assembly who decided guilt or innocence had been taken in by a loutish pack of brats and came to give this folly the name of justice? Well agitated, she stamped a foot in the dirt and thought of several she would like to see pinned in the pillory in William's place.

Not far away the Reverend Josiah Bellingham watched and marked the charity of Glory Warren. The girl's beauty was rare enough, but to have such a face and also a kind heart was rarer still. Though he did not doubt William Cook deserved his punishment, Glory Warren's compassion touched him. She was a many-faceted diamond among lusterless pearls, a treasure to behold.

Always concerned over how he was viewed by his flock whatever he was about, Bellingham prudently peered up and down the street. Seeing that none paid him any mind he continued a rapt study of the comely maid, allowing his hungry eyes to take him where they would. They led him from the top of her head to the dainty, leather-clad toes occasionally visible as she tended William.

As if he observed a living work of art, Bellingham studied every part of her. The wisping strands of hair that trailed from beneath her cap were black as a raven's feathers and with a sheen to match. He knew from observing her in his congregation that her fine brows and long lashes were equally black and luxurious. Her skin glowed with a soft olive hue, her cheeks with the pinkness of good health. Her mouth fascinated him; the lips were as red and full as a ripe cherry. Nor could he forget the eyes, a dazzling blue that more than once had distracted him from the text of his sermon.

The minister warred with his emotions as he noted her tiny waist, the full, round curves of the breasts beneath her criss-crossed kerchief, and the hint of shapely hips beneath the folds of her gray dress. She was by degrees the fairest female in these parts, even in the colony, he would dare to speculate.

The tightening in his loins reminded Bellingham it had been close on a year since his wife Esther had died in childbirth. The year had been a hard one for him, deprived of a woman's care and of a husband's rights in the marriage bed. Had there not been comments from the women attending Esther that her birthing might have gone well had her husband not used her so late into her time, he would have already sought out another bride.

Bellingham sighed heavily. He had done enough penitence for that with fasting and meditation and countless hours of prayer on his knees. To take his wife was, after all, a husband's right, and he had not thought it would harm her. How could he have known her protests of pain were any more real than those before she was with child?

So be it. He had spent a year mourning both Esther and the child. It was long enough, long enough too for idle tongues to find other fodder. Thankfully he had been delivered from the vicious speculation by the emergence of a much more absorbing topic. The witch hearings in Salem Village had occupied the minds and mouths of all in Sealy Grove since early March. Almost weekly news came that more had been found practicing the black arts in that parish.

He himself had been among the ministers first called to observe and question the afflicted girls. Following that experience and an intensive period of study he had written several tracts on the supernatural and diabolical phenomena of witchcraft. To date his writings had been well received; many believed they equaled those of Cotton Mather, a recognized authority on the metaphysical world.

The result of it all was that he had no reason to worry. Soon he could marry again and hopefully to a wife who would enjoy connubial rites and bring enough dowry to pay his mounting debts. The charge he currently held at Sealy Grove was a poor one, more so for a man without a wife, and beneath his talents to boot.

Across the commons Glory smiled at William Cook. Bellingham could see how her countenance soothed the troubled boy. Again he felt the painful tightening in his loins and breathed deeply to temper the pull of it.

"Good day to you, Reverend."

Masking his startled expression with a mirthless smile, Bellingham turned abruptly, not anxious to be caught with the thoughts he had of Glory Warren showing on his face. This night he would be long at his prayers against weakness of the flesh.

"God's peace to you, Goody Warren. I was observing your daughter tend the simpleton." He swept the hat from his head and bowed slightly. "The lass is surely among the pure at heart," he remarked smoothly.

Maudie Lair warmed to the praise of her daughter, surprised as she was to hear the usually stern Bellingham speak in such a manner. It was comforting to learn he did not share the opinion of quite a few in Sealy Grove who believed Glory was a trifle too opinionated for a female.

"She is a joy to me, sir. And surely as kind a child as ever a mother held to her breast."

Bellingham inwardly wondered how one as beautiful as Glory would have been spawned by the goodwife Maudie Lair Warren. What charitable works might have rewarded so plain a woman with such a daughter? His eyes narrowed slightly as he turned the high-crowned beaver hat in his hands. His mind always at work for his own betterment, he took note that the girl was late issue of Goody Warren's womb.

The mother's face was much lined and the gray in her hair equal to the brown. Moreover, her narrow shoulders had begun to stoop from years of toil, though that did not slow her step. Nevertheless, the time would soon come when the responsibilities of a large farm would be more than she was equal to.

The minister's eyes went momentarily back to Glory as she hastened away from the stocks as if bent on an important mission. Her graceful gait was a pleasure to behold and he was reluctant to let go of the vision, but before he need add a fast to his prayer time, he forcefully swung his attention back to her mother.

"She is hardly a child now, Goody Warren. How old is the girl?"

He had a voice that could charm like a song or lash like a whip, and he used it always to his advantage. If Glory was a beauty, Bellingham was her counterpart in the stronger sex. He stood a good six feet tall and his hair was as golden and thick as a field of ripe wheat. His hazel eyes were softly shadowed under thick blond brows, his nose bore an aristocratic curve, and his high cheekbones stood out prominently above a good strong chin. His form had the powerful look a man might gain by much hard labor, though he had not gained it that way, to judge by the softness of his palms.

Maudie Lair responded easily to the handsome Bellingham. "She reached her eighteenth year last month, Reverend."

A sudden joining of thoughts created a ripple of pleasure in Bellingham as he considered Goody Warren's reply. For the briefest moment of meditation his eyelids shut. The girl was indeed old enough to wed. He was in need of a wife. Her father Noble Warren had left no other heir. Except for the widow's third, the Warren farm, not the largest but one of the choicest near Sealy Grove, belonged to the girl when she came of age—or married. A deeply drawn breath rolled slowly out of him. It appeared that God had again looked down on his various dilemmas and granted him a single solution.

"She is old enough to wed, is she not?" he ventured.

Goody Warren smiled faintly. A like thought had crossed her mind lately and she feared she had only selfish cause to put it aside. "There is time enough for that," she replied. "Glory is my only child and I would keep her with me awhile longer."

"Come now, Goody Warren," Bellingham chided. "You would not make the girl a spinster."

Maudie Lair pondered Bellingham's words since they hit so close to the mark. Noble Warren had been a good provider and a kind man, but she knew many women who had not fared as well. Ten or a dozen years of wedded life and the endless childbearing that came with it sapped the health. A woman was fortunate to see her children grown. It was more usual for them to be reared by a husband's second wife or even a third. Had she not found herself barren but for the single blessing of her daughter she doubted she would have lived so long herself.

Forgetting for a moment that the minister expected a reply, she mused on. No, the truth was she would not hasten Glory into just any match. A man from the mold of her Noble was needed, and she knew only one. But she took note that if Bellingham had noticed the girl's coming of marriageable age there would be scant time before others did too; they would covet both her daughter and the property she had inherited.

"I would have her choose wisely, sir," she answered at last. "I would have her wed a man with a care for a woman's lot."

Bellingham colored, uncertain if the remark contained a barb meant for him or if it was innocently said. He would have to treat carefully with Maudie Lair Warren for the hand of her daughter and he preferred not to have her forewarned of what was on his mind.

Pleading that he must be about his business, he donned his hat. "I am of the school who believes the choosing is best done *for* a daughter. I bid you God's peace, Goody Warren," he said and moved on down the street.

Maudie Lair had one more stop to make, at the house of Thomas Leonard, whose wife Rachel lay ill. Since no physician resided in Sealy Grove the sick were tended with home remedies and herbal preparations passed down from one generation to the next. Maudie Lair Warren was much prized for her knowledge of herbal medicines and for treatments that worked when no others did. Rachel Leonard had suffered a burn that quickly festered and poisoned her blood. The poor woman was in danger of having her hand amputated, but before she would give it up she had sent for Goody Warren.

"How do you fare today, Rachel?"

Four children, the oldest perhaps eight, crowded around their mother's bed. The youngest, a toddling two-year-old, pulled the covers up to hide a small, pinched face.

"I am improved, praise God," Rachel said weakly, with a flicker of light in eyes dulled by illness. She had been a sturdy woman and her squared features bespoke an inner strength. Still pale but now strong enough to sit, the bedridden woman pushed up on her pillows. "Whether the hand is better I can't tell but there seems to be feeling in it now. I have hope it will be saved," she added. "Without it I will be of poor use to four little ones. Mercy, sweet girl," she pointed to the oldest child, "is worn down trying to do my work and tend the others. Thomas cannot neglect the fields to stay with me."

Maudie Lair peeled off the plaster she had made by boiling and pounding the bark of the hemlock tree. She was grateful to see Thomas Leonard had found time to keep the plaster moist with the oil she had entrusted to him. The wound underneath was much better as Rachel had hoped; the festering was almost gone and the streaks of red which had previously spread like spider's legs from the sore were not to be seen.

Rachel looked at the hand and saw the change in it. Much of the swelling was gone and for the first time she could work her stiff fingers.

"You have wrought a miracle," Rachel whispered, tears forming in her eyes as the fear of losing her hand subsided.

"Not I," Maudie Lair declared as she bathed the wound and then spread a paste made from alder bark over it. "The miracle is from God and this concoction."

"'Tis true," Rachel agreed. "But I will never forget your part in bringing it about. Would that I could repay—"

Maudie Lair shushed her. "We are friends. 'Tis enough."

Half an hour later Maudie Lair left Rachel with a fresh plaster and medicines to see her through until the next visit. Bidding goodbye to the grateful woman's children Maudie Lair turned from the Leonard gate toward the Collier household where she expected to find Glory waiting. The journey from Sealy Grove to the Warren farm was just over two miles and she hoped to make it home before sundown.

Glory and Sarah Collier left the Collier house, for once without taking with them Sarah's two sisters. The Collier family was a large one, with three sons and three daughters. Sarah enjoyed the rare hours she had away from her chores and the five younger children.

Towheaded and freckled, Sarah was pretty enough, but her looks dimmed to plainness when she was with her friend. She didn't seem to mind being overshadowed, since Glory was more a sister to her than either of the two related by blood. Besides that, she counted Glory as her dearest friend and as the only person with whom she felt confident to discuss her hopes and wishes. The highlights of her week were the days Glory could come into town and the rarer occasions when she was allowed to visit the Warren farm.

"I have a secret," Sarah whispered excitedly. "I am near to bursting for someone to hear it."

Glory leaned her head conspiratorially close to Sarah. "Tell me," she whispered. Secrets were hard to keep in Sealy Grove, where everyone generally knew another's business as quickly as their own.

"Papa says I may take a husband soon, Glory." Sarah's face beamed with feminine pride.

Glory was hard-pressed not to groan. For the past year Sarah had nagged her father to name her dowry and talked of little else but her wish to marry. Glory, who believed there must be more interesting matters to speak of, wriggled a stick at a bug on the path and wrinkled her nose in distaste.

"Do you think of naught but finding a bridegroom, Sarah?"

Sarah scowled and cut her eyes accusingly to Glory. She had waited a week to share her news. To have it squashed by indifference was a bitter medicine to swallow. For the life of her she could not understand Glory's lack of interest. Sealy Grove was a small village and she and Glory the only girls of marriageable age—or at least she was. Glory might look older since she was more filled out and an inch or two taller, but the dark-haired girl still preferred her girlish pastimes to talk of becoming a wife.

Sarah straightened her shoulders and lifted her chin a little higher. "You are not as old as I, Glory, or you would understand how it is to contemplate becoming a spinster." One year separated Sarah and Glory in age. While Glory was left to ponder what might happen in the upcoming year to make her as anxious for a husband as Sarah, the other girl went on. "And your mother has the means to offer a handsome dowry with you. If I didn't have so many brothers and sisters maybe Papa wouldn't be as reluctant to part with my portion. I believe that is why he has waited so long."

"Your papa is said to choke a coin before he parts with it." Glory spoke impulsively, then hastily offered an apologetic look to Sarah. Would she never learn when to hold her tongue? She hoped she had not hurt Sarah's feelings though she had said no more than the truth.

"Aye. 'Tis a fact," Sarah lamented, not in the least offended. "I wonder if any man will wed me for what Papa offers."

Relieved, Glory offered encouragement where she thought it was needed. "You have naught to fear there. I've seen how Isaac Hawkins looks sheep's eyes at you. And Samuel Coventry seems smitten too."

"Posh," Sarah said, stopping her. "More likely they look sheep's eyes at you. But in any case they are both boys yet. I prefer to wed a man who has already settled himself and made his way in the world."

Glory huffed her disdain for this plan. "Such a man will also have a brood of children for you to mother. That will make caring for your five brothers and sisters seem easy."

"Not if I am to have the man I want," Sarah insisted, her eyes looking dreamily into the distance.

"And who might that be?" Glory searched her mind for the name of an unattached man in Sealy Grove who had already made his way and was not also a widower with children. She thought of none she could believe would appeal to Sarah.

Sarah marked the consternation on Glory's face and started to answer, then hesitated, reluctant to reveal her secret yearning. The match she had in mind was a lofty aspiration, even for her dreams.

"Who would you choose, Glory? Tell me first," Sarah said hurriedly.

Glory cast an impatient glance at her friend. "I would choose no one." Nor did she want to talk of weddings and husbands anymore. The thought had just come to her that if Sarah did wed soon she would lose her friend. Undoubtedly the man Sarah longed for lived in another village. If she married and moved away Glory might never see her again. Even if she married and stayed in Sealy Grove, they would have little in common once Sarah became a wife. "I do not desire a husband," Glory announced emphatically. "Nor can I see that matrimony recommends itself so as to make me wish to hasten into it."

"But if you did," Sarah goaded, unwilling to let go of the topic that had ousted all else from her mind, "who would you choose?"

Reluctantly, Glory thought it over. Such a light of interest shone in Sarah's eyes that she hated to disappoint her. She truly preferred the company of her pets to that of foolish boys. But if she had to give Sarah an answer she could think of only one name that would do.

"He is not one you would know," she said as her expression became almost as dreamy as Sarah's. A memory of dark hair and dark eyes and a ready laugh came to her in a flash. "He was my father's friend. They trapped together. I knew him when I was a small girl and again when he stayed with us two years past. Alas, I have not seen him since."

"He must be old," Sarah surmised. Her slim body relaxed as the anxiety which had held her in a tense grip fled before an overpowering wash of relief. Quite surprised, Sarah noted as well the slight slowing of her pulse. She hadn't known she harbored any jealousy of Glory or that she feared her friend would name the same man she favored.

"No. Not so old," Glory replied at length. The face, at first a shadowy image, became clearly visible in her mind, the rugged, handsome, and decidedly youthful face of Quade Wylde. She had not forgotten one feature or even one word that had passed between them as she watched and he worked on the dowry chest that now rested at the foot of her bed. If the truth were told, the trapper was the reason she found the young men in Sealy Grove a dull and unappealing lot. That truth, however, had not yet taken shape within her mind.

Sarah's curiosity was even greater than Glory's had been a moment before. "Does this fine fellow have a name?"

Now it was Glory's turn to feel foolish about what she was thinking. She evaded the question just as Sarah had done, her voice taking on a teasing note. "Will you tell me who it is you have set your cap for if I do?"

Sarah's heart fluttered, her half-shut eyes grew serious, and the name hovered on the tip of her tongue. She had spoken it to herself a thousand times, written it covertly beside her own as many more. On Hallow's Eve she had hidden her mother's hand mirror in the dark cellar. It was said that if a girl stood before a mirror alone at midnight on Hallow's Eve the apparition of her future husband would appear. But Sarah's chance to see the cherished face had been lost. Her father had been about and she could not risk leaving her room.

"No. I think not," Sarah responded at last, deciding that to say the name aloud might be like telling a wish. To hope so high was frightening enough. To name her hope might ensure it would never happen.

"Then I'll not name a name either," Glory answered in like fashion.

The girls continued lazily along the street past the town

church. To Glory's relief Sarah seemed willing to talk of other things. They made plans to talk after meeting on the Sabbath. Glory was just noticing the lateness of the day and realizing she should find her mother when the sound of a ruckus stopped both girls in their tracks. A moment later, bonnet strings streaming, Glory raced toward the stocks. Sarah followed haltingly.

"Stop! Stop it!" Glory's voice rose up in the street against the gang of boys who had earlier spattered William with spoiled fruit and eggs. "Leave him be!"

William's time of confinement was almost up and the boys had returned with new ammunition which they had no intention of wasting despite Glory's warning. Still admonishing them to leave, the irate girl hurried past the boys and stood defensively in front of William. One against six, she faced them as Sarah hung back on the path, hesitant to join in the fray. Glory eyed them in surprise. Four of the lot were from the finer families in Sealy Grove, the other two the sons of merchants of no small means.

"Step aside, Glory Warren! Let us pelt the fool!" Francis Stevens, a boy of William's age and the oldest in the group, shouted, his cheeks reddening. Of all who should catch him at his mischief, why did Glory have to be the one? His too-large hands dangled indecisively at his sides. When it became clear Glory was not going to do as she was told, his lips tottered between a nervous smile and a seditious smirk. If he could do it without losing face, he would willingly be the one to step aside.

With downturned eyes which gave him a constant sleepy-headed look, Francis glanced about. The other boys' eyes were on him, looking to him to handle a girl who did not know her place. "Damn," he said beneath his breath. Senior by two years to any of the lads with him, he had hoped to win Glory's attention in another way, one which might gain him a favored look or a chance to sit with her on the commons. Then he would have a thing or two to brag about to the older boys.

Glory's hands went defiantly to her hips. Her blue eyes blazed with hot anger and in spite of his wish to appear in control, Francis flinched beneath her angry stare.

"No I won't, Francis Stevens. And shame upon you. You of all are old enough to know better. What's more, if you strike me I promise tomorrow it will be you in the stocks." While she could make no complaint against the boys for tormenting William while he was confined, she knew they dared not strike her instead.

"You're a spoilsport, Glory." Embarrassed to be so threatened in front of his younger friends, Francis shuffled his feet and stuffed his hands into his lumpy pockets. He was uncertain whether Glory would take him before the magistrate, but unwilling to find out. Bad enough she looked at him as if he were merely a bothersome brat. He would die of shame and humiliation should he find himself in William Cook's place.

"We'll plug him when you're gone, Glory Warren," shouted another boy, his smudged face askew with annoyance that his fun had been interrupted.

"You will not!" she retorted, planting her feet wide apart in the dusty ground. "I will stand firm until he's freed."

A third boy, Joseph Allyn, who looked as if he was the kind to drown cats, stepped behind two friends. Seeing Glory was occupied with the others, he took the opportunity to let loose an egg which hit the crown of the tattered hat she had earlier retrieved to shade William's face. Just behind that egg he tossed another which fell short of hitting William but spattered the hem of Glory's skirt.

"Vile boy!" she cried, her eyes searching the line of smirking faces. "I'll present *you* to the magistrate for that."

"Ha!" proclaimed Francis, looking around to see that Sarah had hurried off. "You don't know which of us threw it."

"Indeed I do," Glory answered hotly as several heads dropped in shame beneath her angry glare. All were not subdued; two others returned glazed looks of innocence. But it was not necessary to read guilt from the boyish faces; plainly only one among them had empty hands and pockets.

"Who then?" Francis taunted. If he could not impress her he would at least show her up as the foolish girl she was. "Who?"

The boys laughed but were quickly silenced in collective shock.

"It was Joseph Allyn." She pointed a finger at the gawky, blushing youngster.

Joseph's mouth dropped open and his Adam's apple bobbed out of control. He was sure Glory hadn't seen him throw the eggs and had no guess how she could tell out of the bunch of them that he was the guilty one. The others, more brazen than bright, were equally puzzled.

Glory shook her finger at Joseph. The color left his thin face as he made a few furtive steps backward. "For shame," she said. "You ought to be whipped."

"What's happening here?" Reverend Bellingham's voice was unmistakable. He got no response to his question, but a quick look at the pillory, Glory's ruined skirt, and the gang of boys with strangely bulging pockets provided his answer.

Joseph's face paled more under Bellingham's scrutiny. Worse than the stocks would be having the reverend aim a finger at him in church and call out his sin. Worse yet would be the beating his father would give him after that humiliation.

"I didn't mean to," he whined, seeing the other boys cringe and hang their heads. Even Francis was quiet, leaving him to do the talking. "I aimed to hit Daft William," he blurted out. "I didn't mean to hit Glory Warren."

"Go on! Get away from here! I'll see you're dealt with later," Bellingham ordered, his voice at a pitch he did not usually reach until midsermon.

Joseph turned and fled, glad for a reprieve. He would pray tonight that the minister's finger did not point his way tomorrow. Francis Stevens followed and was so quick behind Joseph that he stepped on the first boy's heel and stumbled into him. Francis heard a crunch and felt his pocket but with little need. The awful, sulfurous stench of a rotten egg told him the one he had hidden when Bellingham came was crushed inside his pocket.

Glory was as surprised as the boys to have Bellingham's aid. When Sarah had left her she thought she would have to contend with the whole pack of youths alone.

"You are unhurt?" the minister asked as he knelt at her feet and with his snowy linen handkerchief wiped from her hem the odorous spatters of egg.

Angry color still flushed Glory's cheeks. "I am unhurt but I will have to ask God's pardon for my temper," she answered.

Bellingham rose, folded the soiled handkerchief, and fastidiously stuffed it in his coat pocket. "God will see only your sweetness," he said. "As I do."

Glory was taken aback. Reverend Bellingham was not known to heap praise on the heads of children. Even for a good act he was generally capable of finding some fault. She thought him in truer character when he spoke to William.

"As for you, lad," he said sternly, "keep to the straight

and narrow that you bring no more trouble on those who would aid you.''

William, worn out by the day's ordeal, promised in a squeaking voice to be good. Glory thanked Bellingham for his assistance but quickly realized he was not done with her. Her cheeks reddened when the minister gallantly took her elbow and steered her across the narrow street to where her mother and Sarah stood watching and waiting.

A worried frown settled on Maudie Lair Warren's face as she anticipated public criticism of her daughter's behavior. Sarah's face flushed with livid color as Bellingham delivered Glory to Maudie Lair. He had only a quick nod for both of them before he looked down at Glory with the warmest of smiles.

"You are as good as you are fair, my dear.'' He nodded to Goody Warren, barely noticing that Sarah stood beside her. "A pleasant afternoon to you all,'' he said and walked off.

Sarah's eyes narrowed at Bellingham's words. She had come close to screeching when he squeezed Glory's hand before letting it go. What sin had she done that she must see her dearest friend receive the affection that should be hers? Sarah's eyes darkened as she said a hasty farewell to Goody Warren and Glory and then hurried off, jealousy growing within her like a cankerous sore.

Two houses away, Francis and Joseph hurried around the corner of a picket fence, stopping only when they were out of Bellingham's sight.

"How did she know?'' Joseph demanded, gasping to catch his breath. "How did she know it was me who threw the eggs?''

"Ha!'' Francis scoffed as he picked bits of eggshell from

the mess in his pocket and wondered how he would get this past his mother. Not wanting to appear more witless than he already had, he offered the first explanation that came to him. Every night his father prayed that Sealy Grove would be spared a plague of witches such as the one that infested Salem. The deeds of those accused were talked about at his dinner table enough to fuel a lad's fantasies. "Glory Warren has witch's eyes," Francis said, with an air of indignant authority. "Witches can see all the way around their heads. That's how she could see you."

Joseph's own eyes grew unnaturally bright and wide. Why had he not realized it himself? He never failed to read the accountings of the Salem hearings posted weekly on the meetinghouse door.

"To be sure," he agreed, his regard for Francis having returned to its former height. "Glory Warren has witch's eyes."

CHAPTER
4

She blamed Sarah for starting it all and then leaving her with no one to talk to about it.

With Paddy blissfully quiet on her shoulder, her back straight and jaw tight, Glory rode the bay mare toward the river crossing. She had been there frequently in the past weeks, since that day in the village when Sarah awakened her hazy memories of Quade Wylde. It seemed since that moment she had not known an hour of peace without the trapper intruding in her mind.

Really, it had been the most peculiar turn of events. One instant she was chiding Sarah for thinking only of a husband and the next she was just as giddy with thoughts of a suitor. How she wished she could talk to Sarah about it, but Sarah seemed to have no time to spare lately. If she did not know that it was unlike Sarah to be unkind, she could believe her friend was angry at her. She wanted to ask if this was what had happened to Sarah, this boundless yearning for a man's attention. Did this affliction come upon all girls at eighteen?

If so, why had her mother not forewarned her as she had about the other burdens of womanhood?

At a grassy clearing she dismounted, hobbled the mare, and slipped the bridle from the animal's head. Her destination was the site of the Narraganset camp, a place she had avoided for so long and now favored above all others as a secret retreat. Below the bluffs where the wind whistled and whispered an ancient tune was a good, secluded place to sit and think of the handsome trapper. The shallows at the bend of the river were excellent for wading or taking the sun. Often since the weather grew warm she had refreshed herself with a dip in the cool waters.

The danger of Indians at the spot was no more. Less than a month after Quade's departure, the goodmen of Sealy Grove had loaded their muskets and launched a surprise attack on the unsuspecting village. The few Narraganset not slain had fled and not been seen again. Perhaps those few had completed the journey to their homeland, though a similar welcome must have awaited them there. Near the river where the lodges had briefly rested only charred rings now marked the ground. Those, a few shattered clay pots, and faded drawings on the bluff walls were all that remained to show that Indians had ever claimed the place.

"Have a care, Paddy," Glory called to the soaring crow as she skipped over the mossy stepping-stones where she had once been wrenched from her feet by a pair of savages. She had kept her word to Quade and never told the events of that day. It was almost as if it had not truly happened. Very likely those braves who had held her and worried over her fate and theirs were long returned to dust. Her memories of the occurrence, some two years later, were largely monopolized by the part the trapper had played in the tumultuous episode.

An otter splashed into the water from the opposite bank,

startling her for a moment. Seeing there was nothing to fear, Glory tossed her head and gave a little laugh, freeing her dark hair from the confining cap in a shimmer of waves around her shoulders. How thickheaded Quade must have thought her for going to the Indian camp, for getting caught. How silly and childish she must have seemed the week he stayed at the farm, pestering him with endless questions, forever at his heel like an adoring puppy.

He must have wished for a moment of peace, for an hour without a fatuous girl underfoot. In a listless mood, Glory paused in the middle of the river for a moment of contemplation. Had there not been quiet times, though, when she had felt his eyes upon her and seen a look on his face she had not understood? Pondering this new matter, Glory hastened on over the stones. Since then she had seen that particular gleam, that look, and placed the source. It had been in the eye of Asa's stallion when they had taken the mare to him for breeding, and on Rich Doty's face on the day last summer when he wed Patience Towne. It was the look a man had for a woman he desired as mate. Lust or love? A bit of both, she supposed.

Glory reached the sheltered cove below the bluffs and paced along the water's edge, her bare feet moving swiftly along the path. Paddy swooped to her shoulder, his small claws hooking into the fabric of her watchet blue bodice. The hot sun beat down on the deserted ground and warmed her back until a mist of perspiration dampened her skin and made the clothing she wore cling as if it had been spread thick with paste. Perhaps the heat was to blame, but recently she had felt warm and restive in the coolness of night within her bedroom. And always Quade Wylde's face was there behind her closed lids, stirring her blood, making her wonder about the mysteries of man and woman.

"Ah, Paddy," she said to the crow who had left her shoulder to find a shaded perch. "Would that I were a sleek black hen who could lift my wings and fly away with you. Would be simple then, would it not?"

"Caw!" the crow called and ruffled his gleaming feathers.

It was as good an answer as any and brought a quick laugh to her lips. Her humor, however, was short lived. She quickly grew pensive again and started a search for some diversion to lighten her spirits. The pretty pebbles strewn along the ground caught her eye. She collected a handful and slipped them in her pocket, and then added a drawing of her own to those the Indians had made, but all to no avail. Her mood showed no sign of slackening, nor could she put a name on what it was that made her restless.

Finally, with a heartfelt sigh, Glory began loosening the fastenings of her gown. If she could not ease her mind, she could at least conquer the heat. A moment later she stood clad solely in her chemise, a linen garment she had daringly dyed a light red color with berries from the poke bush and a mix of alum. As she hitched up the hemline and tucked the ends into the waist strings so that they would not tangle around her legs in the water, a slight pout appeared on her lips.

She had wanted to show Sarah the brightly hued chemise with tiny flowers embroidered on the bodice, perhaps persuade Sarah to tint a garment of her own that they might share a secret they could whisper about as they walked among those who disavowed any show of color or frivolity in clothing. Lately, however, on every visit to town Sarah had this chore or that and could not stop to talk.

Glory tested the water with her toes but hardly noted the temperature. She missed her talks with Sarah, and Paddy was a poor substitute. Just as much, she longed for the days when nothing more serious than a day spoiled by rain had worried her. If all this newfound misery came with being a woman she wasn't sure she wanted any part of it. As if she hadn't enough to worry about, that bumbling Francis Stevens acted as if he wanted to court her. She kicked ruefully at the water. Did he think she would give him so much as a smile after the way he had treated William? Still he might have been tied to her apron for all the times she had turned to find him at her elbow last meeting day.

Worn out with it all, Glory waved her arms in a dismissing gesture and waded beyond the shallows to where the water was deep enough for swimming. Oblivious to Paddy's anxious cawing she gulped a breath and dived beneath the surface for as long as her lungs would allow.

High on the bluffs a lone rider swung from the saddle and tied his mount out of sight. With a stealth few could equal, the man made his way to a narrow crevice and crouched unseen on the rocks. Entranced, he watched as a black-haired Puritan girl shed her modest gown and pulled the skirt of her chemise high on shapely thighs. Her legs were longer and more alluring than he remembered. The exposed length of them gleamed like burnished gold. She had changed in other ways. Her breasts were fuller and thrust temptingly against the thin chemise. Her hips were more rounded and swayed hypnotically as she walked into the water.

A look of satisfaction softened the stony face. Glory Warren had become a woman, her beauty more polished, more pronounced. No man seeing her curved perfection would mistake her for a child.

Like a hunting animal he watched and measured her moves. How well he knew them, though now there was a womanly grace about her which the younger Glory had not possessed. The smile of one who has trapped his prey curled his lips.

She was yet an impulsive female, a flittering firefly, or she would not have come here alone. He could not believe she had her mother's approval. It occurred to him she might instead have arranged to meet some swain in this secluded place. Would not any within a day's ride be rutting after her? His keen eyes swept the cove, the path, the far bank of the river and saw no other. She was alone.

Quade Wylde listened to the hammering of his heart, felt the furious pounding of blood in his brain. Two years he had spent getting her off his mind. Two years he had spent burying himself in the wilderness, going where no man had dared. Whiskey and women he had used trying to forget her. Neither had worked. All the months, all the miles had brought him circling back to this place where it had all begun, and to her.

She swam and splashed until exhaustion drove her to a large, sun-warmed rock. Atop it she stretched out her slim legs and set about squeezing the water from her hair and then combing the tangles from it with her fingers. When the long, silky tresses were as smoothed out as she could get them, Glory leaned back on her elbows and turned her attention to the high drifting puffs of cloud overhead. Watching them was as soothing as counting sheep, and shortly she had eased back and allowed a pair of heavy lids to close over the bright blue eyes.

"You do not learn a lesson easily, Glory Warren."

With a shriek and a gasp, Glory bolted upright and would have thrown herself into the water and fled had not a hand gripped her wrist and held her back. She saw a bare chest and a twist of black braid and concluded in her confusion that fate had repeated itself.

"Unhand me!" she shouted and sent a kick flying at the

broad and muscled chest. The blow missed and the following swing of her fist at the ominous dripping face resulted in both her arms being held fast. Shortly she was snatched from the rock and found herself waist deep in the water, face-to-face with her captor.

"Easy, girl!" Quade laughed and jerked her close against him and with such an impact that the ribbon fastenings of her chemise gave way, exposing the soft mounds of her breasts. Quade groaned, regretting the need to handle her roughly, but it was the only way to protect himself from a furious flurry of kicks, one of which he feared might do lasting damage if properly aimed. "You need not cripple a friend," he shouted, pinning her arms behind her so that she was held tightly pressed against his chest.

Glory writhed against him like a caught eel, not giving up the fight until at last she heard the sound of his voice through the fog of her fear.

"Quade!" she cried. "Quade Wylde! 'Tis you!"

"Aye," he said, letting her hands loose. "'Tis me or what's left now that you've pelted me with bruises from head to toe."

"Quade!" Glory flung her freed arms around his neck, tormenting him much more with her sudden embrace than she had with her ferocious kicks. "You nearly scared me to an early grave." She sobbed and clung so tightly he felt every curve and hollow of her woman's body mold against him. "I thought you a savage," she whispered perilously close to his ear. "It was as before. You springing from the water the way the Narraganset did."

Quade gave a ragged sigh as he felt a jolt in his loins. "Was a foolish plan," he said hoarsely as she tormented him further by laying her weight fully upon him. A tremor he could not contain shook through the muscle and sinew of his large frame. "I should have called from the bank and made myself known."

"Aye," she said, twisting her bare legs on his as she struggled for sound footing on the river bottom. "Would have saved us both a bit of wear."

For all the time she burrowed against him he held his arms stiffly at his sides, his hands clenched tightly against his tense thighs. When he should have pushed her away, he could not bring himself to end the sweet torment of having her arms twined about him. His plight was great. Should he join the embrace he feared he would not stop with a brotherly hug and kiss, and he dared not go beyond that mild show of affection.

Had it been only her arms about him he might have endured the storm, but the nearly bared breasts heaving against his shirtless chest, the warm fanning of her breath at his ear, and the silken feel of her cheek resting on his bare shoulder were more than he was equal to. Before he knew his motive his arms crossed her back, a palm resting lightly on the curve of each hip, and lifted her tighter against his aroused manhood.

As her fear fled Glory became aware of the hard, masculine feel of the body that supported her and the alarming impropriety of being alone with a man and clad only in a wet and revealing chemise. She would have pulled away in dismay had not the abrasive feel of the dark fur on his chest spurred her on to cling a little closer. The warm strength of him, so insistent against her, coaxed her to wait a moment longer. The feel was new as was the tingling warmth which spread from the core of her in a slow burn outward to the tip of every limb.

"I have thought of you much," he said, his voice low and husky in her ear. His hands climbed her back, along the spine, beneath the torrent of hair. He looped his fingers in the lengths of black silk, reveling in its luxuriant feel, pulling her head back that he might look into the eyes that had burned in his dreams at every hour of sleep. He had seen them nightly, been lured to them as a child is lured to fireflies at dusk.

"And I of you," she answered haltingly, tipping her head obediently and gazing into his dark, amber-sprinkled eyes. She shook and would have blamed the coolness of the water if it hadn't been for the heat surrounding her. "I—we have wished for your return."

Her lips quivered and parted. The look was in his gaze, the longing, wanting look. She believed he must see the light of it reflected in her eyes as well. What else could have brought such a flush of warmth to her skin? And then there was not another moment to think. He whispered "firefly" and repeated the word in a rhythmic Indian tongue as his head bent to hers and their lips met.

She made a soft sound, lost beneath the onslaught of his mouth. Her arms tightened about his neck and he crushed her in a fury he had not begun to explore in his mind. His lips twisted on hers; the fury was gentle there as he took the time to enjoy the timid softness and untasted sweetness of her mouth.

Glory's pulse pounded. No man had touched her in this way. No man had touched her at all. Reason fled and she relied completely on the instinct nature had given her in response to his kiss. Her lips molded to his, her tongue entwined with the soft probe of his in the sweet, dark hollows of her mouth. It was a heady, honeyed feeling which grew and deepened as his hands roamed tantalizingly over her rib cage until they met the soft undercurves of her breasts.

A new surge of heat rose in her as his thumbs slowly stroked higher, finding the tight, aching peaks. The strange, exquisite pleasure of his touch lit a still hotter fire inside her and took the last ounce of strength from her legs. Glory sagged against him, her cheeks burning, near to fainting from the wonder and suddenness of her arousal.

His heart thundered, his body demanded that he sweep her from the water to the shore, tear away the chemise, and take all the sweetness her nubile body would yield. Instead he tore his mouth away and groaned a refusal to the hot demands. He needed several quickly drawn breaths to regain control of his senses.

This wasn't what he wanted from her, not to dishonor her by taking her with no words of love or promises of forever. He didn't know if he could ever give her that. He wasn't sure exactly what it was he wanted from her or what it was that had brought him winding back to her. Until today. Now he knew she wasn't safe alone with him.

"Glory . . ." he whispered, seeing her flushed face, her lips puffed from the force of his kiss.

Glory gasped for air and looked up at the lean, handsome face stunned, still too weak to stand without the aid of his arms. His eyes were heavy lidded, burning with desire, his heartbeat like thunder against her breast. A sense of what had taken place between them struck her like a blazing bolt of lightning. Moaning softly, she pushed feebly at Quade's chest and staggered back, suddenly aware that her bare, swollen breasts and their hardened buds revealed her need as clearly as the tight, wet buckskins did his.

With fumbling fingers she tied the ribbons of her chemise to cover her nakedness, though when it was done it was of little help since the wet cloth was transparent and showed the outline of both tight, dusky nipples. Quade's gaze lingered where the cloth strained most; Glory felt the hard aching tips tighten more. With arms crossed over her chest for a covering, she backed and stumbled away.

"I have to dress," she cried as she broke from the water and raced toward the pile of clothes discarded on the bank. She was in her petticoats and fastening her bodice when Quade came to her again. She trembled, afraid he would kiss her a second time and that she would allow the kiss and more.

"I wouldn't have you ashamed," he said, taking hold of her slim shoulders. His devouring gaze took in the whole of her and found her as pretty clothed as she had been in her chemise. The glowing blue eyes were downcast but he forced them up by gently lifting her chin with his fingertips.

"What else could I be?" she lamented, hardly daring to meet his eyes now that her blood had cooled. He was still bare-chested, still as appealing as he had been in the river. Rivulets of water coursed down his chest, streaming through the black thatch of hair covering that powerful part of him. Her voice quaked. "Nearly naked, letting you fondle . . ."

"Hush, girl." He shook her gently, and the black hair tumbled on her shoulders and spilled sensually over his hands. "I've seen you in the altogether when you were a small thing." His lips curled wryly at the memory of a curly haired waif gaily splashing in a tub, then unashamedly bounding out and racing her mother around the kitchen before a towel could be wrapped around her.

"Aye," she answered. "Was a different matter then. Now 'tis something else again."

"That it is," he said, hoping the lightness in his voice would cheer her. "I must admit it's a difference I like. You are a woman now. I am a man. 'Tis not the same to see you in the altogether. The outcome is unpredictable, as we have found."

"You mock me." She wrenched away before he could see a tear form in her eye. Her back to him, she hurriedly finished dressing.

"No, Glory Warren." He caught her by the shoulders and whirled her around, forcing her to stop and listen. " 'Tis you who mock me. Two long years I've ridden away from this place, cut deeper into the forests than any man has before me, trapped where no other would set a snare, held my life within a hairsbreadth of death a hundred times and all to rid my mind of a beguiling black-haired girl." He dropped his hands from her lest he again plunge beyond an affectionate touch. "Aye. You've plagued me, girl. Vexed me. Taken the pleasure out of the life I'd have for myself. Even in my sleep you've filled my dreams with that sweet face, haunted me with those blue, blue eyes. You have been my lodestone, albeit a lovely one, calling me over and over back to a fate I would not have."

Glory gasped softly. His speech stunned her as his kiss had done. She was a soft-hearted creature and could not bear the thought of bringing hurt or distress to anyone.

"I never meant . . ." she stammered. "I never knew."

"How could you know?" He shook his head, sending droplets of water flying from the braid that bound his dark hair. "You were hardly more than a child when I left here. Hardly more than a child and I longed for you then, longed for you all the time since while I knew you were ripening into the woman you are. 'Tis not by chance I've come to this place." His deep voice fell lower and one outstretched hand caressed the smooth skin at her throat. " 'Tis not by chance you were here this day." He smiled and brought his hand higher to stroke her quivering chin with his knuckles. A long silence ensued and when it appeared Glory would not break it with a reply, Quade's brow furrowed in a bemused frown.

"You know not what to make of me now, do you, Glory Warren?"

He did not add that he had not wanted to return to this place, that he had been driven ever toward it by a power he could not overcome. Had he been in possession of his faculties he would have arranged for an agent to see to her welfare and her mother's and in that way satisfy his oath. He would not change his life for a woman. That he had sworn as steadfastly as the vow made to Noble Warren. Yet here he stood, so close his shadow fell across this woman's features, shielding her alluring face from the hot sun.

What could he say for himself regarding the second vow? Now that he had seen her, held her, kissed her, it would be next to impossible to leave her again. He had a half-hearted hope she would make it easy for him to go away again. Would she tell him now once and for all time that his longing, his return were both in vain?

Glory wrung her moist hands. He was half-right by any judgment. She did not know what to make of him or of what had happened with meteoric speed when they first touched. Still somewhat shaken, she felt a need to sit and found a log to serve as a seat. Quade fetched his shirt and donned it, then stood with one foot resting on the log, his hands at work lacing the fringed buckskin garment.

Her fine brows knitted, Glory studied the tall, lean trapper who had blown back into her life with the intensity of a gale. Half-right, she concluded, meant he was also half-wrong. She had known of his longing, as best she could within her inexperience and youth. She had seen the signs of it the times his quiet, hooded gaze had been as hungry as that of a bird of prey. She had known.

Her blue eyes glistened. If there was a moment when the last step was made between girlhood and womanhood, Glory made hers then. "You are off the mark, Quade Wylde," she told him boldly. "My heart is open to you."

It was his turn to gape and be struck speechless, though the spell lasted but a moment as he pondered that the brunt of his predicament had been swung back to him with full force. No easy way out would be given him. He must see it through openly and honestly. He had run from her and from himself as long as he could.

"We should start for the farm," he told her, smiling ever so lightly as it occurred to him one obstacle might yet prevent that which he had inadvertently set in motion. Maudie Lair Warren would have a say in who claimed her daughter's affections. "My horse is tied beyond the bluff. Are you afoot?"

"Nay," she answered, starting for the path. "The mare grazes across the river in the same clearing as before." Such an air of wonder filled her she marveled that her voice did not croak. What would Sarah think of her now? She had just agreed to be courted by Quade Wylde.

Quade, leading a horse whose saddle was weighted with a cumbersome pack, walked at her side quiet and thoughtful, a man caught in a trap and seeking the means of escape before he came to consider his prison a palace.

At the stones they parted. Quade rode a quarter mile downstream to where the rocks were fewer. There he swam the big roan gelding across the river, then mounted and turned the horse back toward the clearing where Glory waited. By the time he reached the spot, she had bridled the mare, tucked her damp hair beneath a crisp white coif, and tied a kerchief across her bosom.

Her bare feet covered with buckle-trimmed shoes and hose as well, she looked as prim and modest as any Puritan maid. Had he not seen it for himself he would not have guessed that beneath the sedate clothing she wore a chemise of a sassy rose color. The thought was one to savor and call to mind at quiet moments of enjoyment, since he had determined there would not be any repetitions of what had happened back at the river.

Glory might be unaware of it—he fervently hoped she was—but he had come dangerously close to carting her to the sandy bank and doing much more than kiss her. As much as he would like to carry through with what had been in his mind, he wouldn't subject Glory to the harsh punishment that might come should that action occur and be made known. The penalty for such misconduct was ten lashes or more in the public square. His lips were tight, set in stern determination. No whip would mark that beautiful skin, not for any action of his, not for any reason while he drew breath.

They talked little on the ride. Both had much to occupy their thoughts. The crow flew ahead, gliding, diving with the wind. At least for him, Quade mused, the path was straight and sure.

The afternoon was yet young when Quade and Glory rode up to the Warren house. The farm was unchanged as was Maudie Lair Warren and the warmth of welcome she had for the young trapper. She was polite enough or wise enough not to inquire how it happened that he had brought her daughter home after another soaking. Since half his clothing was wet as well, Quade was particularly grateful for her restraint.

"You are back sooner than I expected," the older woman told him as she took the gelding's reins and looped them over a hitching post.

"And sooner than I am needed by the looks of things," he replied, carrying the momentum of his swing from the saddle into a hug and a spin which swept Maudie Lair from her feet. "I glance about me and see you are a wonder among women, Goody Warren," he teased as Glory hurriedly dismounted and tied her horse beside his. "I passed fields planted with fall crops, a pasture filled with fat cattle, and I'll wager the larder is full to overflowing."

Maudie Lair laughed and straightened her cap which had gone askew with the force of Quade's greeting. Her blue eyes twinkled in understanding but neither Quade nor Glory caught the look.

"Is it the abundance of my larder which has brought you visiting or have you another purpose?" she asked.

Quade missed the subtle implication of her question as he had already turned to unfasten the pack tied behind his saddle. Voicing a groan, he heaved the heavy bundle to the ground at his feet.

"I have the intent of testing the reserves of your larder and rendering your beer barrel empty by half," he said, a wide grin on his face. Kneeling to tear open the pack, Quade yanked out a stack of fine, thick fox pelts. "To soften the blow of my appetite at your table, I have brought you these." He placed the fox pelts in Maudie Lair's hands, and in Glory's he placed several snowy white ermine pelts.

Maudie Lair rubbed the soft fur. "These will make a warm lap rug, or the lining of a good winter cape, and the ermine a muff or hood," she said, smiling her appreciation of his gifts while Glory, misty-eyed, rubbed the soft fur against her cheek.

The supper time they shared was much like those before except that Glory was quieter and the number of questions she asked far fewer than her mother expected. Quade told of new settlements in the North and of Dutch posts along the Hudson River where he had taken furs for trade. It was clear to the older woman if not to the younger that Quade Wylde loved his rambling life and the lack of ties which allowed him to roam as he pleased. Perhaps of the three she knew best what had brought him back to the Warren farm. She did not yet know if he had the will to stay.

When the meal was done and the flames low in the grate of the stone fireplace, Maudie Lair poured three cups of canary wine. The talk drifted to things of little consequence. All three harbored secrets they were not yet ready to share with the others. When the cups were empty and the conversation lagged, Maudie Lair and Glory tarried only a moment before calling the day at an end. Quade expressed a wish to smoke a pipe and opted to stay below when the women rose to leave.

"Sleep well," he bade them as they started up the stairs.

When they were gone he snuffed out the candles and sat with only the glow of the coals and the soft flicker of the dying flames for light. He sat thus for an hour or more, long after he had put his pipe aside. Even then he wondered if he would give way to sleep.

Still later when he climbed the narrow wooden steps he was no more at peace. He had a choice to make that would get no easier as time went on. He would set a limit, a month and a fortnight more, to live a settled life. At the end of the period his choice would be made. If it was to stay he would ask Glory Warren to be his wife. If it was to go he would ride away from Sealy Grove, from the Warren farm, from Glory, and never return.

At the top of the dark stairwell he paused. The room to the left was the one assigned to him. The one at the right was Glory's. The door was open a crack so that the cat she had carried to her room might go and come at will. In the soft stream of light that filtered from her window to the doorway Quade could see her bed and the soft shape of her beneath the covers. Moving soundlessly he crossed the corridor and pushed the door open wide.

His breath came out in a rush. Her arms had escaped the covering of white sheets; one crossed her breast, the other lay outstretched as if she beckoned. Her lacy sleeping cap lay discarded on the pillow. Her dark hair flowed in a wild tumble around her. Moonlight bathed her skin with pale silver light. Her soft breathing made the gentlest of sounds, sounds Quade would have liked to take inside himself with his mouth pressed on hers.

He suppressed the urge to cross the shadowy floor and hold her in his arms, but had no time to temper his body's reactions. A quickening came to his pulse, a tightening to his loins. For uncounted minutes he stared; finally, he turned his dark eyes away. Quade closed the door to the point he had found it and hastened to the refuge of his room, wondering if fate had decreed him no choice at all.

CHAPTER
5

On Holy Sabbath, the meetinghouse benches strained under the weight of the inhabitants of Sealy Grove. The walls of the square building resounded with the eloquent words of Josiah Bellingham as he admonished his congregation toward a sweeter temper of spirit.

Each and every one of them, sitting stiff and unsmiling, knew the text of the sermon stemmed from the accounting Goody White had given the magistrates of the abusive name-calling she had endured from her shrewish neighbor Goody Henry. From her hard bench Goody Henry bore this second reprisal better than she had the first, handed down by the magistrates with the pronouncement of a steep fine.

"Do not murder the spirit of a neighbor with vile words," Bellingham railed, "as the wicked murder the body of an enemy! Let your discourse as well as your deeds be those that honor God and dishonor Satan!" At that Goody Henry flinched, and six boxes back Goody White gloated behind a fixed and innocuous countenance.

Bellingham roared on, alternately rebuking and praising until his humble flock felt tempest-tossed. Sarah Collier, listening more raptly than any, clung to every word. Of a whole, the congregation counted themselves fortunate to have so learned and pious a minister in their small settlement. Few would have suspected that behind the pulpit the sentiment was precisely the opposite.

Josiah Bellingham considered the small though not unprosperous township of Sealy Grove an unfortunate and temporary appointment. His aspirations were higher; a charge in Boston would please him, but one did not get there without a name or a purse better endowed than his.

His bane was to be the eighth living son of a father whose estate had been reduced to a pittance apiece for all but the eldest Bellingham offspring. Though he had the finest mind and most splendid appearance of all his brothers—and of his three sisters too, some had said—he was no better off for it. His education at Harvard he had earned by scholarship and much deprivation. Family resources had been further reduced by the illness of his mother, who had gone off her head and needed the constant care of an attendant.

With so little to offer a wife, he had been forced to take a bride whose dowry was as meager as his inheritance. He consoled himself with the belief that God had set him back in the early part of his life so that the pinnacle of his success would be all the higher when attained.

He knew the steps he must take for the rise to the loftier position he was meant to have. The way was clear and laid out as patently as the rocky path Moses had been directed to follow up the mount. Greatness was his destiny. It took Josiah Bellingham but a moment to discern that the dark-haired stranger sharing the Warren pew might be another of Satan's stumbling blocks to his ambitions. When his voice rang louder, the high emotion that fueled his zeal was more personal than spiritual.

His congregation was not aware of it. Not even a cough interrupted as Reverend Bellingham recounted, in what had become a standard feature of his sermons, the latest happenings in Salem. "God has judged one witch and smote her with his own hand," he said of the recently deceased Goody Osburn, one of the first to be accused of witchcraft. Old and in ill health, she had died while awaiting trial. "But Satan has sent back ten for one," he admonished, lest any think God did not expect man to do his part in ending the infestation. "Satan's evil has spread like a choking vine—to Marblehead, to Amesbury, to Gloucester, even to Boston. Pray!" he shouted at such a pitch that more than one head drew back and bumped sharply against a pew. "For your neighbor! For yourselves! That God not visit his devils on Sealy Grove."

At the close of the lengthy service, Bellingham hurriedly threaded past members of his congregation engaged in conversations about the plight of those cities beset by the plague of witchcraft. From every quarter came expressions of thanks that Sealy Grove had been spared, and a few speculative comments as to why. He did not dawdle to enlighten any with his opinion on why Sealy Grove had to date remained godly. A more pressing urgency drove him to seek out the newcomer, though briefly as he heard the words of those he passed, he considered how very like sheep they were. With a few carefully chosen words he had the power to lead their minds wherever he desired.

The thought vanished as he came upon Quade Wylde conversing with a group of goodmen, former friends of Noble Warren. He approached, anxious to assess firsthand the strength of the stranger's threat to his plans.

"You are new among us, are you not?" Bellingham held out a hand to Quade, quickly determining that the man was the first he had met in some time with a height greater than his own.

Bellingham found the hand firmly clasping his to be strong and callused, the grip nearly painful to his less powerful fingers. The eyes were unflinching though he gave the man his most righteous stare. The man's clothing brought him some relief. He wore the buckskin breeches of a trapper and an ill-fitting coat and hat. His own clothing, which had cost a large portion of his stipend, was of the finest English linen and wool. He had not yet had to stoop to wearing the rough-woven cloth made by the local women.

Quade granted a more liberal assessment to the minister but could not find the proper traits to lift the man high in his regard. There was too much about him that reminded Quade of another minister who betrayed him to Fisk when he had once taken refuge in the church following a brutal beating. As wary with words as with all else, Quade shrugged and answered Bellingham noncommittally. "I have passed this way before."

Not to be denied, Bellingham's sandy brows lifted. "Mayhap before my time," he responded. "I do not recall your face."

"Nor I yours," Quade returned, at last relenting to the minister's persistence. He could not judge all men of the cloth by the actions of one. Nor was he, after all, in the wilderness where he needed to guard his plans and moves from all and any. Although his first instinct was to distrust the man, he endeavored to be polite. "I am Quade Wylde," he said, bowing slightly, "friend of Noble Warren and of his widow. My business is with Goody Warren. My stay here may be short."

"You are a trapper by your garb," Bellingham remarked, pleased at the prospect of a brief stay, but not slackening in his desire to learn all he could about the stranger.

"Aye. A trapper." Quade did not bother to add that he could as easily have named Bellingham's occupation by the cut of his clothes. Were the man to preach a sermon on vanity, however, he would have to turn his head away from his own finery.

Bellingham nodded. "Of a lot I have found trappers a rowdy bunch prone to drunkenness and swearing," he remarked. "'Tis my belief a weakness of spirit comes from too much time spent living as savages. I pray you are a better man than most of your sort."

Quade locked his hands behind his back and held his tongue for a moment rather than prove the minister right on several points. "I hope you do not wear out your knees, sir," he said at length.

Certain he had the man at a disadvantage, Bellingham continued. "Your people, do they live in these parts?"

Now the minister was treading on ground best left undisturbed. Quade's hands clenched into hard fists. Even he did not delve too far into his past and he would not have Bellingham doing it. Intuitively he felt the minister's questions were not spurred so much by an interest in his soul as in his status.

"Nay. In God's," he answered, leaving the minister to determine if he had been dealt a slight or not. "Your pardon, please." Quade looked toward a man Maudie Lair had told him had a property for lease. "There is a one I would see before he takes his leave." With that he wrested himself from Bellingham's prying, though it had not been his intent to speak to the other man of a business matter on the Sabbath.

Assured that Quade Wylde had all the qualities needed to turn a maid's head, Bellingham shifted his attention to the party Quade had been speaking with earlier. An outsider's history could be easily concealed, but a clever fellow had ways of searching it out. There was more he wanted to know of the trapper, and he thought it best to get the information from someone other than the man himself.

A short while later when Bellingham approached Goody Warren he had the rewards of his labor and was in an improved frame of mind. Every man had his Achilles heel. Quade Wylde was no exception.

"Goody Warren," he called. "How fare you on this fine day?"

"I am well," Maudie Lair said as she left Rachel Leonard and her daughter, Mercy. Goody Leonard's hand had mended good as new and Maudie Lair was elated to see the goodwoman at her duties again.

"I have met your young friend, Quade Wylde," he said smoothly so she would not see the direction he meant to go. "He was indentured to your late husband at one time, was he not?"

"Not to my husband, to another." Maudie Lair detected nothing amiss in the minister's question. Bellingham considered it his obligation to be informed about everyone in his charge. Nor was there any shame in having been indentured. Many in Sealy Grove had paid passage to the colony by that means.

Bellingham shrugged. "I have twisted my facts," he said offhandedly. "His indenture was to a man in Boston, I believe."

"Crossland," she corrected.

"Ah, yes. Crossland." His look of faint amusement was quickly gone. "He is living with you, I understand."

"He is a guest in my house," Maudie Lair answered, now beginning to see there was method in the minister's line of questioning.

Bellingham pressed on, his hands folded in a reverent pose, his voice soft but steely. "Have a care, Goody Warren." He quirked his brows. "You are a widow. Do not give your neighbors cause to comment."

Her voice lifted in surprise. "Quade Wylde was like a son to Noble and is the same to me."

Bellingham smiled to himself. The barb was set. To Maudie Lair his face was penitent. "Forgive me," he implored. "I meant no disrespect. 'Tis only that I would have you guard your reputation and that of your daughter. This Wylde fellow is no relation of yours, is he?"

"Nay, but a dear friend as I have said."

Bellingham turned up his expressive hands. "I am sure there is no reason for concern," he said and nodded effusively. "I bid you peace, Goody Warren."

Pleased with himself, Bellingham walked off, certain he had worn out Quade Wylde's welcome for him.

Maudie Lair sighed long and loud. Just such meddling had caused her Noble to cherish his long sojourns in the wilderness. She understood his need for them more and more. Bellingham might lack diplomacy but he was astute and he knew his flock. A widow must guard against admonishments that a woman under the protection of a father or husband was not subject to. Having a man not related by blood under the same roof with two women was bound to spark criticism. Troubled by the thought of the damage that could be done by a carping tongue, Maudie Lair sought her daughter.

"Sarah!" Glory called excitedly as she saw her friend across the commons. "Wait!"

Sarah gave her a cool glance but nevertheless stopped and waited. "What do you want?" she asked impatiently.

"Why, only to talk and to ask you to come to the farm for a night if your mother can spare you," Glory replied, taken aback by the sharpness in Sarah's voice.

"She cannot." Sarah's gray eyes glowed green as she noted the wounded look on Glory's face. Let *her* hurt a little too, she thought petulantly. Let her know how it feels to be denied. "Excuse me, I must hurry home."

Sarah was off in a moment and Glory left to wonder why she had been rebuffed. Didn't Sarah like her anymore?

Hurt and in need of company, Glory spied a group of younger girls sitting in a circle on the commons while their parents gossiped with friends and neighbors they had not seen the week through. Soon she sat among them on the cool, green grass, teaching the youngsters to weave garlands of the fragrant flowers that bloomed in gay profusion in window boxes and beds around the town. One of the four was Ruthie Collier, a sister of Sarah's.

"Place the blossom here and loop a length of vine around the stalk." Sweet perfume from the petals floated in the air as Glory guided Ruthie's small hands in the work. "I asked Sarah to come to the farm for a visit but she could not," Glory said offhandedly. "Your mother must need her help quite a lot now."

"Nay," Ruthie said, quickly catching on to the weaving and more than happy to have the attention of the older girl. "Sarah has Prudence Oliver for company. They are together much now that you do not come to see us."

Glory hid her astonishment by quickly going to the aid of little Jane Cobb when she made a snarl of the vine she was trying to twist around the stems. Prudence Oliver was a plump, overly talkative girl of sixteen that Sarah had always avoided and on occasion unkindly labeled a silly twit. While she did not begrudge Sarah a new friend, she was sharply hurt to realize Sarah *had* deliberately avoided her. But why? What had she done to offend Sarah that could not be corrected with a word?

Her heart was still heavy when the garlands were finished and the children grew hushed as a gray squirrel hopped across the ground toward Glory. Mary Douglass squealed with glee when Glory held out a hand and the little creature climbed upon her wrist and nibbled a petal from her fingers.

"Let me hold it," Ruthie pleaded, but when she tried to touch the animal it leaped to the ground and scampered up a tree, where it sat barking and snapping its bushy tail like a whip.

Ruthie sniffed. Glory put her arm around the small girl. "Perhaps someday when we are alone the squirrel will be less afraid," she said consolingly. "Then you can hold it too."

It was in that posture that Maudie Lair Warren saw her daughter and heard the disturbing comments of two lads in the low branches of an elm. One was Francis Stevens, known for his sly mischief; the other was Joseph Allyn, another master troublemaker.

Abigail Allyn, Joseph's baby sister, his mother's pet and a royal tyrant in his household, was among those happily playing with Glory. Joseph swung around a limb with apish ability, then balanced and stared a long while at the girls sitting around Glory and holding her hands.

"She is a witch for sure to have Abigail in such a spell. The little imp is sweet as sugar candy."

"Who?" Francis queried, snuffing out the pipe he had been smoking while hidden in the tree branches. He parted some leaves to see what had brought about the pronouncement from Joseph. What he saw made him quiver: Glory looking prettier than the posies she held.

"Glory Warren is who." Joseph did not observe the longing in Francis's look. "You haven't forgotten how she got us strapped over Daft William?"

Francis didn't need to be reminded of the multitude of stripes applied to his backside or that Glory had had no use for him since. He puffed out his narrow chest and gave his opinion of the matter.

"Who but a witch would make merry on the Sabbath?" He marked Joseph's rapt attention and then went on, putting his interpretation on what he had heard his elders speak about. "For all we know she has got them in a kind of witches' circle." Seeing Joseph's eyes open wider, he went on. "Witches charm children. It's happened in Salem. Why Dorcas Good is a witch herself and but five years of age. I heard my pa say."

Joseph, only a notch above William Cook in wit, considered the revelation for a moment. "Well, if 'tis a spell she's cast on Abigail, I hope it lasts," he declared. "If it keeps her quiet."

Francis swung from the tree and landed on the ground with a thump. "Let's go," he said, noting that Glory had spied the two of them and turned back to the children without so much as a nod, "before the bitch witch puts a spell on us too."

The boys ran off, quickly forgetting about Glory Warren and witches. Maudie Lair stayed frozen where she stood for several minutes, a dark feeling of foreboding having settled over her. On little more evidence than what the pair had said of Glory, citizens in neighboring villages were being arrested for witchcraft, including little Dorcas Good the boys spoke of.

Like most goodwives in Sealy Grove, Goody Warren feared an outbreak of the same madness in her village. Perhaps she feared it more since distant kin of her husband stood among the accused in Salem. People were frightened. Harmless incidents which once would have been overlooked were now suspect. Even the prayers Reverend Bellingham had called for were no guarantee for Sealy Grove and its citizens.

How easily a charge could be levied against anyone. For a cross remark remembered, a spoiled tub of butter after a neighbor's visit, a nightmare unexplained, the word *witch* might be linked to a person's name. It took no more.

A shudder of dread shook Maudie Lair from her paralysis. That her Glory should become the target of such accusations was too terrible to contemplate. She would take her daughter home and caution her to be careful of all she said and did.

"Glory," she called, her voice falsely calm. "Bid the children goodbye. We must leave."

Glory returned the children to their mothers and for once made no supplication to stay awhile longer. Without Sarah's companionship there was no need. It was with difficulty that she walked Ruthie Collier to her mother and father and politely greeted them.

Anne Collier was well rounded and claimed the cause was that each of her brood had added an inch to her girth. By the looks of her the trend had not come to an end; she was well along in another pregnancy. Anne took Ruthie's small hand from Glory and clasped it in her own.

"You must visit us again soon, Glory," Goody Collier said. "We have missed your company lately."

More distressed than ever to be reminded that Sarah had

chosen another friend in her place, Glory mumbled that she hoped it would not be so long as it had been and hurried off. Burrell Collier, a barrel-chested and red-faced man not known for his tact, followed her nevertheless graceful departure with a long, harsh stare.

His good-natured wife, the antithesis of her dour husband, laughed softly. "Even you are not immune to a pretty face, I see," she lightly reproached him.

"Humph," he said, uncomfortable that the girl had stirred even a slight notice from him. "One could look for the devil's hand in the making of one so fair. Better a maid wear a plain face like Sarah's than one which would keep a husband from his labor and earn him the envy of his friends."

Goodman Collier's remark, though meant for his wife, also found the ear of Josiah Bellingham, who stood unnoticed only a few paces away at the meetinghouse door, just as intently focused on Glory Warren. He heartily disagreed with Collier. A man bought a horse that was sound of leg, sleek-coated, and comely when pulling a chaise. Should a man not look as prudently to the choice of a wife? It was God's decree that man be fruitful and multiply. Would not any man's virility be doublefold if his carnal appetite could be satisfied with the comeliest flower in nature's garden?

"Sir." Sarah rounded the corner of the meetinghouse as her parents strolled away, in time to see the minister avidly watching the departure of Glory Warren. Her eyes brooded with the misery and jealousy pent up inside her. Where she had been scorched before, she burned again. Was there no justice for the meek? she mused. Her aching heart would have stopped its beating to have Bellingham look at her with the same regard he gave to Glory Warren, but he had yet to acknowledge she had spoken to him. "Sir," she stammered.

Bellingham turned his gaze to Sarah and smiled tolerantly. For a moment she thought her heart had stopped and her voice had stilled as well. Never had she stood so close to the handsome minister without dozens of others gathered around. Never had the warming glance of the hazel eyes rested solely on her. To have him to herself even for a moment almost made Sarah forget why she had sought him out. But it had taken all her courage to approach the minister with her bold request; she could not let the chance slip away.

She licked her dry lips and mentally practiced what she would say before seeking her voice again. It was commonly known he took his meals at the tavern, but she believed he had no servant and must want for the work one could do in his cottage.

"I—I wish to offer my services for the cleaning of your lodgings," she said, wringing her thin hands.

Bellingham recognized the signs of infatuation. Sarah was not the first female to approach him on some insignificant pretext. Though at times sorely tested, he took pride in having bested temptations of the flesh and had to date maintained an unspotted widowhood. As for Sarah he took care neither to offend or encourage her.

"That is thoughtful of you, Sarah." He nodded graciously. "But Goody Cobb lends her serving woman once a week for a shilling. Her service fills my meager needs."

His voice enthralled her so that Sarah was slow to notice his words were a refusal of her offer. At last the meaning sunk in. "I would work for no charge," she hastened to say. "Perhaps you have washing or mending I could do."

Bellingham considered her proposal in a new light. He was not one to refuse what he might have for free and there were stockings and handkerchiefs in need of a stitch and shirts with lost buttons.

"Have you your father's approval for this charitable act?" He would not incur the wrath of Burrell Collier for all the buttons and mended stockings in existence. Though not of the gentry the man had some small influence in the colony and his recommendation would be essential when the time came to move to another post.

Sarah's pale cheeks flamed red. Was she so close to what she wished for? Her tightly clasped hands trembled. "My father is in agreement that I should give of my time. Too much of it is idle in his eyes," she added in a tinny voice. "He has given his approval."

Bellingham indulgently patted her head as if she were the merest child. "Very well, Sarah," he agreed. "I accept your generosity. On Thursday afternoons when I am abroad, you may come to the cottage. I will leave the mending out. When that is done we can discuss other chores."

While she was disappointed that he would not be at the cottage when she was there, she was not entirely so. A bit of privacy would suit her purpose well, and there would be times he must wait to tell her what was required.

"Thursdays will be convenient," she said, hardly able to contain her jubilation. "I have been told I sew a fine stitch." She spoke truthfully. The courting piece she had embroidered and hung in her corner of the room she shared with her sisters was the envy of many more experienced with a needle. "You will be pleased with my work."

"I am sure you are right," Bellingham responded, looking impatiently past the slim girl. He was certainly pleased to have his mending done at no cost.

He gave the fawning Sarah a parting smile. He had an inkling what her misguided purpose was. Before Thursday came he would confirm with Burrell Collier that the girl had permission to do as she said; he took no risks with his reputation. He would no sooner allow interference in his plans, not from a skinny, moon-eyed girl, and particularly not from an unkempt trapper.

The wind stirred with a promise of rain and blew much of the heat from the afternoon. Along the roadside, blue-edged violets and the white, bell-like blossoms of bindweed drooped a little for want of a drink, as did the young crops in the furrowed fields. A bank of dark clouds, thick and heavy with their baggage of moisture, swirled in over the clear blue sky. A whorl of dust, teased by the wind, kicked up from the dry roadbed as high as the traces on the cart moving slowly along a pair of well-worn ruts. The rain was needed and would be welcomed, but the three traveling beneath the unsettled sky hoped the downpour would hold off until they reached their destination.

Quade divested himself of Noble Warren's old doublet, the one Maudie Lair had saved from the rag basket and which he had put on to make himself presentable for the Sabbath. The borrowed hat was a mite too large but he would shortly see to getting one with a proper fit. Meanwhile the fur cap he preferred would serve well enough as would his mean buckskin garb.

The problem was not that he lacked the coin to purchase proper clothing; a trapper lived frugally and he had acquired a hefty purse. Unfortunately no shop in Sealy Grove dealt in apparel. Homespun was the order of the day and until he could commission a suit made by a local seamstress, what he had must do.

For all the thought he gave it, clothing was the least of his worries. He sensed an antagonist in Josiah Bellingham and could not fathom what had set the man against him even before they were acquainted. The matter would require careful feeling out. He groaned inwardly and kicked his feet free of the stirrups for a time as he considered that this new life he was testing might have all the rigors of the old. But why should that surprise him? His experience proved that in some ways "civilized" men were more barbarous than the savages they detested.

The thought did not set well with him. Soon his jaw was clenched tight and his mind in a testy mode. Better men than Bellingham had set themselves against him and he had risen to the challenge. What did he care if he had gained the enmity of one foppish minister? At the least a bit of opposition would prevent life from becoming unbearably dull.

And there were rewards. From his seat astride the roan, his gaze went to Glory sitting in the cart beside her mother. Only a glance at her face, the soft blush on her cheeks, the way the color deepened to rose when she caught his gaze upon her, and he was ready to meet all obstacles that might prevent having her ever as a feast for his eyes.

Glory's skin warmed as, from the corner of her eye, she saw Quade had given the big gelding his head while he covertly studied her. She had been lost in thought, but since Quade was the focus of it she gave herself over to forthright perusal of the trapper. Could he be unaware of the change he had made in her? Of how his kiss, so unexpectedly bestowed, had sent her spiraling out of her girlhood?

Abruptly, Glory dropped her eyes to the folded hands in her lap. Did he still feel the same? Or could that kiss have meant so little to him that he had forgotten the words spoken in the heat of the moment? Surely they had been heartfelt and he had not said them simply to ease her conscience. But if so, why had there been nothing more from him, not a single indication that he had any more purpose at the Warren farm than that of a casual visit?

A soft, troubled sigh slipped out. She had expected to be courted or at least to have a companion in whom she could confide. How she needed that since Sarah's withdrawal of friendship. No. That was not it. Glory cut her eyes to the trapper and sighed anew. She must be honest with herself. She wanted more than friendship from him.

"'Tis a quiet lot we are," Quade remarked when nearly half the journey to the farm had passed without a word uttered. The silence made him edgy and Glory was looking at him in a curious way. He was not good at pretenses or in guessing what was on a woman's mind. Nor could he think of a simple way to tell Glory exactly how he felt or what a battle raged within him over the decision he must make. Until the right words came to him he would wait.

"Aye," Maudie Lair replied at length, shaking herself out of the gloom that hung about her like a heavy mantle. "Would seem none of us are uplifted for the hours spent at meeting."

Quade nodded in agreement, then looked toward the deepening clouds overhead as the first rumble of thunder sounded in the distance.

"Nor will our spirits improve if we don't make haste." He clucked to the roan and swatted the cart horse on the rump. Both animals speeded to a fast trot. As the first slow drops of rain splattered down, the party tromped into the farmyard.

Maudie Lair yanked the horse to a stop near the back entrance and scurried out of the cart. Quade drew his mount up beside the other horse, his intent to allow the women a respite from the rain while he stabled the animals. Glory, however, had other ideas. Before Quade reached for the reins she snapped the leather leads and sent horse and cart speeding toward the barn. Astonished, Quade touched his heels to the gelding's sides and followed through the wide barn doors just as the deluge came.

"You do me a disservice, girl." The trapper bounded from the saddle and was at the cart when Glory started to climb down.

"How so?" she asked, pausing to accept his assistance as if she were accustomed to the aid of a strong arm.

"You do not allow me to play the gentleman," he scolded, swinging her from the step and lowering her to the narrow space between the cart and the wooden rails of a stall. "I would have brought the horses in and allowed you to keep dry."

"Would you?" Glory stood only inches away from him, not deigning to move. She blocked his way unless he wished to leap over the cart to tend the horses. When she made no move to step aside Quade gave her a questioning look and noted that in the dim light her eyes shone like a cat's. "You play the gentleman too well as is," she said coyly.

He met her demanding stare with a quick look of surprise. "For a backwoodsman that is a novel complaint."

"'Tis true enough," she said petulantly, hands settling on her hips. "A good day, a nod, a door held open. 'Tis all I get from you, Quade Wylde. Is there not more you wish to say—and do?"

"Hmm," he responded. "You're a saucy wench, aren't you?" Glory huffed. Laughing, Quade caught her by the shoulders to gently move her aside so he could unharness the cart horse. She thwarted him by catching his sleeves and holding fast.

"Saucy enough to want an answer," she snapped. "You were quick enough to take your liberties at the river and to talk of longings and yearnings. Since you've had naught for me but a comment or two on the weather. I'll have my answer," she said, sliding her arms upward and locking them around his neck.

"Glory." He tried to pull her arms away but she laced her fingers tightly together and refused to let go. When her uplifted breasts seared him with sudden heat his attempt to get free became halfhearted. Each day near her had been a torture of wanting and denial. Still, he had not forgiven himself for making bold with her at the river. And now she would chastise him for his restraint. "Watch what you do, Glory," he warned. "'Tis not a youth you dally with, leading on then walking away."

"I have no wish to walk away until I have heard the words I desire." She lifted her face, full of entreaty, to him.

Quade forgot his resolve to keep his distance. His fingers hastily loosened the string holding her cap and pulled it away. The ebony hair piled underneath tumbled in a dark curtain around her shoulders.

Above, the rain pounded a thousand drumbeats on the cedar shakes. At the door it formed a floating wall of silver, shutting them into a world all their own. The horses, forgotten for the time, stood patiently in wait of release from harness and saddle. Paddy, perched on a high beam, twisted his head under a wing and slept, giving a rare moment of privacy to the two below.

Quade's arms eased around Glory, drawing her tightly against him, his face poised an inch away from hers. "If you have been this forward with another, Glory Warren, I wonder you have not been tossed on your backside in some haystack."

His mouth was so close his lips grazed hers as he talked. Glory returned the pleasure with her answer. "I have been forward only with you, Quade Wylde, and naught has come of it except that I am treated as some old thornback spinster you will not come near.''

With that she pulled his head low and pressed his lips to hers. He needed no more urging. His mouth played recklessly on her supple lips, locking them together in a swell of rising passion. Hungrily, he kissed her cheeks, her soft eyelids, her throat, then returned the sweet assault to her mouth and lingered there greedily drinking in the nectar of her kiss.

Glory savored the heat of his mouth, the gentle teasing of his tongue across her lips, and gave herself completely to the enjoyment of the shared bliss. Her heartbeat quickened and the surroundings became a blur. She believed she had changed her mind about not enjoying being a woman. Such pleasures as this would make it all worthwhile.

For need of a breath Quade moved his mouth away. ''You're all sweetness, Glory,'' he whispered, his voice husky and low.

Glory, too, drew a much needed breath. ''And you are all fire, I think. Or fire and flint,'' she amended to account for the feel of hot sparks on her skin. ''I like the way I feel when you kiss me. I wonder if I would like . . .''

''Glory! You little strumpet!'' Quade clamped his hand across her soft mouth. He scowled but his dark eyes flashed with amusement. ''You'll drive me over the brink with talk like that.''

She playfully nipped his hand with her teeth. ''I'll be happy just to drive you to tell what you're here for. You said you came because of me. Am I so disappointing you wish you had stayed in the forest?''

Quade shook his head as he dragged his fingers through the tumble of silken hair. ''Nay, love, 'tis just the other way around. You are more than I dreamed, more beautiful—and sweet as I have said, but with enough vinegar that I will not smother in sweetness." His voice fell lower, huskier. " 'Tis not you who disappoint."

"What then?" she demanded, her arms now snugly around his waist. Before he could answer the first question she asked a second. "Do you want to wed me or not?"

He gave a rollicking laugh and hugged her to him. Never had he encountered such an impudent woman. Was there no way to win with her? He thought not. When his laughter died down he shook his head, then looked purposefully into her glowing eyes. "Glory," he entreated. "Give a man time. We have not laid eyes on one another in two years and you were a child when I last—"

"I know all that," she interrupted, not pleased that he found her questions cause for laughter. "But I have the feeling that if I do not get my answers now, you may ride away again. I would not wait another two years to know your intentions."

Quade sighed in resignation. His hands were at her throat, caressing the satin skin. Her brilliant eyes shone like firebrands. He had to glance away for fear that in a moment he would be able to refuse her nothing. All was going awry here. He hadn't meant to share his reservations with her, but since she pressed him, he had to try to explain why he believed they should approach the matter slowly and cautiously.

"If I could but have you, Glory, it would all be easy enough," he said. "You are beauty and light, all a man could want in a woman. 'Tis this life I must lead to have you that holds me back. I am a trapper, a wilderness man. I like to see the sun rise over my head in the mornings, see the moon shining in the sky when I go to sleep at night." He held her face between his large but gentle hands. "As much as I wish for you I find it hard to live with people at my elbows."

"We could go away," she offered. "We need not stay in Sealy Grove."

He caressed her cheeks, running his fingers along the fine bones, stroking the rose-petal softness of her skin. She made it very hard for him to remember what needed to be said. "Where could we go that would be different than here? One town is very like another and equally as filled with people."

Her mind raced for a solution to the problem and quickly came to one. "I could go with you," she said abruptly. "I could learn to hunt and trap. We could live in the wilderness."

"Nay." He shook his head so that the hair tied in a queue swished across his back. "'Tis no life for a woman. If you were mine I would want you to have as good or better than you have here. I could not give you less. 'Tis I who must change. Until I am sure I can learn to live among others I can ask no pledge of you."

Not happily, but with a sense of fairness, Glory accepted Quade's explanation. Her father had suffered from the same restlessness Quade expressed and had found a way to live in both worlds. She believed Quade would too. He only needed time to get used to the notion. She could wait. If not patiently, she could wait.

A spark of innocent mischief lit her face and she tapped a finger lightly on his hard chest. "There is no reason in the meantime why we cannot share a kiss when we want."

Quade groaned. How was he to explain the danger of that? She was too soft and warm against him, and if she was not aware of his body rousing to her it was because she was more naive than her sauciness would lead him to believe.

His hands tensed on her shoulders as he sought to make her understand. "I am accustomed to living by my own rules, Glory, of taking what I would have."

She gave him a puzzled look. "What has that to do with a kiss if I am willing?"

He shrugged and tried another inroad. "A kiss, you see, is but a step toward . . ." She placed a finger on his lower lip, feeling the rise and fall of it as he spoke. Quade gently pushed her hand away. Having failed again he tried still another way to warn her. "A kiss is not an end in itself, Glory, my sweet. The danger comes . . ." Her finger ran about the rim of his ear and on to enticingly stroke the lobe. "Ahhh," he moaned, giving up the cause as she pursed her rosy lips and hugged him more tightly within the bond of her arms. "You will know soon enough, I fear."

Conceding, he crushed his mouth to hers, twisting, turning, taking her breath, losing his. Where he had held back before he had no hope of doing so now. His hand skimmed her sides, nudging her ever closer.

Glory settled against the stall gate, bracing her back as Quade bent to her. A soft cry slipped from her lips as he nuzzled her throat and buried his face in the dark, tousled curls cascading over her back and shoulders. Lazily he parted the kerchief crossing her bosom and skimmed his fingers over the high swells of her breasts.

Writhing in ecstasy, she thought she could not endure the delectable feel of his hands on her flushed skin, nor could she imagine why anything that felt so wonderful should be forbidden. She would ask him about that sometime when she had nothing better to do. But not now. Now she preferred to feel the tingles of pleasure every place his hands roamed.

Quade bent lower for another drink of her sweetness. His mouth slanted across hers, his tongue sampled the dewy lips, his teeth nipped as if he nibbled at a confection. Glory leaned heavily against the gate that she might use all her strength to meet this new attack of bliss. Not latched, the gate groaned and swung inward. The pair, clasped together, tumbled behind it, landing in a tangled embrace on the clean straw lining the stall.

"Damnation!" Quade swore, raising up on his elbows. Glory, wide-eyed and open-mouthed, lay half-buried in the straw beneath him and he worried that his weight might have bruised or otherwise injured her. He attempted to roll free but found her skirt had knotted around his legs and he could not pull away without rending the garment. "Are you hurt, girl?"

For an answer she gave a strangled cry and waved her arms in a helpless fashion.

"Glory!" Quade rolled to his knees, pulling her up with him. Alarmed, he brushed the disarray of hair from her wan face and gave her a gentle shake. "Glory, love, speak, will you?"

She gasped and pressed a hand to her heaving chest. "'Tis all right," she said weakly. "The fall knocked the breath from me. 'Tis nothing more."

"Bloody hell," he moaned, giving her another shake. "I thought I'd broken a bone or worse. How would I have explained that to your mother?"

The color came back to her blanched face. She laughed as Quade helped her to her feet. "Be glad the gate gave way," she jibed as she picked straw from her clothes and straightened her bodice and kerchief. "Else you might have a more serious matter to explain."

Quade scoffed and spun her around to brush more wisps of straw from the snarls of black curls. He feared she did not know how much in earnest her jest was. "You're shameless, Glory Warren," he said sternly, glad she could not see the gleam of enjoyment in his eyes.

"Aye," she said softly, turning to face him as she tucked the black silken tresses beneath her cap. "And the fault is all yours. Was your kiss that taught me how sweet a morsel a man's lips are. Now I would eat again and again of that treat."

His hands at her waist he gave her a quick fierce hug. "Mind your ways, Glory," he whispered huskily. "What you feel is new and easily misunderstood. I would not willingly lead where you might not wish to go." He halted and smiled dubiously. "But believe me, my sweet, there are moments when my will yields to a greater force."

"Aye." Glory turned her face up so that her eyes met his. She gave a long, wistful sigh. Within, she knew the rightness of what he said. "I would not trap you by playing fast and easy," she whispered. "I would have you by your own choice and not by a chance forced upon you. I will give you the time to choose as you must," she promised, and then with a ghost of a smile and a merry twinkle in her eye added, "Let it not be said I have robbed any man of his will."

Quade quietly set about the long overdue task of tending the horses while Glory clucked and cooed to Paddy. Often his gaze was on her as she stood framed in the misty light of the doorway. She was a pretty bundle of trouble, that one, more than he had bargained for. He had expected a shy little virgin, one who would tremble at a brazen glance, a girl he could easily walk away from once he had satisfied himself that the Glory of his dreams was little more than imagination.

He gave a frustrated groan but only loud enough for the horses to hear. The flesh-and-blood Glory was much more than the vaporous girl of his dreams. She was hot-blooded and sweet, a temptress who did not know her powers. He feared he was helpless should she ever truly learn to use them. But that might not be so bad, he considered as he made short work of tending and feeding the horses. By the time he was finished the rain had slackened to a drizzle.

"Shall we go, love?" he called, taking Glory's arm and dashing across the farmyard, hoping after all he had endured Maudie Lair Warren would not greet him with the muzzle of her musket.

CHAPTER
6

Anne Collier boasted of four crystal wineglasses, those remaining of a set of eight handed down from her grandmother to her mother and lastly to her. They were prized possessions kept on a high shelf and brought down only on special occasions, most often the christening of the newest child born into the family. For daily use the family drank from pewter or wooden cups. None of Goody Collier's brood were allowed to touch the crystal.

It was for that reason Sarah crept across the kitchen floor like a sly mouse and with agonizing care positioned a footstool under the storage shelf. Hardly daring to breathe she climbed to the stool's seat and used her memory as guide when she reached for the stems of two glasses. Grasping them with the utmost care, she crept back as she had come, not daring to light a candle until she was back in her room. A few moments later, a wineglass trophy in each hand, Sarah eased through the blackness to the foot of her bed.

"Do you have them?" Prudence Oliver whispered. Sitting

cross-legged on the feather ticking with her hair tucked neatly into her nightcap and her full white gown wrapped about her legs, Prudence had the look of a fat goose awaiting a scattering of corn.

"Both," Sarah's nervous whisper returned.

"Can I light the candle now?" Prudence's voice trilled with excitement.

"Shhh," Sarah whispered. "Let me be certain my sisters are still sleeping." Prudence sat quietly, tucking the hem of her nightgown securely under her chilled feet while Sarah peeked around the quilt she had strung across her corner after Ruthie and Judith had fallen asleep. The slow and measured breaths of the two younger Collier girls came distinctly and reassuringly from the darkness. Sarah pushed the edge of the quilt against the wall so no line of light would show through when Prudence lit the candle. "Go ahead," she whispered eagerly.

Since they had not dared bring a lighted brand through the darkened house, Prudence began the painstaking process of striking a light from the flint and steel in Burrell Collier's tinder box. The job was made no easier by the lack of all but the palest glimmer of moonlight shining through the oiled paper in the bedroom window. To her credit, and as a result of much practice at home, Prudence caught a spark less than a quarter hour later and quickly thereafter had the stump of a tallow candle glowing.

Nearly bursting with anticipation the two girls slid to the floor in the space between the bed and the wall with the candle and the two precious glasses positioned between them.

"Heat the water." Sarah pointed to the small porringer set out of sight behind one footpost of the bed.

While Prudence took the vessel in her hands, Sarah

stretched an arm beneath the pillow and withdrew a napkin concealing the two fresh hen eggs she had retrieved from the chicken coop late in the evening.

Holding the pewter porringer with a folded cloth to protect her hand, Prudence moved it over the candle flame until the water within was warmed.

Sarah tested the temperature with her finger. "Pour carefully," she whispered, worried that the hot water might crack the delicate crystal. Had there been another vessel of clear glass in the house she would have used it instead. But there was not and what she was about to do was too important not to take the risk.

For all her chubbiness Prudence had a steady hand and poured the glasses full without spilling a drop. "Done," she whispered, her eyes dancing gleefully. "Shall we do mine first, or yours?"

"Yours," Sarah answered, enjoying the anxious anticipation too much to bring it to a fast end. Ceremoniously she produced one of the eggs and handed it to Prudence. "You must close your eyes and think very hard for a whole minute, then crack the egg—"

"I know the rest," Prudence interrupted. A moment later she held the brown egg clasped in both plump hands. Her eyes were shut so tightly the eyelids looked as if they were sealed for good. Sarah wondered if her friend was not meditating so hard she would crush the egg before the minute passed.

"The time is done," Sarah mumbled when she had counted the seconds away.

Prudence opened her eyes slowly and proceeded with the next step. Gently she cracked the egg and split the shell, maneuvering the yolk into one half, the white into the other.

The half with the white she held poised over one glass. Barely loud enough to be heard, Prudence whispered a rhyme as she poured the white of the egg into the water.

"In the glass, spin and spell," she chanted conspiratorially. "Tell the trade my sweetheart holds."

Two sets of eyes zealously watched the opaque egg white swirl in the water and then congeal into a nondescript shape. Where common sense was lacking, whimsy took root and each imagined the floating mass contained what she wished most to see.

"'Tis a hammer or hook of some sort?" Prudence's plump cheeks twitched excitedly. "What does it seem to you, Sarah?"

"Neither hammer nor hook," Sarah answered, studying the shape as if she observed the secrets of the universe. "'Tis an anvil, I believe." Prudence gave a dubious look. Sarah promptly remembered she had three years' wealth of wisdom and experience beyond that of her friend. "An anvil I am certain," she said imperiously. "See the base." Her smile was convincing. Her hand squeezed Prudence's wrist. "Your sweetheart is a smith."

The image of a strong, handsome fellow at the forge was enough to dash all the doubts Prudence harbored. One of that description only recently had begun to learn the trade from her uncle. A lad named Eli.

"A smith!" she cried, squirming with joy. "I'll wed a smith!"

"Shhh," Sarah shushed her and knew a moment of terror. She did not like the thought of what her father would do should he find her practicing what he termed sorcery, particularly now when witches roamed the land. But the test was true, even if it relied on the black arts. Everyone knew the test was true. Had not Patience Towne sworn such a reading had foretold she would marry a wheelwright? And six months later she wed Rich Doty, who had sold her mother a spinning wheel.

"'Tis your turn," Prudence prompted when it appeared Sarah would never come out of the daze she was in.

Sarah unwrapped the second egg. As Prudence had done minutes before, Sarah shut her eyes for sixty seconds of intense meditation, then with trembling hands, cracked the egg, separated the yolk and white, and dropped the white into the glass of water. Sarah's head reeled with the swirl of the gelatinous mass. Her warm palms dampened with perspiration. She desperately needed this confirmation of what was in her heart, especially since her father had hinted that bucktoothed Isaac Hawkins had much to offer as a mate. Sarah shuddered. As if she would consider wedding such a stick.

When the egg white firmed and stilled in the glass, Prudence could hold her tongue no longer. "What do you see, Sarah?" she queried, twisting her head to take a look from every direction. "'Tis all naught to me."

Sarah too bent her head this way and that, looking at the cloudy clump of egg white in the glass. "'Tis a book," she said softly, her heart beating unsteadily as she convinced herself it was true.

"A book? What could that mean?" Prudence impatiently bent low for a closer look. "A scholar? A teacher?"

"Nay," Sarah whispered, tears of happiness beginning to well in her eyes. "'Tis the good book you see." She stretched out a thin finger. "Note that part which resembles the cross."

"Aye," Prudence whispered, seeing it all clearly now that it had been pointed out to her. "'Tis a minister you will wed, Sarah." She sat back on her heels. "Fancy that."

Fancy it was exactly what Sarah did, long after the glasses

were rinsed and returned to the shelf and the wastes of the eggs buried beneath a bush outside the kitchen door. Her eyes did not shut for a long, long while, not for hours after Prudence slumbered beneath the quilts on her bed. A face appeared to her so clearly that it might have been by some magic etched into the darkness. Sarah's heartbeat skipped each time she thought on what she had learned in the waning hours of the night. She would wed a minister. The test was true.

"I will wed Josiah Bellingham," she whispered, voicing her dream at last.

The week passed with what seemed half its normal duration. Quade took it upon himself to be on guard in the moments he was alone with Glory since it took a mere glance, a chance touch from her to fire his passion to the point of dashing all reason. Her beauty, he was sure, increased threefold each day. Soon he began to feel he needed the sound of her voice or the smile she was quick to give more than he needed nourishment for his body.

Her open ways and honesty he acknowledged as sweet and rare prizes but there was a delightful tartness about her too. A shopkeeper in Sealy Grove had called her willful because she had once demanded he wait on William Cook in turn instead of overlooking the boy for a customer with a bigger purse. "Turned those wild eyes on me and spoke as if she was the magistrate," the man had complained. "The girl has too much idle time," he went on. "She roams the country on that horse as if she was a man. A female ought to be afeared of something."

Quade had listened but not entirely agreed. Was it not to be expected that the only child of a well-to-do widow would be more outspoken than other girls? As for being idle, she did her chores. But her mother could well afford to hire others to ease the load of work on the large farm. And none could say she was not devoted to her mother or that she had not a quiet, gentle way with children and animals. If sprinkled with spice, Glory was nevertheless an openhearted girl who gave freely of her affection.

Quade grinned. Such a girl would inevitably inspire envy in a few like the loose-tongued shopkeeper. If Glory had flaws they were tiny ones. For his purposes he might have preferred that she had greater shortcomings; then he would have a just reason for the restlessness he felt, for the urge to leap astride his horse and lose himself in the forest. As it was, he had to admit that his urgency stemmed from a flaw in him, one that manifested itself as a fear that his heart, so long cold and closed, was growing soft with love.

In a compromise with himself Quade decided to leave the Warren farm for a short time. He did have his possessions, meager though they were, stored in a cave some miles north of the settlement. Since he had committed to renting a cabin from Asa Douglass, now was an opportune time to fetch them.

"I see no reason for you to go away." Glory's petulant face taunted the trapper as he sat astride the roan gelding. She appeared to be biting her tongue to avoid demanding he stay at the farm.

To hide his humor at her displeasure, Quade scrutinized the pack animal Maudie Lair had loaned him, checking needlessly to see that the straps and halter were securely hooked.

"There is a need," he said, after a time daring to meet the flashing eyes. "I have a store of skins and goods two days' ride away. If I am to enjoy any comfort in the cabin I will need them with me."

Glory sighed heavily as she reached out and stroked the roan's muzzle. "I do not think you should move to the cabin at all.'' Though she had resolved not to, she brought up a matter that needled her as much as the trip Quade was about to take. ''Our house is plenty big for three.''

To begin with, she did not like the idea of Quade going off. What if he should decide not to come back? Provided he did, she didn't like the plans he had made to lease the vacant cabin at the back of the Douglass' property, even though it was easily within walking distance of the Warren farm. She did not think her mother would allow her to visit him there and she had quickly grown fond of having him ever at her beck and call.

''That is just the case I make,'' he said. '''Tis your house. A man should have a place he calls his own, whether a clearing in the wood or a rough cabin.''

'''Tis not your cabin either, if you but rent.'' Her brows lifted. ''And if 'tis but to rent which makes you feel a place is your own my mother and I will put a charge on the room you now occupy.''

Maudie Lair frowned at her daughter but Glory ignored her.

Quade chuckled. If he had thought to find a woman who would be agreeable to his every whim he had missed the mark with Glory. She *was* a bit spoiled and too accustomed to having her own way.

Glory's hand rested on the roan's neck where she stroked the animal beneath the silky mane. Quade gently placed his hand over hers.

''Your mother has been more than kind to let me stay so long,'' he said, clasping her hand and giving it a squeeze. ''But I would have a place where I am not underfoot, where I am master of my castle.''

''But . . .'' Glory started, then hushed as her mother gave

her a look too sharp to ignore. "When will you be back?" she asked instead.

Quade straightened in the saddle, pulling his hand away. "In five days or perhaps more," he told her. "Whatever time it takes."

Glory's brow furrowed with a frown and the bright eyes clouded momentarily as the sky does before a storm. "'Tis only two days' ride, you said." She cocked her head to one side. "Why . . ."

This time Maudie Lair did not stop with a glance. Now at her daughter's side she gave her a nudge. "Godspeed," the older woman bid the trapper. "A safe trip to you."

Glory stepped back a pace, guided somewhat by a hidden tug on her sleeve. "Goodbye," she added reluctantly.

Quade nodded and offered Glory a mercurial grin as he turned his mount to the trail, the pack animal ambling along behind.

Glory bit down sharply on her lower lip. She had the feeling she was in for a lecture the minute Quade was out of earshot. She also had the uncomfortable feeling that what her mother was about to say was right. Dreading what was to come she waited the long minutes it took for Maudie Lair to enter the house, stir the fire to flame, and brew a pot of herbal tea.

When they were seated at the table and each had taken a sip of the tea and just as Glory had begun to believe she might be spared, her mother drummed the table with her fingers, a sign she had something of consequence to say. Glory flinched beneath Maudie Lair's composed stare.

"What is it you want of Quade, daughter?" her mother asked. Glory smiled uneasily. The answer to that question came too quickly and readily. Nevertheless, she replied with what had sprung into her mind.

"What I want," she said, "is that he prefer me to the wilderness. I would be first with him. First in his thoughts and first in his heart."

"You care for him."

Not sure if her mother had asked a question or stated a fact as she saw it, Glory paused a moment before offering her reply. "Aye," she said, blushing, but as she had rarely found it necessary to be less than honest with her mother did not hold back exactly what she felt. "And he cares for me though he is too stubborn to give himself up to what he feels."

"He fears losing his freedom." Maudie Lair stilled her fingers and leaned back, surveying her daughter with knowing eyes.

"I would not take his freedom," Glory countered, her brows flickering. "'Tis his love of adventure which sets him apart from other men."

"Aye," Maudie Lair said. "And would such a man tie himself to a shrew?"

"A shrew? Nay," Glory said indignantly. "He would not tolerate—" Her eyes flew open wide.

"Aye." An inkling of humor showed behind her mother's placid face. "He is like your father in that. And like your father there will be times when he must go where there are no boundaries for a man. When he must go, step aside and let him go freely. Give a parting smile and a fond farewell and trust to that to turn his path home again."

Glory nodded. "A shrew." She tried the word again, this time picturing herself the way Quade must have seen her, demanding, directing, prodding. She hoped she had not made him long for even more freedom.

Three days following Quade's departure, Glory found herself alone at the farm, her mother having been called along with a number of other goodwives to help bring another life into the world. Since there was no way to predict how long Maudie Lair would be away, Glory worked diligently to complete both her chores and her mother's before evening. She could not, however, resist on several occasions climbing the attic stairs to see the litter of kittens Tansy had tucked in a space among the dried ears of corn stored there.

She was at the top of the stairs on her third pilgrimage to the attic when a rap sounded from the brass knocker at the front door. William, she supposed, having failed to rouse her at the kitchen. He would be wanting to know what work she had for him.

But it was Josiah Bellingham who stood on the stoop of the Warren house. While he waited for an answer to his knock he took the opportunity to closely examine the structure. He had visited the house before but now his interest was personal.

Keen, solicitous eyes ran over the clean lines from the stone foundation to the cedar shakes on the roof. He also assessed the spacious barn, the well-stocked coop, the smokehouse, the dovecote, and other outbuildings. Altogether a self-supporting farm.

Bellingham liked what he saw. The place had a definite look of prosperity. The grayed clapboards of the farmhouse were well hewn and tightly set to keep out the weather. The windows had good glazing and the door hinges were of iron instead of leather. Only one or two other houses in Sealy Grove were larger or finer. All in all a fitting residence for a minister, a trifle far from town, but with a good horse that was no hindrance.

"It will do nicely," he mumbled to himself as he straightened his coat, checked his starched white cuffs for any speck of soil or stain, and determined that his stockings were free of wrinkles. He was not expected but he was sure the widow would welcome him.

A satisfied smile broke the satirical look on his handsome face as he awaited Goody Warren. The trapper had not been in meeting on the Sabbath past. He credited himself with that and with making William Cook an invaluable informant. How easy it was to extract news of events here from the idiot boy. No Catholic priest in his confessional could be more adept at uncovering secrets. In a spare five minutes he had learned from William that the Wylde fellow had packed his animals and ridden off.

Bellingham gave a low and caustic laugh. There was a problem easily dispatched—and before he had received answer to his inquiry in Crossland.

The door swung open but it was not Goody Warren who stood to greet him. Glory, her hair uncovered and bound back with a bit of yarn, gasped in surprise.

"Reverend!" she stammered. "I did not expect you." Her hands flew to her bare head. "Forgive me," she said, alarmed that if she had to be caught with her head uncovered it must be by the minister himself. "I'll get my cap." She half whirled away, then as quickly whirled back, remembering her manners. She could not leave Reverend Bellingham on the stoop.

He removed his hat and made a polite bow.

With her mother away she would have refused entry to any other man. Since the visitor was Reverend Bellingham, and as all knew, a person above reproach, the proper thing to do was to invite him in. For her, Reverend Bellingham was a person in a category by himself. Although she acknowledged he was of the male sex, she simply did not think of him as a man.

He was a person she admired in many ways. His sermons

at times stirred her heart or at worst set her head to thinking when she found his sentiments disagreeable. For all that, he was to her a part of the church, as inanimate as the pulpit he stood behind on meeting days. She did not assign him human feelings and urges.

Not the same for herself, caught barefoot and bareheaded, it was with forced calmness that she invited him in. "You must have had a dusty ride—perhaps a mug of cider would refresh you."

An eager gleam in his hazel eyes, Bellingham nodded and quickly stepped over the threshold. Before Glory spun away he tapped her lightly on the shoulder.

"'Tis of no concern that your head is bare," he said, admiring the fall of raven locks streaming nearly to her hips. Poor Esther's hair had been thin to the point of embarrassment and lacking any distinctive color. Glory Warren's was thick and long enough that she might be a modest Mistress Godiva if she chose. "Leave off your cap," he implored as his mind illustrated what his thoughts had brought forth. He would let her play the legendary lady for him when they were wed— and he would serve as her steed.

"As you wish." She smiled sweetly.

Bellingham noted with approval her gown of watchet blue that made her lighter eyes all the more brilliant. The linen fabric was finely woven and flowed over her generous curves like a soft Eastern silk as she turned to shut the door behind him. She was met by gentle gust of wind which slipped into the foyer and whipped her skirts high on her calves, revealing trim ankles and dainty feet. For Bellingham, who did not miss the display, it was another lovely bit of femininity long denied his hungering eyes.

His lips thinned and pressed tightly together. He was grateful for the long coat that hid the outcome of the sudden surge in his loins. Nevertheless, his hat held strategically in front of him, he made an abrupt turn as if to admire a sampler hung on the wall.

"A fine piece of work," he commented, mopping his brow with a hastily withdrawn handkerchief. Though the house was cool, he felt the temperature had abruptly escalated by several degrees, the unhappy symptom of a body insistent for relief and victimized by the desires boiling within it.

"'Tis middlin' fair," Glory said. "A work I did for my father. 'Tis not so neat as I do now but he was pleased."

While Bellingham's back was turned she shook her head in bemusement that he should find the ragged stitches she had done as a child of admirable quality. Plainly he knew nothing of needlework. Although she was quite adept at spinning and weaving, she had never been as clever with her stitching. Uncomfortable to have him continue goggling at the childish work, she invited him to the parlor.

Breathing heavily, Bellingham walked stiffly behind Glory as she led him into the cozy room, deeming to stand before the mantel when she bid him take a seat.

Since he would not sit she did not either and, skirts swaying, crossed the room and stood quietly, framed by a window sash, her face in profile, her features backlit by the sunshine seeping through the panes. Bellingham gawked in earnest as he had pretended to do at the sampler, his mind totally absorbed with the delicate lines of her face, those of classic perfection.

"If 'tis my mother you seek, she is out."

Bellingham detected the soft murmur of her voice but it seemed his sense of hearing had shut down that his eyes might more fully appreciate her beauty. With the light on it her skin glowed like soft ivory satin; he laced his fingers together to restrain the itch to touch it. A smell of lavender, from the tied bunches hung on the beams, permeated the room and did much to make his yearning all the more acute. He must remember the lavender and put bunches of it around the room on their wedding night.

Had the girl any inkling of the effect she had on him? Nay. His shrewd eyes narrowed. She was naive. She would know little of what passed between a man and a woman and that was best. He would teach her to be a submissive and obedient wife.

It was a rare occurrence for Bellingham to be dumbstruck, but for several minutes he could not pull his eyes away or recall just why he had come. "I would speak with your mother," he announced at last. "I would speak to her on a matter of some urgency."

Glory frowned. Had he not just heard her say her mother was out? Bellingham was not so old that he should be hard of hearing. She believed he must be less than a score of years older than she was.

"Goodman Tilden's servant fetched her this morning to midwife Goody Tilden. 'Tis her time to be delivered," Glory explained.

"So I have come in vain." Crestfallen, he took no pains to hide his disappointment as he made to leave.

He had not counted on a delay in making his purpose known to Goody Warren. He considered waiting for her return, but who could guess how long it would be before Goody Tilden's baby arrived? Besides, it was not fitting to remain alone with Glory. She was far too desirable. Were he a less honorable man he might choose to stay, but he had his reputation to be concerned about.

Still he moved slowly, all the while contemplating his situation. Privy to all the talk in town, he knew he was not the only one to have determined Glory Warren a plum of a match. Even now, fathers were thinking how to fund their sons with a settlement proportionate to her dowry. While he did not think she would choose another over him, he preferred not to take the risk.

He sighed hollowly. Not until after the next Sabbath would he be free to return to the Warren farm. He did not relish the wait. But such was his lot. A widower's life was sorely trying for a man who would not dishonor himself by turning to base or vile women. He must wed soon or find himself tried beyond what any man could bear. Prayers and fasting had ceased to quench the flames of need inside him. Well, he contented himself, at least the trapper was gone.

To Glory it seemed the minister was acting strangely. It was unlike him to say so little. She hoped he had not come to report some infraction of hers. She could think of nothing she had done amiss except to gallop the mare through town when she had been sent on an errand. Nay. Who could complain of that?

"I'll tell my mother you called," she said as she led him out of the room.

"I would be grateful. Mayhap on the Sabbath I can arrange with her a convenient time to return."

Bellingham followed purposefully to the door but found himself crossed by temptation by the time he reached it. Here was an opportunity, a part of him cried. He should take it. The mother would be far more willing to agree to the marriage if the daughter wished the match. Besides, the worst that could come of a compromising situation was that he would have to wed the girl and that was, after all, his wish.

"Aye, she will be pleased," Glory said matter-of-factly, having convinced herself the visit had nothing to do with her after all. She was set to show him out when he reminded her she had offered a mug of cider.

"Would ease my thirst before I start home." His voice was slightly strained.

"Your pardon, please." Glory's face reddened. How could she have been so thoughtless? Her mother would be horrified. Again offering apologies, Glory hastened to the kitchen and quickly filled a mug with cider for the minister. As she corked the spout on the cider barrel she was astonished to find Bellingham had followed her into the room.

"No need for you to make unnecessary steps," he reasoned, taking the mug from her small hands and managing to brush his fingers over hers in the process. "Will you not share a cup with me?"

"Aye," Glory answered, lest she appear even more impolite. A minute later she had filled a mug for herself and was insisting Bellingham sit until he finished drinking.

He chose the backless form running the length of the table on one side, hoping she would sit beside him. Instead she sat in a chair across the board from him. Bellingham smiled and sought to engage her in conversation. On a shelf he noted flour had been spread and a bowl sat covered with a cloth.

"You are making bread, I see."

"Aye," she answered. "With the last of the wheat flour. After that it will be rye and 'injun' until next harvest."

"Even that is better than the tavern offers. 'Tis all of injun corn and a taste I tire of." Bellingham sipped the sweet and potent cider, deciding he felt quite at home in the Warren kitchen with Glory attending him. "I am pleased to find you are an industrious girl," he said. "'Tis a fitting trait for a female."

Her laughter rippled gently through the air. "I fear I am not so commendable as I should be. 'Tis easy to find a diversion and be tempted to gad about when the day is a bonny one."

"I have heard naught but good of you," he assured her. "Indeed, 'tis commonly remarked you will make a fine consort when you wed."

The rosy color in her cheeks deepened. Could the minister read her mind and know her wishes concerning Quade? "I hope 'tis not said of me in error," she stammered. "I would endeavor to be a good and meet wife to my husband."

"You desire to wed soon then?" Bellingham ventured to ask, seeing the high color in her cheeks and the nervous way she wrung her hands beneath her apron. But of course. He almost laughed aloud. How had he missed the signs before? The girl was smitten with him. Holding his laughter, he gave her instead an expression of tender understanding.

Glory averted her eyes from the strange look in Bellingham's. "When the time is right," she answered. "When the one I favor desires the same as I do."

The expression on the minister's face had not changed. She hoped he was not about to ask who it was she favored. The time was not right to reveal that.

Bellingham relaxed as much as was possible on the backless bench, relieved by the assurance he would meet no resistance when he made his plea to the girl's mother. No doubt Glory hungered for a word of encouragement that he felt similarly disposed toward her, but that would be inappropriate until he had negotiated with Maudie Lair for the dowry.

"I am sure it will all come to pass as you wish it."

"Aye," she said, relaxing visibly. "I must believe that is true."

He patted the hand she rested on the table. "Patience is a virtue. Keep that in—" In the midst of his sentence he stopped and jerked his knee upward, bumping the table and spilling cider from the mug. Muttering "What's this?" he bolted to his feet and looked down at the black and white cat that had brushed affectionately against his leg.

Glory sprang from her chair and hurried around the table to pick up the cat. She hugged the animal to her breast.

"Your pardon if she has upset you. 'Tis only Tansy though."

"The creature startled me." Bellingham's smile was tight-lipped. He could not abide cats and would not allow one in his house, but since she seemed fond of the beast he prudently held his tongue. Some matters were best aired after vows were spoken.

"She meant well." Glory put Tansy safely aside and grabbed a cloth to wipe away the spilled cider. "No doubt she's hungry again." While the minister further composed himself she removed a porringer of milk from the cupboard and set it on the floor for the cat. "She has a new litter in the attic," Glory explained as she watched Tansy lap up the offering of milk. The kittens were adorable and they fascinated Glory with their endless play. She suspected she was almost as proud of them as Tansy was. "Would you like to see them?"

He was about to refuse when he thought better of it. She had warmed to him so; no doubt this was a shy ploy to make him stay a little longer. "Aye," he said reaching out to pet Tansy but changing his mind when she flattened her ears at the approach of his hand. He drew back quickly lest he incur a scratch. "Let's have a look."

Glory led the way up the dark attic stairs. Bellingham resigned himself to a long night of prayer for the thoughts he had as he watched the graceful swing of her hips as she moved up the steep steps. In the attic, a long room laced above with pine joists, a narrow window was the only source of light and it took a moment for their eyes to adjust to the gloom. Once she could be sure of her footing Glory led on. High overhead the sharp pitch of the roof was dimly visible; the heart pine summer piece supporting it was a long dark shadow stretching from one gable to another.

Bellingham had to bend his head to prevent himself from bumping it on the low beams. Shucked ears of dried corn lay on the plank floor, some in baskets, some in rows on the bare boards. One basket had been cleared to serve as a bed for the kittens whose mewling cries had started with the first footfalls. Glory knelt at the basket; Bellingham reluctantly followed suit and knelt close beside her, his shoulder deliberately touching her sleeve.

While Tansy settled herself in the basket and scolded her noisy offspring Glory stroked the silky fur of each little one. Bellingham gave the kittens but a cursory glance. He had a better resting place for his eyes.

"We can't keep them all," she said, unaware the minister's gaze all but raked the clothes from her back as, spurred by the darkness and the unaccustomed closeness to a woman, he fought a hot surge of desire. Glory picked up a squirming kitten and held it for Bellingham to see. "Would you like one when they are old enough to go?" she asked. "They'll be good mousers. Tansy is."

"Nay," he said, his breath coming raggedly as it seemed a torch had been lit in his loins. The shadowed room, the nearness of her, the scent of lavender here, too, sweetening the air; it was a maddening combination. "Though 'tis kind of you to offer," he stammered. "I have not had good luck with cats."

With that he rose, fearing he no longer had the resolve to keep himself in check. Temptation swam around him like a thousand tiny devils let loose. Sweat poured from his brow and he was certain he could not trust himself a moment longer in this dark, secluded place. He was a man obsessed and so thoroughly so that he forgot the low beams as he stretched to his full height. As a result his skull rapped painfully against a joist directly above. Clutching his aching head, Bellingham groaned loudly and had pause to consider that punishment for sins was sometimes swiftly handed out.

"Oh my!" Glory came quickly to his aid, untying her apron and doubling it into a compress should there be bleeding.

Still rubbing his head, Bellingham assured her his injury was nothing more than a goose egg and had left him only momentarily dazed. The hurt, a small one, faded fast as it dawned on him that another opportunity had presented itself in an odd way.

"Nevertheless, I fear I may be somewhat unsteady on my feet." He groaned and braced an arm on the offending beam, then nodded affably to Glory. "If you would be so good as to give me your arm until we are down the stairs it would be of great help."

"Certainly." Glory was only too glad to oblige and quite anxious to get Bellingham from the attic. He was behaving strangely. Perhaps the attic was too hot for him. Downstairs she could ascertain the seriousness of the blow and if it was minor hurry the man on his way. She had made a mockery of hospitality as it was, forgetting to serve him a drink then sending him off with a lump on his head.

"Wrap your arm about my waist," he rasped, draping a long arm over her shoulder so that his fingertips grazed the curve of her breast.

Feeling just a spark of alarm, Glory hurriedly brushed his

hand aside. Wary of any other misguided touches she hastily directed the minister to the steps.

"Would you like a damp cloth for your injury?" she inquired when they reached the foot of the stairs where the light flooded in freely. She could see Bellingham's hair was mussed, his collar askew and his face florid. It had not been that hot in the attic. Furthermore there was no sign of swelling on his head. Odd. The blow could not have been so severe as to give his eyes the peculiar glint they had. What was wrong with the man?

"Nay," the minister said, impulsively crushing Glory to his side so that her soft curves pressed all the more enticingly against him, then hastily releasing her as the bright light flooding through the window reminded him who he was and what he was about. His face coloring to a deeper shade of red, he straightened his clothes and cleared his throat. "The throbbing has stopped and I am good as new."

Glory shook out her folded apron and in a snap had it tied around her waist. "You are certain?" she asked haltingly, feeling the spark of unease flicker within her. He looked as if he wanted to devour her. And why had the man pulled her so tightly against him? It was the sort of thing that forward Francis Stevens would do if presented with an opportunity. But nay. She was wrong. Bellingham was a man of God. Nevertheless, she had to force a smile.

Bellingham struggled to halt the turbulence of his passion. Never had he known such an explosion of feeling. What a match she would be for him, doing his bidding, warming his bed. Nay. She would set it blazing as she did him. His eyes narrowed to slits and he wet his lips with the tip of his tongue. The girl looked flustered too. Pleased it was so, his eyes took on a hawkish gleam. It was his destiny to have her, else he would not have this depth of feeling.

With his back to the door, he bowed. "I look forward to seeing you in meeting on the Sabbath," he said courteously.

To himself he began counting the days until Glory Warren would be his in every way.

CHAPTER
7

The scream sounded human. Quade snatched the roan to a full stop and listened, his hands automatically flying to the musket strapped to the saddle. Eyes and ears alert for anything else out of the ordinary, he prepared the weapon for firing. The roan was well trained and responded to a touch of his knee, moving on at a slow walk. The trees were so thick the horses could hardly maneuver through them, the underbrush so heavy it was difficult to determine the direction the sound had come from.

The second scream set the position as clearly as a compass needle. Quade let go of the pack horse's lead and urged the roan into a trot.

"Damnation," he grumbled aloud. Someone was in trouble and, sure as sin, in a moment he would be too.

Another scream pealed before the last died down, this time echoing from only a few hundred feet in the distance. The voice sounded shrill and high-pitched. A woman, he thought, though a woman alone in this country could only bode more ill. A moment later he broke through a thicket and saw he had been wrong. There was no time to decide if the small Indian boy up a tree boded more or less trouble than a woman; he had his hands full keeping his mount under control.

"Steady now," he called to the fidgeting horse.

The roan was afraid of very few things, but a black bear of the staggering size of the one attempting to snatch the boy from the tree ranked in that small minority. The gelding's muscles quivered beneath the saddle as it snorted and made several steps in reverse before rearing. Quade had to choose between voluntarily dismounting or getting off the hard way. Deciding his chances were better if he swung from the saddle on his own, he quickly cleared leather and bounded to the ground.

Relieved of his rider, the roan whinnied and bolted away, but the ruckus he'd caused had already drawn the bear's attention. Its grizzled head cocked, the crazed animal let loose a growl which rattled leaves and branches as he lumbered toward the trapper. Short of time to aim and fire, Quade ducked behind the broad trunk of a tree, surely the only one in the forest with no low branches.

"Back off, you damned bloody Goliath!" Quade hoped his shouts would at least startle the animal into slowing down the attack. For an instant it seemed he was in luck. The big creature stopped and raised up on his hind legs as if deciding which quarry he wanted most.

A fleeting glance at the boy showed the youngster scrambling to a limb high enough to be clear of a swinging paw should the bear return to him. That, however, was not the most immediate danger. The enraged creature, now intent upon him again, swung at the trapper. Claws longer than a man's fingers whizzed by, inches from his eyes. Quade ducked. The big paw missed and hit the tree, ripping off a thick strip of bark.

Had he ever wondered, Quade now knew for certain that fear was as cold and biting as the icy north wind. The swipe of that huge paw had been meant to take off his head. The next was likely to find its mark.

"Here, you bloody beast!" Musket raised, Quade bounded away from the tree and took aim as the animal snarled and bore down on him. He underestimated either the animal's speed or the range of the devastating paw. Before he could get off the shot, the musket was ripped from his hands and the impact of the blow sent the trapper reeling to his backside. The fall saved him from the deadly counterswing of the other paw but left him with no room to escape the next.

A devil's roar tore from the creature's mouth. Quade snatched the knife from the scabbard at his side, a feeble weapon against the bear, but he would not die without inflicting some damage on the beast. Screaming an oath, the trapper scrambled to a defensive crouch for the bear's assault, but the animal, instead of carrying through the charge, stopped in midstride and slapped violently at one shoulder.

Eyes red with rage, the bear spun around, bent on finding the enemy who had inflicted the sudden, burning pain. Quade spotted the shaft of an arrow protruding from the shaggy back, a small missile better suited for downing a bird than a bear, but thankfully powerful enough to grab the beast's attention.

The boy had saved him, at least for the moment. As Quade gasped for a breath to start his heart beating again, the Indian lad slid another arrow from the quiver on his back, fumbling to keep a hold on the limb as he fitted the wooden shaft into his small bow.

The bear sighted the boy again and, roaring, clawed wildly at the air between them. Quade dove for his musket while the animal was diverted. He doubted he had more than a few seconds before the animal returned to the prey within easiest reach. He was right on that score. With yellowed teeth bared and flecks of foam flying from its mouth, the animal shifted its massive body and full menace back to the trapper. With no time to take a proper stance, Quade braced the stock of his musket on the ground and aimed the barrel at the animal's heart.

For the fraction of a second before he fired it seemed there was no sound in the world but the thunder of the bear's feet and rasp of his own breath. The hairs on the back of his neck stood rigid. He could ill afford a miss. Having fought bears before he knew he would have no opportunity to reload. Either this shot did the work or Quade would be the trophy from this encounter.

Hoping the fierce roar of the bear would not be the last sound his ears heard, Quade fired off the shot. It occurred to him as the gigantic animal seemed suspended above him that he would much prefer the last sound he enjoyed to be the sweet ring of Glory's voice. The thought of what he would miss with her hung in his mind as the bear shuddered and stumbled and fell. When the dust had settled about him, Quade, feeling weak as a willow branch, clambered to his feet, pulling a pinned leg from beneath one of those stilled paws.

The curved claws had left only tatters of his legging. Quade looked gratefully at the spared flesh underneath. Another inch and his leg would have been rent to the bone. Groaning, Quade steadied himself against the trunk of a tree until the fierce pounding of his heart slowed to near normal. Only then did he notice the second arrow in the dead animal's back. The plucky youngster was a sure shot.

A word of thanks froze on his tongue and his heart fell a good foot in his chest at the cracking sound of another heavy body moving toward him through the brush.

"Be damned," he muttered beneath his unsteady breath as he took cover in a thicket. He hadn't taken the precaution of reloading the musket and from the nearness of the sound, he didn't now have the time to do so.

"Climb down, you bloody little scamp! I ought to kill you myself!" a rough voice bellowed from beneath the boy's perch.

The choked cry of the Indian boy propelled Quade into action as quickly as had the lad's screams. Many times as a boy no older than this one he had cried out that same sound of distress and most often got kicked or cuffed for his misery. White or Indian, he would not see this lad abused by some savage-hating woodsman.

He slid from the brush and into the open. "You touch one hair on his head and I'll split you from gizzard to crotch," Quade said icily, the broad blade of his hunting knife glinting the truth of his threat.

The burly, red-haired man in trapper's garb like his own threw up a hand in a friendly greeting instead of taking up Quade's challenge.

"Put your steel away, stranger," he said, lowering his ready musket. "The lad's my own son. For the life of me I don't know whether to skin or cuddle the rascal for gettin' in such a scrape."

It was a hug nearly as strong as a bear's that the boy got when he shinnied down the tree. The mist of a tear in the big trapper's eye was all Quade needed to see no abuse would be forthcoming. He sheathed his knife.

"I owe you, stranger, for savin' my son," the man said, hoisting the boy to his broad shoulder so he could offer Quade his hand.

"I seem to have a calling for it." Quade clasped the man's hand, then briefly told of the Narraganset boy he had once rescued from the ice. "Else there's a host of lads in need."

The trapper cut his eyes up to the boy. "Or a host who don't mind their pas." His words came out in a snort. "John Bayard's the name," he said more clearly. "John 'Bear,' the injuns call me. I hunt 'em." He kicked over the head of the downed beast. "This one's called Choke. Meanest varmint ever crawled the earth. Seen him squash the life out of two cubs last spring. You did a good day's work bringin' the cuss down."

"It's not work I favor," Quade said, at last breaking into a grin. "Beaver and fox are more to my liking and don't put up half the fight."

Bayard bellowed with laughter. "Good pelts there," he said. "But a bear's got a lot more hide. Good eatin' too. We'll have this one for supper, if you're agreeable." His eyes turned questioningly to the man who had come to his son's aid. "'Tis your kill."

"The meat's yours," Quade said, collecting his musket and the powder pouch he had lost in the fray with the bear. "The hide I'll keep."

Bayard slid the boy to the ground. "That's generous of you." He nodded between groans of effort as he rolled the big bear over. When he'd succeeded in flopping the dead animal on its back, a nervous whinny sounded from far off in the woods. "Get your horses," Bayard said. "I tied 'em up a ways back when I was lookin' for the boy. They're a mite skittish yet." He jerked a knife from a leather scabbard beneath his buckskin shirt. "I'll start skinnin' the bear."

Quade nodded and left to collect the frightened horses. The scent of bear was still strong and the pair balked at coming too close to the carcass. To keep them from trying to break loose, Quade tied them securely upwind of the spot Bayard and the boy worked stripping the hide from the big animal.

"Looked for a while like I might be his supper," Quade remarked as he squatted beside Bayard and slid his knife between the tough bear hide and the layers of fat beneath it.

Bayard snorted. "Wouldn't surprise me if this one has had a taste of some poor devil who wasn't as straight a shot." Bayard's words seemed confirmed by a rounded scar on the animal's flank which looked as if it had been made by a rifle ball.

When the hide was clear of the carcass, Quade wrapped a pair of claws in a large leaf. "For you, lad. If you hadn't put that arrow in him, I don't think we'd be hanging his hide up to dry." He offered the claws to the boy. "What's your name, son?"

The boy looked eagerly at his father before answering or accepting the claws. Bayard gave his son a wink of consent.

"Johnnie," he said, clutching the leaf-wrapped prize. "I'm Johnnie Bayard and my mother is Clemmie."

Quade gave the elder Bayard a questioning glance. Clemmie was an English name, but the boy he had identified as his son was evidently a half-breed.

Bayard laughed, guessing Quade's thoughts. "Clemmie's the name I gave her. She's an injun woman. My wife."

"Married?" He wondered how the trapper had managed to find a clergyman to wed him to an Indian.

"Injun married," Bayard explained, wiping his knife blade in the grass. "'Tis all the same to me. She's a good woman. Don't mind livin' out here or goin' where I go." He began tying strips of bear meat to a stick. "Had an English wife who stayed in the colony a year then went home to her family. This one suits me better.'' He tapped the boy's shoulder with the back of his bloodied hand. "Get your ma,'' he said. "We'll smoke some of this meat here.'' The boy nodded and started off in a trot. "And watch out for yourself this time,'' Bayard shouted after him.

Quade digested what the woodsman had said. Bayard had found a way to live as he liked and have his woman with him. Noble Warren had done the same by different means. Why was it he had never been able to embrace either solution as workable for him? Was there something that bothered him about settling down with a woman besides having to change some of his ways?

Within a few minutes the boy returned at a trot followed by an Indian woman. Clemmie Bayard had the distinguishing flat features and blue-black hair of her people. Her face was plain but Quade detected a glow that made her seem pretty when she looked with adoring eyes at the burly trapper she called husband. Clearly the pair had a loving relationship, the proof of it in the boy Johnnie and the rounded belly beneath Clemmie's buckskin dress.

Immediately Clemmie began gathering twigs and sticks for a fire, her gaze, however, never straying far from her young son. If John Bayard had taken Johnnie's narrow escape as part of a day's work, Clemmie evidently took it less well. She kept the boy close beside her while she worked stringing the meat for smoking. Now and then she paused to gently scold Johnnie for following his father on a hunt.

"You are first child, first son,'' she said to the boy, placing one of his hands on her rounded belly. "This one cannot take your place. You take care of Johnnie so Johnnie can take care of Mother in old age.''

The boy laughed and his eyes lit with wonder as he felt

the kick of a tiny foot within his mother's womb. Quade, watching the exchange between mother and son, felt his throat go dry and tight as a long-suppressed memory racked him with torturous pain. His hands fell still on the knife embedded in a hunk of the bear's flesh. In his mind's eye he saw a small boy, somewhat older than Johnnie. The lad stood in a grand room, his cap courteously tucked beneath his arm. He was smeared with dirt and his riding jacket was torn. A woman, a beautiful woman with golden hair, scolded lovingly.

"Quade Wylde," the woman said firmly but fondly. "Look at you." She turned him, slowly examining the soiled silk breeches and the rip in the brocade coat. "Such a disgrace," she said. "Your father has warned you not to ride the pony at a reckless pace. 'Tis dangerous to the animal and dangerous to you."

"Yes, Mother." The boy dropped his head and dragged the toe of a scuffed boot on the thick carpet.

The blond head lifted quickly. " 'Yes, Mother'? Is that all you can say?"

"I'll be more careful in the future, Mother?" He turned his dark eyes entreatingly to the woman.

She shook her head, sending golden curls swaying. "Don't turn that soft look on me and think I'll let this go," she said, brushing a smudge from his cheek. "You'll be more careful in the future or you'll be banned from the stable permanently."

"Mother! You wouldn't!"

"Aye," she said sternly. "Indeed I will before I'll risk losing my son." At that she dropped to her knees so that she seemed to be floating in the pool of silk her emerald gown made on the carpet. Her lovely face was level with the boy's. Small hands took the lad's hand and brought it to her tight, rounded belly. "You're my firstborn, Quade. Even this one could never take your place. Take care, my little love," she pleaded. "I would have you to wait on me when I grow old and feeble."

Quade's hand tightened on the knife handle until it seemed the stock of horn would shatter beneath his grip. Still he could not rid himself of the feel of a tiny foot kicking against his palm. His brother—or sister. The child had never been born. Madelyn Wylde had not lived to be feeble or old. She had died with her husband before the month was done.

Quade stabbed the blade of his knife into the earth and bounded to his feet, turning his back on Clemmie Bayard and her son. Only when he was sure he had banished the ghostly images in his mind could he face them again and return to his work. If the others saw anything amiss in his behavior they made no mention of it. Each worked diligently to save what could be used of the bear and to bury what would not be kept so that it would not draw hungry scavengers to their camp.

Late that night the work was complete and the last of the meat smoked over the embers of the fire. Clemmie and Johnnie slept beneath the thatched shelter of a lean-to. Quade and John Bayard sat at the smoldering fire, sharing what news they had from recent travels.

"Any injun trouble where you've come from?" Bayard asked.

"Nay," Quade answered. "'Tis quiet near Sealy Grove. What of the country you've passed through?"

Bayard guffawed. "None but what Clemmie gives me." He slapped the young trapper's knee. "And what mischief a band or two of renegades from the North make taking captives and cartin' 'em to the Frenchies." Bayard filled a pipe with tobacco and lit it with a brand from the campfire. "Keeps the mosquitoes away," he said, offering the pipe to Quade.

Quade accepted and Bayard pulled a second clay pipe from a pouch at his side, then filled and lit it. "The worst trouble is this business in Salem. Witches," he said. "And any who sets his mouth wrong stands to be accused." He drew heavily on the pipe. "Those who seek witches will draw more blood than the savages, I fear."

Quade nodded and chewed the stem of the pipe. "'Tis a waste of a man's time to try such foolery as that."

Bayard puffed until the clay bowl glowed red in the darkness. "And a waste of a good woman's neck if the verdict is wrong." He blew a small cloud of smoke which divided and drifted away. "I'd rather take my chances with an injun than sit under judgment in Salem."

"Aye." Quade stirred the dying coals of the campfire and added more twigs. A small blaze kindled and spread, flickering in the men's eyes and casting darting shadows on their faces.

"You stayin' in these parts?" Bayard asked hopefully. He did enjoy an occasional parley with a man after his own heart. "Clemmie and meself are building a permanent camp up the river. The huntin's good."

"Nay." Quade stretched his legs out and leaned back against his saddle. "I've come to claim my stash and head back to Sealy Grove. I've leased a cabin out of town and aim to stay awhile."

Bayard chuckled. "Got your eye on petticoats, I'll warrant. Naught else will take a trapper from the woods and put him under a roof. Must be a fine lass."

"Aye. Uncommonly fine." Quade puffed on the pipe for a few moments, then told Bayard about Glory Warren. When he was done he was surprised at how anxious he felt to get back to Sealy Grove and Glory.

John Bayard was smart enough to realize when a man needed quiet more than talk. He kicked back and closed his eyes, enjoying the nip of the strong smoke from the stem of his pipe. After all, what could he say? He would be the last man to tell another that a woman was not a good part of a man's life.

Quade locked his hands behind his head and stared up at the heavens. An opening in the thick foliage overhead gave a clear view of the midnight sky studded with limitless blinking, teasing stars. His mother had loved to watch the stars. Many evenings he had sat at her side on her balcony and recited the names of the constellations. Orion, with a sword, a club, and a lion's skin. The seven sisters. The sailor's protectors, Castor and Pollux, known as the heavenly twins.

Suddenly restless, Quade shifted and pushed the saddle to a more level spot, but found himself no more comfortable than before. After a time he acknowledged that his uneasiness came not from the hard ground but from the discontent inside him. Seeing the tenderness the Indian woman Clemmie had for her young son had opened up a valve of emotion he had managed to keep closed for years. It had also made him realize his hesitation to wed Glory wasn't because he hated giving up a trapper's life. Noble Warren and John Bayard had proved that obstacle could be overcome.

His reluctance stemmed from a fear that too much happiness could only lead to tragedy as it had for his parents. They had loved him, each other. That abundance of love had led to treachery and devastation, the loss of their lives, and his loss of the life he had known. And yet, neither would have traded a chance to live forever for the few years of happiness shared.

In the glow of the firelight John Bayard saw a slow smile

spread on the young trapper's face. Content to let the man slip into whatever dreams awaited him, Bayard shrugged down beneath a blanket and fell asleep.

When Bayard's snoring roused him Quade again opened his eyes to the stars. He felt peculiarly light, as if some weighty burden had been lifted from his back. It was strange. He had killed a bear, then learned he faced a greater foe within, a small boy's fear of giving his heart to anyone after those he had loved most had been cruelly wrested from him.

He sighed, more at rest then he could ever remember. Not a man to back down in the face of any enemy, he would beat this one too. Contentedly, he stretched his long limbs, feeling as free as the anchorless stars above. Aye. It was mostly done already. The feel of Glory in his arms again would see the deed complete.

In Sealy Grove on the second Thursday spent at Josiah Bellingham's cottage, Sarah found herself in a state of nervous excitement so strong she could hardly control the needle she used to mend a cuff on one of the minister's good bag holland shirts. Several times she was forced to stop and breathe deeply or, she feared, go faint. The tiny silk packet hidden in the pocket beneath her skirt weighed like a stone against her side.

She sat alone in Bellingham's study. The cottage had only two rooms, the other a common room where he ate and slept. The study was furnished with a table and a few books stacked beside the Bible case. An inkwell and quill had been swept aside to allow her room to work. Stacks of parchment tied with string lay on a shelf—a collection of Bellingham's sermons and copies of several tracts he had written and had published. The minister was in the garden speaking with her father; otherwise she would not have to wait to do what must be done before she left the cottage.

Under the gentle rays of the morning sun Burrell Collier and Josiah Bellingham rounded the rock-strewn path in the minister's unkempt garden. The night before Sarah had stunned her father by suggesting he look into arranging a match between the minister and herself. Now that he had gotten over the shock of her proposal, Burrell Collier admitted the idea was a good one. His house overflowed with children. With another on the way it was time to marry off Sarah. Plainly Bellingham needed a woman to tend his garden and table, to do the chores a man could not.

Shrewd merchant's eyes assayed the minister's cottage and humble grounds. Bellingham had little property of his own, so he could not expect much in the way of a dowry. Here was a way to rid himself of one mouth to feed without parting with valuable assets as well. The line of his mouth softened into a rare smile. The match had possibilities. Evidently the girl had inherited some of her father's wit. Nevertheless, he would first feel the minister out carefully.

"Do you find my daughter's work satisfactory?" Collier asked Bellingham.

Hands clasped behind his ramrod-straight back, Bellingham paused on the weed-riddled path. "She is adept with her needle and does not shrink from a task."

He might have said more of the diligent Sarah, but too much praise might bring a request for compensation. On her last work day she had finished the mending he left and voluntarily embroidered his initial on one of his handkerchiefs. The stitchery was exceptional and today he had put out more handkerchiefs for her to begin work on.

"She is the finest of my pack," Collier returned. "A great

help to my wife in the care of the younger ones. Nigh as good a cook as Goody Collier herself. We will regret having her leave us.''

Bellingham's brows rose in surprise. ''She is not going into service?'' he queried, concerned that he might lose this gem before all that he wished done was completed.

''Nay.'' Collier studied the minister's face for a show of interest. ''''Tis time she wed. I do not believe in keeping a girl until she is overage. Better a malleable young bride than one who has her head set her own way. Do you agree?''

''Entirely.'' It was exactly the way he would have put it. Bellingham thought of Glory and how young and ripe she was for a man's hand to shape her into a proper helpmate. Who would Goodman Collier treat with for Sarah's hand? Isaac Hawkins? He had heard the lad was interested.

''Then we're of one accord,'' Collier said, encouraged. Give the man time and he would ask for Sarah's hand. Better if it came about that way; then the setting of the dowry would be to his advantage. ''But let us not wear the topic out today.'' With what was close to a smile on his face he made a dismissing gesture. ''You have calls to make, I believe.''

''Aye.'' Bellingham nodded as he followed the older man through the garden gate. There were three who had not attended meeting the past Sabbath and one family whose youngest child lay ill with a fever. ''Good day to you, sir,'' he said as he and Collier took separate paths.

From behind the window Sarah watched her father and the minister depart. As soon as both were out of sight she hurried from the study into Bellingham's spartan living quarters. Shortly she was kneeling by the bedstead, a simple square-backed piece with a single feather mattress atop it. The coverlet was faded, the pillows in need of new coverings. The room begged for a woman's touch, that of a woman who cared for the man she served, not simply that of a disinterested servant who only dusted and scrubbed.

With a great deal of care Sarah eased the packet taken from her pocket beneath the bolsters on the bed. Her heart fluttered and her stomach churned with anticipation. Tonight Josiah Bellingham would dream of such a woman. Tonight Josiah Bellingham would dream of Sarah Collier as his fair head rested above a lock of her hair and the parings from her nails.

Sarah did not know how long she stayed beside the bed with her hand resting on Bellingham's pillow. At length an imagined noise at the door sent her scurrying to the study. There she remained until the shirts were mended and the handkerchiefs adorned with flourishing monograms and all were neatly folded for Bellingham's inspection.

Disappointingly, the minister failed to return before her time to leave.

Sunset lent a glow of orange and amber to the fading blue sky. The green caps of trees in the distance darkened to black with the thinning light. Paddy and the chickens flapped to roosts that would keep them safe from owls and weasels through the night. The goats were milked and fed. Glory had also spun fifty knots of linen and made two straw brooms. She would rather have been about any of those tasks than throwing swill to the hogs when she saw Quade riding in. Hurriedly emptying the contents of the bucket into the trough, Glory raced to the water barrel by the kitchen door and washed her hands, drying them hastily on her apron.

"'Tis Quade!" she cried, rushing inside the kitchen where her mother scrubbed potatoes and dropped them into the wrought-iron boiler. Maudie Lair protested when, giving a squeal, Glory grabbed her arm, intent on tugging her outside to see the rider and horses outlined on the horizon.

"I cannot leave this goose to scorch," she insisted as she turned the crank that rotated the spit over glowing coals. "Find a bit of patience, daughter."

Glory paced and pouted until the hot coals were pushed aside and her mother was satisfied the bird would not be ruined before she got back. Then, still making no particular haste, Maudie Lair followed her daughter out the door.

"See. 'Tis him. He's come back," Glory said softly, her mood now one of mellow satisfaction.

Maudie Lair gave her a cool glance. "Did you think he would not?"

"I must say the question gave me pause to think." Glory laughed, recalling the ungracious send-off she had given Quade. "He'll stay for good, I think. What say you?"

Maudie Lair understood that her daughter's question arose from more than an ordinary interest in the trapper. While she knew she could easily lend her consent to a match between the two, she believed that some seeds were better left to sprout on their own. With the shadows of evening falling softly over her wise face, she took a long moment to consider her reply. "He may not stay, but he may not leave alone," Maudie Lair said sagely. "You have put a curb on that carping tongue of yours, I hope." She wagged a finger at Glory.

"Aye, Mother." Her smile was wistful. "He is a good man, do you not think?"

"Good enough." Maudie Lair brushed a dusting of meal from her apron. "He has much to learn of sharing himself with others. 'Tis a caution born of pain, I suspect."

The thought that Quade might have endured some hurt she was unaware of struck a tender spot in Glory's heart. "What pain?" she demanded.

"That he will tell in his own time," Maudie Lair said, her soft voice soothing her daughter.

"Aye," Glory said quietly. There was much she longed to hear him tell. But for now it was enough that he was back. She could wait. He loved her whether he was ready to admit it or not. That she knew as surely as she knew she loved him. Her heart stirred with the sprightly feel of a bird taking flight as the handsome trapper rode in.

Quade swung down from the roan. His eyes, starved for the sight of her, saw only Glory until she was caught fast in his arms. He had not shaved in the days he'd been gone and the dark stubble of a beard shadowed his face. Glory squealed when he nuzzled his bristly cheeks against hers and gave her a quick kiss. Unthinkingly she pushed him away, then instantly regretted having broken free of his arms.

Maudie Lair threatened the trapper with no supper if he dared rub the bristly cheeks against her. Instead he whirled her from her feet and spun her around so quickly she had not the time to offer another threat before it was all over and he had set her down again.

Maudie Lair laughed at his antics. "For that I'll feed you twice," she promised.

Quade swept the fur cap from his head and bowed. "Goody Warren, you go straight to a man's heart," he teased. "I've had naught on my mind this day but a big porringer of your stew."

"'Tis roasted goose you'll get," Glory cut in. "I think Mother knew you'd be riding in today." One dark brow arched suspiciously. "She has a way about her."

"Aye. She does." Quade wrapped an arm affectionately about each of the women. "As does her daughter."

Behind them the pack horse snorted and pawed the ground.

"He feels the weight of that load now that he's home," Maudie Lair said, observing the cumbersome bundle of furs strapped to the animal's back. "Store them in the house if you like." With a sudden look of dismay she hurried toward the kitchen. "And if I do not get back to my cooking we may all come up lacking at suppertime."

Glory helped Quade loosen the straps on the pack animal. "'Tis a bigger load than before," she said.

"Enough to buy a man a cabin and a scrap of land," he said, swinging the bundle free.

While Glory hung anxiously on his words, Quade carted the furs into the house. Almost beside herself, Glory waited with the horses and gave the animals a drink while he was inside.

"Do you mean to do it?" The question burst from her the minute he cleared the door. "Buy the cabin? Stay here?" She dropped the horses' leads and caught hold of his shirt. "Tell me."

Quade shrugged as if it were no great matter they spoke of, but a telltale twinkle shone in his eyes. "If Douglass will sell. A man should have a place to call his own," he said, catching a lead in each hand and hemming Glory in between the horses and himself.

"Oh?" Her blue eyes flashed as her ire started to rise. That reasoning was not what she had hoped for.

"Aye." Quade nodded and dropped his hands on her shoulders. He smiled as he felt resistance in her muscles. "A man must have a little something to offer a woman," he whispered. "A soft bed, a warm fire."

"Oh." The corners of her mouth curved softly as her flattened palms eased up his chest. Had she known going away would change his mind, she would have sent him off sooner instead of trying to prevent his going.

Beneath his hands he felt the tautness drain from her shoulders and a radiating warmth come in its stead. The quickening in his loins was instantaneous.

"Do you agree?"

"I do," she answered, brushing her thighs against him, lifting her face temptingly. "I'll help you stable the horses," she whispered, her lips skimming his as she spoke.

"Nay," Quade chuckled softly as he felt the soft lips puff into a pout. "Your mother asks that you come inside and help finish the supper," he explained.

Glory nodded woodenly, disappointed she would not have a few minutes alone with Quade. Her sense of loss, however, was short lived. Her rosy, pouting lips were too much for the trapper to resist. Shielded by the horses, he closed Glory within his arms and seared her mouth with a kiss that seemed to pour through to the farthest depths of her. Flushed and trembling she braced against one of the horses when he pulled away.

"Quade . . ." She mumbled his name, the start of a question she didn't know how to phrase.

He understood. "Soon," he whispered. "Soon, my bright, burning firefly."

CHAPTER
8

The man was enough to drive a woman mad. Soon, he had said, but now days had passed since he returned with his belongings and not another word about it. What was soon to Quade? A month? A year? Forever?

Glory tied on a clean apron and dutifully pinned her hair beneath her cap. What was worse, now that he was staying at the Douglass cabin she hardly saw him at all. Bounding over Tansy, who had chosen to take a nap in the middle of the kitchen, Glory hurried from the house.

"Stay home, Paddy," she warned the crow who sat atop the back of the cart seat as she hitched the mare between the traces. "Or some fool with a slingshot will make you a target."

Well, perhaps she exaggerated a little. Quade had been to the house each day since his return. Her real complaint was that she had found no more than three minutes on each occasion to be alone with him. That was hardly enough for a sound kiss, but plenty to make her wish for an hour or two to learn just what it was those brief kisses made her yearn for.

"A blight on the man," she swore to the crow. "I will make him tell me what I want to hear if I must hunt him down to do it."

For all her bold words Glory had to admit it was opportune that her mother was sending her into town to deliver butter and eggs and medicines she had made for two of her patients. Only yesterday Quade had mentioned having business that would take him into Sealy Grove as well. If the sun did not fall from the sky she would find him and he would ride back to the farm with her. Let him avoid speaking to her of love and marriage then.

She had another purpose as well, that of seeing Sarah and insisting the rift between them be mended. It was silly. Childish. They had been too close, shared too much sisterly love to have their friendship ended without so much as a try to save it. All her life Sarah had been like a part of her. She wanted to share what was new in her life, to make Sarah understand that whatever had offended her could not be greater than the love they had shared.

Making sure Paddy obeyed, Glory stowed the basket of goods in the cart, then climbed in herself. Ordinarily she had too much regard for the mare to be careless, but today her mind was occupied. She did not realize what a fast trot she had urged the horse to keep, or that she had ceased to watch the road as she lapsed deep into the pleasurable depths of a daydream. When the animal gave a terrified whinny and jerked the traces so hard to the right that they cracked, Glory was caught hopelessly off guard.

"What—" she cried as a great, blurred shape surged from

the shadowy brush lining the road. She had not the time to see what was upon her before another followed the first in a mighty leap and the cart went careening to its side.

Glory hit the roadbed with a painful thump, dazed but clearheaded enough to see the mare bolting into the woods. She had but an instant to look up and see the cart tumbling her way and to know that it was bound to land on top of her. Letting out a scream, she put all her might into a roll which she hoped would take her out of harm's way. She could only pray she was fast enough as the move sent her skirts billowing and her black hair flying.

"Whose hair is black as Hallow's Eve?"

At the Collier house Ezra, at eleven eldest of the three Collier sons, sat beneath a maple tree in the garden, whittling a six-foot birch staff down into a splint broom. While his jackknife slivered the green wood into small, flat strips, Ezra mumbled over and over one line of a ditty he was trying to recall.

At length he pocketed the jackknife and made for the house, certain a bite of food would improve his memory and the other lines would come to him before the first wore a hole in his mind. A moment later, bread and cheese in hand, he found the cure had worked as he repeated the whole of the verse.

> Whose hair is black as Hallow's Eve?
> Who looks with craft through deepest guise?
> Who is the one with witch's eyes?

The abrupt scrape of stool legs set the boy back on his heels. "Where did you hear that?" Sarah, whom Ezra had failed to note at her spinning wheel in a far corner, caught her brother firmly by the collar and demanded a reply. "'Tis a wicked rhyme!"

The boy stiffened. He had no fear of Sarah, but she judiciously reported his infractions to his father and Burrell Collier's wrath was best unstirred. His skin reddened as he tried to hide the pilfered bread and cheese inside his shirt.

"Joseph Allyn taught it to me," he responded promptly. "'Tis a harmless riddle. Nothing more."

"And who is the one with witch's eyes?" Sarah insisted, using her free hand to pluck the food from Ezra's grasp. As her mother did when disciplining her offspring, Sarah tapped her foot soundly on the plank floor. She would not put it past Joseph Allyn to have marked some poor crone for ridicule. "Who?"

"'Tis no one." The boy squirmed, twisting his collar into hopeless wrinkles. He would not meet his sister's demanding gaze.

"No one? Perhaps you would like to recite for Father."

"Joseph would not tell," Ezra blurted out. "'Tis a riddle only he knows the answer to." Cautiously he cast a glance at Sarah. "Likely there is no answer. 'Tis just some banter of Joseph's. I won't say it again," the boy added, certain he heard the stern Burrell Collier entering the house. The thought of arousing his father's dander made him cringe. The man could wield a birch rod like no other.

"See that you don't," Sarah warned, releasing her brother who immediately disappeared out the back door.

Sarah shivered. Only a week before the witch Bridget Bishop had been hanged in Salem. Leave it to her brother and Joseph Allyn to imagine witches in Sealy Grove.

"Who's the one with witch's eyes?" she murmured to herself as she returned to her spinning wheel. The line was a catchy one but neither it nor dread of witches was strong

enough to dim the pleasant thoughts she'd had before Ezra interrupted.

Soon her wheel hummed again. One day she would spin in her own house. One day. Taking a moment to roll back her hunched shoulders, Sarah dipped her fingers into the gourd-shell cup tied to the wheel. Her foot rocking on the treadle, she spun the spread and drawn flax fibers into thread. Though there was a certain serenity to spinning, it was an endless job, as endless as the passage of time which of late slid by so slowly it seemed days were held overtime by some covert force.

She sighed. Today was Thursday. The best day of the week. Another hour at her spinning and she would go to Reverend Bellingham's. At least she had that to look forward to. She would see Josiah again, talk to him. On the Sabbath there had been no chance to ask Josiah—Sarah stilled her thoughts to whisper the treasured name.

"Josiah," she said over and over with the steady rhythm of the turning wheel. Josiah, whose hair was as light as the flax wrapped on her spindle, whose eyes were lanterns to a girl's yearning heart. Had he dreamed of her each night since last Thursday? Goose bumps rose up on her skin as she pictured him at rest, the packet containing a lock of her hair hidden beneath the bolster. Of course he had dreamed of her. He must have.

In a fanciful daze, Sarah spun until her spindle was empty and she had to stop and concentrate on joining a new thread to the one dropped. Only a little annoyed that her attention had strayed from her work, Sarah soon had the fine linen floss flowing from her wheel. She wanted the skeins to be the choicest she had done. Washed and bucked with ash, the bleached skeins would be ready for the loom. Once the linen webs were woven and the fabric bleached again to take out the color the bucking had left, she would cut and sew a gown.

Sarah imagined the soft, white linen swathed around her on her wedding night, a gown with embroidered rosebuds and hearts, and a nightcap to match. Perhaps her mother would buy silk thread for the needlework and a ribbon for the trim.

Sarah dreamed her dreams and spun. The nightdress would be a long time in the making. Months. Other work had to be done too. Winter, though, was a good time for a wedding. There was not so much to be done out of doors then. By winter the special nightdress would be finished. By winter she would be Goodwife Bellingham.

In pursuit of that end Sarah had spent every spare minute at her wheel spinning linen thread. Those minutes were few. Her mother, after a dozen pregnancies, was not faring well with the present one. It did not help that Ruthie had been taken ill with a fever and was confined to bed. Sarah and her sister Judith, to spare their mother as much exertion as possible, assumed more and more of Goody Collier's work. But she did not mind the extra chores Not as long as she had Thursdays at Josiah's, among his things.

Sarah could not quite wait out the time. Less than an hour found her hurrying along the footpath to the minister's house. Nearby in an alder tree a catbird made its mewling cry. Overhead a bobolink skimmed the air and dipped low, chirping with morning gaiety. Sarah's step was light, her spirit buoyant. For a week her charm had rested beneath Josiah's pillow. What man could overcome such a spell as that? He would not notice Glory Warren again and, more important, he would not look at Sarah Collier with indifference any longer.

"You are early, Sarah," Bellingham said irritably as he answered the knock at his door.

"Not so early that I have disturbed you, I hope." Sarah blushed and stammered and swallowed at the tightness in her throat.

Bellingham wore the shirt she had mended. He had not yet donned a coat and it appeared he had halted his shaving to answer her knock. A folded cloth lay across his shoulder and one cheek still shone with a bit of golden stubble.

Hands hidden behind her back, Sarah rubbed her thumbs over her fingertips, imagining how that start of a beard would feel beneath her hands. The tip of her tongue shot out to dampen her dry lips. Never had she seen the minister except in full garb. To find him in so casual a state of attire was like sharing an intimacy.

"'Tis no matter," he said, looking past her to the deserted street. With the end of the towel he wiped a speck of soap from his chin. "But as you can see I am not yet dressed. If you will but wait a moment . . ."

"Aye," Sarah bobbed her capped head and answered hurriedly. "I'll sit in the garden till you've finished."

He shut the door, but if he had opened it within the next few minutes he would have found Sarah transfixed to the spot where he had left her, her eyes glowing, her hands clenching the edges of her apron. He did not, however, discover Sarah still enraptured at his door or engrossed in what followed— her counting petals plucked from a daisy in his garden.

Josiah Bellingham promptly dismissed the girl from his mind and completed his shaving. Afterward he took the time to brush the dust and soil from his coat and hat and to inspect the last clean bands and cuffs in his wardrobe before he donned them. Satisfied with his appearance, he sat a few minutes glancing over notes made while writing a sermon. Only then did he recall that Sarah waited in the garden.

Sarah had put her imposed wait to good use. At her feet lay a pile of weeds pulled from an edge of the garden which had been planted with herbs before weeds choked out the edibles. She was sure Bellingham would notice her industry.

"Bless you, Sarah," the minister said solemnly, eyeing the weeded plot of ground. "You are ever vigilant. I was set to say you might just as well take the mending home. You could do it as easily at your house as mine. I know you are needed there more than here with Ruthie ill. How fares the girl?"

"No better. My mother fears she may have come down with measles. But 'tis too early to tell and as yet there are no spots."

Bellingham studied her for a moment before going on. "Your mother may have hit on the cause. Ruthie is not the only one ill. There is Mary Douglass and Abigail Allyn come down with fevers too. But if 'tis measles they will all be well soon enough."

"Aye," Sarah agreed. "And as yet there is no reason I cannot continue here."

"I will ask that of your mother when I stop by to visit Ruthie." He glanced about, seeing the work she had done in his garden, and nodded. "For now you have shown there is a reason you might continue here."

Too enamored to perceive anything other than what she wished to hear in the minister's words, Sarah smiled and agreed. "Would take some doing but it could be a serviceable garden again," she said eagerly. "And I could do your mending in the evenings along with my other needlework."

Bellingham nodded his consent for the plan. "That would

please me," he assured her, his eyes following a tiny garden spider which crawled from Sarah's white cap to her forehead. He flicked it away. "Lest it bite you," he explained, hurriedly brushing off his hands. "Some have a dreadful sting."

"Thank you." Sarah's hand crept to the place on her forehead that Bellingham had grazed with his fingers. The spot felt warm and tingly. Her eyes nearly filled with tears. She had felt affection in that tender gesture. He cared for her. He did. She was sure of it.

Bellingham, concerned only with preventing a mishap, quickly found his attention drawn to several plants nearly crowded out by an especially thick growth of weeds. "In that patch," he said, pointing to blue-tinged leaves. "Is that lavender?"

"Aye," Sarah said, boldly standing close to him. "A few good plants. The smell is pleasant and lingers even when dried."

"Aye," Bellingham responded, a sparkle in his eyes as he remembered how the heady lavender perfume had permeated the air in the Warren attic. "I am partial to the scent of lavender. Clear that patch first if you would."

"As you like," Sarah answered ardently. Cheeks bright with excitement, she lifted her beaming face to him. "Will you be abroad today?"

"Aye." He removed his beaver hat to check for any leaves or particles of debris that might have fallen onto it as he walked beneath the trees. "'Tis a strict schedule I impose upon myself. Thursday is for visiting those in spiritual and physical need. In the evening I fast and devote myself to prayer for those in want of God's mercy." As if to emphasize the importance of his mission, he cocked his head to one side. "Would be remiss of me to vary from what I have pledged to do."

"You are an inspiration to all," Sarah replied fervently, imagining this was the way they would talk as man and wife. He discussing the demands of his ministry, she listening with understanding, and devoting herself to easing from him the sundry demands of daily life.

Bellingham slowly traversed the garden path, winding his way to the gate that opened onto the street. "I can only hope all view me as you do, Sarah."

"How could they not?" Sarah kept pace, enjoying the feel of being at his side.

Bellingham stopped at the gate and, in a humble gesture, turned his palms up. His face showed a quiet assurance that he believed himself well thought of. His treatises on the supernatural were gaining him recognition throughout the colony. Only this week he had been awarded an increase in his stipend. Not so much as he had requested, but enough to make a presentable offer for a wife. He wondered how his flock would respond to his plans to wed.

"The mending is on the table in my study," he said, deciding to test Sarah on the topic. A girl of her age would surely keep abreast of the latest gossip. If skillfully questioned she could provide insight into the disposition of the people concerning his matrimonial state. He reached for the gate as if he meant to go, then turned back. His expression was impassive. "You must have concluded by now that I am a man in need of a spouse."

Sarah suppressed a cry of astonishment that he should speak of marriage so soon. Her reply came in a stutter. "T—'Tis said a man without a wife must be near to death from lone-liness." Her chin quivered. She dared not move lest she reveal her rising emotion. "And 'tis for certain you are in need of a woman's care." Awkwardly she spread her arms and pointed to the surroundings. "The garden is in a sad state and the house cries for a woman's hand. I think you must tire of the tavern's stew.''

She longed to say he must also wish for a wife to warm his bed, to rest her head beside his on the pillow, and that he must wish for sons. But she dared not go so far.

"Is it so apparent then?" He felt relieved. Perhaps he had been wrong all along to think any would question his re-marrying. He must remember most widowers married again promptly; indeed, it was expected of a man. Still, his brow furrowed speculatively as he sought more reassurance. "Per-haps I am slighting those I serve by requiring too much of my time to tend my person. Perhaps it would improve my service to have a helpmate."

"Clearly that is so."

His exuberance briefly getting away from him, Bellingham reached out and squeezed Sarah's arm. "You have convinced me 'tis so," he said.

"Then you wish to wed soon?" she ventured, feeling so light with happiness that she believed she might at any mo-ment find herself adrift in the clouds. This was beyond her greatest dreams. She might not even have long enough to complete the nightdress before he wished to wed. An inward smile brought a wondering light to her eyes. Would that matter so much?

"As soon as is feasible. 'Tis a matter of some delicacy as you might guess. There is the question of a dowry and other negotiations which might be required." He drummed a finger thoughtfully against his chin. "Sarah," he continued, cap-turing her totally with a strong look. "I must ask you not to reveal what has been said between us today."

She stiffened a bit. "I should not tell anyone?"

"Not for a time."

"If 'tis what you want," she agreed reluctantly, her high spirits dashed a trifle.

"You understand the need for discretion, do you not?" His brow furrowed. "Consider your position," he said, recalling that Burrell Collier had mentioned Sarah would soon wed." "Before your father names a dowry 'tis difficult to conclude a negotiation. And should there be no agreement forthcoming, unbridled talk could be injurious to both parties."

Sarah's eyes grew wide with alarm. "My father will be generous, I assure you," she said briskly.

"I'm certain that is the case," Bellingham replied. "Goodman Collier is equitable in all his dealings." He gave Sarah a heartening smile promptly followed by a gesture of dismissal. "Before I am late beginning my work, let me be on my way. A good morning to you, Sarah."

Her heartbeat increasing with such rapidity she wondered if it could stand the pace, Sarah watched her beloved leave the untidy garden. Only when he was too far away to hear did she whisper a reply to his farewell. "A pleasant day to you, Josiah, my beloved."

Several hours later, the garden well on its way to being free of weeds, the items for mending tucked under her arm, and the recovered packet of hair and nail parings hidden in her pocket, Sarah slowly strolled home. One day she might tell Josiah how she had used a dab of magic to turn his thoughts in the right direction. For now she would keep the miraculous method to herself and take the time to believe all this was true.

She was to marry Josiah Bellingham. And soon. He had said as much in the garden. Why had she ever doubted it would come to this? To think how she had burned with jealousy of Glory! Perhaps they could be friends again. Nay. She recalled the way Josiah had once looked at the ebony-haired girl. Never. Let Glory have her turn to be jealous when she heard this news.

Head held high and virtually skipping with joy as she entered the Collier house, Sarah considered that everyone, in fact, would envy her such a fine husband.

Halfway through the day's rounds, Josiah Bellingham passed the Allyn house. Not far from there he came upon the boy Joseph pushing a barrow of corn to the mill. While the rasp of the barrow's wheel drowned out the sound of footsteps to Joseph's ears, it did not dim the hearing of Reverend Bellingham.

> Whose face is fairer than any maid's?
> Who charms the creatures with clever sighs?
> Who is the one with witch's eyes?

Rocking his head from side to side, Joseph sang out the new verse of the riddle which had so far stumped everyone who heard it. The exception was Francis Stevens, but Francis had known the answer before the verse was penned. Francis would not tell and to date both boys had enjoyed the consternation of their friends.

Joseph laughed aloud. Let them have their bedeviling old hags in Salem. Sealy Grove could boast of the prettiest witch of all.

"*Who is the one . . .*" Joseph yelped with pain as a hand clamped his shoulder and jerked him back. Off his feet for an instant, the boy's arms and legs flapped like loose sacking as he struggled to see the face of his tormentor. Recognition of the minister turned him white and stone stiff.

"Who?" Bellingham demanded.

"I do not . . ." The harsh lines of the minister's face threatened what might follow a lie or evasion. Joseph felt a lump grow large in his throat and impede the flow of air to his lungs. "Glory Warren," he croaked. "She is the one. 'Tis because her eyes are outlandish blue and her stare gives a shiver."

Bellingham made a sound like a growl deep in his throat that this ill-mannered youth should sully the name of his intended. He gave the boy a rattling shake.

"'Tis a guilty conscience that gives you pause, Joseph Allyn." The deep voice cut like a jagged blade. "Keep in mind the penalty for bearing false witness, lad."

An accusing finger dangling in the boy's face, Bellingham loosed his clawlike grip. Joseph nearly crumpled when let go.

"Aye, sir," he sputtered. "Was all in fun. Be assured I have not spoke her name to any. No harm was meant."

"Are the words your own, lad?" A forbidding sight towering over the hapless boy, Bellingham needed only to observe Joseph's fallen face to know the rhyme was his invention.

"Aye," he squeaked.

Bellingham glowered. "Then malice was intended." Joseph cringed, fearing the naming of some terrible recompense for his misbehavior, but the minister only saw fit to delay the penalty. "Promise you will stay to the straight and narrow, Joseph Allyn," he warned. "Else I will speak to your father of your vicious tongue."

"Nay, do not," Joseph pleaded, ready to agree to anything now that it appeared he might again escape the minister's ire. Most often his mother begged off his punishment when his father was set to whip him. But if Reverend Bellingham accused him there would be no reprieve, and unless he was so lucky as to be wrong, Bellingham was even now on his way to visit Abigail who was sick in bed. "You have my pledge," he insisted, his gangly knees knocking together. "I have forgot the words by now."

Bellingham sent the boy packing. A sly piece, Joseph no more than turned the corner out of Bellingham's sight before he hissed defiantly beneath his breath. "Glory Warren has witch's eyes."

With his head twisted over his shoulder to be certain the minister had not followed, he missed seeing the scrawny cat that had just escaped a pursuing dog by running through the slats in the fence. The hissing creature ran beneath his feet, upsetting both him and the barrow and spilling the corn into the dirt.

It was as if a cord had been wrapped around his ankles, Joseph was to say later as he related the incident to Francis Stevens.

Seething with outrage, Bellingham watched Joseph scamper off. While he would have liked to see the hide flailed from the boy's back, he determined that to pursue the matter would assuredly bring the riddle and Glory's name to light. The girl was to be his wife and he would not have her name slandered by making the boy's offense public. He shook his head. What foulness could have led the lad to think such vile thoughts?

Witch's eyes? Nay. An angel's eyes. There was naught of Glory Warren that could not be admired and praised. The Allyn brat would see that if he were a few years older. As for him he would hold his piece and make no mention of the incident while he called on Goody Allyn.

* * *

When he left the Allyn household his mind was made up. He would not delay in asking Goody Warren's permission to wed her daughter. Mentally making adjustments in his plans that he might see to the matter right away, Bellingham proceeded down the main street of Sealy Grove, past the several business establishments that were at its core. Beyond those he came to the fellmonger's shop where he spied a roan horse tied to a rail out front. He had seen the animal once before and if he was not mistaken it belonged to the trapper Quade Wylde.

Bellingham's lips thinned with anger. Was there no end to his troubles? He had thought himself rid of the trapper yet here the man was to nettle him again. Making an abrupt turn he entered the building. The trapper, clothed in his fringed buckskins, stood haggling with Goodman Wharton, the dealer in hides.

"Are you here yet?" Bellingham said in way of greeting. "Was said you had departed Sealy Grove."

The voice was unmistakable, nor was there any misreading the irritation in it. Smiling sardonically, Quade turned about.

"For a time," he replied, pushing a bundle of raccoon pelts to Wharton. "I had business which called me away."

"He plans to purchase a cabin from Asa Douglass," Wharton, a man whose ruddy complexion and exuberance offset his marked thinness, volunteered. "And means to stay among us."

Bellingham's brows rose swiftly. "Will you now?"

"Aye," Quade answered, hearing the challenge in Bellingham's voice. "A time comes for a man to end solitary ways."

Bellingham's shoulders tensed. That was true enough, but

if the trapper meant for Glory to quell his solitude he would come up short. "Preposterous! What good can a trapper do here but cause trouble among those who are refined persons? What woman will be safe?"

Nostrils flared, Quade gave him a hard stare but kept a rein on his tongue.

"Aye." Wharton, who had mistaken the animosity between the minister and Quade for lighthearted jesting, laughed so heartily it shook his spare frame. "The maid Glory Warren will not be safe for long if the trapper stays. But good will come of it," he added. "If it can be worked to satisfaction, he will be a partner with me." Days of deliberation had brought him close to an agreement with the trapper. Smiling, the lean fellmonger stowed a bundle of pelts on a shelf and came around the plank counter.

Veins stood out in the temples above Bellingham's narrowed eyes. "What could a maid such as Glory Warren see in an uncouth trapper?" He snorted.

Still keeping his temper in check, though with growing difficulty, Quade turned his back on the pair and saw to the sorting of some skins. At least now he knew why the man despised him. He had his eyes on Glory too.

Oblivious to what was happening, Wharton spoke up again. "Uncouth or not, Wylde's a man who knows skins and those who trap. We expect to do well. Should he drive as hard a bargain with others as he has with me, our profits will be great and he'll make a fine catch for any dewy-eyed miss."

Needing some way to vent his rising vexation, Bellingham seized on the handiest one. "A man must not be ruled solely by a desire for profits, sir," he chastised. "Let us not forget there is a higher purpose than temporal pursuits for man."

"Aye, Reverend," Wharton agreed, only momentarily

subdued. "But 'tis easier to reach a higher purpose if there is a sound profit for footing."

Bellingham snorted. "And 'tis easier for a camel to pass through the eye of a needle than for a rich man to enter heaven," he returned, without for an instant stopping to con-sider his own mercenary motives in seeking Glory Warren as a wife. "I shall address the matter of meekness in my sermon next Sabbath."

Wharton nodded knowingly to Quade.

"Wharton and I will both be the better for hearing it, sir," he said in a conciliatory tone. If he was to live in Sealy Grove he preferred not having the minister disposed against him, though from the looks of him it would be an uphill ride to change the man's mind. He could, however, understand how a man would be irked to lose his chance to have Glory.

When Bellingham had left them, Wharton shook his bald pate in disdain. "Plainly Reverend Bellingham has forgotten his sermon on last Holy Sabbath. Was titled 'Prosperity in Reward of Godliness and Industry.' "

Laughing, Quade and Wharton concluded their negotia-tions, agreeing that Quade would act as the fellmonger's agent in the purchasing of furs and pelts. The bartering would take place in the wilderness where Quade would establish an out-post and periodically travel to it to conduct his business. Wharton believed meeting trappers on their own ground would give him an advantage over his competitors in other towns. The plan was bold and would take a knowledgeable man to carry it through. He was convinced Quade Wylde was such a man.

Wharton, pleased with the prospect of success, poured two tankards of beer. "'Tis sealed between us, then," he said.

"Aye. Partners we are," Quade agreed. Like Noble Warren he had found his way to have the best of both worlds. Manning the outpost would take him to the wilderness for days, occasionally weeks on end, but not so many that he could not spend most of his time with Glory.

Hours later, after papers detailing the workings of the partnership had been drawn and signed, Quade mounted his horse and rode out of Sealy Grove. Now that he was assured he could earn his living in Sealy Grove, he could ask Glory to be his wife.

The ride to his cabin took him past the Warren farm. It was the part of the trip Quade most liked. Generally he could not pass the house in under an hour. That time he would linger to talk with Glory and her mother, helping them with the chores or, as was often the case, taking a meal at their table. Occasionally too, he found a moment to steal a kiss from Glory's rosy lips. Those sweet kisses were harder and harder to live without.

On this morning there had been no time to stop as he had the appointment with Wharton and could not be late. Nevertheless, he looked forward to spending a pleasant afternoon with Glory and to tell her his plans. A fence in the cow lot needed mending and it was as good a reason as any to give for stopping in.

With Glory on his mind, Quade nearly rode up on the cart sitting lopsided in the lane before he noticed it.

"Ho, Red!" he called to his mount. The cart was off the ruts; one wheel had split and run from the axle and lay on the ground next to a large stone. The traces were broken and empty as was the cart itself. On the ground lay a spilled basket of butter and the shells of broken eggs.

Quade's lax senses came quickly alert. Either Glory or Maudie Lair had started for town, but clearly whoever had driven the cart had met with an accident or worse. Indians had been seen in the area and there was the ever present danger of attack. Quade dismounted cautiously so that he would not disturb the tracks that would tell what had befallen the driver.

Eyes to the ground, he felt an easing of his tight muscles. Besides the horse's hoofprints and several sets of deer track, only one set of footsteps marred the ground. He knew the small track. Glory's. The cap he found nearby was hers as well. By the signs the mishap had been a simple accident, and from the firmness and evenness of her tracks Glory had not incurred injury. What worried him was that instead of leading the cart horse home she had followed the animal off into the woods.

Quade mounted and followed the easy track. The cart horse had been at a run with harness dragging.

"Glory!" he called. "Ho! Glory Warren!"

Ahead he heard the rustle of a skirt and the snap of a twig before he saw her rise from behind the trunk of a fallen tree.

" 'Tis a fright you gave me," she said breathlessly. "And that close behind another. The cart wrecked," she explained, approaching the roan.

"So I've seen." He stayed in the saddle. The dark eyes smiled, though his tone reproached. "Most would not attempt to drive over a boulder."

Glory halted and snapped her hands to her hips. She gave him a menacing stare. Having rolled from the cart and then chased the horse through a thicket of briars and brush, she was in no frame of mind for criticism.

"Most would have no choice if a stag jumped from the bank and landed right beneath the cart horse's nose," she informed him smartly. " 'Tis a wonder my head is not split as well as the wheel."

A flicker of amusement lifted the corners of his lips. " 'Tis a wonder I do not break it that you took the risk of doing so." His voice hardened but the tender notes came through.

Glory detected the concern and smiled, realizing Quade had only been baiting her as he was so fond of doing. "You would not dare," she warned, reaching enthusiastically for his outstretched hand and shortly finding herself swung up behind the saddle.

"Give me another cause and we will see," he returned, his voice falling low as Glory eased her hands around his waist, another strain on his self-control.

"The horse went through there." Glory indicated a deer trail through the trees. "A doe and fawn bounded by just as I unhitched the horse. The poor animal was already in a state and bolted as if she had wolves at her heels."

"I know," he said matter-of-factly. The tracks near the wagon had made the scene as clear to him as if he had witnessed it firsthand. The cart horse's fright would have been intense but short-lived. He touched his heels to the roan and followed the crescent-shaped prints which indicated the runaway horse had soon slowed to a walk. "She won't be far. There is a stream near, is there not?"

"Aye," Glory answered. "And I must still ride to Sealy Grove to deliver the goods my mother sent, though I think some must wait on the eggs." She was in no rush, however. There were still plenty of daylight hours and for now it felt good to lean her cheek against his hard back. The tanned buckskin shirt felt smooth as velvet against her skin; beneath it she felt the play of muscles as he reined the horse around a gully.

Quade groaned softly. Her fingers drummed teasingly on his belly. Her round breasts pressed tormentingly into his taut muscles. Against his thighs her knees bounded and prodded as she sought to slip her toes into the pockets between the stirrups and his boots. He believed the girl had no idea what a woman's touch did to a man. Or if she did she must want him to burn to ash with unrequited desire. Not trusting himself to speak until the heat of his ardor could be conquered, Quade cast his eyes on the winding trail.

"I think you are naught but trouble, girl," he said when it was evident the fires would not cool as long as she clung so closely to him. When she did not willingly relent, he tugged her laced fingers apart and shrugged away from her embrace. "Give a man space to breathe."

"Nay," she answered, snuggling nearer and intensifying his agony. "I like the feel of being close."

The nearness of his warm, hard body made her breasts ache in a tantalizing way. Her nipples nudged wantonly against his back and tightened till they were hard as pebbles. The warmth that always came when they touched spread along her thighs, unlocking a rousing and sensual curiosity. Just where would these wonderful feelings lead if she let them run free? Did Quade feel this same gnawing hunger?

"Sit back, Glory," Quade ordered, his voice husky, his body tight enough to shatter.

"Nay." She slowly rubbed her chin along the hollow beneath each shoulder blade, giggling as the length of dark hair tied with a leather thong tickled her nose. "Tell me what you feel. I want to know."

Quade, at his breaking point, wrenched around in the saddle, wresting free of Glory's grip. His arms snaked around her waist and snatched her from her seat, swinging her around so that she might sit sideways across the front of the saddle. In that position he could keep her at a safe distance.

Glory, believing Quade meant to set her on the ground, clung like a cat and nearly unseated him in the process. Shortly she found herself half-in and half-out of the saddle,

Quade much the same. When the struggling ended she was straddling the horse and facing Quade.

He groaned anew. This was more an assault on his senses than having her mounted behind him.

"I feel you will drive me out of my wits before I have you properly wed," he complained. It was an awkward position, face-to-face, her knees crossing his, the horse's smooth gait rocking them intimately together.

Glory threw her arms around his neck and squealed with delight. "Are you asking for my hand?" He had hinted he would marry her but this was the closest he had come to naming it as fact.

"Aye." His arms slid with infinite care around her waist. "Your hand and all of you, Glory Warren. Else I will have my neck stretched for taking what I have not pledged for."

Glory laughed softly and clung to him even tighter. Restraint forgotten, Quade dropped the reins and let the roan find the way as he added his other arm to the embrace and claimed her lips in a gentle union, clinging, savoring, until both flushed with warmth and want.

Bare beneath her petticoats, Glory felt his heat and rising hardness through the smooth buckskin breeches. Quade drew a deep ragged breath and slowly eased his hands over her hips and beneath her buttocks, pulling her closer. His mouth played again on hers in light, feathery kisses, his teeth at times gently raking her lips.

She took to the play quickly, trying what he taught her even to the gentle sucking of his probing tongue. All the while Quade rocked her against his loins, bringing that intimate part of her against his swollen manhood.

Feeling a strange, shocking ache spread in a slow tide of heat from the center of her body to her limbs, Glory hastily opened the buttons fastening her gown tightly around her throat.

Quade nuzzled his face into the sweet-smelling curls tumbling loose around her neck and shoulders. His lips found the warm flesh beneath the opened collar. "I am twice a fool ever to have thought I would walk away from you," he whispered.

"Nay," she said, her voice rippling sweetly at his ear. "You were right then. No child bride could have felt . . ."

"Ahhh, Glory." His kisses fell into the soft hollows of her throat. "What is it you do not think of?"

One hand slid beneath the petticoats and found the silken flesh between her thighs all wet and dewy. The lean fingers explored for a torturous minute then fitted around the sensitive nub of flesh already aching and aroused. For Glory a rapturous shuddering started where his fingers moved.

"Not this," she gasped as the pulsing heat built and splintered, then built again even hotter than before. "I never thought of this, love," she cried as a flare of light flashed behind her closed lids and she rose to heights of unbearable, unbelievable pleasure.

Quade clasped her against him, his agony still at a peak, as well it would remain for some time, he suspected. Already he had done more than he meant to.

The roan broke from the trees on a crest overlooking the farm. The runaway horse had circled through the wood above the barn, taken a drink from the stream, and headed home.

Breathing a heavy sigh, Quade swung Glory around so that she sat sidesaddle across his lap. Sated, she lay drowsily against his chest, making a sound rather like a purr. She was too happy to speak. She had gotten most all she had set out for this day.

"Damnation," he said, finding no way to get comfortable in the saddle nor any way he could justify to himself finding a springy bed of moss and continuing what he had begun until his own satisfaction was reached. He wished fervently that he was as uncouth and dishonorable as Bellingham had accused him of being.

But he was not. And Maudie Lair would be worried with the harnessed horse coming in alone. He had best get Glory home. Gently he kissed her and handed over the cap which she grumbled about having to put on.

Quade grimaced as he started the roan toward the house. The ache in his loins would subside in time, but he believed if he did not wed soon he would find himself useless as a husband.

"Well, Glory girl," he whispered as she smiled up at him and gazed wonderingly into his eyes. "You are not still untouched, I fear. But you are yet whole and much loved."

"Aye," she said. "Until the next time."

CHAPTER
9

Her duty half-done with the butter delivered to Rachel Leonard and a jar of medicine dropped off at the Allyn house, Glory guided the mare toward the Collier residence. She kept her fingers crossed that Sarah would be as eager to end their estrangement as she was. In her mind she had all she would say mapped out and waiting.

"We have been too close, Sarah, not to speak of what is between us. Surely you know that whatever I have done to slight you was not done with intent. You are the sister I never had by blood, Sarah. Let us mend this hurt. Let us be friends as we were before."

Surely Sarah would not refuse her plea. She was too good-hearted not to hear out even an enemy. Besides, what could possibly be a great enough offense to permanently tear down the friendship they had held?

Anne Collier, looking as if she lacked for sleep, opened the door. "Glory," she said warmly. "You have brought the medicine for Ruthie. I am glad of it. Your mother's remedies are always good to break a fever. Come in, will you not. I'll call Sarah while I take this up to Ruthie.''

"I have wanted to see her for some time," Glory replied.

"No doubt she feels the same. She has told me you have been too busy to visit these past weeks."

While Glory was left to ponder the twist of truth Sarah had told her mother, Anne climbed the stairs and called for her eldest daughter. She was late by some minutes. Having heard the clattering approach of a horse, Sarah had hurried to her window and seen the arrival of Glory Warren. Not anxious to explain to her mother why she did not want to see Glory, she had hurriedly tiptoed down the back stairs and by the time her mother called was shutting the garden gate behind her.

Anne was back in the time it took to administer to Ruthie a draught of the medicine. "Sarah is gone," she offered with a look of dismay. "She must have set off to do an errand I had for her. Though 'tis unlike her to go without saying a word."

Glory declined a mug of cider and took her leave. She knew why Sarah had left. So this was the way it was to be between them. For the life of her she could not fathom the cause, but it had all started that day she had defended William at the stocks.

The sun was beginning to slide from the sky as she rode away from the Collier house. Deep in thought, she did not notice Josiah Bellingham standing with a gathering of church elders on the meetinghouse grounds. Nor did she see Sarah in the doorway of a shop across the street; thus she did not know that as Bellingham's eyes followed her departure the gap of enmity between two who had been friends grew ever wider.

* * *

Josiah Bellingham wished as he prepared for a journey that he had not been engaged when Glory rode through town on the previous day. He would have liked a talk with her. But if his business went well today, soon he would have all the time he desired with Glory Warren.

Hours later he arrived in the village of Crossland and, after obtaining directions to the residence of the cooper Avery Fisk, rode down the tree-lined street to the man's house. The weathered, planked, two-story structure stood apart from a large barnlike building he took to be the cooper's workshop. He pulled his horse to a stop. The ride had been long and his steed had not the smoothest gait. Hopefully the arduous ride would prove worth the effort and he would find the means to rid himself of the irksome trapper once and for all.

The man was not what he seemed. Something about him rankled and did not ring true. Whatever it was he hoped to learn from Fisk. He did not like having to put off parleying with Goody Warren.

A crudely etched shingle confirmed that he was indeed at Fisk's. His backside aching, the minister dismounted and tied his horse to an iron loop atop one of several waist-high poles in front of the place of business. Taking from his saddlebag a letter delivered to him from Crossland only days before, Bellingham unfolded the paper and again read the words written upon it.

The letter had been long in coming, though he had quickly found the cause of that. The man responding to his inquiry had signed with his mark. Like so many in the colony, Fisk did not read or write. Thankfully, the man had found someone to pen a reply, though he had but disappointingly few words to say about Wylde. But there was an additional note that had brought Bellingham the twenty-five miles to Crossland —a puzzling request from the cooper.

Seeing a portly man intently at work inside the cavernous doors of the building, Bellingham pocketed the folded document and approached him. The man, working with a hammer and chisel, made so much noise he did not hear Bellingham cross the dirt floor nor notice the minister's shadow as it fell across his workbench.

Bellingham, unaccustomed to being ignored, cleared his throat loudly. "I am the Reverend Josiah Bellingham of Sealy Grove," he said, bowing officiously to the cooper.

The man lifted his head, showing a broad, fleshy face with the flushed, red-veined look of one who has overindulged in strong drink. His eyes were deep set and strained out of fat cheeks to observe that his visitor had a prosperous and genteel look. Hoping the man had come to place a sizable order, the cooper stopped the work of smoothing a barrel stave and wiped a pair of sweaty palms on his leather apron.

"Avery Fisk," he said. "At your service."

Though generally long-winded, Bellingham also knew how to get right to the point when he wanted to. "You are the cooper Avery Fisk who owns papers of servitude on one Quade Wylde?" he asked.

Disappointed, Fisk's smile gave way beneath his heavy jowls. "The same," he said, lifting a pair of craggy brows laden with the wood dust he produced as he scraped. "Came to me for a span of ten years. A lad full of promise."

"Which was not proved out?" Bellingham queried. "You mayhap found yourself burdened with a lad who was not worth his keep?" Ten years was uncommonly long and meant Wylde had been put in service at an early age, probably by some wretch of a father who had got himself in debt to the cooper.

Fisk came around the bench. The smell of the sweat raised by his labor offended Bellingham's nose. "Oh, it was proved out," he said, wiping his flecked brow with his sleeve. "And the lad was the best ever in my service. He had a clever hand and a quick mind and did a man's work when he was still a boy."

Not having ridden so far to hear the trapper praised, Bellingham cut to another topic. "'Tis rumored he ran away before his time was done."

"'Tis no rumor. 'Tis truth," Fisk said. "He was a strong-spirited lad and would not be broken even with a well-applied rod. The lad ran off after a beating and has not been seen in Crossland since." The craggy brows crowded together. "Left me in a bad way for help, he did. I was forced to hire a man for wages, which was not to my liking."

"Still, you did not make an effort to retrieve a runaway bond servant?"

Fisk shrugged. "I advertised where I could. But how could I leave my work to chase a servant?"

"Indeed." Bellingham could find no fault with the cooper's logic. A man could not be expected to leave his family or let his work go undone while he followed a slave. "That being the case, why are you now anxious for word of Quade Wylde?"

The cooper sensed he had found a kindred spirit in the minister. "After the lad fled, a letter came from England containing a purse sufficient to pay off the indenture."

His curiosity piqued, if not pleasantly so, Bellingham urged the cooper to go on with the story. "Who would be so generous? A relative? A friend?"

Fisk shook his gritty apron, filling the air with floating motes of dust. "That I do not know. The letter was signed and sealed by a barrister and named no other person. Another has since arrived addressed to Wylde himself but I dared not break the seal; 'tis registered with the magistrate.''

Feeling a disappointment he could not account for, Bellingham continued his questioning. ''And 'tis for this reason you wish to see Quade Wylde? To tell him the debt is paid? To give him the letter you hold?''

''Nay,'' the cooper said gruffly. ''The lad did me a wrong by running off. I would leave him to think the debt still owed and he could have his letter when he came looking for it. Were there not a better reason I would let him stew, believing himself still a fugitive. I seek him because half the purse cannot be claimed until Wylde has signed a document verifying its receipt.''

''So.'' Bellingham scratched his chin. ''Quade Wylde still vexes you though it has been many years since he left your house?''

''That is one way of putting it.'' Fisk fanned his perspiring face. ''Have you news of the lad?''

Bellingham guffawed, picturing the tall, well-formed trapper. ''He is no lad now. Until recently the *man* Quade Wylde has occupied himself as a trapper,'' he said tersely. ''No doubt that is why you failed to trace him. He is newly settled in Sealy Grove.''

Fisk's deep-set eyes lit up. With Quade Wylde found he would soon have the money that for years had dangled just out of reach like fresh meat hung before a hungry dog.

''Perhaps you could be of service to me, Reverend. Perhaps you could take the letter and the document to Wylde. Have him send the reply stating he has not these past twelve years been in my service.''

Bellingham pondered the proposition. He had hoped to find evidence from the trapper's past that would discredit the man and make him less appealing to Glory. The news Fisk had given him was of little help. A true disappointment. But had his indenture not been paid, Quade Wylde would yet be considered a fugitive.

"Mayhap we could be of service to one another," Bellingham replied, as his resourceful mind clicked out a plan. Recompense was due for every wrong. "It seems to me you are owed something for the years you have had to wait to collect the second part of the money due you. Mayhap even for the wages you were required to pay the man hired in Wylde's place."

"Aye," Fisk agreed, liking the sound of what the minister said and failing to mention that the sum sent was more than the amount of the debt the lad's indenture was to cover. The tempting purse which was soon to be his grew fatter and fatter in his imagination. "The lad did flee service before the payment was received."

"A man, even a boy, must live up to his obligations," Bellingham said with conviction. For the first time since he had arrived at the cooper's Bellingham smiled. "Have you an hour to spare?" he asked. "I believe we should see the constable, you and I."

"Jacob! Come here!" Fisk shouted. A youth, stumbling over his own feet in his haste to obey, rushed into the building. "Finish here," Fisk ordered, indicating the work he had put aside. "Reverend Bellingham and I have urgent business with the constable."

"Aye, sir," the boy replied, steering his way carefully around Avery Fisk, having been cuffed enough to know how far the beefy arms could reach.

The wind died and the heat of the day clung to the air late into the evening. Seeking a cooler place than the kitchen and seizing a chance to be alone, Glory and Quade strolled first through the garden and then into the orchard on the hillside below the house. Maudie Lair had declined to join the pair and chose instead to sit by the open window in her parlor and read beneath the flickering light of a fragrant bayberry candle. She needed the rest. She had spent long hours making a new supply of the fever elixir for the Collier and Allyn girls and for Mary Douglass.

And there were the whispers she had hoped would never start in Sealy Grove. Whispers that the girls were tormented. "Was it not true," Goody White had asked, "that if they had been afflicted by measles they would be well by now? And are they not getting worse instead of better?" But Goody White was given to hysteria at a change in the weather. It was enough to make one weary. Still Maudie Lair had not forgotten the Allyn boy's words. She could only hope he had.

In the orchard, dark shadows cast by trees bathed with the silver light of a full, high moon sat in still, dark splotches on the bare ground. Finding the most respite from the heat beneath a large apple tree, Quade and Glory reclined in the dry grass, using the limblike roots that ran above the ground as seats.

Glory, cooling herself with a turkey-wing fan, had discarded her high-necked bodice for a linen shirt she could open at the throat. Quade unlaced the front of his buckskin shirt and rolled the sleeves to the elbows. Pushing aside a pouch tied at his waist, he heard the crackle of paper. His face clouded with anger.

"Damnation! Fisk!" he said, recalling what was contained in the summons he carried. "I thought myself done with the bastard." Quade swore again as he opened the shirt to the waist, revealing a triangle of sweat-dampened skin and a patch of dark, curling hair. "I would rather have the pox than set eyes on that bloody lout again."

Only that morning Bellingham had advised him of the summons sent in care of the magistrate in Sealy Grove. *There* was a question worth finding the answer to. How had the minister come to be meddling in his business?

"You will be done with him for good when you have signed the receipt," Glory said, leaning comfortably against the stout trunk of the tree. She stretched her long legs out in front of her and hitched her petticoats up to her knees, hoping to find some coolness in the tepid air. "Are you not just a little curious as to who sent the payment and who has written to you?"

Quade settled himself down cross-legged, as an Indian might. "I have a thought who is responsible for both." A muscle jerked in his tight jaw. "If 'tis who I believe, 'tis naught but a crack in his black conscience that has led him to pay off my service. Was he who placed me with Fisk. As for a wish to correspond with the bloody bastard I would sooner comply with the devil."

Even in the shadowy spray of moonlight Glory could see that his face was set in hard and rigid lines. "You have a great grievance against this man," she said softly, hoping to draw him out on the troubling subject. To speak of it might ease his mind. "Is it perhaps your father?"

"Nay." Quade crossed his arms firmly over his chest. "Were my father alive, no son of his would have been placed in service. 'Tis my uncle I speak of, though it pains me even to claim kin with such as he. He was my father's brother, a half brother and the younger son. When my grandfather died, my uncle was given a portion of the estate. 'Tis my understanding he quickly squandered the money and ran up large debts. Finding himself hounded by creditors, he sought to have my father assume his obligations. My father would have no part of it and ordered him to move out of our house."

Quade's eyes rolled up as he searched old memories. "My father was a kind man," he went on. "Now I think there was more to their estrangement than money, but as a youth I was not aware of another cause."

Quade halted again to fill and light a pipe. The story of his past had been locked inside him for many years and rarely had he delved into it himself. The telling was difficult and could not be done without reliving some of the hurt of those days. Only because he wanted Glory to understand his earlier reticence to enter family life did he reveal his secrets at all.

Glory likened Quade's telling of his story to the removing of sharp thorn deeply embedded in the flesh. Getting it out would be painful, but until it was removed it would continue to fester and pain the one afflicted. Not wanting Quade to stop now that the process was begun, she spoke in a soft, soothing tone and gently coaxed him on. "How is it you came to be in your uncle's care?"

Quade pulled the stem of the pipe from his mouth. "My parents died in a fire. I was my father's heir. My uncle assumed guardianship of his brother's only child, not for any love of me but to get his hands on the property he coveted. There must have been legal obstacles. I know not the particulars. Only that my father was a man of wealth and that to have access to that wealth my uncle thought it necessary to rid himself of me."

"So he sold you to Fisk?"

Quade shrugged as if that gesture might shake some of the hurtful barbs from him. "I was locked in my room a long while, weeks, months perhaps. Then I passed through many hands before I came to Fisk. I know not the workings of that arrangement either. Whether my uncle claimed I was dead or had run off, I believe it was all done that he might gain my father's estate, which by now he has doubtless squandered as he did his own portion."

Glory felt the welling of tears in her eyes but blinked them back, fearing Quade would not go on if he saw how it pained her to hear of his mistreatment. "Have you no other relatives who might have learned what your uncle did and sought you out?"

"No relatives," Quade answered. "Doubtless my uncle lied to my father's friends as to my whereabouts. He dismissed the loyal servants and hired those who would do as he ordered. There was no one to help a small boy, and when Fisk had me he would not let me out of his sight. I once tried posting a letter to my father's solicitor but Fisk caught me at that. A few months later he brought me with his family to the colonies, where I had no recourse but to remain in his service until I was old enough to go out on my own."

"'Tis no wonder you despise him," Glory said, her anger stirred that anyone could be so heartless to a child. "But you have no need to fear Fisk anymore," she added. "You are no longer a boy Fisk can rule. You are a man now." She placed a hand gently on Quade's arm. "And the debt has been paid in any event."

Quade cupped a hand over hers. "'Tis not Fisk I fear," he said hoarsely. "'Tis myself and what I might do to the man. His cruelty went beyond reason. As for the debt, I could have paid it many times over myself. But the debt was not mine, nor was I placed in his service by any legal right." His eyes blazed in the darkness. "'Tis he who should pay me for the years he took and the pain he gave."

"Aye," Glory said, her voice choked. Her heart ached that Quade should have suffered so when her own childhood had been filled with happiness and love. "Will you refuse to go to Crossland then?"

"I cannot." The muscles in his arm grew taut beneath her hand. "The magistrates have summoned me to stand before them. Should I not appear they would issue a warrant." He swore, then drew deeply on his pipe. "This is some ruse of Fisk's to pick my pocket," he said bitterly. "The greedy bastard."

"I wish I could go with you." Glory snuggled against his side. It was unfair that Quade should have to answer to Fisk or the magistrates when clearly he was the one wronged. Yet once it was done she was sure he would feel relieved of part of the burden he carried.

Quade's callused palm gently stroked her smooth, small hand. "I would not subject you to that, love, were you already my wife."

Glory laid her head on his shoulder and gently nuzzled her cheek against the soft buckskin shirt. A deep sigh sent a fluttering of warm breath to his cheek.

"I fear I will grow old and unappealing before that day comes," she teased.

"You will grow old by my side," he told her, relaxing his rigid muscles in response to her caress. Arms unfolded, he wrapped one around her waist. "But never unappealing. When I have put this matter in Crossland behind me, we will make our plans. 'Tis nigh time the saucy Glory Warren had her wings clipped."

Her pulse skipped and leaped at the thought. "'Tis time my reluctant suitor had his feathers plucked," she said, catching a handful of the silky hairs on his arm and giving a sharp tug.

Quade groaned and flung his glowing pipe aside. "That is a game two can play," he threatened as he snatched the linen cap from her head and caught a generous handful of lush black hair. Laughing, he tipped her head back so that the moonlight caught her full in the face, showing bright, burning eyes full of challenge and a wide, mischievous smile. The reaction of his body came as swiftly as a flame to oil touched by a fiery brand.

"I would play any game with you, love," she teased, easing her hand into the open front of his shirt and slipping her fingers threateningly into the thatch of silky hairs on his chest.

His muscles tensed and quivered beneath her fingertips. The fire reached his loins and flared like a torch. "'Tis no wonder you call me reluctant," he said in a gritty voice. "I fear my ardor will be met by some torture of yours that would make Fisk seem a tame old dog in comparison."

"You need not fear me." Her soft, cooing voice sent another quiver through his flesh. Slim, smooth fingers splayed over his chest, then slowly curled and swirled in widening circles. The torture was not pain but a sweet agony that brought a heavy groan from his lips. "I would only love you, Quade Wylde," she whispered.

"Aye, Glory girl." He rolled to his knees and bent over her, his arms looped across her back. His hands glided over the damp fabric of her shirt. "I would only love you. But I fear if I am not careful I will have you with child before you take my name."

"I would not mind that," she crooned, easing her hand low to his belly and feeling it jerk tight beneath her touch.

Feeling as if he had been doused with flame, Quade sat back on his heels, pulling briefly away from her soft stroke to strip the buckskin shirt from his back.

"Nor would I mind seeing you grow big with my child," he whispered. "But to have you flogged for delivering a babe before its time would only earn me a noose. I would kill the one who wielded the whip, I believe."

His chest lay bare, his skin like gleaming copper in the moonlight. Glory lifted her hands to him, placed her palms over the tight male nipples and teased the hard nubs with her lithe fingers. Sitting straddled over her outstretched legs, Quade cupped her face in his hands and stroked her velvet-skinned cheeks with his fingertips.

A low moan broke from his lips when she slid her hands slowly down his rib cage again, reaching his hard, rippled belly. She hooked her searching fingers inside the band of his breeches, finding the hidden flesh burning hot to her touch.

"Have you no mercy, girl?" Quade shuddered and dropped his weight onto her thighs. "I've had it said of me that I've stayed in the wilderness so long I've become half-savage. Do not put me to the test."

Glory slid her hands with punishing slowness inside the waistband until she found the laces that secured his breeches. She tugged gently at the knots.

"Nay," she said. "What good would a savage, even half a savage be to me?" Quade gave her a puzzled frown and another tortured moan as she loosed the leather ties at his waist. "Savages never molest the women they take—or rape them."

"Aye." He groaned, clamping his hands over her wrists to stay her hands from wandering lower. The light in his dark eyes fused to hers. "But I believe 'tis what they want. 'Tis certainly what I want at this moment."

Her lips, full and inviting in the moonlight, parted softly. "You could molest me just a little," she whispered, struggling to free her hands from his steel-hard grasp. "You could let me touch—"

"Nay, Glory." He ground out his reply as her wiggling fingers teased at the springy hair low on his belly. "Can you not understand what you ask is not a thing that can be done by degrees? 'Tis a thing which once started cannot be turned back from.''

Her lips formed a fetching pout. Not to be outdone, Quade mocked her, but she only smiled and made a purring sound as her pale eyes grew luminous with desire. Focusing her gaze accusingly on the bulge prominent at his loins, she whispered, "You want. I see the proof of it."

Quade wet his hot lips with his tongue. "Aye, Glory. I want. Enough that I am near to bursting with the need of you." He shook his head slowly. "'Tis not a feeling to be toyed with, love. I am a man parched with thirst and tied on the bank of a cool stream. If you cut my bindings I will plunge into the water and drink the stream dry."

"Would that I had a knife," she whispered, wriggling beneath him so that her skirt rode up and her bared thighs brushed seductively against his groin.

A shudder wracked Quade's anguished body. For a moment he lost his grip on her hands and his control. He reached for her breasts, softly highlighted by a covering of soft white linen. Glory's hands slid inside the breeches to cup his buttocks, finding them hard and tight and slick with perspiration.

Quade was unaware of opening the buttons on her shirt or of sliding the loosened garment over her shoulders. He only knew the sight of her full breasts scantily covered by the rose-colored chemise was one he would never have enough of. Soon that garment, too, slipped below her shoulders and her perfectly rounded, dusky-tipped breasts lay uncovered for his touch. His large hands cupped her soft flesh, his touch at first as delicate as that of a gossamer cloth, stroking, exploring the satin curves, the silken valley.

Glory moaned, wanting his touch everywhere at once, wanting the same kneading pressure she applied to his firm buttocks. Lips parted, she whispered his name as his hands moved responsively over her. Squeezing, nudging, tugging the rock-hard nipples, his caress sent a rippling heat through her.

"'Tis magic," she cried. "I am set afire."

"You are fire, love. The sweetest, hottest fire a man could wish for. Would that I could burn forever in your flame." His hands beneath her arms, he pulled her naked breasts against his bare belly, then cried out at the searing pleasure of having her softness crushed to him.

She nuzzled her face to his chest, her lips playing over the hard muscle, her tongue darting out to cool the heated skin. She savored the salty taste of him and the tickle of the crinkling hair leading like an arrow to his loins. Her mouth followed the furry line downward, lips caressing, teeth nibbling the hard flesh.

When she reached the thickening hair at his belly, Quade groaned and swung clear, giving Glory a moment of dismay until she found his head nestled in her lap and his arms around her neck, pulling her down to him.

"I am a drowning man," he whispered, his mouth at her breast. "A burning man plunging into a hotter current." His fingers softly holding her breast, he took a tight, aching nipple into his mouth and sucked gently.

Glory gave a soft moan and pulled loose the leather thong that held his thick, dark hair. A flush stained her skin as if it had been touched by a white-hot flame.

"I would let you burn," she whispered, "that I might burn with you."

His loins strained at the loose laces holding his breeches. Glory's heavy-lidded eyes fell to the swollen erection surging against the tight buckskins. Overcome with lustful curiosity, she nudged the breeches low on his hips and before Quade knew what she was about, slid her hand inside.

He gave a sharp cry as her fingers closed around the pulsing, erect flesh. "Glory. No." His voice was gritty and hoarse as he buried his face in the silken softness of her breasts.

Glory hastily wrested open the breeches' lacings. "I want to feel you, to see," she whispered, running her fingers in a wondering touch over the length of the heated shaft. Never having seen a grown man naked, she could not tear her eyes away from that powerful male part of him, so awing, so eagerly throbbing beneath her hand.

For a moment Quade was too weakened to speak or move in protest of her explorations. His strength came back in a surge. Moaning her name, he rolled atop her, his damp, glistening chest crushing her breasts tightly against him. His erection lay hotly against her thigh as his mouth sought her soft lips. His kiss was hard, a hungry joining of mouths that sent shocks of desire plummeting like a chain of lightning from one to the other. With his knees he nudged her legs wide while his hands slid her skirt clear for his fevered manhood.

It was as he raised himself above her that he saw a light swaying in the doorway of the house. Cursing, Quade flung himself from her.

"Sweet Jesus!" he said. "In God's truth you are safer with savages than with me." He rose hastily and pulled his breeches over his straining erection, and with much discomfort drew in the tight lacings.

"Quade?" Glory lay at his feet, legs and breasts bared, her breathing ragged, her eyes wide with astonishment.

He groaned and shut his eyes, rubbing his hands over his aching loins. A moment later he quickly bent down and pulled Glory to her feet. With trembling hands he jerked the chemise and shirt over her surging breasts.

"Your mother calls," he said hoarsely, finding his shirt

and plunging his arms into the sleeves. "Straighten your clothes and go in."

"Aren't you coming too?" Glory fumbled with the buttons on her wrinkled shirt and managed to get them lined up right. She tucked her cap in her pocket and shook her hair to rid it of grass.

"Nay, I want to live," he said. "By all rights your mother has cause to kill or castrate me."

Glory hurriedly placed her hand over his mouth. "I would not let her do either," she said. "Come in with me. We'll tell her we are to be wed. The banns can be posted tomorrow. We can marry next week."

Displeased with himself for having come so close to taking her when he had vowed to himself he would not until they were wed, his voice sounded harsh. "Nay, Glory. Not as soon as that. I have only just settled with Wharton and that cost me most of the money I had. Will be some months before I have saved enough to buy the cabin and land from Douglass."

Taken aback, the glow quickly faded from Glory's face. "What does it matter if you have a shilling or not? We have the farm. Is that not enough?"

"Nay. Allow a man his pride, Glory. I cannot come to you in marriage with naught but a pack of furs."

"'Tis plenty."

"'Tis enough to keep us perhaps three months. Then what?"

"Then you might come to your senses and have what is yours for the taking. Can you not understand I care not if you have naught but that buckskin shirt? What I have is enough for both of us."

Quade sighed. What a muck he had made of things. Instead of seducing her, he should have been explaining his plan to build a business which would support a wife in proper fashion. "Have patience, love," he said, softening his tone. "I am only asking that you wait until the venture with Wharton turns a profit."

"Nay!" she said in a high voice. "I will not wait!"

His brows flickered. "Aye. You will unless you plan to wed another in the meantime."

Glory's eyes flashed hotly. "Perhaps I will. Perhaps you are too stubborn for me."

Quade's fingers splayed out and gripped her shoulders. "Or perhaps you are too spoiled and too accustomed to getting your way," he returned. "But if it helps your feelings I will speak to your mother tomorrow before I leave and ask her permission to wed you in six months' time."

"Nay!" Glory whirled away. "Do not bother. Go to Crossland and stay for all I care."

"Glory!" he called after her, but she was off in a run and would not stop.

Quade stood at a hearing before the two magistrates in Crossland, a deep rage boiling within him. His case was not helped by the eagerness of the magistrates to dispense with the proceedings so that they might journey to Salem and witness, after a long delay, the renewed witch trials. A breach of the law that occurred twelve years back was insignificant compared to stopping the spread of witchcraft.

By concentrating on some pleasant event, Quade held his temper in check. The method of control was one he had learned from Indian friends and he'd found it to be useful when he was pushed beyond natural bounds.

The cooper Fisk, his gap-toothed jaw exposed in a vicious smile, faced him and slung an accusing finger in his immobile face.

"'Tis the same Quade Wylde who fled my service twelve years and some months ago," Fisk said, addressing the magistrates, a somber pair of men clad in black. "An unruly lad, he left my house in the dark of night and has not been heard of since, till this day."

"I took naught of yours, Fisk," Quade returned. "Nor had you ever any legal claim to my service. I was placed with you against my will and to pay out no debt of mine."

"Have you proof of this claim?" one of the magistrates asked.

"Nay," Quade replied. "I was but a lad and could not defend myself against grown men who set themselves above me."

"Then 'tis your word against his on that matter," was the reply.

Fisk shook his beefy jowls with a smirk. "I have the document which laid you to my service for a period of ten years, five of which were not worked out," the cooper volunteered quickly.

Quade directed a withering stare at the man. "You have said you accepted payment freeing me of indenture," he pointed out.

"Half-payment," Fisk corrected, shuddering beneath those menacing eyes. "Half is yet held in abeyance and must be paid—if not, 'tis my requirement the remaining time of service be fulfilled."

"Good sirs." Quade turned to the magistrates. The thick-headed cooper would have to do better than that if he expected to coerce Quade into his domain again. "The man accepted half-payment for the indenture. Half was served as we have both attested. That being so, only half was owed and the man has received that amount. The other half held in abeyance is not his by any just calculation."

The magistrates conferred and agreed the indenture was cleared and the money in question could go to Fisk only if the unknown benefactor agreed to release it after hearing the terms under which it was received.

Fisk snorted and turned redder in the face, seeing the expected money no nearer his grasp. "The payment came a full year after Wylde fled my house," he snapped. "This man owes me reimbursement of the wages I was forced to pay a hired man. 'Tis also a fact he fled when the indenture was yet in effect and was, regardless of his present state, a fugitive for the period of those twelve months. 'Tis my belief the payment at a later date does not erase the crime previously committed."

Again the magistrates' heads went together. "You are right, Goodman Fisk," was the concurrence. "For fleeing service it is our judgment that Quade Wylde be confined in the public jail for a period of one month."

"Sirs!" Quade started, but the magistrates ordered him silent. Lips sealed shut, he shook inside as if he were a cannon filled with powder and ready for firing. To his credit, none of his seething anger showed outwardly.

"Goodman Fisk," the magistrate continued. "It is further our opinion that should additional payment be released to you for the indenture of Quade Wylde, that amount is more than sufficient to cover expenses you incurred by the hiring of a worker. Should the money be denied, then Quade Wylde, formerly of your service, shall pay you the amount equal to one year of wages for the worker hired."

Fisk gloated and fairly danced in front of Quade and the magistrates. "You are not so cocky now, are you, Quade Wylde?" he said in a low voice. "And you will be less so when you have spent a month in the jail living on molded bread and sour swill. Aye." His deep-set eyes gleamed from his fat face. "You will long remember you cannot get the best of Avery Fisk."

Quade gritted his teeth and clenched his hands lest he strike Fisk with hard words or hard fists. Were it not for Glory who would be waiting while he served his sentence, he would have risked breaking the bloke's neck right in the courtroom. Uncertain how he would manage from the confines of the jail, he hoped he could find a way to send a message to Glory. Otherwise she would wonder why he did not return when expected. He regretted having left with a quarrel between them. He needed her now. Certainly he had no friends in Crossland. Fisk had seen to that.

The magistrates penned a document verifying that Quade Wylde was indeed free of indenture to Avery Fisk and further stating that Quade Wylde was alive and in good health. Afterward the constable escorted Quade to the jail and locked him in a room with a single narrow window. The furnishings were two buckets, one for water and one for the call of nature, a three-legged stool, and a broken-down cot with stained ticking which, by the crackle it made when sat on, was filled with dried corn shucks.

Fisk saw him shut inside, then offered a yellow letter though the door slot used for handing in a trencher.

"The seal is unbroken, as you can see," the man shouted. "I hope 'tis bad news."

Quade bit back the fierce retort poised on his tongue. He accepted the letter rather than have Fisk hold another thing that was his, but when it was in his hand he tossed the sealed envelope across the room. He was in no mood to read his uncle's lies.

CHAPTER
10

Josiah Bellingham rode purposefully to the Warren house. He was only mildly disappointed to learn Glory was away at the Douglass farm helping to tend the ailing Mary.

"Goody Douglass has sat at Mary's bedside until she is near weary to death herself. Glory will relieve her a few hours so the poor woman can rest. 'Tis fortunate the child is fond of my daughter."

"Aye," Bellingham agreed. "I am on my way there when I am done here. 'Tis curious, this illness. One or two have questioned if 'tis caused by malefaction."

"Do you agree?" Maudie Lair clenched her trembling hands, afraid he would next say Glory was the one accused. Bellingham quickly relieved her fears.

"Nay. I have assured them Sealy Grove is too godly for witches to breed here. But it does not help those who doubt that another child was taken sick last night, the youngest in the Cobb household." As she beckoned him inside, he doffed his silver-buckled hat.

"Jane?"

"That is the one. She is fevered like the others and covered with whelps none have seen the like of. But what of you? How do you fare, Goody Warren?" He deftly changed the subject for he had not come to talk of illness or sorcery.

Maudie Lair invited him into the spacious parlor. "God favors me," she replied. "I have no infirmities."

Bellingham took a seat on the high-backed wooden settle near the fireplace. He had been expected and a teapot sat steaming beside a platter of jam and bread. Maudie Lair poured tea for each of them, then sat in the rocker her husband had lovingly made to fit her small frame. Her duty done, she looked expectantly at the minister. He had not tasted his tea and appeared anxious to speak. But if not of what she had feared, then what?

Though he was perfectly capable of talking all day on any topic, Bellingham wasted few words in getting to the crux of his visit. "I have come on a matter of great significance." He sat straight-backed and stiff. "'Tis a matter in which I beg your cooperation."

For all her intuitive understanding of people, Maudie Lair was unprepared for what he would ask. "It has long been my purpose to help where I can," she replied.

Bellingham's straight shoulders relaxed a little. "'Tis obvious your daughter, Glory, is of marriageable age. 'Tis time she took a husband."

Maudie Lair tensed slightly. Had someone complained of Glory's carriage, or observed her conduct as too forward? Had Bellingham come to chastise her about her daughter's behavior?

"She approaches her nineteenth year and has shown some interest in marrying," Maudie Lair said cautiously.

"And you are willing to see her wed?" Hiding his keen interest in the widow's answer behind downcast eyes and the rim of his teacup, he sipped the hot, fragrant liquid.

"If 'tis her will to wed, I would not stand in her way."

"I see you have given the matter some thought." Encouraged, he sat the cup aside and proceeded with new vigor. "Have you set the amount of her dowry?"

Genuinely puzzled by his query, Maudie Lair could only stare. Was the amount of a dowry a matter to be discussed at large? Or was there some reason for haste she was not aware of?

"The farm is hers by two-thirds. A part of that will serve as dowry," Maudie Lair replied at last. "And when I pass, my portion will come to her as well."

Bellingham swelled with anticipation. It was as he thought, and even rented the Warren acreage was sufficient to keep a man satisfactorily if he had no other income. But then there was the matter of what he could offer a wife.

"'Tis no trifling amount," he remarked, feeling his collar chafe his neck as he considered how pitiful his resources were in comparison. Ordinarily a groom would put up an amount corresponding to half the dowry. "Would be a difficult amount to match."

Maudie Lair laughed softly, deciding Bellingham was as fond of gossip as any of the women of Sealy Grove. She now believed speculation had arisen as to whether Glory would wed the trapper Quade Wylde, and the minister wished to be the first to confirm or deny the truth of the rumor.

"I think my daughter will expect only that her intended match her love."

Bellingham gripped the arm of the settle. He could not have asked for a better answer. "That she will have," he said boldly.

"Your pardon," Maudie Lair mumbled, completely confounded by his comment.

"Have I not made myself clear?" The minister sat proudly, aware that his handsome face and good carriage were often remarked upon. If not a tidy purse he had his looks to trade on.

"Nay. I do not follow you."

" 'Tis Glory," he said, smiling as if he bestowed a gift on the woman. " 'Tis my wish to wed your daughter."

"I—she—I cannot speak for my daughter, sir," she replied with some difficulty, Bellingham's request having robbed her of reason for a moment. Indeed she could not speak for Glory, even though a match with Quade would please her far more. But as yet the trapper had not made a request for her daughter. In fairness she must allow Glory to consider the minister's petition as well. "She must make her choice of a husband." Maudie Lair pulled her breath in sharply. " 'Tis only my blessing I can give her."

"Then I have your permission to ask her consent?"

Again Maudie Lair stumbled for words. "I—as I have said, 'tis her consent alone you must have. Ask if you will." She sat in stunned silence for a long moment more, then added, "I believe, sir, you will take her by surprise with your proposal, as you have me."

Bellingham smiled knowingly, recalling how Glory had warmed to him the last time he had been in this house. "Perhaps you will be surprised in that, too," he said.

Maudie Lair Warren shook her graying head. "It would surprise me no small amount. That is for sure."

Bellingham left the widow a short time later, having been told by her the time Glory would depart the Douglass house. He knew the path she would take and, being in a state to deny himself nothing, determined to meet her along the way.

It was as good a time as any and better than most to ask for her hand.

He saw her in the distance, her gait light, her arms swinging gaily, her cap in tow in one hand. He would never fault her for that. The dark hair hung in a charming array of ringlets over her shoulders. Even from far off he could imagine the satiny feel of it in his hands, the look of it lying against her bare skin, and his. He did not reproach himself for his lustful thoughts. Today was different. Soon Glory would be his and there was no sin in lusting after his own wife.

Not having expected to meet anyone on the trail, she cried out a greeting. "Good day, sir. What brings you so far from town?"

Bellingham halted his horse and as she walked nearer gazed fondly at her. "I am on my way to call on Goody Douglass and Mary. How fares the child?"

"She is improved. Well enough to complain of the broth she is fed."

"Good. Then there is no need for haste. And I have another purpose in being here. Is that not so?"

As he dismounted Glory gave him a puzzled look that would have equaled the one on her mother's face a short time earlier.

"Aye, sir," she said. "If you say, though your purpose eludes me unless 'tis me you have come to see."

"You have hit upon it." Bellingham turned aside to tether his horse to a bush. "Sit a spell," he said, indicating a large, flat rock a few yards away which could be used as a bench. "I would talk with you awhile."

Glory waited as he tied the horse, then walked with him toward the rock, her face lighting up in awareness as she recalled her mother mentioning that Bellingham was to call.

"I remember," she said at once. "You wished to see my mother on an urgent matter."

"So you remember that." The hazel eyes observed every detail of her appearance and found nothing that did not please. "Tell me, have you an inkling what that matter was?"

"I have none," she replied, concluding the minister was behaving in a most peculiar manner.

With girlish energy she hopped up on the rock. Her feet, crossed at the ankles, swung clear of the ground. Bellingham sat close beside her, his longer legs allowing his feet to remain solidly planted.

"My business concerns you."

"Me?"

His clouded eyes made her shiver. Her mind followed the same vein as her mother's had. She was as aware as Maudie Lair Warren that any behavior, even if done innocently, was subject to misinterpretation. She sought to recall what action of hers might have invited the minister's correction. Though she could think of several, she was sure they could not have come to Bellingham's attention.

"You are a lovely maid, Glory Warren." He edged closer.

"I thank you, sir." Thinking he needed more room, she scooted over a bit.

"You are the sort of woman a man would be pleased to have as wife."

Glory blushed lightly. "I hope that is true, sir." She also hoped Quade would feel the same on his return from Crossland, though she could hardly blame him if he did not, considering the send-off she had given him. The bit of cheer she had felt over Mary's improvement diminished. She had been unfair, but she would make it up to Quade.

Misconstruing her musing, Bellingham plucked her small

hand from her lap and held it within his own. "'Tis true," he assured her. "Is it in your mind to marry, Glory?"

"Aye," she said boldly, all her reticence gone. "The thought has been much with me."

Now he held her hand crushed between both of his. "I thought as much." He spoke in the mellow tones that so effectively enthralled his congregation. "I ask you to be my wife, Glory Warren."

"Sir!" Jolted, Glory's jaw popped open and her eyes grew round as moons. For what seemed an endless time she could only sit and stare at the bemused minister.

"You seem undone, my dear." Bellingham again caught hold of her tense hand, brought it swiftly to his lips and kissed the warm back of it.

Finding her voice, Glory responded brokenly. "You have astonished me, sir. I know not what to say except that I would make a poor wife for a minister."

Chuckling lightly, Bellingham nodded. "That is for me to decide. 'Tis only natural you would feel unworthy." His smile was warm; he admired modesty in a woman. "I will teach you the proper carriage for a minister's wife. 'Tis not so different than being any ordinary man's helpmate," he assured her.

Glory shook her head, sending the black hair shimmering around her face. "I fear I would not take to it," she declared. "I do not learn quickly."

Black, silken strands of Glory's hair brushed his hands. His skin prickled at the soft, sensual feel of it.

"I am a patient man, an erstwhile teacher," he insisted, though the surge of desire in his loins gave a double meaning to what he said next. "You would learn well under my tutelage."

"Nay. I could not. I am not the meek sort a minister's wife should be. I am too outspoken. And what is more, my heart . . ."

"Your heart is in a flutter," he interrupted, allowing himself the liberty of slipping his fingers into the tousled curls on each side of her head. "I understand the workings of a young girl's mind. You are concerned about your shortcomings. You must have time to ponder what has been asked of you. You must consult your mother, of course. We have discussed the dowry, she and I."

Glory gasped. Her mother could not have consented to this. Not before Quade had spoken for her.

Her eyes flashed. Her words came rapidly. "You do not understand. I love . . ."

Her words were lost in a gasp of surprise, which Bellingham took as eagerness for his kiss, as his mouth forcefully covered hers, bruising her lips, cutting off her breath. Aghast, she pushed at his chest but found her strength ineffective against a man filled with a year's worth of craving for an intimate touch.

For Bellingham she was an earthly paradise, her lips hot and soft, and if they were not as yielding as he would like, that was another thing he would enjoy teaching. His own response came with the speed and recklessness of a whirlwind. It was in his mind to let his hands roam where he so wanted them to be, to feel her creamy skin beneath them, but he was a moral man and subjected himself to the same limits he would impose on any other. Warring with himself, he pulled away.

"We will make our plans soon," he called, leaving her too stunned to speak as he hurried to his horse.

Her lungs were empty and burning. She gasped for breath

to fill them. "Wait!" she cried when at last she had the clarity of mind to speak.

But Bellingham had mounted and ridden off. Glory fell back against the rock, certain her legs were too wobbly to carry her home. Her swollen lips ached; she tasted a fleck of blood on the lower one. What madness was this? The man believed she would wed him. Bellingham. Josiah Bellingham.

Glory moaned softly and started unsteadily to the house. This was a time she could use a friend to help her sound out a problem. She thought of Sarah and felt the heaviness of her loss. She thought of Quade. She needed him. She hoped he would not be long in getting back.

Having touched her, having kissed her, Josiah Bellingham burned with the fever of his desire to have Glory Warren as consort. Of all the advantages the marriage carried, it seemed to him the greatest was the physical person of his intended. Her skin was as smooth and unblemished as the finest silk. He longed for the day he would see her in naught but the splendid covering she had been born with. Sweat dripped from his brow and ran from his heated body as he imagined having Glory submissively beneath him on a soft feather mattress.

Overcome with his thoughts, Bellingham twisted in the saddle, the hard leather seat more a torture than a convenience for the condition he was in. Were he a less righteous man he would be tempted at such a time as this to provoke his lust by his own hand. Instead he would pray for a quick deliverance from his widowed state. Until his prayer was answered he would count himself twice blessed that a woman who inspired such intense feeling was also endowed with the wealth to make his life one of veritable ease.

Bellingham spurred his horse to a trot. She would bear him children, but not too soon, he hoped. He would like to enjoy the use of her a long while before her body was misshapen by pregnancy. A servant could be employed to tend the babies once they came so that they would not take all her time from him. His mother-in-law could continue her duties as well.

His smile lasted a long while. The arrangement was ideal. He would have the liberty and the resources to develop his mind, to have his papers published and distributed where they would do him good. Eventually he would be called to a large charge. In the meantime the parlor in the Warren house would make a fine study. Perhaps he would need to make adjustments in his schedule in the beginning. Indeed, it would be necessary. To neglect a new bride was unforgivable.

Bellingham mopped his brow with his already soggy handkerchief. The wedding must be soon. Only a fortnight's delay at most. He did not think he could endure longer without her now that he had her answer. Much needed to be done. The elders must be advised of his plans; he would need their approval though it was but perfunctory. That at least he could attend to immediately. Burrell Collier was chief among them and when told would notify the others.

Yes. He would report his plans to Goodman Collier as soon as he was done at the Douglass place.

The sky had taken on a dusky hue when he got under way again. But it was not so late that he need postpone the visit with Burrell Collier. Picturing Glory on his arm as he strolled the streets of Sealy Grove, Bellingham turned his horse toward the Collier dwelling.

He was shown into the parlor and offered a glass of canary, which he accepted. Neither he nor his host were aware that another was interested in what had brought the two of them together. But Sarah, risking her father's wrath should she be discovered, sat at a turn in the stairwell, a spot the Collier children had long ago learned gave them a clear and undetected view of the room. She could see Bellingham seated in the slat-backed maple armchair, his face turned to her father. Her heart thumped excitedly, fanned by the belief that the minister had come to plead for her father's permission to ask for her hand.

Bellingham's flaxen hair, dampened by sweat, glistened beneath the wavering candle flames. He crossed one leg over the other, showing a well-turned calf clad in snug hose of dark green worsted. Sarah eyed him longingly, wishing for the interview with her father to be quickly over, so that hers—the much-anticipated one in which he would beg her to be his wife—would soon begin.

A few minutes passed, during which Bellingham inquired of Ruthie's condition.

"She is some better since you were last here," Collier said.

Assuring the father that Ruthie would be mentioned in his prayers, Bellingham turned to other business.

"Goodman Collier," he said, modulating his voice with the proper mix of authority and humility, "'tis my wish to make certain plans of mine known to the elders, though not yet make these same plans common knowledge."

His interest aroused, Goodman Collier inclined his head toward the young minister. "You may count on my discretion unless 'tis a matter which should be decided by the congregation."

"Nay, 'tis a personal matter." Bellingham sat back. "Nevertheless, it has some bearing on my calling." Slowly swirling the wine in his glass, he paused until he saw Goodman Collier was near the edge of his chair in anticipation of some privileged tidbit of information. "I have determined to take a wife."

At her hidden watch Sarah stifled a gasp with both hands. It was all she could do not to fly down the stairs to throw her arms around Josiah's neck.

"'Tis past time," Collier said, a satisfied look settling over him. In a celebratory frame of mind, he poured a refill of Canary for Bellingham and for himself, thinking of the toast he would make when the bartering was done. He smiled, pleased he had been proved out by waiting to speak to Bellingham about Sarah. Here was the man about to ask for her hand, giving her father the advantage in arranging the dowry.

"A man was not meant to live in solitude," he said loudly. "'Tis unnatural."

"Aye, that is my thinking," Bellingham agreed. "My solitude will end before a fortnight is past. 'Tis my intent to wed Glory Warren."

"Glory Warren!" Collier sputtered and sprayed a swallow of canary back into his glass. That girl. "I thought—Glory Warren, you say?"

Goodman Collier's mind leaped to a quick series of calculations. Not without placing himself in the poorhouse could he match a dowry such as Glory Warren would bring to a marriage. Sighing heavily he dabbed his stained band with a handkerchief. There was no help for it. Sarah would have to set her cap elsewhere. He would not make himself look foolish by bargaining where he had no chance to succeed.

Altogether pleased with himself, Bellingham rubbed his palms together. "A comely maid, do you not agree? And of unspotted reputation."

"I have not heard otherwise," Collier stammered.

"Nay and you will not," Bellingham stated. "She is a good and modest girl, a fitting choice for a minister's wife."

And richly endowed, both in looks and land, Collier thought to himself. Well, if God had guided the minister to one such as that, it must be to test his mettle. Let him make the best of it. Josiah Bellingham was not so pious that he was blinded to realities. And Collier could not blame the man for making the best match available to him. Were he to find himself a widower, he would do no less.

Having been assured the elders would rejoice to have their minister rightly wed, Bellingham left the Collier house and returned to the cottage which had begun to look remarkably humble to him as he anticipated the pending change in his state.

With the wine decanter sealed and the candle flames snuffed, Burrell Collier left the darkened parlor. After he passed below her on his way to the kitchen, Sarah, one hand pressed to her heaving abdomen and the other over her mouth, crept down the stairs. Outside in the garden she hung her head over the spines of the picket fence and spilled the contents of her stomach. When the retching ceased, she slumped to the grass and wept. Feeling cruelly and pitilessly abused by fate, the brokenhearted girl sought a reason for what had happened to her.

Why had she not been born with brilliant blue eyes? Why had she not been born with a face cast from a perfect mold? It was not fair, not fair that Glory should have her Josiah. Had not the test of the egg shown she would marry the minister? Had not the spell she'd made ensured the prediction would come true? Had she not shown Josiah what a devoted and loving wife she would be?

Sarah sniffed, then wiped her nose and eyes on her apron. How how had it happened that he chose Glory over her? How?

Sarah choked back more sobs rather than bring unwanted attention from anyone in the house. This was not the way it was meant to be. Something had gone terribly wrong. Still sniffling, Sarah turned her eyes to the heavens and saw what appeared to be a shadow on the moon. A shadow such as a witch might make, one who had come to spy and mock. One would think an evil eye had been cast upon her.

All at once Sarah stopped her crying and sat upright. Perhaps, she considered, there was more to this turning of the minister's head than a pretty face and a pair of besotting eyes.

Oh, yes. As Sarah removed her tear-stained apron and balled it up the answer came more clearly to her. Glory Warren had used a spell, a spell far stronger than that of hair clippings and nail parings. She had charmed Josiah in some new and terrible way. Why, Glory Warren need only look at a man with those . . . witch's eyes.

The lines of Joseph Allyn's riddle came drumming into her mind. Sarah supplied the elusive answer. *"Glory Warren has witch's eyes."*

Gasping, the horrified girl shuffled to her feet. The truth had been before her all along. Josiah had not chosen Glory over her. The choice had not been his to make. He was bedeviled, bewitched with a spell born of a dark power no mortal could wield alone.

Glory Warren was a witch.

Glory Warren blotted tears from her reddened eyes. "Where could he be? He is overdue from Crossland." She sniffled as she pared the brown peel from a potato. "Do you think he has returned to the wilderness?"

"Nay," her mother said. "If 'tis as you've said between you, he would not leave without telling you, not even if you quarreled. He has been delayed. 'Tis nothing more. He will be back in good time.''

"In good time," Glory moaned. "That is what he said."

"A lack of patience has ever been one of your faults, girl." Maudie Lair gave her daughter a playful whack on the behind as she passed the shelf where Glory worked.

"Aye, Mother," Glory said in a calmer voice. "'Tis a fault I will endeavor to improve. But tell me, please, what am I to do about Reverend Bellingham? The man as good as thinks I have agreed to wed him."

Her lips set tightly together, Maudie Lair stopped stirring the soup that was boiling in the blackened kettle hooked to the iron backbar. With a poker she skillfully spread the fire so that only glowing coals remained beneath the kettle.

"'Tis truly a thorny mess," the older woman said at length. "I fear he will not take a refusal lightly."

"If only he had listened," Glory wailed. "Instead of assuming I would not reject him. Now that he believes his proposal accepted, the blow of a denial will fall doubly hard."

"Perhaps a letter is best," her mother suggested. "I believe our Reverend Bellingham would prefer to have your refusal in private. By any means it must be worded with care. It would be unkind to offend the man more than is necessary."

"Of that I am not so sure." Glory rinsed the last of the peeled potatoes in a bucket of water, then began to dice them into cubes to be added to the soup. "'Tis because I sought to spare his feelings that the misunderstanding arose. Better I had been blunt than kind."

"Do as you must." Maudie Lair took the chunks of potato and stirred them into the simmering broth. "But do not delay. He must know you will not have him before he has made his intention widely known."

"Aye," Glory agreed, dreading what was ahead of her even if she was spared doing it face-to-face. "I'll pen a letter before I get into bed."

The dawning day matched Glory's mood. The sky was heavy, clouded, and gray as a summer storm blew in and whipped the land with fierce winds and heavy rains, soaking the roads, flooding creeks and streams, and making the fording of those ordinarily trickling waterways hazardous. The storm was ferocious but brief and by afternoon the rain had slowed to drizzle. Ordinarily neither she nor her mother would have ventured out until the roads had dried. But storm or no, she would go. The letter to Bellingham could not wait.

A storm of another sort had settled over Sealy Grove, and it was one that even nature's fury could not hold back. It began with a mere whisper to Prudence Oliver and a chance conversation with Joseph Allyn.

"I know the answer to your riddle," Sarah told him. "'Tis Glory Warren."

Joseph, wary, weighed his response. "Why do you think 'tis her?"

Sarah looked at him as if he were a fool. "Because she has worked her sorcery on me. She has by design taken a thing which was mine."

"What?" Joseph demanded.

Her pride would not allow her to tell him. Defensively she searched for another charge to bolster that one. Recalling a rumor, she added Glory's name to it. "She is a witch! She torments my sister."

Joseph's face was as blank as a wall for a moment and then he remembered something he had seen one Sabbath several weeks back. Glory on the meetinghouse grounds with a group of girls, Ruthie : . . "And Abigail," he said. "And Mary Douglass and Jane Cobb. I saw her with those very four. And since, all suffer with the same illness."

Pondering what Joseph had added to what she said of Glory, Sarah went on her way, debating whether or not she should relay the charges to her mother. But though she was brave enough to voice her feelings to Prudence and Joseph, she lacked the courage to make the same charge to Anne Collier.

Joseph had less discretion. By late in the day, half the residents of Sealy Grove knew what had been said. Some chastened him for having an artful tongue. Others listened with rapt attention, all too ready to believe their village no less susceptible to a plague of witches than Salem.

Enjoying his celebrity and having forgotten the admonishment from Reverend Bellingham as well as the promise of silence made to the minister, Joseph added another verse to his riddle:

> Who charms a child and charms a man?
> Who brooks no wrong to kith and kin?
> Who holds a key to Satan's den?

The words caught like fishhooks in minds denied the pleasure of frivolous songs or entertainment. Soon the witty rhyme was recited throughout Sealy Grove and only a few stumbled over the name of the person described.

"'Tis said she has a crow which rides on her shoulder and does as she bids," Goody White told a neighbor who had come to beg a firebrand since the coals in her fireplace had grown cold during the night.

"'Tis said she works a spell which tames the wild creatures, that they seek her out and nibble crumbs from her hand," the other woman said.

"None but a witch could do that," Goody White insisted. "With my own eyes I have seen her entice children into idle play, and that done on the Sabbath on the meetinghouse grounds."

"And what was she about with that? Would she deliver our children to the dark one?"

Altogether unaware that Glory's name was slandered about the town, Glory and her mother drove the cart to the house of Rachel Leonard, where Maudie Lair planned to leave a portion of the butter churned earlier in the week.

Glory left her mother talking with Goody Leonard while she walked the few blocks from the Leonard house to Bellingham's cottage. If her luck was good Bellingham would be out and she could leave the letter in the message box affixed to his door.

The street was muddy and the air filled with the rank odor of decaying matter that pigs, chickens, and other animals that ran freely about the streets had contributed to the mud. Wearing a pair of high clogs to protect her leather shoes, Glory passed only two or three others whose business required them to brave the foul streets. One of those hastily crossed the street before reaching her. Another turned into a side lane and hurried away without returning the greeting she gave. The third entered a house just off the street. As she passed she saw a child pulled away from a window. Glory thought little of it. The miserable weather was enough to make people irritable. Not until she saw Sarah did she wonder if those others on the street had sought to avoid her.

"Sarah. A good day to you," Glory called out as she

saw the girl gathering a basket of carrots in the Collier garden.

Sarah took a rest from her work and sat on the brick-lined path, staring aimlessly at the sky as she chewed the stem of a plant she had just plucked from between the rows of carrots. Hope welling up in her heart, Glory slowed her steps, praying that Sarah had gotten over whatever had upset her. While she must first deliver the letter to Bellingham, she was not opposed to stopping in on her return. If only they could be friends as before, and she could tell Sarah that the girl who had once scoffed at her desire to wed now yearned to be the bride of Quade Wylde.

"I have missed seeing you," Glory called out as she drew nearer. "And I have news which will surely surprise you."

Sarah, watching her rival pass her house, was overcome by an outpouring of envy at Glory's announcement.

"Witch," she hissed as she angrily leaped to her feet. Sneering at the black-haired girl leaning against the picket fence, Sarah tossed the stalk of jimsonweed to the bricks and ground it to pulp beneath her foot. She knew what the news was. Glory wished to gloat over her betrothal to Josiah Bellingham.

An image of Glory locked in the arms of her Josiah swirled wildly in the haze of her troubled mind. It was more than Sarah could take. In such an agitated state that all reason escaped her, the distressed girl made a piteous moan, shielded her eyes, and turned her back on her former confidante and friend.

"Sarah!" Glory had not understood what Sarah said, but it was impossible to misunderstand the meaning of the stiff back presented to her. Hurt to the quick, she cried out, "How is it you treat me so? Have I abused you in some way, Sarah? Tell me if I have and I will make amends."

Sarah, aided by the delusive potency of the herb she had inadvertently ingested, by now believed all that her twisted imagination had conjured up concerning Glory. Screeching loudly, she dashed off for the house. While Glory, heartsick over Sarah's barefaced disdain of her, moved on slowly down the street, Sarah, shaking and mumbling incoherently, tumbled into her mother's kitchen.

Her head spun like a wagon wheel. Muted colors and images flashed and faded in her mind. "She has cast her spell on me!" Sarah cried, throwing herself prostrate at her mother's feet.

"Who has, Sarah?" Anne Collier demanded, alarmed to see her daughter thrashing on the floor like an errant child. "What is this you babble about?"

Sarah writhed and groaned and beat her fists on the floor. "The witch," she mumbled. "Poor Ruthie."

Getting no sense from Sarah, Goody Collier hastened as best she could, burdened by the heaviness of pregnancy, to the door and looked out. She saw a dark-haired girl, head drooping, ambling down the street

"'Tis only Glory Warren," she said, shaking her head. "Has your sanity slipped?"

Sarah continued to pound her fists on the floor and cry out, "'Tis unfair! Unfair! She is a witch!"

Unable to stop her daughter's ravings with words, Goody Collier caught Sarah firmly by the arms and endeavored to pull the struggling girl to her feet.

"Get up, Sarah," she ordered, bending her back to better lift the resistant girl. "Get up and tell me what all this is about."

Sarah did get up but only after her mother stumbled over her and shrieked with pain.

"Mother! Mother!" she cried.

Goody Collier clutched frantically at her swollen abdomen and pleaded with Sarah to get her to the bed. "My time is upon me," she moaned. "And early by two months." Groaning as a sharp pain tightened like an iron clamp around her belly, she cried out in alarm, "'Tis too early. I fear for the child."

A baby squalled. Rachel Leonard lifted her youngest, a toddling boy, from the standing stool where he played. The other children she had sent outside in Mercy's care.

"You have been my friend since Thomas and I came to Sealy Grove," Rachel said solemnly. "'Tis for that reason and the loving care you gave when all else had given up on saving my hand, that I am bound to tell you what has been said of Glory."

Maudie Lair cringed. She had noted the strange sidelong glances as she and Glory rode through Sealy Grove. She feared she knew what Rachel Leonard would say.

"What is it, Rachel?"

"'Tis whispered she is a witch." Rachel spat out the dreaded words as if they stung her mouth. "'Tis wicked talk and scandalous," she went on, "but no less harmful for being wrongly said. 'Tis remarked she afflicts the four girls who are sick."

"Who could believe that?" Maudie Lair cried.

"If but one does, it is enough for trouble," Rachel warned. "'Tis also remarked that Glory has an unholy alliance with sundry creatures. One has claimed to see her shape giving suck to a black bird between her fingers."

"The crow is a pet. 'Tis commonly known."

"The sad part of it is," Rachel explained, "that 'tis the common things which become suspect. What way is there to defend acts one has always practiced without question?"

"None of it is true," Maudie Lair declared. "Glory is no more a witch than you or I."

"It matters not. You or I or any goodwife or maid might as easily be named a witch. We have all heard what happens in Salem, where the wicked cannot be distinguished from the just. Arm yourself," Rachel warned. "She has not yet been accused; 'tis only rumor for the time, but 'tis a rumor which incites fantasy. What one says, another feels bound to best. If one claims she has spoiled a batch of beer, another claims she has caused a cow to run off. And so the rumor grows."

"I fear there is no way of ending it."

"It may end as it started, on idle tongues," Rachel offered. "But if it should become more, if someone ventures to make a charge, Glory must know what she will say in answer."

"Aye," Maudie Lair said sadly. "But is there any defense to being named a witch?"

CHAPTER

11

Josiah Bellingham spent a day of fasting in meditation and prayer—prayer that whatever calamities came upon him might count for the good of God. A calamity was precisely what he considered the rash of malicious gossip concerning his intended bride. If it was a test of faith for having given too much thought of late to temporal affairs, he would withstand the ordeal. Locked in his study, he did not hear the gentle tap of feet on the stoop or the click of the cover on the message box as Glory Warren deposited a letter within it.

At dawn of the following day when he read the refusal she had penned, his desire to have her was not dashed one whit. If anything, his resolve was strengthened and the challenge taken as a personal affront not only to him but also to the divine plan for his life.

He crushed the letter into a ball and tossed it on the grate where the glowing coals quickly set it aflame. "She believes her name sullied and would spare me the association of it," he told himself as he broke his fast with a meager meal of beer and bread.

Not long after the sun rose, Bellingham, a stark figure in the morning mist, rode to the Warren farm, his cause clearly set in his mind. This time he was glad Glory was in the forest gathering fresh herbs and roots for her mother's medicine box. He needed an ally in the mother and could best win her to his cause by speaking to her alone.

"You are aware of what is said of your daughter?" His face clouded, he drank steaming coffee from an earthenware mug. Though not at all pleased by the circumstances he found himself in, his confidence did not wane. Seeing other people at a disadvantage, as Maudie Lair Warren was now before him, had a way of bringing out a feeling of extraordinary power in him.

Maudie Lair's fingers tightened around the mug she held. "I have heard some cry out against her. I know not the extent or how much is believed." Her look was pained. "Surely you do not believe these rumors."

Accustomed to standing at the pulpit when he made a point, Bellingham rose and looked down at Goody Warren. "If I believed them I would be the first to speak against her. Who better to confront a witch than one who holds fast to the hand of God? Nay," he said, rocking back on his heels. "Of all in Sealy Grove I alone am qualified to name a witch. I have seen those tried in Salem. I have studied the writings of experts. This talk about Glory is largely a pastime, I believe. An attempt to have our humble village gain the same notoriety as those afflicted ones in Essex. Or 'tis but some device of Satan's to gain a foothold in Sealy Grove. Either way it will pass with no lasting harm done if the right remedy is used."

Maudie Lair shook her head in consternation. "How are we to know what remedy is right and what is wrong? There is no way to predict how people will interpret any action when they are disposed to believe the worst."

Hands clasped behind his back, Bellingham turned and paced the room as if using the time to gather his thoughts, though in truth he had come prepared to say what he spoke next. "If Glory were my wife, none would use the word *witch* in the same breath as her name."

Had he come to gloat? Was this his way of offering a rebuff to Glory for refusing his offer of marriage? Or was it a renewal of the proposal? Maudie Lair rose from the leather armchair and paced where Bellingham had. For her, a gathering of thoughts was the purpose of the exercise. Reluctantly, she admitted the minister was right. Josiah Bellingham was respected and feared and though many found him stilted and unyielding, all agreed he possessed a pious spirit. Where gossips would easily banter the name of a pretty maid, particularly one who had no father or husband to turn to, they would think twice of linking Bellingham's name to witchcraft.

At last, finding no solace in aimless movement, Maudie Lair stopped and faced the minister. "Have you read the letter she left at your cottage?"

His nostrils flared slightly, but he gave no other indication that Glory's refusal had disturbed him. "I have read it," he said. "And I have given consideration to the climate in which it was written. I must say Glory endears herself to me by wishing to spare me any link to this debasement." His voice became deeper. "I do not hold her to it."

Maudie Lair struggled with the choice of telling Bellingham the truth or finding a tactful way to allow him to continue believing as he did while convincing him the refusal was final. Given the circumstances, saving face seemed less important than truth.

"She spoke what was in her heart. She wishes to give her pledge to another."

Bellingham held his breath a long, dangling moment. *Quade Wylde.* Anger flared within him, but he willed it away. The trapper was no threat while imprisoned in Crossland. Besides, this was a moment for calm and levelheadedness. He prided himself on being possessed of both. He need only impress upon the mother the importance of acting promptly.

"She is young," he said. "She cannot understand as you and I do the significance of what occurs in Sealy Grove. Without my protection she will shortly find herself the subject of examination for malefic witchcraft. Already there are those who hint of taking their evidence before the magistrates. Little Jane Cobb is close to death. Should she die, or one of the other girls Glory is said to afflict, it will be too late to counter a complaint."

Maudie Lair's cheeks paled. "It cannot be!" she cried. "She has done nothing to justify these charges."

"It can be. It will be if you do not aid her."

"Aid her?" Maudie Lair chimed incredulously. "She is my daughter, my only child."

"She has one chance." Bellingham said the words in a slow and steady cadence. "She must become my wife before a charge is made against her."

Maudie Lair collapsed to the armchair. Glory was all she had. All that mattered to her. "I do not know . . ." she started.

"Goody Warren!" His voice bellowed, his eyes flashed. "You trifle with your daughter's life! This is not the time to

give way to a girl's foolish whims. Count yourselves fortunate
I am yet willing to wed her.'' His sandy brows lifted high
on his forehead. ''And give note that five more witches were
hung in Salem. Do not let us begin such events here with
Glory.''

''You know she is innocent. Even if she is not your wife
you could defend her.''

Bellingham's voice softened but his eyes grew cold. ''Pre-
pare your daughter to wed. Tomorrow I return for her.''

''A witch!'' Glory cried, her cheeks burning with indignation. ''If I were a witch I would put a spell on them all—
including Josiah Bellingham. He cannot force me to marry
him even if they dare try me as a witch. I love Quade! I will
wed him and no other!'' Having spilled her anger, her defiance flagged and a shadow of fear passed over her. ''If only
Quade were here.''

''He could not stop this evil talk,'' her mother said, fearing
Bellingham had hit another truth. Glory did not realize the
seriousness of a charge of witchcraft. Mere denial was useless
as a defense.

''He could take me away. He could take me to a place
where good people are not called witches.''

''Then go to him. Go to Crossland. Tell him what happens
here.''

''What of Bellingham? He expects me to be waiting tomorrow.''

''If you love Quade, go to him. Leave Bellingham to me.''

Glory jumped to her feet. Shortly she had a bag packed
with food and a cloak to keep her warm should she find herself
on the road after sundown. When the mare was saddled, her
mother gave her a parting kiss.

"Remember the dangers on the road. You are a woman alone. . . ."

Glory laughed bitterly. "Am I in more danger there than here?"

Maudie Lair held Glory tightly to her. "Nay. But you are my daughter and I love you. Take care."

"Aye, Mother," Glory said tenderly. "The same to you."

By hard riding, a good rider on a good horse could make the trip in under a day. Though she had both advantages, she had not begun early. The rigors of such a journey did not concern her. It was whether she would find Quade in Crossland that pricked her mind sore as she covered mile after mile of the rough trail.

Only when the mare showed signs of exhaustion did she halt and dismount. Even then she did not risk a fire and ate her bread and cheese beside a small brook while the hobbled horse grazed and drank. Stiff and aching, Glory finished her meal and lay down beneath a tree, wrapping the voluminous cloak around her. Though she had meant only to rest a few hours, fatigue soon carried her deep into a troubled slumber.

The first pink rays of dawn brought her awake and anxious to make up the time she had lost. Soon she had the mare saddled and on the trail once more. As it turned out, she had spent the night only a few miles outside of Crossland. Another hour's ride took her into the town. She had visited Crossland once before. That had been when her father lived. She remembered the friendly apothecary and it was to his shop she went. If Crossland was like Sealy Grove, any merchant would know if a stranger had passed through the town.

Having purchased a small glass vial which she knew her mother could use for storing herbal preparations, she asked offhandedly of Quade. "My father's friend was to journey to Crossland. A trapper called Quade Wylde. I have not yet inquired at the inn," she added. "I thought perhaps you would know. . . ."

"Do not waste your time asking at the inn," the elderly, bespectacled apothecary said. "Quade Wylde has taken his lodgings in our jail."

"On what charge?" Glory demanded, forgetting she had meant to make her inquiry seem but a passing thought of an old friend.

"Your father's friend is guilty of fleeing his master while bound to the cooper, Avery Fisk. Though it has taken many years, his crime has found him out," the man informed her.

Getting the name of the constable, Glory rushed from the shop, almost forgetting the bottle she had purchased. By much pleading and persuading she obtained permission to see Quade.

Quade, who felt himself more trapped than trapper, sat cross-legged on the floor of his cell with his face turned to the thread of light from the high window. He detected the sound of two sets of footsteps entering his cubicle, but did not turn to see who intruded. The jailer, a man named Bray, was not overly friendly, nor was his wife who on occasion brought the prisoners' meals. Only the Indian servant, Sam Hawk, showed an interest in his welfare.

Quade heard the thump of a wooden trencher dropped on the bench and the thud of Bray's steps as he left the cell. He wheeled slowly around. Two had entered, one had left.

"You have got yourself in quite a fix." A scarlet hood covering her hair and the soft folds of a cloak streaming from her shoulders, Glory stood within the shadowed enclosure.

For Quade, a winged angel could not have been a more beauteous sight. "Glory!" He was on his feet in a flash, at her side in another, and before time could be measured again, wrapped her tightly in his arms.

No amount of worry could supersede the rush of love Glory felt on seeing the joy on Quade's face.

"'Tis I," she said, tilting her head so that the hood fell back and her face was lifted to his. Quade kissed her quickly and soundly, thrusting his tongue past her lips as if to extract the sweetest nectar from her mouth. The effect on Glory was the same as that of lightning exploding the sky in a blaze of brilliant light. It was over as quickly, Quade pushing her to arm's length.

"Bray will not leave us alone for more than a moment," he said, knowing the man kept watch by peering through the knotholes in the ceiling. Several times, dust had filtered through from the room above and once even a skein of Goody Bray's wool. "How is it you are here?"

Glory sat on the splintery bench, her hands folded in her lap. Quade propped a foot on the opposite end, afraid he could not resist taking her in his arms again if he sat beside her.

"I came in search of you," she said softly. "We expected you back days ago. How is it you are confined?"

His composed voice seemed to come from far away. "I expected to be here but a day. As you can see 'tis not by choice I tarry. That bastard Fisk brought charges against me which the magistrates saw fit to believe. I am jailed a month for having fled service. 'Tis of no consequence to any that Fisk has been paid in full for my servitude."

"Have you learned who paid him?"

"Nay!" Quade pounded his palm. "I would have paid him with a fist if the chance had been given."

Glory's eyes swept the small, dank cell. The cracks in the floor were wide enough to accommodate all manner of vermin; the cot was bare of any covering. Quade looked well enough, but she was concerned that he might have been deprived of food, having no family nearby to provide for him.

"How have you fared?" she asked anxiously.

Quade lifted the napkin covering the trencher and showed a generous portion of stewed chicken and bread. A wooden tankard of cider accompanied the meal.

"Goody Bray is a fair cook," he said, offering to share his food. Glory declined to eat and Quade set the trencher aside for later. He laughed as he returned to the bench. "Goodwife Bray would put me in the almshouse with what she charges."

Glory attempted a smile but failed to convince Quade there was any merriment behind the curve of her lips.

"Ah, my sweet," he said teasingly. "I detect there is more behind this visit than concern for my welfare." Glory sniffed. Quade's tone turned serious. "Something is amiss, Glory, love. Tell me."

Chin quivering, she lifted sad eyes to him and said, "How would you like finding yourself wed to a witch?"

Quade crossed his arms over his chest and pressed his lips tightly together for a moment. He cocked his head to one side and looked her up and down.

"I can see there might be certain carnal benefits in such a match. Are you telling me I am in for a whirl of witchcraft when we marry?" Making sure Bray was not watching, he bent low and kissed her forehead. "Are you a witch, Glory Warren?"

She pulled a handkerchief from her pocket and dabbed her nose. "'Tis what is said of me in Sealy Grove," she answered. "My mother fears I will be summoned for examination. I have been informed I can avoid it only if . . ."

"If what?" Not a trace of mirth remained in his voice or

in the expression on his face. Bray had talked of little but the recent hanging of five witches in Salem. People throughout the colony were suspicious of anyone who had ever given them a cross look. It was not preposterous to believe that in Sealy Grove Glory could meet with the same fate as those taken in Salem.

"If I wed Josiah Bellingham," Glory choked out the words. "He has offered the protection of his name."

"Bellingham?" Quade caught her by the shoulders. "So that is his ploy."

Never had she seen such a blistering look on his face. Though she knew it was not meant for her, she felt a small shudder just to see him so angry.

"'Tis no ploy," she said, not understanding Quade's meaning. "Since you left he came to me and asked my hand in marriage. I refused. Now he has renewed his proposal as a means of saving me."

"As a means of having you," Quade corrected, his scowl deepening. In that moment it seemed the walls of his cell moved in closer. "It was Bellingham who delivered me to Fisk."

"Bellingham? But why?"

"I'm sure he convinced himself that he acted out of a sense of justice. But it was most convenient to have his rival removed while he sought your hand." The anger in his voice softened. "Do you wish to wed him, Glory?"

Glory jumped up. "Nay! 'Tis you I want. I would rather be hung than wed Bellingham."

"You will not hang." He kept his voice low, imagining Bray with his ear to the floor. "But you must not return to Sealy Grove. Ride north. I have a friend—"

Glory wrung the handkerchief in her hands, her expression grim. "I cannot disappear without giving my mother word," she insisted. "She would die of worry. I have to go back for her."

Quade could not persuade her otherwise. He knew in part she was right. If Glory disappeared, how quickly would Maudie Lair be accused of aiding her? Both women had to get away.

"Stay only long enough to load a horse," he told her. "John Bayard is near Arkport. He will help you." Quade snatched the white napkin from the trencher and took up a piece of charcoal he had found among the litter in the room. I'll make a map," he said. As he bent over the drawing, Quade told her about John Bayard and the camp he'd made in the wilderness. "You will be safe with him until I have served my time and can come for you."

Glory strolled about the cell, pausing when she came upon Quade's pack rolled into a corner. Beneath it she saw a piece of paper and, thinking the scrap might serve better than the napkin, pulled it out. The sealed letter bore Quade's name.

"You have not read this," she said, taking the letter to Quade.

He looked up from his drawing. "'Tis from my uncle," he said. "The best use for it is to light a fire."

"The writing appears to be a woman's hand," Glory observed, noting the graceful curls and swirls in the lettering. "And that of one well schooled."

The map finished, Quade obligingly took the letter from her. Because she insisted, he broke the seal and opened the paper. The message was short but poignant. Quade's mouth fell open as he read the first lines.

My dear brother,
    You must wonder who calls you brother, for of course you left our father's house without knowing of my birth.

Or is that another of Uncle's treacheries? I only learned
of your existence when I was fourteen, but I feel a part
of me has always known of you. I pray my letter will
find you and that we can be reunited. You may write to
me in care of our father's solicitor. There is so much ·
we must share of ourselves.

> Your loving sister,
> Eden Wylde

The solicitor's address was given. Quade recognized the
name.

"You have a sister." Glory placed a hand on Quade's arm.

He shook his head slowly. "He told me the child my mother
carried died with her. All these years I believed my family
dead. I never went back because there was no one there I
cared for."

Briefly, Glory forgot her woes and thought only of Quade.
"You must go to her. You should see her, know her."

"Glory, love." He risked placing an arm around her shoulders. "You would forget your trouble to tend to mine. When
I can I will write to her," he said. "And I will see her when
I no longer have to worry about a rope stretching your lovely
neck."

"But you will see her," Glory insisted. "You must."

"I will see her and so will you." Quade folded the napkin
carefully and gave it to Glory to conceal in her pocket. "When
I am free, we will sail together, your mother, you, and I."
He kissed her quickly and sent her hurrying to the door. "I
hear Bray coming," he said.

Glory donned her cloak and hood and said a sorrowful
goodbye to Quade. A short while later, having raised many
a brow in Crossland, she rode the mare out of the village on
the long journey home.

* * *

Obtaining a special license to marry had taken the better part of the day before. The remainder of it he had spent praying at the bedside of Goody Collier, recently delivered of a son. The child was small and weak and though the mother was reluctant to admit it, showed little sign of surviving his early arrival into the world. There was one note of hope. Ruthie Collier was improved so much it was believed she would soon be well.

As he had hoped, word of his pending union with Glory Warren had spread rapidly over the town. Already the vicious talk about his intended had begun to die down. Several of those in attendance at the Collier house had congratulated him on the coming marriage.

Briefly he recalled that Sarah had not been present while he prayed for her mother. He had intended to tell her to forego working at his cottage the following day. He considered sending a message but, finding his mind occupied with more serious matters, dismissed the oversight from his mind. She would be finished with the gardening and gone before he returned with his bride.

Having given his toilette special attention, Bellingham dressed in his best doublet and bands. The marriage would take place at the meetinghouse. It was fitting and would save Reverend Stibbins a longer ride.

Though domestic tasks were distasteful to him, Bellingham spread the feather mattresses on his bed with fresh, clean linens. He and his bride would spend the wedding night at his cottage where they could be completely alone. The sheets stretched tight and the coverlet turned down invitingly, he pictured Glory lying atop his bed, her dark hair streaming over the pillows. Just the thought of her strained his loins.

His breath rattled from his chest as the ache of desire grew greater. His lips stretched into a thin smile. The day would be a lengthy one. He had his rounds to make; the sick and the sinful must be attended to first. Rubbing his hands together, he smiled; the evening's reward would be worth the wait.

Before leaving he placed a bottle of canary and two cups on the scarred tabletop which begged a covering. Soon such trivial worries as the lack of table linens would belong to Glory. Another advantage of having a wife. *Wife*. Did Glory Warren know what a service he had done her? He would tell her tonight. Let her show her gratitude as she would.

Late in the afternoon, having made his rounds and completed arrangements for the ceremony, the minister rode along the lane to the Warren farm, reminding himself that he would soon make this same ride with regularity.

"Goody Warren!" he called when no immediate answer came to his knock. "'Tis Bellingham."

"Come in, sir." Her eyes red-rimmed and dark-circled from a sleepless night, Maudie Lair showed the minister in.

"Mother," he tried the word on the small-boned woman who stood before him, "I know it pains you to give up your only daughter to another, but you must think of this joining together as a happy act." With what was meant as a tender touch he clasped one of her hands and patted it. "Matrimony is the crowning event of a woman's life, as well you know. Shed no tears over it." The condescending tone changed when he looked into the empty parlor where he had expected to find Glory waiting. "Where is my bride?" he demanded.

Maudie Lair led him into the room, bracing herself for what she dreaded telling the minister. Her voice was soft but firm. "She is not here."

Bellingham flung out his arms. "Not here! Where has she gone?" He imagined Glory in a flurry of activity, preparing for the wedding. "To borrow some item she felt a need for? I hope she will not be long. I have arranged for Reverend Stibbins to meet us in Sealy Grove."

"Reverend Stibbins?" Maudie Lair said in alarm. Did Bellingham believe Glory would wed him today? "Surely you did not arrange—we did not expect—what of the banns?"

He smiled in the arrogant way reserved for those he felt were below his intellect. "Waived by a special license," Bellingham explained, bemused that his future mother-in-law should fail to realize he was a man of some power and connection. "Did I not make myself clear?" he said. "The marriage will take place this evening. It has all been arranged."

"You are mistaken," Maudie Lair replied, galled that he should be so presumptuous even under these circumstances. "Glory is not here. She has ridden to Crossland."

"Crossland!" Bellingham's face filled with high color. "To see that Wylde fellow, I presume." He expanded his chest like a strutting cock. "It will do her no good. The man is in the jail."

Another time she would have asked how Bellingham knew that fact, if it was one. But presently making the overbearing minister understand that her daughter would not marry him seemed more pressing.

"Sir," she said crisply. "My daughter and I have the highest regard for you, but 'tis not her wish to wed you."

"It may not be her wish, but 'tis her destiny." His mouth twisted and his eyes glared hotly at the small woman. "I will not be denied, Goody Warren. I have lent my name to her defense. Do not oppose me." He glanced suspiciously at the stairs. Very likely Glory had not gone anywhere at all, but hid upstairs in her chambers. His eyes came accusingly back to Maudie Lair. "Send the girl down," he said curtly. "I will make her understand since you will not."

"She is not here," Maudie Lair repeated.

"I think she *is* here." His eyes narrowed and his gaze sliced into the widow. "I think she is hiding in her room, hiding behind her mother's skirts. Does she think that will save her? Does she think the magistrates will not search her out?" His jaw twitched. "Does she think she needs saving from me as well as from the hanging tree?"

"She is gone," Maudie Lair said quietly.

Something in Bellingham gave way. He brushed the woman aside and tore up the stairs. When a search of the upper rooms did not turn up the girl, he raced up the second flight to the attic, that spot that had haunted his memories and dreams since he had been with Glory there. The room was empty as the others had been. With mounting rage, he rushed down and encountered Maudie Lair in the second-floor hallway.

"Where is she? In the barn?" He gripped her narrow shoulders.

Maudie Lair gasped at Bellingham's daring to lay hands on her. "She is gone, I tell you."

He gave her a hard shake. "You lie! Find her! I demand you bring Glory to me!"

Maudie Lair gripped his wrists and pushed his hands from her shoulders. "Sir! You overstep! I demand you leave my house."

"Not without my wife! You cannot keep her from me."

Outraged at the minister's treatment of her, Maudie Lair whirled around. "Consider what you say and do, Reverend Bellingham," she warned. "Even a man such as you can find himself before a court."

Bellingham lifted a fist to shake in her face, incensed that she dared threaten him. Maudie Lair, perilously near the top of the stairs and believing he meant to strike her, made a step back.

Seeing the danger, Bellingham shouted, but his warning came too late. A misstep sent her tumbling backward. Bellingham lunged and grasped for her but caught only the band pinned at her collar. The loosely attached linen ripped free and Maudie Lair Warren, unable to stop her fall, rolled down the steep staircase.

"Goody Warren!" Bellingham flew down the stairs and knelt at the woman's side. His face ghostly pale, he placed a palm before her face and failed to detect a stir of breath. The woman was limp, arms and legs sprawled loose, a large, purple bruise marring her temple. "You cannot be dead," he cried aloud as he slapped her cheek in an attempt to revive her. She did not respond. "Mercy of God!" The minister mopped his streaming brow and sat back on his heels.

The woman *was* dead, but it was the sudden complication of his life that concerned him most. He had not pushed her, but what did that matter? Even an inquiry concerning her death could mean the demise of his career. A minister linked to a questionable accident would lose his charge and all hope of attaining another.

His eyes rested pensively on the lifeless form. Without thinking, Bellingham pulled her twisted limbs straight and folded the hands over the still chest. Now she looked like a fallen saint, peaceful and serene in death. Abruptly he looked away, feeling himself tainted in comparison.

A shrill cry from overhead brought the minister to his feet. Fearing the worst—that someone else had come to the Warren farm—he felt his breath congeal in his lungs. The cry rang out anew. Bellingham frantically sought the direction of the sound until he spotted the blue-black crow perched high on the beams. The weight of worry fell from him. Only a bird. The only witness was a bird. Who was to know what had happened here? Only God, and it was plainly his will that Maudie Lair Warren's life come to an end. Who could question that?

An impulse seized him. Acting on it, he said a brief prayer for the dead woman. He would do no less for anyone. Moments later Josiah Bellingham galloped his horse toward Sealy Grove. Reverend Stibbins would have to be told the wedding was postponed.

In the early hours of the morning, Glory unsaddled the weary mare and locked the animal in a stall. Her body was tense and sore from the days of abuse. When the mare had been fed and watered, she limped from the barn to the house, thinking she would have to sleep a few hours before she had the strength to ride out again. Her clothes were covered with dust, her face by a layer of grime. She would not be surprised if her mother refused to allow her in the kitchen until she had washed.

Glory called out wearily as she entered the back door but got no answer except the pitiful meowing of Tansy who ran to meet her. She bent to pet the cat.

"Did you miss me so much, Tansy?"

The cat would not be consoled by a pat on the head. She wrapped herself around Glory's ankle and kept up the pitiful cry. Glory picked her up and stroked the wriggling animal's shiny fur. Glancing around and finding the kitchen otherwise deserted, she muttered a cry of surprise. The fire had died behind the hearth; she could not remember another time when that had occurred. Her mother should be up by now, baking the day's bread.

Alarmed, Glory rushed from the kitchen to the front hallway and stumbled to a stop when she saw the crumpled figure lying at the foot of the stairs.

"Mother!" The cat fell from her arms as she sped to her mother's side.

The hand she clasped was rigid and cold, the skin gray like marble. Still Glory chafed the icy cheeks and tried to rub life into the unyielding limbs. Finding her efforts of no use, she fell across her mother's body and wept.

She could not tell later how long she had stayed that way. Paddy's relentless cawing alerted her that she must act. She must get a quilt; she could not leave her mother uncovered. Friends and the authorities had to be notified. And of course she must go to Josiah Bellingham and arrange a service honoring her mother. She stood, supporting her weight on the stair rail until she felt fit enough to move. Her heart thudded too slowly in her chest, heavily burdened with guilt that her mother had been alone when she died.

The sun was high when Glory rode to Bellingham's cottage. That he had recently asked for her hand in marriage was far from her mind as she knocked on his door.

"My mother is dead," she blurted out when the minister, freshly shaved and dressed, answered his door. She was too distraught to notice the fleeting look of relief that passed over his otherwise solemn face.

"Come in, child," he said placatingly. "Tell me what has happened."

"I hardly know," she said, accepting the firm clasp of his hand on her arm. "I returned home from a journey and found my mother beneath the stairs. She had taken a fall, though it is difficult to believe—she was ordinarily sure of foot. She had been dead awhile."

"My poor, dear Glory." He pressed her arm tightly. "To have been alone for that. You are a brave child. Come here and sit.'' He took her into his study where the bottle of canary that had been meant for another purpose sat on his table. He poured a small amount for her. ''Have you told others of this tragic event?''

Glory dropped weakly into a straight-backed chair and accepted the draught of wine. It warmed her throat and returned some color to her cheeks.

''I have come from Goody Leonard's. She would have accompanied me here, but I wished a moment alone.'' She lifted her eyes to him and though they burned with the pain of her loss, Bellingham was no less stimulated by their brilliance. ''I would have you commend my mother's soul to heaven,'' she said.

Bellingham opened his mouth to say he would willingly comply with her wishes, but found his vocal cords strangely paralyzed. He coughed and clutched his throat, then hurriedly downed a swallow of wine.

''As you wish, Glory.'' His normally smooth voice was as raspy as rusty metal.

CHAPTER
12

Rachel and Thomas Leonard comforted Glory before the service. Goodman Wharton paid his respects. William was there to do the chores that could not be postponed. But where were the others, Goody Tilden, Goodman Douglass, all those her mother had tended over the years? Did they fear a "witch" so much they would forget a woman who had cared for them and their families? So it seemed, but at the burial it was a different matter.

Glory sprinkled a handful of soil into the open grave in the churchyard, then stepped back as the diggers tossed in spade after spade of dark, moist earth. If any in the town failed to attend the service, it would have been difficult to name them. Had it not been an outward show of respect for her mother, Glory would have chased them away, the curious who came but to stare and whisper.

But she was wrong about the reason for their coming. The rumor that she was betrothed to Bellingham had drawn them. If it was true and he did wed the girl, none wanted to be named as one who had shunned the minister's wife. Fear of crossing Bellingham did not silence the whispers following his final prayer.

The large crowd quickly thinned. Many left with heads together, low voices asking questions none dared express aloud.

"Where was Glory Warren on the eve her mother died?"

"Flying cross the moon on her broomstick," quipped the sharp-tongued Goodwife Henry, less awed by Bellingham than the others.

"Did anyone notice the girl's eyes, the way they burned through her tears as if a strange light blazed behind them?"

"'Tis the devil's light," was Goody Henry's answer to that. "We ought to send for one of the afflicted girls from Salem. Young Ann Putnam was taken to Andover and uncovered witches there. Bring her here, I say. See what she makes of our Glory Warren."

"We do not need Ann Putnam," her companion replied. "If the girl is a witch she will prove herself so."

Josiah Bellingham, who moved among the thinning crowd, did not hear the conversation between Goody Henry and her friend. Those wayward remarks he did hear were quickly curbed by his presence alone, as it took but his approach to stop in midstatement those who saw him. To them he gave an undisguised lecture on the sinfulness of gossip. He knew the artless workings of their minds and how those whose thoughts were weakest sought to link sick children and the death of Maudie Lair Warren to witchcraft.

Stretched to his full height he towered above the best of them. Let their tongues wag a few more days. He would give Glory that long. He did not want her morbid on their wedding day. But before the week was done he would silence the village busybodies for good by taking Glory Warren as wife.

When the grave was filled and all had gone but those few who had proved loyal friends, Bellingham slowly shook his head in disdain. Pity them, he thought; were they so blind they could not see there was a purpose in all that had happened here? They had a lesson to learn and he would not neglect giving it to them in his upcoming sermon. He sought Glory out and with a final comforting word to her, took leave.

"Stay with me, Glory," Rachel Leonard pleaded when he was gone. "You should not be alone."

Glory consented, then regretted it as she passed a restless night in the Leonard house. Rachel was kind and coddled her as if she were the new baby of the family. And though she was grateful and could not have been made to feel more welcome, when Rachel made the same plea the following day, Glory insisted on returning home.

"I thank you for your kindness. Perhaps later I will need your company and that of the others who have offered help." She dropped her head as ever-ready tears formed in her eyes. "Tonight I wish to sit in my mother's house and remember. Let me have this time alone to think of her."

"If you must." Rachel looked intently distressed and would have liked to ask Glory about her feelings for Reverend Bellingham. Out of regard for Glory in her bereavement, she refrained. "I do not like it, but Thomas and I will drive you home if you feel you must do this."

"I must." Glory bit her lip. As fond as she was of Rachel, she did not feel she could burden the woman with her anxieties concerning Quade and Josiah Bellingham. The problem was hers and with her mother gone, she would solve it alone.

Glory passed the second night following the burial in her mother's house, her house. She rested no better than she had at the Leonards'. Her mind could not be eased or her thoughts pulled from the memory of her mother lying broken at the foot of the stairs, hands crossed on her chest.

"Her hands!" she exclaimed involuntarily. How had they come to be in that peaceful pose? It was as if someone had placed them that way. But that was impossible. Her mother had been alone. Perhaps, Glory thought sadly, she had not died immediately and had drawn them into that position herself. Or was that too unlikely, a mere wish to believe her mother's end had not come in a moment of violence? But then it was no better to believe she had lain there in pain, waiting, hoping to be found.

Bleakly, Glory roamed the house and then sorted through the things in her mother's room, touching her mother's comb, looking into the mirror above the washstand. Nothing brought her any contentment. At last, when she had been through each room half a dozen times and more, she realized what she needed could not be found in the house.

William had cared for the animals while she was away. Glory found the mare in her stall, anxious for an outing. Before the sun had shed light on the gray morning sky, she saddled the horse and rode into town.

The oblong mound of fresh earth stood out from the older, grassy graves in the churchyard. Glory knelt by the newly hewn cross at the head, her eyes downcast. For hours she sat by the grave and spoke to her mother as she was accustomed to doing when she lived.

"What am I to do, Mother? I am alone, without you, without Quade. There is the farm to see to. What am I to do?" The answers were her own, but in this place they began to come more clearly through the drift of haze in her mind. Quade had not wanted her to return to Sealy Grove. She had come back for her mother. Now there was no reason to stay.

She would do as Quade wanted. She was sure her mother would insist on exactly that if she had lived.

John Bayard near Arkport. The map showing the way to Quade's friend was in her room. William could be persuaded to stay at the farm and continue caring for the animals. She would leave as soon as she made the arrangements with William, as soon as she could pack her belongings.

"Goodbye, Mother. For a time."

As in prayer, Glory sat exceedingly quiet and still, a dark figure in the bright sunlight, kneeling at the grave. She was not alarmed when a king snake slithered toward the rise of dirt at her feet. Her father had taught her those snakes to fear and those that did good deeds for man. The king snake was a harmless creature looking for the warmest spot in the churchyard. He coiled where a ray of sunlight lit the heap of earth.

Her farewells finished, Glory picked up the brightly marked snake and removed it from the grave. "Go," she said. "Find another spot."

Whatever business had brought Goody Coventry and Goody White walking past the churchyard at that hour was quickly forgotten when they saw a lithe girl lift a brightly banded snake into the air and carry it to the edge of the woods.

"'Tis Glory Warren," Goody Coventry whispered, alerting her friend, then abruptly shielding herself behind a tree.

Goody White's eyes were enormous as she concealed her bulk behind a prickly holly bush. "What does she say?"

Not noted for keen hearing, Goody Coventry cupped a hand behind her ear and relied on imagination to supply words where there was only the rattle of a leaf or the bump of green limbs rubbing together in the breeze.

"She bids the serpent lead her home."

Trembling, Goody White clutched her immense bosom. "'Tis true as said of her. She is a witch."

Goody Coventry clapped her hands over her hot cheeks. Her voice shook. "'Tis her shape we have seen above the grave."

"And her familiar, a serpent."

Goody Coventry hissed and shrank back behind the tree. "Do not let yourself be seen. 'Tis unsafe. She will torment you."

Goody White, suffering palpitations, crouched behind the holly bush, no mean feat for a woman of her size. Fearful the witch's shape would discover her, she edged closer to the foliage. The dark, pointy leaves of the bush jabbed through layers of petticoats into her large buttocks. Afraid to move, the woman endured the pain by chewing her jaw until it was raw and bleeding. Her wide eyes bulged from the sockets. She believed herself pricked with pins like the afflicted girls in Salem. It was horrifying torture. Goody White could bear it only a moment longer before she went flying down the street sounding an alarm.

Glory had left the churchyard and was on the mounting block, her foot lifted to the stirrup, when she saw she was surrounded by a group of women. Startled, she cried out the name of the goodwife whose face she first recognized.

"Goody White. What brings—"

"Avoid, witch!" Goody White shrieked and swung at Glory with a stick. "Take your serpent and get away!"

"Avoid, Satan! For the name of God, avoid!" came another hysterical voice.

A pebble struck Glory solidly on the chest. "What is this?" She threw her arms up defensively as she braced against the skittish mare. "You call me witch. I am the same as you."

She stretched out a hand to Goody White. "You know me. Have I ever done you harm?"

"You pricked me!" Goody White screamed and slapped her stick against Glory's threatening palm.

"You afflict the children," shouted Goody Partridge, whose offspring Glory had minded on many occasions.

Another pebble, well aimed, struck Glory sharply on the ankle. She cried out in pain and twisted to see who had cast it. Her heart shattered, the defiance went out of her eyes.

"Sarah! Are you against me too?"

Sarah could not look Glory in the face and instead fell on her knees and began shrieking and striking the ground.

"Witch!" Sarah cried. "Vile witch!"

As if a mirror image of Sarah, Prudence Oliver fell upon the ground and struck it with her fists, her voice even louder and shriller than Sarah's. Their peculiar behavior, though alarming, proved a blessing. It distracted the women long enough to allow Glory a clear moment to mount the mare and kick her heels in the nervous horse's sides. The animal bolted into a gallop.

Tears flooding her face, she kept the mare at a breakneck pace all the way to the farm. William was in the barn when she galloped in. She gave him the winded mare and asked him to give the animal a drink and a rubdown before putting her in the stall. In a choked voice, she enlisted his promise to care for the stock while she was called away for a time. When William pressed for the day of her return, she could not tell him.

"I will be gone a long while, William. Stay here and if you cannot, find another to care for the animals." William assured her he would remain at the farm until her return. Glory nodded. "I will pay you now and if it is not enough to last until my return, the cart horse is yours to keep."

William smiled and in his dim way wished her journey would be a long one. His eyes, set to the task of rubbing the mare, glinted. The possibility of having a horse of his own was enough to make him promise his life, though Glory assured him that was not necessary. Instead he promised to leave as soon as the mare was fed to collect his belongings. He would return by sundown.

Though her heart felt broken into a thousand jagged pieces, Glory refused to cry anymore. She had thought those who called her witch would hush in shame after the death of her mother. Now she had learned that fear and suspicion respected no bounds or persons. Her situation was worse than before.

The women—friends—had attacked her and driven her from the churchyard. By now they were at the magistrate's, crying out against her. Her first instinct was to ride back into town and demand justice, but recalling how quickly those she thought friends had turned on her, she doubted there was any justice to be had.

Her dazed eyes filled with indignation. One of them had seen her pick up the snake. Was it suspect to show kindness to God's creatures? Was that all it took to make a witch? Nay, she recalled; she had "bewitched" children too.

Crying out bitterly, Glory pushed open the door and entered the deserted house. She pitied her sisters in Salem. What simple deeds had they done that had brought the wrath of a village down on them?

She rubbed her throbbing temples. What did it matter? If she did not misjudge her enemies, the constable would shortly come for her. She had no time to waste wondering why she was hated. A few minutes might make the difference in slipping away unseen and being caught. Hurrying about in the kitchen she filled a skin with cider and a traveling bag with bread, dried meat, coffee, and a sack of corn that could be ground into meal and which would sustain her a long while.

When he was free, Quade would find her with John Bayard and his family. With Quade at her side, perhaps she would return and face the charges made against her. Until that time she might have to endure loneliness and dread, but she would not do it here.

Her provisions ready, she hastened to her room to pack the clothing and other articles she would need for the journey. It was at that task Josiah Bellingham found her, having entered the house and climbed the stairs with such stealth she was unaware of his presence.

He saw what she was about and guessed what she meant to do. For a minute or two he stood in the doorway and watched. She was frightened and perhaps a little angry too. He found he liked the look high emotion gave her, the deep color in her cheeks, the almost unnatural brightness in her eyes. He had come to make a sensible and charitable plea for her hand, but the tempo of his desire was anything but sensible. The need to quench the fire in his loins was great.

"You need not flee, Glory," he assured her, his voice too husky to be consoling. "I will see you meet no harm."

Not up to another shock, Glory gasped and darted behind the bed. But seeing the intruder was the minister and that his expression, though puzzling, bore her no malice, she returned to her packing.

"'Tis too late," she told him. "I have been pelted with stones and with words which wounded me even more sorely. I am despised by all in Sealy Grove."

"Nay." He took a cloak from her hand and laid it aside. "I have heard what happened in the churchyard. A few hysterical women acted out of fear, but they can be dealt with.

A word of reason will set them straight." Brooking no resistance, he took her hands gently in his. "I give my pledge
you will suffer no more from word or deed."

Glory pulled her hands from his grasp and slumped listlessly to the bed. If the minister spoke the truth, there was
no need for her to leave.

"If you have that power I pray you will use it in my behalf.
I am weary and heartsick," she said. "And I fear for my
safety."

Bellingham drew near, convinced her words were proof
they shared a common goal. "Trust me, Glory, my sweet."

He bent to one knee and took her hands in his, resting both
pairs on her knee. Her hands were warm and trembling and
he let himself believe it was his touch and not her distress
that made them so.

As if a door had shut in his mind and another opened, he
found himself at once in a frenzy of wanting. They were
alone; she had led him to her bed. His lust, long pent up,
roiled and erupted, consuming him with a madness which
pushed the last remaining traces of reason aside.

In another day she would be his wife. What harm in lying
with her now? With a jerk he pulled her hands to his lips and
kissed them, his tongue darting out to stroke her palms. His
groin ached as a sudden rush of blood brought him to a state
of full arousal.

Glory gasped in alarm as Bellingham looked furtively
around the room. She tried to wrest her hands away but he
would not let her go.

His face contorted with agony. Nay. He could not lie with
her. It was a sin. And yet, as quickly as his face had clouded,
it brightened. There was a way. He had the license. He could
perform the ceremony himself. In a rush he told Glory of his
plan, then, as she sat frozen on the bed, his hand snaked out

and brushed the linen cap from her head. The black hair, loosely pinned underneath, tumbled down her back.

Glory shrank from the minister's too-familiar touch, her faced lined with fear and disbelief.

"This cannot be!" She sought to stand but Bellingham held her back.

"It has been done. It would be a legal bond."

"Nay!" she cried. "I love another."

A last thread broke in Bellingham's mind. Too much had rested on having Glory Warren as wife. He would have her now or be damned.

His twisted face frightened her. Finding a reserve of strength she flung away from him, but he caught her by the waist and pulled her to the edge of the bed. His arms wrapped her like great bands, pinning her weaker limbs to her sides. With a twist of his torso he pushed her knees apart so that he could press his face against her breasts. As she cried out in protest, his cheeks rolled wildly over the soft mounds of flesh, moving from one to the other.

His hot breath penetrated her bodice, his voice rasping, "You are my love, Glory Warren. My destiny."

Legs thrashing, breast heaving, she fought him. For Bellingham every move she made was an enticement. His body ached and boiled for the raven-haired girl so much that he forgot all that he was except a man who had been too long deprived of a woman. Holding her flailing arms in one hand, he ripped open her bodice with the other. His mouth fell hot and wet on her bared throat.

"Love me, Glory!" he demanded. "Be my wife!"

"Nay!" she screamed and, jerking her hands free, clawed at his face. "Stop this! I will not have you."

Bellingham was a man possessed, all arms and hands and hungry, seeking lips. While he pinned her wrists he split her chemise with a gnash of his teeth. A groan tumbled from his mouth when the forbidden flesh, soft, rose-tipped mounds of beauty, lay naked to his eyes.

"You know not your own mind." He moaned and wretched open his breeches. "'Tis a joining of flesh you need, Glory Warren. Once mated you will not doubt you belong with me." He groaned as his erection sprang free of the confining clothes.

"You are mad!" Glory screamed as he seized her skirt and dropped his weight upon her. She was thankful for the layers of petticoats that kept the thrusting shaft from reaching her before she could slam the hard bone of her knee into him.

Bellingham screamed like a soldier shot in the belly. He fell to the floor and doubled over, clutching his exposed groin. Glory rolled to her feet and darted for the door but was jerked back as if caught on a leash.

"By Judas!" he roared, his hand like a claw on the hem of her skirt. "I will have you!"

"I would die first!" She spun and struck out with her foot, landing a powerful kick on the minister's chin. His head flew back and struck the bedpost, sounding a dull thump in the sudden quiet. He slumped to the floor. Leery, but fearful she had dealt the man a death blow, Glory approached the unconscious figure.

Bellingham made a groaning sound. His eyelids flickered and one hand twitched. That part of his anatomy that had been heated and threatening now lay as limp and deflated as the man himself. On his face, scarlet weals grew more livid by the moment. He lived.

Seeing she had not killed him, Glory could not be sure she was glad of it. He was a monster, a hypocritical one, and more dangerous than the women who had cast stones at her.

Forcing her chaotic thoughts in line, she backed away from the downed man. His breathing was steady and strong. He had ceased moaning and looked as if he might awaken at any instant. She dared not wait until he was conscious to leave.

Though every part of her trembled, somehow she kept her head and brought unsteady fingers to work, closing her open bodice. She even remembered to pick up the bundle of garments she had packed before she fled the house.

The mare could have used more rest but she was not to get it. Glory hastily saddled her, certain Bellingham would be gone before William returned. She believed the errant minister would go quietly and surely be too ashamed of his actions to speak of them.

A scant ten minutes after she had run from the house, Glory mounted and rode out. The crow Paddy, sensing the distress of his mistress, stirred from his barn perch and, high overhead, floated through the darkness, following wherever Glory Warren led.

Long after the sound of hoofbeats died, William returned to the farm. He was late. The sun had sunk in the western sky, leaving it tinted with fast-fading streaks of purple and orange. Ordinarily he did not venture out after sundown and would not have done so on this evening except for his promise to Glory. Goodman Douglass had kept him, warned him of keeping company with a witch, and, finally accepting that William would not be dissuaded, insisted the chores of the day be finished before the boy left his place.

William started for the barn, where he could light a lantern and shut out the encroaching blackness. Halfway across the yard he stopped. A peculiar lowing sound came from the direction of the house. At first he believed one of the cows had gotten into the garden but quickly realized the sound came from inside the structure. Frightened by anything out of the ordinary, William cowered in the shadows.

The noise came again and had the sound of distress, but with the windows dark and an empty feel to the place, William hesitated to make himself known to whatever was responsible for it. Several minutes passed before his nerve reached heights that would allow him to investigate. At that, he ventured inside solely out of concern for Glory. She and her mother were the only persons who had ever shown him kindness.

The kitchen was dark but for the lingering glow of a few coals in the fire pit. William cautiously lit a lamp and proceeded up the stairs. Legs quaking, he followed the noise, a pitiable moan from the upper floor.

Bellingham saw the glow of a lamp and started to call Glory's name but let out a curse instead. Moving his sore chin caused an agonizing pain. Nevertheless, the minister's shout was adequate to shake William Cook into spilling hot oil on his fingers gripping the lamp handle. The boy yelped. Bellingham recognized the voice of Daft William and quickly recovered from his belief that Glory had repented of her callous rejection and come back to aid him.

"Bring the light here," he said groggily.

William, accustomed to obeying, especially when admonished by the minister, hurriedly complied, but not without exhaling a great sigh of relief that the noise that had drawn him to the house had come from human lips.

"Aye, sir. I am glad 'tis you. I feared to find a wounded creature had wandered in the house."

"Hurry yourself," Bellingham said stormily.

William, mumbling that he was hurrying as best he could, rested the betty lamp atop a low chest. Light filled the room as did the foul odor of the burning tallow grease.

"Reverend!" The astonished boy nearly tripped over his own feet at seeing the minister sprawled on the floor of Glory Warren's bedroom, his face marked by long red scratches, his clothes rumpled, and his breeches half-off. A quicker mind might have known at a glance what had occurred, but William's lumbering thoughts brought only bewilderment.

Bellingham hastily closed his breeches and combed his hair from his face. The long fingers tested his aching chin and found it intact. "Bring a bowl of water and a cloth," he ordered.

William found the needed items and brought them within Bellingham's reach. The firm chin was swollen and had turned a shade of blue. " 'At's a nasty bump," William observed. "Did you take a fall?"

Bellingham gave the boy an incredulous look and proceeded to bathe his brow with a cool, wet cloth. Only then did he realize how ponderously close he had come to ruination. He had been within a hairsbreadth of disaster. But it had been avoided; he had a guardian after all, a deliverer.

Refusing William's assistance, he struggled to his feet. That ungrateful girl. She was to blame for this, for temptations no mortal could overcome. He could believe she *had* bewitched him.

Assuring himself that all parts of his anatomy were yet intact, Bellingham straightened his doublet and repinned the bands that Glory had wrenched from his neck. In spite of his aching head and groin, he still desired the black-haired beauty, his body still burned for want of her. He supposed she had fled to the Wylde fellow, for all the good that would do her.

William Cook was easily mollified. When he was recovered enough to ride, Josiah Bellingham returned to his cottage not in the least concerned that the simpleton would mention the condition in which he had found the minister. Glory Warren was another case altogether. If she came back and wished to, she could make a charge and his ruin would be a certainty. Or would it?

In the privacy of his cottage he drank, considerably more than he had ever allowed himself at one sitting. Later, his head reeling from the effect of the spirits, he flung himself into bed, forgetting the lengthy prayers that usually preceded his retiring. Even as he fell asleep lusting for Glory Warren, for the feel of her honey-colored skin and the glance of those brilliant eyes, he asked himself, who would believe a witch?

Witch or not, it was Glory Warren's radiant image that filled his slumbering mind and tormented his body as he slept. Like an opium-besotted wretch, he tossed upon his bed, coming time and again to the point of losing himself in the rapture of unfulfilled wishes.

No matter how he turned, he saw Glory's face tossed about in his dreams like a shining silver moon. The black hair waved about him like silky banners, the lips full and inviting called lovingly to him. The blue, blue eyes burned like stars through a hazy sky. His hands sought the soft, satin breasts but again and again found only emptiness. Even in sleep it was his fate to be denied the fulfillment his loins demanded.

He awoke late, aroused by a strange, soft sound, lust still heavy and burdensome in his loins. His eyes sleep-laden and his head pounding from overindulgence in drink, he saw the blurry figure of a girl stepping over the threshold. His haggard face bore a smirk of satisfaction. Glory had returned to him after all.

"Come here." He beckoned with a soft roll of his hand.

Sarah stood transfixed. She had stopped by to return Bellingham's mended shirts. It was midmorning and finding the minister in his bed at such an hour was beyond belief. Without

a doubt she should leave the cottage immediately. Nevertheless, when he called her to his bedside, she was too overcome
by her amorous feelings for Josiah Bellingham to do anything
other than what he asked. Shivering as if hit by a cold blast,
she crossed the cottage floor.

Bellingham propped up on his pillows, prepared to forgive
Glory Warren for her transgressions. She was spirited, but
that was not such a bad thing if controlled and directed.
Everything could be mended. His vision, blurred by the af-
tereffects of drink, would not rub clear no matter how many
times he passed the back of his hands over his eyes. Seeing
but a woman's shape, he reached out for a wrist and pulled
her down beside him.

"Josiah," the girl whispered, seeing the razed cheeks and
the blue mark on the center of his chin.

Soft fingers stroked soothingly over the scratches and traced
temptingly around his lips, but the unexpected voice gave
him a mild shock. His vision cleared in a shake.

"Sarah! 'Tis you!"

"Aye. 'Tis me," she said. Her fingertips grazed the stubble
of his beard and when stilled, shook visibly. "What is it you
want of me, Josiah?"

She could not have made a worse choice of words to a
man aroused and brutally denied. He wanted a woman and
since the one he preferred was not at hand, Sarah would do.
He groaned and pulled her closer. "Only a kiss, Sarah."

She obliged with a nervous, feathery peck on the cheek,
never knowing it was not her pale face and hair he saw
hovering over him. Instead he imagined a rosy-cheeked face
and black, black curls. It was that image he begged for another
kiss, one upon the lips.

Sarah was glad to supply all the kisses he wanted, though
she had little practice in the art. Her lack of skill mattered

little to Bellingham. The inner blindness that had set him
upon Glory Warren took hold of him full force. His arms slid
possessively around Sarah's back and soon he had snatched
her beneath the coverlets.

A girlish giggle ended when his mouth clamped bruisingly
to hers and his hands wandered beneath her bodice to find
soft feminine flesh. Sarah moaned and made a halfhearted
attempt to free herself, but she had longed for his attention,
dreamed of his touch for so many nights that she could not
bring herself to restrain his boldness.

"Sarah, Sarah," he crooned and then filled her ears with
meaningless endearments as he tore her clothes loose.

Sarah would have given herself to him on the street if he
had asked, but she did long to hear a promise of lasting love
as well as the sweet nothings he mumbled.

"Do you love me, Josiah?" she whispered when his hand
plunged beneath her chemise.

"Aye," he lied. His rampant fingers slid between her
thighs, his eager mouth claimed her breast.

Sarah cried out, partly from shock, partly from pain, but
the brash fingers only probed deeper and his teeth nipped
more viciously. In a moment he had pushed her remaining
garment, her chemise, up over her hips and thrown the bun-
dlesome nightshirt he wore from his shoulders.

Alarmed and jolted out of her romantic mood by the realization of what was about to happen, Sarah slithered away.
This was not the kind of initiation she had hoped for or
daydreamed of.

"Nay, Josiah," she cried, seeing the compassionless set
of his face. "We should wait."

Her pleas were wasted. Josiah Bellingham could not have
controlled himself on the basis of what was morally right or
even what was considerate to an innocent girl. Long, hard

fingers clamped her shoulders and jerked her back within his reach.

Sarah screamed and fell into a faint when he took her. Later, when she was barely conscious she heard the gritty whisper at her ear. "Glory," he murmured. "Glory, my love."

Crushed beneath the now leaden weight, her body aching and violated, Sarah's hatred grew, but not for Josiah Bellingham. She loved him too much not to forgive even the brutal taking of her virginity. It was Glory Warren she despised for stealing the heart of the man she loved. Could any doubt the sable-haired girl was a witch? Or that her evil shape had connivingly gripped Josiah's heart through no will of his own?

Nay. Glory Warren was a witch. How else could she have intruded into a moment, an intimacy, that should have been Sarah's alone?

CHAPTER
13

"Yer a popular man, Quade Wylde." Goodman Bray, a lean and sober-faced man in black garb, showed Goodman Wharton into Quade's cell.

"So 'tis here you have been keeping yourself." Wharton wrinkled his nose at the musty smell of Quade's quarters. "The place has nothing to recommend it, partner."

Quade shrugged wearily. He wholeheartedly agreed. Since Glory's visit he had mentally taken the cell apart brick by brick. Still, there was no need to burden Wharton with his misery. He managed a smile. "Nay, but if there is ever a demand for rat pelts I have found the source of wealth."

"I see your wit is not dulled." Wharton, a tidy man, brushed off a space on the wobbly bench and seated himself. "You will need it when you hear what I have to say."

"Tell me." A tightening came to the pit of his stomach; his expression changed to one of apprehension.

"'Tis the girl Glory Warren." Wharton paused, reluctant to go on with the delivery of bad tidings.

262

"Yes. Speak, man," Quade insisted, his brows tight.

Wharton, flustered, blurted out his news. "She has fled Sealy Grove. Three days ago and not before time. The girl is charged with witchcraft and a warrant has been sworn out. 'Tis a pity," he added. "Coming on the heel of her mother's death."

Quade's eyes darkened. "Goody Warren! Dead? How?"

Wharton frowned. He had forgotten Quade could not have known of that event either. "'Tis said she tumbled down the stairs in her house and broke her neck. But there are those who claim the girl is to blame and that the mother's death was caused by her black art."

A look of outrage covered Quade's face. "They have not found Glory?"

"Nay. She has vanished and that has only led to more belief in her powers. 'Tis remarked she has taken the shape of an animal to escape. 'Tis reputed to be her special power to change herself at will. The constables found a cat on her bed and believing the beast to be her, one of them wrung its neck."

Quade paced, though the smallness of the cell allowed but a few steps in each direction. "Do they yet look for her?"

"Aye. In Sealy Grove. The minister Bellingham chief among them. He stands as one of her accusers, claiming she set upon him as a seductress."

"If there is a devil, 'tis him. The lying dog!" Quade swore in stronger terms but kept his voice low so that Bray would not overhear him.

Bellingham again. There was a man to examine. How had he gone from wanting Glory as wife to charging her as a witch? Quade stopped his pacing and put his mind to work, knowing he could not wait for his sentence to be up. Glory was in danger. It was only a matter of time before they looked beyond the town. He hoped she had gone to John Bayard. But how could he know if she had reached the trapper's camp safely?

Quade listened to a recitation of all the evidence given against Glory. Some of the charges were trifling matters, others so severe he wondered at the sanity of those who made them.

"'Tis the death of Jane Cobb which has set the town on its ear. The Allyn child is near death and her brother claims 'tis because he made a rhyme about the witch.'' Winded from his long oratory, the fellmonger rose weakly from the bench. "The girl is no sorceress and I will attest to it if she is brought to trial. I have known her since she was but a child. There is no evil in her.''

"Aye. And you have done me a good deed as is, Wharton.'' Quade's knuckles were white as he clasped the fellmonger's hand. "I will not forget it.''

"'Tis no more than you would have done for me. I regret I could not have helped the girl, but she was gone before I knew of the threat.''

"You have done well enough,'' Quade assured him.

Sam Hawk came to let Wharton out. Quade had found a friend in the Indian slave. Sam could sympathize with a man of the wild held against his will. He was the same himself and had spoken to Quade of his wish to fly from his master.

"Sam Hawk,'' Quade spoke in a low voice. "Are you willing to leave this place?''

A man of few words, Sam Hawk nodded.

"Help me and I will take you to a place of safety,'' Quade promised. "In the French lands you can live as a free man.''

Looking about to be sure no one overheard, Sam Hawk agreed and Quade told him the plan for leaving that same night. As the day stretched out, Quade waited with all the impatience of a caged animal, pacing, climbing to the window, thinking only of Glory alone on the dangerous trail between Sealy Grove and Arkport. When Sam Hawk returned hours after darkness had fallen and long after Bray and his wife had gone to bed, Quade was as edgy as a cornered mountain cat.

It would have been difficult to tell who moved more quietly, the trapper or the Indian. Nevertheless, both men stole out of the public house unnoticed by the keeper or any of the other prisoners. Quade's horse was saddled and waiting in a cove of trees just beyond the building, another feat the Indian had accomplished without alerting anyone. Quade swung into the saddle and the Indian swung up behind him. By first light they were miles out of Crossland, heading north to find the trapper, John Bayard.

"You are a stranger, are you not?"

"Aye," Glory said to the woman sitting in the shade of a tree near a public well on the outskirts of a tiny village. "A traveler. I am bound for Arkport but am not sure if I am on the right road."

The woman pulled a pipe from her mouth and as she spoke emitted wisps of smoke. "You cannot miss it if you bear to the left ten, twelve miles on where the road splits."

Glory thanked the woman and rode on past the scattering of rude buildings that made up the village. She thought nothing of it when, as she reached the far perimeter, Paddy swooped from the sky and lit on her shoulder. The woman with the pipe thought about it over and over and each time she shivered. Had not just such a bird hovered over the head of the witch Martha Cory? Nay, that had been a yellow bird or so said the afflicted girls who could see it. The pipe dropped from her mouth and spilled hot ashes on her shoe. *She* had seen the black bird. What did it mean? Had Salem's curse come to her village? Who was the girl with the strange blue eyes?

Glory's gaze was on the road. She believed she had ridden ten miles since the old woman told her the way, but she had not yet come to a fork in the road. She stopped the mare and dismounted to allow the animal a rest. She did not know who was more tired, the horse or she, but neither were slated for rest. From the way she had come, a clamor of pounding hooves raised a cloud of dust she could see before she could make out the riders. Did they seek her? She dared not wait to find out. Without remounting she led the mare into the woods, running and pulling the animal after her until she was sure they could not be seen from the road.

Glory bit the back of her hand as the riders thundered past. When they were gone she felt no safer and feared returning to the road. Instead she led the mare deeper into the forest until both she and the horse were too weary to go on. When the mare was unsaddled and hobbled for grazing, Glory sunk down beside a tree. Paddy, the only friend she had left, perched above her. She could take no pleasure in this second escape, if it had been one. She could not get beyond the emptiness she felt. What had she done to any in Sealy Grove that they should turn on her? She had only tried to be a friend, a good neighbor to all.

At length she stirred and got her cloak from her bag. She had only wanted to be a wife to Quade, to bear his children. And now she had nothing, nothing but fear, not even the certainty that she would find John Bayard or that Quade would find her. Too heartsick to eat, Glory lay back against a tree and watched the darkness come.

The night flowed in starlessly, the sky dark and heavy as black velvet. A chill hung in the air and there was a damp hint of rain. The hobbled mare, full from grazing, snorted contentedly amid the nighttime clamor of crickets and tree frogs. Glory, much less relaxed, lay curled beneath her heavy cloak shivering, wondering if she was lost in addition to her other troubles. She did not know how far she had come from the road or even if she could find the way back. Arkport had not looked so far on Quade's map.

If the camp of John Bayard was as difficult to find, she might be rambling through the wilderness for weeks. That thought seemed to make the chill more unbearable, the night darker. She would not have minded if Quade had been with her, but alone she was not sure she could endure another day without seeing a friendly face. Surely John Bayard and his wife would welcome her as Quade had said.

Hours must have passed before she drifted into sleep. She was groggy and stiff with cold when the mare's anxious whinny brought her awake. She heard nothing else extraordinary in the cacophony of night sounds, but a deep-seeded and instinctive feeling brought a shiver that had nothing to do with cold.

Glory drew herself up into a tight ball and pulled the dark cloak over her eyes. It was a childish ruse to shield out danger and, though it made her feel marginally less visible, she did not deceive herself that it made her any safer. The dangers in the midst of a deep wood were innumerable, among them wild animals and Indians. It was even possible a party from Sealy Grove had set out after her. She would have looked about for a place to better conceal herself had she not feared any movement of hers would only add to the risk of being discovered.

The sound of a branch being pushed aside came quietly as a whisper. Someone was near, not an animal but a man. She knew that without knowing how she made the distinction.

Biting her lip to prevent a cry of fear, Glory folded herself even smaller beneath the cloak, hoping that anyone who passed could not distinguish her from the darkness. Even as she counted her quickening heartbeats she knew the unlikeliness of that. The mare would give her away. The skittish animal snorted and pawed and had it not been for her hobbled feet undoubtedly would have bolted off into the forest.

Glory held her breath. Had the men on the trail doubled back and followed her tracks? She heard footsteps or imagined she did. Almost at once the mare quieted and calmed as if someone had given her a reassuring pat. Someone who would now be searching for the animal's rider.

Glory chastised herself beneath her burgeoning fear. She had her mother's musket but had foolishly left it with the saddle. Little good it was to her six or eight feet beyond her reach. And yet, having come so far to escape a fate she did not believe she deserved, she refused to cower and shrink without a fight if someone meant her harm. Hidden beneath her cloak, she moved like a great, bow-backed cat toward the musket.

Like a cat caught by the scruff of the neck, Glory found herself snatched up. No feline could have hissed and fought more furiously. Armed only with nails and teeth she sought to tear her unseen enemy to shreds.

It was a credit to his quickness that none of her strikes drew blood. "Damnation!" He caught her wrists fast and pinned her head against his shoulder where the worst she could do was to rip a mouthful of fringe from his buckskin shirt.

"I believe 'tis a wildcat and not Glory Warren I have caught."

The familiar, teasing voice penetrated her fury. "Quade! Oh, Quade!" she sobbed, cinching her arms around him with all the might she had put into resisting him. "Hold me, please."

He did not need the invitation. He had thought only of finding Glory since fleeing his cell in Crossland. In a rush he wrapped his arms tightly around her back, his hands kneading and caressing as if he wanted to assure himself she was really there in his embrace.

"Forever," he whispered. His mouth slanted over her soft, waiting lips, twisting against them with all the fury born of worry and need. Their kisses branded them together. Glory felt the heat from his body seep into her like a mystical potion that could shield her from all the evils and ills the world might toss her way.

Quade clung to her as if he would draw her inside him, needing the soft, sweet feel of her body as reassurance that she was not lost to him. He nuzzled his face in her hair and whispered his promise over and over in her ear.

To Glory it seemed all her troubles had melted away like the last snow of a cold and bitter winter. Her glacial world turned green and bright and warm. She longed for the feeling to last.

"I wished for you," she said wonderingly. "And here you are." Abruptly she flung her head back and looked into the dark, glowing eyes. "Though is it possible you have been let out before your sentence is done?"

He would not free her from the circle of his arms. "I let myself out when I heard what had happened to you." His brow furrowed. "A warrant has been issued for your arrest. Are you aware of it?"

She lay her head against him. "Nay, but I guessed as much. We are both fugitives, it seems."

"A matched pair," he told her, his teasing tone deliberate as he sensed despair in her voice. "I care little what we are

called. 'Tis enough that I have found you and you are safe.''
Now his voice grew soft and comforting. "It pains me that
your mother is dead, Glory, love."

Sheltered in his arms and feeling a strength she had lacked
all the days she had been alone, Glory told him how her
mother had died or at least all that she knew of it.

"She was alone," Glory sobbed. "I blame myself."

"Nay. 'Tis no fault of yours."

Glory shook her head in disagreement. "You would have
spoken for me before you left had I not quarreled with
you. Had we been betrothed naught of this with Bellingham
would have come about. I would not have set out to find
you and my mother would not have been alone. Had I been
there . . ."

"Nay, you must not think as you do." He kissed her brow
and kissed the salty tears from her eyes. "She would not
want it. She was a strong woman and she would have you
be the same."

"I am not so sure I have the courage I need." Her head
rested snugly against his chest. His soothing warmth had
served her well; even as she spoke, she felt the last vestiges
of anxiety drain away.

"You have it, love. Else you would not be here."

Glory sighed. "Perhaps I should have stayed and faced my
accusers in court. There is no evidence to prove I am a
witch."

"There is no evidence to prove you are not. In Salem a
handful of addled girls swore they were tormented by the
accuseds' shapes. On that testimony six were convicted and
hung. 'Tis worse for you."

"Worse? I have not harmed the children. I did not prickle
Goody White. I but moved the snake from my mother's grave.
Nay," she said. "I believe all can be explained."

Quade held her tighter. "You do not know," he said softly. "Jane Cobb worsened and died. You are blamed. Goody Collier and her newborn babe died the day you left Sealy Grove. Her daughter says the mother looked on you and went into an early labor. She blames you for those deaths as well."

"Sarah?"

"Aye. Sarah Collier. She claims she is afflicted with fits when she looks on you herself."

"'Tis but lies!" Glory gave a pained cry. "'Tis lunacy!"

"Aye," Quade agreed. "But 'tis what you would face in Sealy Grove."

Leaning against him, she wept a long while. Quade held her, but when it seemed the tears would never cease flowing down her flushed cheeks, he tilted her head back and brushed the streams away with his fingers.

"'Tis said a witch cannot cry," he remarked. "Would seem you are a mortal woman for all the claims made against you."

The tears and sobbing stopped. She was warmed through with his heat and now her body had come alive to feel the corded strength of the muscles supporting her.

"I am mortal," she whispered, nestling all her weight against him. "And woman. With all a woman's needs. Take me, Quade. Love me," she pleaded.

For once Quade could muster no opposition to her pleas that he make love to her. He gathered her in his arms and would have carried her to a soft bed of leaves had not large, pelting drops of rain begun to fall. A frustrated groan slipped from him as he gently eased Glory to her feet and hurriedly saddled the mare. In a moment more he had slung his pack and her bundles over the saddle.

"I know a sheltered place not far from here," he shouted above the tumultuous downpour.

Glory pulled her hood over her head and, holding tightly to his arm, trotted alongside as he threaded through the forest with an ease that made her suspect he could see as well in the darkness as she did in daylight. By the time they reached the shallow cave in a rocky hillside there seemed little need for the cover it would afford. Both were soaked. Quade's buckskins clung as if painted on. Glory's layers of skirts dragged on the ground with the weight of the water contained in them.

She wrung water from her hair as he tied the mare's lead to a stone then started a fire. The blaze caught and sent out an immediate glow, which for all its brightness did not penetrate the cold of her wet clothes.

"Take them off," Quade ordered as he stripped away soggy leggings and boots. "It seems we are ever destined to be wet to the skin if we are together."

Glory nodded and hesitated but a moment that she might watch the reflection of the nimble flames move on his skin as he pulled the fringed shirt over his head. Soon she had laid aside her ruined bands and cuffs and had her bodice spread over a rock to dry. Her petticoats, once off, required squeezing and, as she suspected, the water wrung out made a small stream that inched across the rocky floor of the cave.

"I am cold yet," she complained, moving near the snapping fire, her shoulders hunched, her chemise plastered to her skin like so many pink rose petals. Her dripping hair hung in an untidy braid over her shoulder and from its end a rivulet of water streamed a curvy path across her breasts.

Quade, resting on his knees as he added more of the branches he had gathered to the fire, threw in a last stick and turned to his pack. Casting a sideways look at Glory, he withdrew several lush pelts and arranged them on the cave floor near enough the fire for warmth but far enough back that they would not be scorched.

"Come closer." He motioned to the shivering girl. When she was within arm's reach he raised to his haunches in front of her and nimbly unbraided her wet hair. A blast of wind sent the flames at his back dancing and twirling and made a spiral of the rise of smoke climbing toward the rocky roof overhead. Golden lights flickered in Glory's raven hair. Quade combed his fingers through the damp tresses and watched in wonder as she shook her head and the silken strands sprung into tendril curls. There was an odd look in her eyes as he kissed her softly on the lips, then sat back and gently caught hold of the wet chemise at her sides. "Lift your arms."

Glory did as told, wondering if it was possible to be warmed by words, for she felt a sudden infusion of heat although the fire had not yet driven the damp from their small shelter.

Quade, skimming his hands along her sides, pulled the damp, clinging garment over her head, his breath coming out in a rush of astonishment as he uncovered a treasure of honey-eyed skin and satiny curves the equal of which his eyes had never seen. It was no wonder he dropped the wet chemise in a heap at his side instead of spreading it to dry; he was lost to all but the divine beauty of the woman soft and naked before him.

"Warm me," she whispered, stretching out unbidden atop the thick bed of furs.

Quade watched, his fascination growing, as she positioned her weight on one side, her knees slightly bent, her head resting on one arm. Her full breasts stood out proudly, the peaks nipped tight with cold. For a full minute he sat and stared and, though he voiced no answer to her request, his eyes told her that he would do as bidden.

"Over," he said at last, gently toppling her to her tummy, so that her curvy bottom temptingly presented itself to his view.

She could have told him she was no longer cold, that in fact she was hotter than the flames leaping and spitting at his side. She did not, however. She was discovering there were all kinds of heat, that which came from a glance, that which came from a tender word, and that which came from a loving touch. She liked the fire in his touch best. It warmed and penetrated as if he had broken open a white-hot star and poured out the shimmering heat on her skin. That was what she imagined, eyes dreamily shut, as he rubbed her feet and toes and small, round heels before moving on to her slender ankles and calves.

"I like it." She purred like a lazy cat, her limbs limp and yielding to his deft fingers.

He worked, it seemed, to the primitive rhythm of the drumming rain and the howling wind. Now and then a peal of lightning flashed and chimed and lit the shadowed cave with a burst of silver light. Glory cooed in delight as he kneaded her dimpled knees and, when he paused at his work, obligingly shifted her weight to give him room to reach her tingling thighs. When he left her wanting and switched to massaging her arms and shoulders instead, her relaxed face tightened with a frown.

Quade laughed softly. "I see you *are* easily spoiled, Glory Warren."

"'Tis true if you are the spoiler," she returned quickly, lacking the will to lift her head from the pillow of furs.

Her soft moans came with regularity as he worked every hint of tenseness out of her back. The pleasure of that, however, was nothingness compared to the feel of his hands moving like fluid heat on her buttocks and thighs. Mumbling her approval, she rolled over with gentle ease when he gave the command for her to lie on her back.

"Glory, my lovely Glory," Quade whispered as again he fed his hunger by running his eyes slowly from the ten dainty toes to the black cloud of hair falling freely over her glowing skin.

Firelight sparkled in her eyes and made an enticing play of shadows over the whole length of her. She was not a witch, he could plainly see. The people of Sealy Grove were wrong about that. She was a goddess sent down on a beam of light, and were the lot of them anything but fools they would spend the remainder of their days worshiping her as he meant to do.

"I am warm enough," she said, breaking into his thoughts. Her arms were outstretched, her fingers curled in invitation for him to join her on the furs.

"Nay, not yet," he answered, feeling his control slip a notch. Having been deterred from his purpose by the sudden downpour, he had thought better of it and sought to put a check on his passion. She could not be in a state to think clearly, no matter what she believed. He wanted to give her his love when he could be certain no regrets would follow. Dropping his gaze, he took a tiny foot and rested it on his thigh as he began rubbing the smooth instep.

Glory pulled her foot free. "Your breeches are wet," she said softly. "And cold enough to give me another chill." She rose to her knees and reached for the laces at his waist. "Take them off. I will warm you."

Quade caught her hands and held them pressed against his sides. "Nay, Glory," he said huskily. "You know not what you ask."

She shook her head slowly and edged closer so that their knees met. Her nipples grazed his chest and sent a tremor through him.

"I know," she whispered. "Do not deny me, Quade." Her uplifted face filled with entreaty. "I have lost all else that mattered. I have naught else left to me." Her warm breath ruffled the soft fur covering his chest. "If you love me as you say, do not deny me the full measure of that love."

His answer was a hungering kiss which fed her desire and cut away the last of his reticence. Conceding, Quade placed his hands on her shoulders and allowed her to unlace the leather ties that held his breeches. When they were lose she pushed the wet buckskin from his hips. Quade shrugged them over his knees and feet and hurriedly tossed them aside. With some measure of discomfort he hurriedly sprawled on his belly and submitted willingly to the soft onslaught of her hands.

"I will be about this all night," she said as she picked up a foot which was bigger than the two of hers.

"You are quick to find fault," Quade remarked as her fingers exerted a soothing pressure on his tight muscles.

Laughing, she plied the firm sole with her fingers, then hastily moved on past a sturdy ankle to a well-muscled calf.

"I see naught that does not please me," she replied, gliding her fingers through the crinkled hair covering his calves and thighs. Unlike Quade she continued the massage to the curved base of his buttocks before switching from the right leg to the left.

Kneeling beside his long, bronzed body, her loose hair dusting his skin like a dangling tassel of silk, she rubbed his arms, learning the sinewy shape of well-muscled forearms and powerful biceps. Quade sighed raggedly at the pleasure of her tender ministrations, relaxing until his eyelids threatened to slip low over his eyes. They snapped open quickly when Glory gently slipped astride him, resting her bottom on his as she began stroking his broad, sinewy back.

Moaning, Quade jerked in blissful agony beneath her. "Damnation! Glory!" he cried brokenly. "You torture me with sweetness."

"'Tis the best way to reach you," she explained as she leaned forward and kneaded his taut shoulders.

He groaned and clinched his fists around the pelts as her soft Venus hair tickled his buttocks with every move she made. His tolerance for her brand of torture proved short-lived. Soon he had nearly unseated her by twisting beneath her legs until it was his front side she sat astride.

Her slight weight rested on his thighs; her hands pressed his chest to keep upright. Her eyes froze on his erect manhood which throbbed and jerked on his belly. Lips parted to whisper his name, she touched him tentatively, running two fingers down the length of him, reveling in the feel of the smooth hardness of the heated shaft.

Words choked off in his throat as one of Glory's hands closed around him and the fingers of the other gently stroked and explored him. It was all he could do not to lunge up and toss her to the pelts and savagely drive himself into her. He fought down his lust. She was the woman he loved and he wanted this first time for her to be beautiful and entirely pleasurable.

"I love you, Glory," he whispered as he gripped her waist, easily spanning the narrow breadth with his hands. He held them at that point but a moment before finding a more tempting resting place in the pertly rounded breasts.

" 'Tis all I want," she murmured. "To have your love.

To give you mine.'' Crying out at the rapturous feel of his hands upon her, she twisted her torso, grazing his palms with her hard, rosy nipples.

Quade, unable to endure that bit of play, grasped the soft, tantalizing flesh and gently caressed the pebbly peaks with methodical strokes of his thumbs.

"If so little makes you happy, I will keep you blissfully so forever."

A quiver ran the length of her. When it ended Glory shook her head slowly so that her hair shimmered like a silk banner teased by the wind. " 'Tis no small thing to have your love,'' she whispered.

He smiled and, sliding his hands around her rib cage, pulled her down on him. Her arms crept around his neck, her fingers finding the leather cord that tied back his hair. She loosened the knot, then slid her hands into the thick, dark strands.

Quade's hands fitted over her tight, round bottom and pressed her firmly to his loins. She gasped softly at the feel of his aroused manhood pressing against the sensitive spot at the apex of her thighs.

"Glory, Glory,'' he rasped as she rolled her hips upon him. "You are a lusty wench for an innocent.''

"Hmmm,'' she murmured. "You must find a way to reconcile my two natures.'' Her eyes sparkled with the shifting light of the fire. "Make me a woman,'' she whispered.

"As you wish.'' A shudder of desire ran through him. His hand rose to cup her face and bring her mouth down upon his own. His kisses held a fierceness that was hard to temper. Glory met them with a matching ardor which fueled him on. Only the realization that she gasped for air brought his passion skidding to a momentary halt. Breathless, she lay her cheek on his and murmured soft words of love in his ear.

Quade kissed her again, slowly, softly, then, as if she were weightless, lifted and slid her up the length of his body so that her breasts were positioned within reach of his greedy mouth.

A soft, keening sound came from her as she guided a dusky nipple to him and felt the pressure of his lips tug it within. His gentle suckling shook her with pleasure. Passion budded and bloomed, spreading like the petals of an awakening flower from the core of her, warming her skin as if she lay naked in the hot sun and not in the growing darkness of a cold, damp cave.

His erection lay hotly against her thigh and though she rolled and twisted he would not allow her to settle upon him. She thought she would die of wanting and told him so. He chided her gently for her impatience and with a quick but skillful roll brought her beneath him.

"Bide your time, love," he whispered.

"I think I cannot." Her eyes burned brighter than the fire. Her nails raked his bare back, urging him to yield.

"Let me teach you patience," he whispered and, seeing her dubious look, added, "Will be an enjoyable lesson, love."

"Then I am your willing pupil," she returned.

Quade taught her well, beginning with a rousing kiss upon the lips, then shortly bringing his soft lips to her throat. Her breasts he teased with a velvet touch, circling the pliant flesh with kisses, dampening the peaks with the tip of his tongue and rendering them tight and red as cherries with a gentle nip of his teeth. She begged him not to stop but his mouth moved on and rested upon her belly, his tongue plunging into the dimpled navel as his hands crept maddeningly inside her thighs.

A rasping groan tore from his mouth. He found her slippery and wet and felt a shudder ripple through her as his fingers explored the satiny folds of womanly flesh. As his mouth moved across the soft nest of black curls, one finger slipped inside, stretching the tight web of membrane within. Eyes wide with wonder, Glory lay spellbound as he gently moved and stroked, and she experienced the bewildering start of sensations that felt shockingly good. Soon she was lifting her hips to him and guiding his other hand to the sensitive little nub which ached for his touch.

Quade whispered her name as his lips nuzzled her thighs. When he felt the first small shudder begin in her body he quickly but gently slid another finger inside, opening the virginal veil at a moment when she would feel no pain.

Her eyes had a languid look, her lips a satisfied curl. "You learn quickly," he said huskily, stirred to a new pitch of desire by her release. Breathing unevenly, he knelt beside her, his hands on her hips.

"I know so little," she murmured sweetly. "Teach me more. Teach me everything," she pleaded.

"Aye, my love," he answered, gasping as she brought her hands to his manhood and stroked the hard, burning length of him. "All that I know and then we will learn new lessons together."

He braced his arms beside her head, allowing her to guide him into the primed and ready sheath of her body. Exercising a steel will, he entered her slowly, taking care that she feel only enjoyment as their bodies united.

Nevertheless, for Glory he was like a brand within her, full and deliciously hot. He moved so slowly at first, pulling from her, entering again, she thought she would scream from the building anticipation of what was to come. He did not disappoint. Her eyes luminous flames of desire, she readily met his gaze and held it.

His thrust quickened. Glory rose to meet him, clasping his hips, crying out his name as a molten heat rippled, then raged, then burst into a thousand tremors inside her. Quade caught her ecstasy and drove a last shuddering thrust into her, his breath rasping her name.

Glory whimpered with pleasure as she felt his liquid fill her. The flexed muscles beneath her hands grew still. Only then did they know the rain had stopped, the storm had stilled. The fire had died to a mere glow, but neither cared; both were flushed with enough heat to last through the night.

The mare, anxious to get to the tender green grass outside the cave, woke them as she sought to drag off the rock she was tethered to. Quade slipped from beneath the furs and found his rumpled buckskin trousers. He tugged them on, then took the mare to a spot where she could nibble grass to her heart's content.

Glory sat up in the bed of furs, covered only by a fox pelt haphazardly draped over her lap. Her hair hung in a tangled mass over her shoulders and breasts. While Quade splashed his face with water caught in a recess of rock, she slowly stretched her arms over her head. Her soft nipples peeked through the dark curls.

"You tempt me, love." Face dripping, he combed his own tangled hair with his fingers and quickly twisted it into a single short braid which he fastened with a leather tie.

"Good. 'Tis what I meant to do." She flung her hair to her back, exposing her breasts. Beneath his hot gaze the peaks grew hard and rosy.

His loins tightened. "We will be midday leaving this place if you display yourself so openly," he warned.

"Would that matter?"

"Nay," he said. "John Bayard will not care if we arrive at morning or night." He stripped his breeches off and joined her on the soft furs. "Nor do I."

Early in the afternoon, after partaking of the food Glory had packed, the pair mounted the rested mare and rode toward John's camp. It occurred to Glory as they set out that Quade had somehow misplaced the roan.

She queried him about that from atop her pillion behind the saddle.

Quade laughed. "I traded him to an Indian who helped me shorten my sentence. Without a horse the man had little chance of getting away."

Glory looked up at him in alarm, knowing that in addition to his own trouble he had gained more by aiding an Indian slave in an escape.

Quade shrugged off her concern. "I have a soft spot for those who are bound against their will, whether Indian or white."

"And for witches too, I believe." She pressed her cheek to his shoulder.

"For witches especially," he concurred. "If they are black-haired and blue-eyed and warmly willing."

Glory gave a lusty laugh and nipped his earlobe with her teeth. "Where will we go?" she asked, her mood turning serious.

"We'll stay with John for a while if he will have us, till we are sure no one searches for us. Then go on to Canada or New York as seems best at the time. Perhaps to England as now I have business there."

"Promise you will never leave me," Glory pleaded, recalling the emptiness she had felt at her mother's death. "I could not bear it if you did."

"I'll not leave you, Glory, love. Not while there is breath in my body. You are bound to me as surely as if the vows had been spoken between us."

The sun shone hot and golden above and the warming rays lifted a mist of steam from the damp forest floor. It seemed an enchanted place with the soft fog hanging about the lush green of ferns and foliage. The spongy ground cushioned the mare's slow hoofbeats; only an occasional chirp from a bird in the branches overhead or the buzz of bees at work gathering nectar for a store of honey broke the spell.

Glory clung to Quade's back, hoping the peacefulness would last forever. She had known her share of trouble in recent weeks. But even as she closed her eyes to seal in the quiet and beauty of the unspoiled forest, she feared that wishes would not be enough to sustain her.

"Look there. See the lodge fire." Quade pointed out a smoky thread rising to the treetops. "'Tis Bayard's camp. Set your mind at ease, Glory, girl. We are here. We are safe."

CHAPTER
14

The mare broke through a barrier of brush and thorns into a circular clearing where a long, cylindrical lodge formed of wattle and daub and covered with a roof of bark squatted on the bare ground. A fire pit near the entrance was the source of the smoke. A small boy crouched beside the banked flames, turning the crank of a wooden spit run through a pair of roasting rabbits.

The scene was quiet and peaceful but Quade knew the wary John Bayard had not left his camp as vulnerable as it appeared; nor had the boy failed to hear the approaching clump of the mare's hooves. On the back of his neck a ridge of fine hairs raised up as he considered that from some hidden vantage point a musket barrel or the sharp tip of an arrow was aimed at his heart.

"Johnnie!" Quade called out loudly.

The lad spun on his heels. A wide grin spread on his brown face as he speedily looked up. "Quade Wylde!" he shouted gleefully. "Look, Papa! 'Tis Quade Wylde come back."

"That I can see for myself." John Bayard, his curly red beard bobbing as he talked, stepped from behind a blind of limbs and leaves. Slung over his big shoulder was the musket he had kept trained on the riders until their faces were clear. His broad grin rivaled the boy's for showing the longest line of white teeth. "Welcome, friend!" he shouted. "I see this time you have brought along a prettier face than your own."

"'Tis Glory Warren of Sealy Grove," Quade explained as he leaped from the saddle.

Bayard shook his hand, then gave the younger man a friendly poke in the ribs. While Quade recovered from the unexpected blow, no less powerful for being amicably given, the burly trapper stepped back, his fur-capped head nodding slowly in recognition of the girl's name.

"Aye," Bayard said and then chuckled. "You spoke of her. The wench who tamed a trapper."

Quade cast Bayard a glowering look but accepted the jibe as he had the poke in the ribs, in the good-natured spirit in which it was given. Glory took note of the teasing revelry the men enjoyed and added her wit to the banter after Quade gripped her waist and eased her from the mare's back.

She brushed her skirts free of horsehair and tugged her bodice over the waist ties while the brawny trapper gave a lengthy stare. Her blue eyes flashed mischievously.

"He is not so tame, I am pleased to say." She smiled sweetly at Bayard, then laughed as his jaw sagged open at her boldness. "I fear he will never take to a leash."

Bayard, whose first assessment had been that so pretty a maid would be shy and retiring, slapped his sides and roared with laughter. Glory joined him, her laughter as sweet as a tinkling bell compared to Bayard's raucous outburst. Quade looked from one to the other, one corner of his mouth downturned in a sure sign that he was rubbed the wrong way to have been made the brunt of their humor.

"You've done a good day's work catching that one, lad." Bayard poked Quade again, nearly knocking him off his feet.

Quade could not hold back a chuckle for all his attempts to appear offended. "As you tell it, I am the one snared." His arm slipped possessively around Glory. "Though I must say if I am truly caught 'tis an agreeable fate."

"Wisely said." Bayard made a comical bow before taking charge of the horse and tethering it a few feet away behind the lodge. He was back shortly to continue where he had left off. "No fur has been found that is soft as a woman's touch." Laughing loudly Bayard made a wide swing of his arm which caught Glory unawares. He clasped her to his side and gave her a ferocious hug. "Welcome, Glory Warren," he said.

Finding the breath nearly squeezed out of her, Glory thanked the rugged trapper and ceremoniously straightened the cap he had knocked askew.

The boy Johnnie, who had rarely been around a female other than his mother, stood at his father's knee, staring up at the bright-eyed woman with childish curiosity, his glance occasionally darting to the dark doorway of the lodge.

Bayard's glance followed the boy's. "Clemmie, come out," the trapper called affectionately.

A slight figure in a pale doeskin dress slipped from the shadows into the sunlight, a tenuous smile softening her brown face. Unaccustomed to friendly whites other than her husband, she nodded nervously at the guests.

Glory smiled warmly and nodded back. "Hello, Clemmie. I hope you don't mind that we've come."

"I am pleased," Clemmie said graciously, her English nearly as good as Bayard's.

"Pleased and surprised. That's what we all are," Bayard

said as he unhooked their bundles from the mare's saddle and tossed them to the ground. "Take these in the lodge, Johnnie."

The boy swiftly gathered up the bags, burdening himself to the point that he staggered under the weight. Though his father suggested he take them one at a time, Johnnie seemed determined to carry all the bundles at once. His bent knees straightened when Quade laughingly lifted his heavy pack from the boy's shoulder.

"Wait," he said. The boy stopped. Quade looked apologetically at Bayard. "We don't want to trouble you." He pointed to a thicket on the edge of the clearing. "We'll make a shelter over there."

"'Tis no trouble," Bayard insisted, urging Johnnie along to the lodge. "There is room aplenty for two more in—" He stopped short as he read the gleam in Quade's dark eyes. "Ahh," he said, and catching the boy by the shoulders, turned him toward the thicket. "Put the bundles there, Johnnie. It's a bit of privacy they're wanting."

An hour later the five of them sat in a circle outside the lodge, finishing the last of the rabbit and tasty pottage Clemmie had prepared. Happy but uneasy with their secret, Quade and Glory could not continue to accept the trapper's hospitality without making him and his family aware of the danger they had brought with them. Quade explained that they might possibly be pursued.

"Not respectable citizens, you say." Bayard stroked the disordered hair on his chin and looked at Clemmie as if he had a mind to toss the two of them out. Glory observed the dour set of his face and knew a moment of worry until Bayard caught her look of alarm. He slapped his knee and guffawed. "You will fit in well here. We are not welcomed in any town either. It matters naught to me, but do satisfy a man's curiosity," he insisted, furrowing his brow. "Just what has made two fine people outcasts?"

Quade leaned back against a stump and lit his pipe, reflecting that all the time he was in Sealy Grove he had not had a conversation with any man in which he did not feel a need to guard his words. Perhaps that was what he liked about John Bayard. The trapper accepted a man for what he was without judging him right or wrong.

"I am sought for having given my jailer the slip. And undoubtedly for aiding an Indian slave to escape as well. Though in truth it was the other way around. The Wampanoag, Sam Hawk, set me free, and if he has been blessed with good fortune is well along to Canada astride my horse."

"You will gain Clemmie's heart with that story," Bayard remarked. "She is Wampanoag." Clemmie nodded that what he said was true. "She was a slave to a goodman in Arkport until I bought her freedom." Anger crept into his deep voice. "'Tis not just one man or woman should be under another's rule except by choice."

"You need not convince me of that," Quade replied. "'Tis for fleeing a bond master twelve years back that I found myself an occupant of the Crossland jail."

"I see," Bayard said, shifting his understanding eyes to Glory, who until now had sat as quiet as a dormouse at Quade's side. "And is your crime the same, lass?"

"Nay," she said somewhat reluctantly, not knowing Bayard so well as Quade and fearing that if he heard what was said of her, he too might fear and reject her. Quade gave her a heartening glance and she went on with her story, though her voice trembled with the telling. "I am said to be a witch."

Bayard's thick red brows arched sharply. "Well, well," he said. "So the madness has spread to Sealy Grove. And your neighbors will tear out the hearts of good families as those wretches have done in Salem?'' He saw her trembling and felt a tenderness for the girl. His booming voice ebbed low. ''Fear not, lass. I do not believe there are witches. But,'' he said, ''there is evil in every man and it is that dark blood we should all dread.'' In a gentle, fatherly way he touched Glory's hand. ''You may both stay here for as long as you wish sanctuary.''

Johnnie had been put to bed. Bayard and Clemmie sat huddled within each other's arms by the crackling fire. From some secret cache, Bayard produced a bottle of good English brandy. He passed the fiery drink around, assuring his guests it was a rare treat for these parts and not the cheap gin colored with molasses sometimes secretly traded to the Indians.

Quade took a long draught, Glory but a sip, though it warmed the tube from mouth to stomach as if she had swallowed half the bottle. Clemmie had a drop, but Bayard drained a goodly portion of what remained, then looked longingly toward the lodge.

If it was a hint, Quade was quick to seize upon it. He was anxious to settle in with Glory beneath the lean-to he and Johnnie had fashioned inside the thicket. When a round of good nights had been said and Quade and Glory had again thanked Bayard for taking them in, Quade linked Glory's arm in his and led her to their fur bed.

Moonlight made a dappled pattern on the entwined pair beneath the leafy roof of the lean-to. Awed by her warmth and beauty, Quade pressed his lips to every portion of smooth, gleaming skin covering the exquisitely fashioned body of the woman in his arms. When he was done his fingertips touched each place his lips had caressed before them. Glory lay blissfully still, astonished that such incredible satisfaction could come from being stroked and touched by the dark-haired, dark-eyed man at her side.

Love and desire for Quade shining in her pale eyes, Glory insisted another turnabout was only fair and slowly did to him the same seductive things he had done to her. She delighted in starting small tremors in his flesh as her lips touched intimate parts of him. When she finished he lay beside her, panting, glistening with sweat, his arousal complete, his need for her skipping beyond control.

He reached for her but she gently pushed him down upon the furs.

"Not yet," she whispered in the darkness. "No yet, my love. I am not finished with you." Swinging long, silky tresses over her shoulder, she trailed the curling ends along his cheekbone, down his muscular neck, over his broad chest and flat, hard belly, tickling, teasing, raising his senses to the highest pinnacles of wanting. "Do you like it?" she whispered.

Quade groaned and grazed the smooth skin of her thighs with an outstretched hand. "I like all you do," he whispered, his voice breaking as she trailed the black, silken strands over his throbbing erection. His breath catching, he reached for her and snatched her down on the furs and in a moment loomed above her in a savage pose. "Now see if you like what I am about to do to you."

With that, he thrust inside her heated, willing body, crying out his pleasure as she linked her legs over his and rose to meet his heavy thrusts. For long, glorious moments all else was forgotten, worldly cares were shut out, as two bodies forged into one. Nor did those cares come creeping back into love-sated minds until long after he had poured his essence inside her.

* * *

"Has she bewitched you?" Before the magistrates, Josiah Bellingham prodded the slow mind of William Cook. "Where is she now?"

William nervously shifted his weight from one foot to the other. Many times he had been brought before the authorities and never yet had he come up with the right answers to their questions.

"She did not say where she would go or when she would return," William repeated, having lost count of the times in the past hour that he had been asked the same question. "Only that the cart horse was mine if she was gone a long while." Though it had not occurred to William before during the ordeal, he suddenly realized that he was not the last to see Glory before she left the farm.

"You spoke to her after me," he offered to Josiah Bellingham, a look of enlightenment shining briefly in his dull eyes. "Perhaps she told you where she was bound."

Bellingham's lean face reddened. He had not meant to lead the boy's memory in this direction. Like a swooping hawk in his somber garb, he leaned over William. "I am here to question, not to be questioned," he returned harshly. "Tell us what you know."

"I know only what I have said." William made a snuffling sound. He was tired and his simple mind strained beyond its limits. "I was hired to care for the animals."

"What did she promise you?" Bellingham's droning voice hammered at the boy.

"Only the horse."

"Did she make you sign a book?"

"Nay." William looked at the minister as if he was the daft one. "I cannot write," he said.

Bellingham shrugged and made an eloquent gesture of despair to the magistrates who had so graciously yielded to his persuasive arguments that he be allowed to question the boy. William was subsequently let go but sternly warned that if Glory Warren returned to the farm he must waste no time in alerting the authorities.

Badgered to the point that he would have agreed to anything, William left the meetinghouse, steering a path through the crowd milling beyond the portals.

She was lost to him. Bellingham shut the heavy doors on those who hovered and waited for some news of their most infamous citizen. Glory Warren had left Sealy Grove. Some in the assembly claimed she had changed her form and slithered away as a black snake, or flown off as a cawing crow. One of the constables had killed a cat in her room but the beast had yielded nothing but blood and bone.

Only he knew she had left the house in human form, whether witch or woman he could not say. He was forced, however, to accept that she had spurned his love and left him in the humiliating posture in which William had found him. If that was not a sorry enough state, she had also left him with the perplexing question of whether she had acted of her own accord or by the will of the devil.

He leaned first one way and then the other. And yet, if she was a mere woman would she have left him? It made no sense that she would. If she was a witch and the devil's hand was upon her, she would surely fear to unite with a man of God. He felt suddenly lighter, as if a yoke had been removed from his shoulders. That had to be it. The devil had singled him out as an adversary, had singled him out because he was the most godly man in Sealy Grove. Satan had entered Glory Warren to spite Josiah Bellingham.

The agitated minister mopped his dripping brow. It explained his loss of control the night he had struggled with

Glory. It explained why he had weakened and yielded to carnal lust for Sarah Collier. It explained the abomination that had happened with Goody Warren. Satan had wanted to make him a murderer, but he had thwarted the Black One in that. Now it was his duty to find Glory Warren and purge her of the fiendish possession.

"She must be found," he said. "At all costs, she must be found and examined."

The magistrates agreed. Sealy Grove's witch must be found and stopped before others died of her torment. Already five persons complained of Glory Warren's shape tormenting them. If absent in person, she was much in spectral evidence throughout the countryside. Before she enlisted others to her wicked cause, she must be found and tried.

"The constables will go on the morrow," the chief magistrate announced. "And sir," he addressed Bellingham, "we would be pleased if you would lead the party."

"Sir?" Bellingham responded with no small dismay. This was not a duty he favored. The hunt might lead anywhere and there was no way of determining how long it took to find a witch. "I do not wish to question your judgment, but surely this is a job the constable can do far better than I." He spread his palms. "I am a man of the cloth, a man of letters, not a tracker or woodsman."

The magistrate shook his head. "Your objection is well taken, Reverend. But it is because you are an educated man and a man of the cloth that I wish you to lead the expedition. This Glory Warren, if she be a witch, is a clever one by all accounts. It will take a resourceful mind to seek her out." Bellingham nodded and graciously accepted the compliment to his intelligence. "And when she is found, who better than a clergyman to confront a witch?"

Bellingham bowed. "I yield to your reasoning, sir. I will do my duty."

Not duty but the heat of an August night drove Sealy Grove's minister into the garden, where a lazy breeze helped relieve the grievous temperature. Though it was past midnight, he sat on a bench beneath an elm, his head still bowed from his prayers. Josiah Bellingham was a man besieged by guilt and fearful his petitions no longer penetrated the gates of heaven. Often when he should be about his prayers he found himself preoccupied with thoughts of Glory Warren.

He could not close his eyes without a vision of her; she came to him in his dreams, not as the gruesome hag some reported seeing, but as the tempting, seductive siren who roused him to lust even in his sleep. It seemed to Bellingham that his yearning was greater than the ordinary desire of a man for an alluring maid. These were no ordinary dreams. Was he not in truth beset by a specter of the girl who had observed where he was weakest and had chosen to torment him in this lamentable way?

What he knew with certainty was that his loins ached to the point of soreness and that at a time when he should be examining the scriptures concerning witchcraft, his thoughts were unclean. Some men, frustrated as he was, would resort to chafing their own flesh to provoke lust, arguing that that sin was lesser than having corporeal knowledge of a willing maid. He was not so sure one was less vile than the other, and already he had the fornication with Sarah Collier as a burden to his conscience.

Finding no ease to his vexation, Bellingham rose and strolled the garden paths. Was it providence he had been charged with finding Glory Warren or was it more of the devil's work, some new torture designed to test him?

WILD GLORY / 295

His long feet scuffed upon the ground as he paced in the
darkness. He ought to be at rest. There was no way of knowing how long he would be on the trail in search of the girl.
If not asleep he ought to be engrossed in meditation, but he
could not bring his mind to ordered thought. He could not
think more than a moment before she was there in his mind,
beautiful, beguiling, causing his body a suffering hunger he
could not ease.

"Glory, Glory," he whispered, feeling his groin tighten
with need.

"Josiah." A soft, pleading voice spoke out of the darkness.

He jerked around. "Sarah?" She was barely visible. Had
it not been for the white band and cuffs catching a sliver of
moonlight, he would not have seen her at all. "How come
you to be here?" he asked gruffly, his unease, already high,
mounting even more.

Since that day he had taken her to his bed, she had acted
as if nothing was amiss. He had gratefully done the same and
hoped the girl would not veer from that course until he had
had time to reconcile himself to that vile act. Now he knew
that was not to be; it was only the deaths of her loved ones
that had delayed the inevitable.

"I was restless and went out to walk," she said. Her voice
had a strength it had hitherto lacked. "Passing your garden
I heard you astir and turned in."

A frown crossed his brow as he considered the unlikeliness
of her having come to his cottage by chance. "'Tis unseemly
you should be here at this hour, Sarah. Should your father
look for you or any other happen by . . ."

Sarah stepped into the splotch of light where he stood. Her
pale hair was unbound and there was a purposeful look on
her face which gave him a clue to her thoughts. She smiled
slyly. Though Josiah might have wished for Glory Warren

in his bed, it was her virgin blood that had stained his sheets. She was not about to let that advantage go unused.

"My father is a sound sleeper," she said wryly. "And I do not think any others will be about at this hour."

Bellingham's body tensed as tightly as that of a man upon the rack. "What is it you want, Sarah, that could not wait until the light of day?"

"Only what I have had from you before," she answered boldly as she gently laid her hands on his chest.

"Nay," he said, feeling a sweep of weakness in his knees. Though it surged into his mind that he should pull away, he did not follow the thought with the act. "You must forget what happened. Purge it from your mind. It was never meant to be."

"I cannot believe that is the truth," Sarah returned. "Else you would not tremble beneath my hand."

His teeth gritted together. "I tremble for another reason."

Sarah's hands slid around his neck. Grimacing, he caught her small, fragile wrists, squeezing them so tightly Sarah had to bite her tongue to keep from crying out with the pain. She would have bruises, but they would heal like the ones he had given her before. And the pain was small compared to having her heart's desire.

Besides, he had inflicted a far greater pain when he did not ask her to wed. After he had defiled her, she had been sure he would seek out her father and ask for her hand. Days had flown by and still he had not come. Not even at the time of her mother's burial had he sought her out. But he would not get off so easily.

Her face hard-set with determination, Sarah again measured the plan in her mind. There was more than one way to catch a husband. She would see herself with child. Then let him hang back.

"I cannot think that a minister would lie so," she whispered. Unable to break his grip on her wrists, Sarah countered by pressing her slight form against him.

Bellingham knew a velvet trap when he saw it. "Stop! Stop, I tell you!" He spoke venomously, finding Sarah not the only foe at hand. His groin twisted with pain. His lust burst upon him like a sudden, raging storm.

Now Sarah trembled with uncertainty, remembering the pain of his last assault. Her will faltered and for one minute she hung limply against him, feeling his arousal grow hard against her belly. For a time she shook like a shivering pup, frightened of what she had unleashed. But from the cold grip of her fear she grasped at a thread. It would not hurt so much this time. The second coupling was never as bad as the first, or so Patience had told her after she wed Richard Doty.

Gritting her teeth, Sarah brought her hips to bear against him. If she must endure more abuse to have him, so be it. She wanted Josiah Bellingham.

Groaning in agony when he knew he had lost the battle with himself, Bellingham wrenched her arms to her back, holding them encased in his own against the swell of her buttocks, lifting her pelvis high against his burning hardness.

Whimpering, Sarah gave herself up to his cruelty. His punishing kiss bruised her mouth and nearly snapped her neck with the viciousness of the attack. When he ruthlessly slashed her lower lip with sharp, savage teeth she gasped and strangled on the taste of her own blood. Sarah choked back her cry though her ribs were straining to stay intact as he brutally crushed her against him.

"Josiah!" she cried, hoping to touch a tender chord.

He answered with an animalistic snarl as he whirled her about and hurled her against the hard trunk of a tree. As Bellingham lunged heavily against her, the craggy bark grated right through the sturdy homespun bodice she wore, scratching the skin from her back.

He had no inkling of her pain and no care that he inflicted it upon her. Like a male beast who had scented a female in heat, nothing could deter him from mating. He snatched his breeches open and with his mouth cruelly upon hers brought her hand around his pulsating erection. Sarah cried out in shock, repulsed by the heat and slippery wetness beneath her fingers. Bellingham groaned and his pelvis jerked as he yanked her skirts high. His hand shot between her thighs, forcing them wide apart.

With her hand still trapped upon him he urged the erect shaft to the gateway of her body and shoved the pillaging head inside. Not having been prepared as she might by any loving caress, Sarah shrieked and believed with all her heart that Patience Doty had deceived her.

Out of control, Bellingham slammed fully inside her, the force lifting the small girl to her toes. His body convulsed; he drove in and out of her; his mouth crushed suffocatingly over Sarah's to snuff out her screams. When he gained his release he snatched from her and like a man tormented fell to his knees, his hot brow held in his hands.

Sarah crumpled at the base of the tree, her back raw and burning and missing much of its skin; the space between her thighs felt similarly abused. She lifted the hem of her petticoat to her eyes to catch the flow of tears. More than all else she prayed he had gotten her with child. Surely then he would treat her tenderly.

Bellingham spoke softly though his mood was one of building anger. "I have it from a goodwife in the town that a maid as I described to her passed through less than a week ago."

"There could be no other like Glory Warren," the constable said to Bellingham. "None other with eyes of that shade." The men were saddle-weary and this was the first news to come to them that the trail they followed was the right one.

"The woman remarked on them," Bellingham said, stretching his legs as he allowed his horse to drink from a stream. "And that there was a crow which lighted on the girl's shoulder as she rode off. She thought it odd since just such a bird was said to frequent the witch women in Salem."

If Constable Gerrish had been a Catholic he would have crossed himself. Just what had he taken on when he agreed to chase a witch so bold that she rode through the center of a town with her familiar? And was it not so that this witch had more than one familiar, a cat and a snake besides the crow? Would she know he was the one who had killed the cat?

The constable shivered in the heat of the day and looked around at the forest which seemed to have come oppressively alive with sound. The treetops bent and dipped from the rush of an inexplicable northern wind. Had not the woman said the girl rode north? He looked to his companions, the minister and Constable Hubbard, and felt relieved. Neither man appeared unduly worried.

"How far to the next village?" Hubbard asked.

"A day's ride," Bellingham replied. Even his desire to find Glory had begun to diminish under the rigors of the trip. "And there is naught between Arkport and there but an Indian settlement and the hunting camp of a trapper called John Bayard."

"Is it likely our witch would go to one or the other?" Gerrish did not like the idea of stopping in either. Indians could not be trusted and trappers were not known for their hospitality to strangers.

"Who can say?" Bellingham responded. "But they may have seen the girl. We will inquire of both."

The Indian village offered no help. The savages had not seen Glory Warren, nor could they grasp the meaning of witchcraft and the threat it was to God-fearing men. What they could give was a guide to the camp of John Bayard. It was decided that Bellingham alone would accompany the Indian since the trapper was reputed to be a surly man and bad-tempered toward unwanted visitors. He was not likely to take kindly to the sudden appearance of three armed men.

On foot and with the Indian guide a few paces ahead, Bellingham followed through the forest, knowing a moment of doubt as the trees grew unbearably thick. Frequently he had to dodge a swinging limb set in motion by his guide. Was the Indian leading him astray to rob or murder him? His answer came quickly as the dark-skinned brave motioned for him to crouch on the edge of a thicket. If his eyes did not deceive him, a shelter of some sort lay ahead in the selfsame thicket and voices emanated from the crude dwelling.

There was the sound of two bodies moving together and then sighs of fulfillment. A while later came words that the seething minister could easily understand.

"Glory, love, I would rather stay with you than hunt with John."

"Nay, love," Glory replied sweetly. "It would be selfish of me to keep you at my side while we both accept John's generosity. Join the hunt. Go with him. Let us make a contribution to the man's larder for what we have imposed on him."

"'Tis right you are that he is generous to a fault. What other would have taken in two such as us?"

"None."

A sound of more stirring came from within the lean-to. Bellingham strained to see what movement caused it.

Glory shrieked. "Ouch," she complained, slapping her bare thigh.

"If you were not so hot-blooded, lass, the mosquitoes would not seek you out."

"Humph," Glory returned. "If that were so, you would be naught but a mass of welts."

Quade laughed. "A point well made."

"Aye. Now give me a kiss before you go."

Bellingham angrily sucked in his breath on hearing such playful banter and such a solicitous plea from the one who had so brutally rejected his affections.

"A kiss? Nay love. 'Tis much more than that I'll be needing to sustain me for a day away from you."

Glory laughed softly. "Again?"

"Again," he said lustily.

The sounds that followed set the minister's teeth on edge. He could easily distinguish Glory's cooing and Wylde's soft moans of pleasure. Had not the Indian guide thumped his shoulder and motioned him away from the camp, he might have rushed in. But the Indian's stony face helped restore reason to his blistering rage.

Wylde was leaving and the trapper Bayard with him. The camp would be vulnerable. He would return with the constables and take the girl prisoner. He had done his best to help her and had been spurned for his charitable efforts. The girl was a witch. Let her hang. If it was not meant that he should have her, then no man would.

A beaver pond broached the edge of the Bayard camp. Clemmie used the flat rocks for scrubbing clothes, and further down where the streambed kept the water moving, she filled jugs with water for cooking and drinking. Glory helped her carry the water needed for the day's activities, then returned to the pond with a bundle of her clothes sorely in need of washing.

With her shoes off and her skirts hitched through her legs and tucked into her waist, Glory squatted in the water, pounding her garments with a smooth rock. Nearby, Johnnie waded and waved a sharply pointed stick, waiting for a fish to appear, boasting to Glory that he would provide their supper rather than Quade and his father.

Both were taken by surprise when three riders galloped in, shouting and brandishing muskets. Glory whirled and shouted for Johnnie to run only to see but the smooth surface of the pond where the boy had been.

Having lost precious moments, she bolted and ran but the riders were upon her before she reached cover, two of them flanking her, a rope carried between them. In a blinding flash of pain she felt the rope grab and cut into her abdomen, sending her reeling to the ground. Before she had recovered her breath and could rise, the men had dismounted and had her in their grip.

"I arrest you, Glory Warren, on the charge of practicing witchcraft," said Hubbard. "Arggh!" he shouted and then gave way on one side as a sharp wooden projectile struck him in the calf.

Gerrish raised his musket and fired at the shimmering water of the beaver pond. "'Ere's a devil in it!" he ranted. "With my own eyes I saw it raise up and hurl a spear at Hubbard!"

"Johnnie!" Glory screamed, fearing for the boy's life. She was not given the opportunity to utter another word or to call for Clemmie. Gerrish roughly bound a handkerchief over her mouth and secured her hands with the rope that had brought her down.

"You'll not summon up another devil," Gerrish gasped, more concerned with assuring himself than her.

"Get her shoes and other clothes. She may have to walk part of the way," Bellingham, still astride his horse, ordered.

Hubbard, having examined his leg and found the wound hardly more than a scratch, did as the minister told him.

Glory, with silence forced on her, let her blazing eyes tell what she could not express with her lips—that of all people in the world she dreaded seeing, Josiah Bellingham topped her list. To her he said nothing, but with relish snapped out the orders concerning her treatment.

Shortly, she was hauled up on a pillion behind Hubbard, Gerrish being too afraid to share his horse with a witch. Besides, he told Bellingham, he would be much better at finding the trail. One of the men caught Paddy, who had flown to his mistress, and put the bird into a netting bag.

Two hours later the party passed through the village of Arkport. Glory hung her head. If the cruel, curious stares were a sign of what she could expect in Sealy Grove, she would fare even worse than she had believed when she fled.

Just out of Arkport, Hubbard removed her gag but by then she had nothing to say, believing her pleas and protestations of innocence would fall on deaf ears. She would save her words for the examination. For now all her energies were focused on thoughts of Quade and of Johnnie. Had the boy been wounded or killed? Her heart tore in two to think she had been responsible for either tragedy.

Quade and Bayard would be hours returning to the camp. And what could they do when they knew of her capture? They could never catch up. And Bellingham, if she knew

him as she thought she did, would take no chances on losing
his captive.

Her fears were borne out when the party reached Crossland
and bedded down for the night. Glory was given space in the
jail and overheard Bellingham directing the authorities on
where to find the man who had recently escaped confinement
in the very cell she now occupied.

CHAPTER
15

Paddy did not survive the journey to Sealy Grove. Stuffed within the netting bag and jostled against the side of the horse, the poor bird succumbed to the ill treatment. Gerrish burned the body.

"Fittin' for a witch's imp," he said, and pointed out to Hubbard that the devilish varmint had not lasted a day when denied the opportunity to suck from the witch. He stood by the fire until the last feather became ash. "'Tis the only way to be certain the creature's black soul 'as departed us."

Glory, heartbroken over the bird, wondered if she would fare better. The heavy shackles she had worn since leaving Crossland bruised and scraped her wrists, but no amount of pleading would convince the men to remove them.

"'Tis commonly known a bound witch has not full use of her powers," Hubbard explained.

Otherwise the men treated her with polite deference, Bellingham having warned the constables that an exceeding tenderness need be shown even an accused witch. Bellingham

306 / *Andrea Parnell*

himself kept a detached air for which Glory was grateful, but there was a look about him, a peculiar glint in his eye that gave her more than one shivery tremor along her spine. At length she realized that look which so unnerved her was strongest when Bellingham caught her glancing back over her shoulder in hopes of seeing Quade.

It was the talkative Gerrish who put an end to the episodes. "If you're lookin' for the trapper 'e won't be comin'," he said bluntly. "Constable Talbie of Crossland took a party out after 'im. By now 'e's coolin' 'is heels in the jail."

What little spirit Glory had left waned at Gerrish's words. Undoubtedly what he said was true. She had heard the men give Talbie the information. Quade would have been caught unawares as she had been. What chance did he have? Listlessly she clung to the saddle to keep her seat, but was too tired and disheartened to feel even anger as she noted a smirk cross Bellingham's face.

She must have slept, but came awake sharply amid the hisses and jeers of those in Sealy Grove who had kept a vigil for the return of the witch-hunting party.

"Look up! 'Tis Glory Warren!" came a rude cry. "Stand back 'ere she strike you with 'er witch's eyes."

Dragged into town bound like the fiercest of criminals, Glory mumbled a thanks for the cover of darkness which at least shielded her from the harsh stares of those responsible for the cries and clamor. When the constables hustled her into the jail she went willingly, hands clapped over her ears that she might escape the stinging taunts and jeers.

By morning the streets of Sealy Grove were again abuzz as people came and hung about the jail like bees at a hive. Fields were left untended, cows unmilked, and stew pots cold as all who could find the means rode in to confirm that the witch Glory Warren sat chained in the most secure cell. Only when the time of the hastily set hearing was announced did the dusty byways empty as most of those gathered hurried to the meetinghouse to claim the best seats.

Inside her cubicle, having been roused from sleep, Glory submitted most reluctantly to a search for a witchmark. In defiance of her objections, the appointed party of goodwives stripped her bare and, armed with pins to poke through any abnormality, began a minute examination of her person. One of them, Goody Elgar, an experienced hand since she had taken part in the examination of several accused witches in Salem Village, instructed the others.

"Look to the soft places, under the arm, between the legs, beneath the breasts," she said in a tinny voice. "For a reddening blemish or any strange protuberance of skin. 'Tis on the soft flesh they are most wont to give suck."

As if her statement gave the others divining power, a woman known as Gammer Pomry cried that she had found such a mark. "'Ere!" the wrinkled crone gloated over her find. "'Ere on the soft inside of 'er thigh. See it!"

Four pairs of hands descended on the red, raised spot, a harmless remnant of a mosquito's bite.

"'Tis but an insect's sting!" Glory pushed the women away and held her legs pressed defiantly together. To have one's body probed and poked down to the most intimate inch by a band of hostile women was humiliating enough, but to have them proclaim that they were about to push a pin through her flesh galled even more.

The women would not be dissuaded from their duty by the protests of a witch. Forcibly they held her legs asunder and Goody Elgar did what was necessary. She pricked the raised spot on Glory's thigh, slowly driving the point through until it emerged with a drop of blood a quarter inch away.

Glory refused to cry out. With her lips sealed she endured the torture, the only sign of her pain the twitch of a muscle beneath the site of the pin.

Goody Elgar, face grimly set, withdrew the tiny lance and with the same methodical slowness inserted it from another direction. That the girl did not cry out did not surprise her. Witches had no feeling in the nipples where they gave suck to their imps.

"'Tis a witch's teat," she pronounced, done with the abuse. "See it that you may give your testimony." When all had peered at that private part of her body, Glory gathered up her clothes and donned them in indignant haste, her pale eyes flashing her anger so fiercely that Gammer Pomry nervously called for the constable to hurry and release the examiners from the cell.

Properly garbed but primed with anger, Glory was led to the meetinghouse which had been converted to a courtroom for the preliminary hearing of the charges and evidence against her.

Sealy Grove rivaled Salem Village in turning out for the examination of a witch. If ever an event in the town had drawn more interest or provoked more comment, it was not remembered. The meetinghouse walls groaned to contain those packed together inside like salted fish in a barrel. Outside the open windows, latecomers grumbled at being kept out as they stretched and strained to see and hear the proceedings within.

Those on the grounds, however, were the first to see the magistrates, Fylar and Jones, ride in. The somber pair, assigned to conduct the examination, arrived with all the dignity and amid all the fanfare that might have been accorded a royal visitor.

Amid a respectful hush the two entered the meetinghouse

and seated themselves behind a long table which had been
brought in to serve as a judges' bench. They were resolved
to insure that the proceedings did not fall into the same chaos
as those they had observed in Salem.

Led by the constable, Glory came down the aisle and
mounted to the bar, her eyes raking the crowd for Quade,
hoping against hope that somehow he had eluded those who
sought him and managed to come to her. Though she searched
every face more than once, the trapper's was not among them.
It was then an unquenchable sense of grief overwhelmed her.
She had lost her mother and not been given time to mourn.
Was Quade lost to her too?

Eyes downcast, hands trembling, Glory took her seat. At
once it seemed as if she had left a wake of sound in her path.
Whispered voices rippled and gathered strength, the pitiless
words lashing at her like so many whips.

Those who stepped forward to give evidence were no
kinder as from forbidding faces they whispered among themselves in the box assigned to them. Only the fellmonger
Wharton and the Goodwife Rachel Leonard who sat apart
from the others recalled that Glory was a compassionate and
thoughtful girl, and like her mother ever heedful of the needs
of others.

A rap from the bench snapped her attention to the magistrates. Fylar, the stouter of the two, raised his head from
the notes before him. A grumbling came from his throat as
he cleared it. When he spoke it was in a forceful manner.
"Glory Warren of Sealy Grove is accused, by witchcraft, of
pinching and afflicting divers persons and of causing the
deaths of three persons, those three, Jane Cobb, the Goodwife
Collier, and her unbaptised child."

Fylar, with his seamed face, gave the accused a solemn
look, taking in the remarkable eyes that were much men-

tioned in the charges. To him it seemed the pale blue orbs, even in the bright morning light, glowed like a cat's eyes in darkness. The similarity troubled the magistrate as he considered the possibility of the girl changing forms within the courtroom.

If biased on the subject of witches, Fylar did not take his duty lightly; in fact, both he and Jones were committed to conducting the hearing fairly. Such was required when the accused had a formerly unblemished reputation.

His face mirroring the burden of his grim duty, Fylar addressed Glory, speaking loudly so that none in the assembly would fail to hear his question. "Are you an innocent person regarding this witchcraft?"

Glory sat primly, her hands folded in her lap. "I am not a witch nor have I ever done harm to any who speak against me."

Her gaze of innocence and entreaty swept over the gathering of people. That in itself triggered a rumble of speculative comments. Glory shuddered as the censorious mood of the people transmitted to her. Her troubled gaze flickered from person to person until it haplessly stuck on Josiah Bellingham who sat at a small table near the magistrates, copiously making notes on the proceedings. She was uncomfortably aware that frequently his eyes lifted from the paper and lingered reproachfully on her.

The anger that had started when the women stripped her began to be replaced by chilling fear as she searched the contentious sea of faces for one that was kindly disposed toward her. She found few—the staunchest, the faithful Rachel Leonard. At that she might have felt confident if she could have hoped for a dismissal of the charges. But that thin hope was dashed by reaction to the first testimony.

"Goody Elgar." Fylar turned his leathery countenance to the matron who had led the search for the devil's mark. "What evidence can you give concerning this woman's person?"

Goody Elgar, her expression showing the gravity of the matter entrusted to her, presented the magistrate with the document attesting to the witchmark and bearing her signature as well as the marks of Gammer Pomry and the other women.

The magistrate Jones, until now silent as he had been designated to keep records of the proceedings, donned his spectacles and read what was written. His grizzled head lifted slowly and his voice sounded with the ring of finality. "You have been found to bear the devil's mark, Glory Warren."

A chorused gasp came from the crowd as the whole of them hung on the edge of their seats for what the magistrate would say next. All knew, having gained a layman's expertise by following the proceedings in Salem, that a witchmark in itself was proof of guilt.

"'Tis but a whelp made by a mosquito," Glory snapped. Could rational men be misled so easily? "Any one of you might have it just as I do."

For little Ruthie Collier, who had survived her illness, Glory's denial triggered the bewildering fear Sarah had pounded into her mind. For days she had heard it said from morning to night that Glory Warren was to blame for the fever that had kept her bedridden for weeks, that the shape of Glory Warren had tormented her mother and baby brother. Her mind had given way to delusion and hallucination. A fly buzzing by her face became an imagined swarm of biting insects. Almost at once Ruthie fell thrashing and writhing to the floor, her hands slapping and waving, her voice shrilly calling out that she was stung all about her body.

The magistrate Jones half rose from his chair, his ruddy cheeks suddenly white. "Why do you afflict this child?" he demanded.

Glory's breath turned cold in her lungs as panic sifted into her blood.

"I do not!" she cried in dismay, sensing that no defense she offered would be as convincing as the antics of Ruthie Collier. Up until the moment the hearing had begun, she had held a hope that reason would prevail and learned men would yield to the power of intellect. Now she shrank in her chair, realizing the outcome was ordained long before she entered the courtroom.

"You send your devils to do it." No longer questioning, Jones's voice came booming back. "Is it not enough you have tormented a mother and one poor child to death and sent another to hell? Will you take this one's life too?"

For a moment she could not find her voice, then abruptly something about the hopelessness of her situation raised her ire. Her cheeks flamed red and her small chin lifted proudly. "I have tormented no one," she burst out. "I have no league with devils. Would you have me belie myself?"

The magistrate was unmoved. "Confess!" he roared.

Her wavering voice grew stronger and more defiant; her eyes flashed across the room like a pair of shooting stars. "I confess I am no more a witch than you are."

A shock wave of silence hit the crowd; Glory Warren was blatantly mocking the magistrate. The lull was brief. Out of the unnatural quiet, the clear, thin voice of Sarah Collier rose like an uplifted sword. "She lies! She is a witch. I saw her shape hover over my sister in her illness, then it hung about my mother's neck and sent her into an early labor."

"Sarah." Glory, her bravado crushed, spoke brokenly. "'Tis untrue. How can you say these things?"

Sarah slowly stood but kept her eyes steered to the magistrates, never turning them to look at the accused. "She did come again in her black form and smother the life from my mother's body."

Fylar's shoulders shook at the horror of what he heard. "Are you certain this is the woman?"

"Certain. Yes," Sarah answered in a flat tone as if she spoke out of a trance. "I saw her eyes burning like a night creature's and they did torture my infant brother until he was killed from it." Sarah paused, then added the most damning testimony of all. "Her shape spoke to me and boasted she would deliver the child's soul to the devil."

If a trial was needed after Sarah's deposition, it was solely as a formality to obtain a sentence to hang this witch who refused to confess in the face of incontestable evidence. Of that the magistrate Jones was convinced. He briefly put his head to Fylar's, then addressed Glory. "It is our determination," he announced, having instructed the constable to bring the still-murmuring crowd to order, "that the devil cannot assume the shape of an innocent person in doing mischief to mankind." The pen still rested in his hand. He pointed it at Glory. "You, Glory Warren, will be tried two weeks hence," he said, and brought the hearing to an abrupt end.

In Essex County and Salem the afflicted girls drew a never-ending line of gawkers. In Sealy Grove, quite the opposite occurred. The witch herself drew the curious in throngs. And though it was claimed that chains diminished a witch's powers, fully one-half of those who came to stare at Glory Warren swore they were pinched or choked by her mercurial shape. But the chains must have had some effect. Both Mary Douglass and Abigail Allyn recovered after Glory was confined, each girl confessing under lengthy questioning that she had been ridden by the shape of the witch while the fever was upon her.

These additional charges against the sorceress were entered into the records daily by the ordinary, as well as others offered by persons harassed in their homes or in fields or wherever the fiendish witch could find them. Joseph Allyn, convinced he had been among the first to observe Glory Warren at her witch's work, achieved some fame when his taunting rhyme was printed and spread throughout the colony.

Glory, whose pleas to be left alone fell on deaf ears, languished in the hot, moldy cell with the burdensome manacles gnawing at her ankles and wrists. Finding no other reprieve for her misery, she gave herself up to thoughts of Quade and to the heartening belief that he would yet come and save her from this mockery of justice.

Having been given a scant hour of privacy that she might attend her personal needs, Glory's hopes leaped when she heard a heavy footfall at the end of that interlude. Quade, her heart cried. But it was the hawklike stare of Josiah Bellingham that greeted her.

The long ride from Bayard's camp had served to salve the minister's rage at finding Glory with Quade Wylde. Convinced she had not acted of her own accord, he was prepared to pardon the transgression; somehow it seemed to equal his own. He had expected her to confess her guilt in the hearing, but since she had not it was left to him to help her exorcise the devils that possessed her. It had come to him only the night before that the very notoriety of a reformed witch as his wife might serve him well if the credit for her deliverance was his.

He spoke a word to the constable to insure they would not be disturbed. The man nodded and let him into her cell.

"You dare come here?" Glory backed to the farthest corner; she did not trust him without Gerrish and Hubbard to intervene. "You are more a devil than any," she said hotly. "You hide under the guise of piety. You preach it to others and do not practice it yourself."

"Stay your temper, Glory," Bellingham said in his mellowest tone. "'Tis not you who speaks."

"'Tis I and no other," she snapped.

"Nay." Having wrestled a long while with himself to understand how his spirit had been tumbled from the epitome of grace to the low depths it now occupied, Bellingham refused to be dissuaded. "Listen to me, Glory. I have made a study of diabolism. I understand how it is with you. 'Tis clear enough you are possessed of a devil without knowing it."

"I am as I have always been," she refuted him.

"Nay, you are a devil's pawn, possessed of wickedness and guilty of offenses against decency."

"And are you not?"

Bellingham shook his head. He had hoped the girl would listen to reason, but now he could see she was less in control of herself than he had believed. Her devils were strong. Already they reached out to him, tempting his flesh, making him want her enough to risk taking her in this public place.

He drew a labored breath. "Can you not see it, Glory? 'Tis your wickedness which infects me. 'Tis your devils which caused me to do that which was profane." Keeping his voice calm, he gestured for her to leave the corner and be seated on the three-legged stool near the foot of the cot.

Since he had made no move toward her and as there was no retreat from the cell, Glory did as bidden, though not without keeping a wary eye on the minister. "If there is a devil in you 'tis yours alone," she said.

Again he shook his head. He might not convince her with ease, but convince her he would. Bellingham, since birth steeped in righteousness, found it impossible to live with the guilt of the terrible acts he had been a part of in recent weeks. His mind, with no room for admission of error, slipped in and out of dementia rather than facing those deeds. But through much prayer and meditation he had found the way to save himself, and it was tied to Glory Warren.

Glory shuddered when Bellingham came to stand beside her. There was a fevered look about him. He was not, she observed, the same man she had fought and fled. This Bellingham had a zealous gleam in his eye and instead of an attack, offered a prayer of supplication in her behalf.

"I forgive you, Glory Warren," he said when he lifted his head.

"You forgive me?" She gave him a wondering look and lifted her shackled arms. "'Tis you who have put me in chains."

Bellingham knelt beside her, but too close. His blood was at once aflame with desire for the girl who had scorned him. His troubled mind was quick to supply a reason. Was this not proof she was a seductress, that she exercised an evil pull on him? His voice cracked. "'Tis I who can save you, Glory. Confess to me. Denounce your devils."

Her eyes grew stormy. "I denounce yours. I have none."

He dropped a hand upon her knee. She shrugged it away but he didn't seem to notice. "Try to understand," he whispered. "All this is a devil's plot designed to keep me from attaining the heights I am meant to have. 'Tis Satan's work but it need not succeed. I have a plan which will defeat him. Help me. Admit you are a witch, Glory."

Bellingham grasped her hands and held them tightly. In her rested his redemption. If she admitted to being a witch, if he could lead her back into the fold, he could be absolved of his guilt.

"Nay!" she said, and tried to snatch her hands from him but could not. "'Tis not true! I will never admit it!"

Her refusal was too much for Bellingham. The veneer of calm he had managed to maintain since entering her cell shattered and fell away. His arms shot around her waist. His head dropped into her lap. "Do it," he cried. "'Tis not too late."

Glory's efforts to get away sent the stool toppling and both of them sprawling on the floor at the moment Sarah Collier, who had slipped past the constable, peered in.

Bellingham pinned Glory down. "We can be wed. All can be as it was meant to be."

Neither he nor Glory heard Sarah's horrified wail or the sound of her footsteps as she ran off.

"Take your hands from me, Josiah Bellingham!" Glory's tone was hard, her eyes ablaze. "Though the devil take me or the hangman's rope claim me, I will never admit to being a witch. As for you," she spat out, "a like fate is preferable to being wed to such a wretch of a man."

Bellingham pushed up to his knees, then rose to his feet. The veins in his throat throbbed convulsively. "You prefer that trapper to me?"

Glory quickly scrambled upright and attempted to straighten her clothes. Though disheveled she held her head high. "I love Quade Wylde. I will wed him and no other."

"Then you will wed no one," Bellingham hissed. "The trapper is dead. The word came from Crossland a day ago." He went on, exhilarated by the look of horror on her face. "The man put up a fight when the constable tried to take him. Talbie was forced to fire to protect himself. Quade Wylde is molting to dust by now."

"You lie," Glory trembled.

"'Tis true. Confirm it with Gerrish if you doubt me." His face was shadowed with rage but he kept it in check as he went on. "Mayhap *now* you regret the hasty refusal of my offer?"

"Nay. Never," Glory responded, though her voice had lost its venom.

Bellingham's eyes became frighteningly menacing. "Then you have sealed your fate." Turning away, he gave a shout loud enough to bring the constable running. "Get me away from this witch," he said, then spun about to leer at her one more time, the last of his love for Glory Warren having turned to bitter hate. She was beyond him, beyond help, but at last all his guilt was gone and he had a firm purpose—to see the witch hang.

Sarah's ears rang with the fast coursing of her blood as she stood on the commons until she saw Josiah Bellingham walk past. For once she did not wish to be noticed by the handsome minister. When he was gone she gathered her skirts and hurried along the path he had come, entering the jail for the second time. With a minimum of persuasion since she was a chief witness against the witch, she convinced the jailer she must have a private interview with Glory.

Glory lay upon the cot, her face covered with her hands. Had Bellingham lied to spite her or was what he said of Quade true? Rachel might know, or Gerrish could tell her when he came again. Though it was doubtful any other could have stirred Glory from her gloomy thoughts at that moment, when Sarah entered and spoke her name, she lifted her head, very much astonished to see who her visitor was.

Sarah hung back at the door where the light was dim, but

her voice came strong and demanding across the cell. "Let him be," she said.

Glory sat up. "Who? Do you accuse me of bedeviling another? What madness is this of yours, Sarah? You know I am not a witch!"

"I know the opposite is true." Sarah slid along the wall that she might have a better view of the girl she had once called friend. "I gave you my trust and you betrayed me."

Glory pushed her tangled hair from her face. "This is nonsense, Sarah. 'Tis you who have betrayed me."

But Sarah could not be reached. "Why do you hate me?" she whispered. "Why do you take all that is dear to me?"

Many times since the hearing Glory had thought she would like to tear Sarah apart for the wrong she had done. But now her anger was burned out and she had only pity for her accuser.

"Sarah. Sarah. I understand," she said gently. "You must remember my mother is dead too." Her heart went out to the lamentable girl who stood cringing at the wall. Quickly on her feet, Glory started toward Sarah but stopped when she saw the closed look on her face.

Sarah's pale brows rose sharply. "What does a witch care about that?"

Glory's hands fell limply to her sides. "How could I know?" she mumbled. "I am a woman just as you are."

"Nay," Sarah said. "Not such as I am or you would not bewitch a man away from another."

Glory, still drained from her ordeal with Bellingham, had ceased to listen and turned back to her cot. Sarah was as irrational as the minister and she lacked the strength for another fight. "Go, Sarah," she said tiredly. "Leave me."

320 / *Andrea Parnell*

It seemed Sarah gained strength from Glory's loss of it. "Nay," she said boldly. "Not until you promise to release Josiah."

A few moments passed before the meaning of Sarah's words sunk in. Glory whirled about and stared incredulously, recalling the mysterious man Sarah had professed to love but would not name. "Bellingham? He is the one you wish to wed?"

Sarah scowled. "Do not play the innocent. But for your wicked interference we would be wed by now."

Glory shook her head in disbelief; Sarah had turned against her because of Josiah Bellingham. It was the cruelest of ironies. "Nay," she said ruefully. "I have not wanted his attentions."

Sarah's pinched face had a cold look, her voice a sharp edge. "Then you admit you deliberately bewitched Josiah to keep him from me?"

Glory, feeling more dismal than when Sarah had arrived, crawled upon her cot and pulled the thin covering up to her shoulders. "Believe what you will," she murmured.

Nothing she said had the intended effect on Sarah. The meaning of every word was twisted, every sentiment misread. As if the life had already been let out of her, she abruptly found she no longer cared what happened to her. If Quade was dead she had little enough to live for.

Sarah straightened her spine and lifted her voice. "I believe you are a witch," she said. "And if I must hasten you to the gallows to have Josiah free of your spell, I will do what I must."

"Go, Sarah," came the soft reply.

Glory did not rouse from her cot all the day long, although droves came and peered in at her and were mostly disappointed not to get a look from the witch's eyes. That she was unresponsive did not mean her audience was the same. Three persons fell into fits and had to be carried from the hallway. Another tripped over a doorstop and swore a black cat with blazing blue eyes had run beneath his feet.

None of this brought a stir from the prisoner. Only for Rachel Leonard, who daily brought food and fresh linens, did Glory become animated. This was the one person she could trust to tell her the truth.

"Is it fact?" Glory cried almost before the door was shut. She clasped Rachel's hands with a desperation that wounded the older woman's heart. "Is Quade dead?"

Rachel's face had grim lines as she nudged Glory from the bed and hurriedly stripped off the sheets, delaying her answer for as long as she could. "'Tis the report that has come from Crossland," she said. "Wharton was told that when the men tried to take the trapper he knocked one of them from his horse and leaped astride it. Another sought to pull him from the saddle and got his arm broke. After that Quade rode at Talbie who stood in his way. The constable fired."

"He would have come for me." Glory slumped atop the freshly made cot, blaming herself for Quade's death. "Where have they taken him?"

"Nowhere, it seems." Rachel sat beside Glory and, with arms wrapped around her, tried to console the girl. "The horse ran off with him hung in the saddle. Near nightfall the animal was found covered with blood."

"Then Quade could yet live," Glory cried, her eyes over-bright.

"No, love," Rachel said gently. "There was such a store of blood on the horse and saddle that no man could live having lost that much. He is dead and his body lost in the forest."

Beneath Rachel's arms Glory's body went limp. She eased the girl down.

"'Tis where he would want to be," Glory whispered. "I'm glad they could not find him."

Rachel stayed as long as she was allowed, knowing that as things stood Glory would most assuredly be sentenced to hang in a few days' time. Though she feared what the answer would be, when she heard the jailer coming, she found she could not leave without making a plea.

"Glory, consider this," she said. "'Tis your life you trade with in the courtroom. Do not give it to these unmerciful men who sit in judgment behind a bench. You need only tell them 'tis true. No confessing witch has been hanged."

"I cannot," Glory said. "Not even now. I cannot belie myself though it cost me my life. If they will shed innocent blood let it be on their consciences."

"You will hang!"

"Aye. If I must," she said apathetically. "But does it matter so much. I have lost all I love, all I wished to live for."

Rachel pleaded with her. "Nay, Glory. Do not speak this way. Your mother would want you to live. Would not Quade want the same?"

Glory nodded. "He would want me to live."

"Then say you are a witch. 'Tis all it takes."

"I cannot," Glory repeated. "If I live it must be with the truth. I will trust God to bring me His justice and deliver me from those who act in ignorance of His will."

Rachel had no rebuttal to faith in God. Bidding Glory a good night and pledging to pray for her delivery, she left the jail.

CHAPTER
16

Rain buffeted the meetinghouse, the slashing drops falling with a ferocity that was uncommon in Sealy Grove. Quite a few reflected that the stormy weather was a sign of God's displeasure at finding witches inhabiting his land. Others were as sure the downpour signaled the displeasure of a darker power that one who served him was found out. What was agreed upon was that neither raging rain nor sky-cracking thunder stopped anyone from attending the trial of Sealy Grove's brazen witch.

The cheerless room was packed tighter than before; those who had braved the rain to travel did not wish to stand in it. Many persons from far off had passed the night in Sealy Grove that they could be on hand when the proceedings began. Among those who had taken lodgings in rooms above the tavern was the trapper John Bayard. He was among the first to take a seat in the meetinghouse and chose a bench near the accused's chair.

Glory spotted him almost as soon as she was brought in. "John," she whispered hopefully, pausing as she passed by.

The trapper's face was immobile, his eyes averted. Her expression, which had peaked with the brief joy of recognition, fell to the blankness of despair when he made no response to her wistful attempt at a smile. She had the dread thought that Bayard blamed her for whatever harm had befallen his son, as well he should. It was likely he too had come to testify against her.

The constable, impatient at her lagging approach to the bar, tugged at her elbow until she moved on and took her seat before the assembly. Her blue eyes, so featured in the charges against her, were disappointingly lackluster. Rachel was the first to note that the girl who had sat proud and straight at the hearing drooped in her chair as if she had given up the fight now that she was brought to trial.

The same could not be said of the magistrates. They approached this new duty with all the vigor they had brought to the old. The difference between the trial and the hearing was the seating of a jury and the addition of a third jurist on the bench; otherwise an observer would have been pressed to find a distinction.

Testimony given at the hearing was presented as evidence. Much of the morning was spent hearing the charges taken down by the ordinary in the interim. By noon the crowd began to weary of the proceedings. The ordinary's tedious voice lacked the drama of a Sarah Collier standing up and in person delivering a shocking charge.

They were not disappointed for long. Goody Cobb testified that her daughter had once, in the midst of her suffering, called Glory Warren's name.

"I did not know then as I know now it was because the

witch hovered over her bed and would not allow Jane to fight off her sickness,'' stated the bereaved Goody Cobb.

"I saw her with the four who took sick,'' claimed Francis Stevens. "Joseph Allyn and I did.''

On the heels of those two, Prudence Oliver, as malleable in Sarah's hands as little Ruthie had been, knew beyond a doubt that the witch hated her for having stolen Sarah's friendship. When her name was called for having cried out against Glory Warren, all her fears of diabolical retaliation came to a head. Prudence hurled herself to the floor and in a shadow play that awed the crowd fought off the ominous shape of Glory Warren.

"'Tis a great black bird,'' she wailed, covering her face, then her neck to void off the invisible attack.

The third magistrate, a man called Dickenson, whom Glory had hoped was possessed of a more sober mind than the other two, aimed a bony finger at her.

"Relieve the girl!'' he shouted.

Unconsciously, Glory pressed her hands to her heart. "I cannot relieve her. I do not afflict her.''

She spoke with cool, forced calm and in so doing added to the weight against her. Would not an innocent person despair of seeing another in sore distress?

"Touch her,'' Dickenson ordered. "If it stays her fit then you prove your guilt.''

The constables brought the aggrieved girl forward, being careful that her head did not roll in a way that she would look on the witch and be more sorely affected. One of them held Glory's hand forth and laid it upon Prudence's trembling hand. Immediately the girl shook and moaned as if coming out of a daze. Miraculously restored to calm, Prudence was led to her seat and troubled the assembly no more.

"Can you now deny you are a witch?" the magistrate demanded.

"I deny it," Glory said, some of the old defiance finding its way into her voice. "I deny there is even one witch in this land."

Her blasphemous retort brought Dickenson to his feet, and but for the prompting of Fylar and Jones he might have charged the jury at that moment. Jones, however, insisted one last person be permitted to give his testimony since he was one who had special insight into matters of witchcraft.

Josiah Bellingham came forward.

"This woman is a witch," he said. No novice to the workings of minds, he aimed his words at the jury lest any one of them still doubt the truth. "She came to me fully a dozen times," he swore. "A beautiful Circe who cast a spell upon me and quite broke my senses." He looked aside to the magistrates.

"A Circe you say?" asked Jones, no reader of classics.

"Aye," Bellingham humbly nodded. "A creature who changes forms. She came to me once like a big black cat whose eyes were live, dancing flames and did wrestle with me on my bed, her long claws flailing the hide from my back."

"You resisted?"

"Aye." Bellingham straightened, his back taut as a bow-string. "And rendered her furious," he revealed. "Afterwards she did then torment me nightly, sometimes in her own form, sometimes in the form of a huge, black-feathered bird, but in place of a beak it had her own face."

The magistrates' eyes widened in amazement. "You never yielded to her?"

"Nay," Bellingham said. "Never. Though once she came and snatched me from my bed and hauled me to a witches' sabbath. There I learned her dark purpose. If she could deliver Josiah Bellingham, a man of God, to the devil, she could be made queen of the witches."

"Why, sir, have you not told this before?" Fylar inquired.

Bellingham shook his head sadly. "When I tried, she put a spell on me. Only now that she is chained and her power diminished am I able to tell what has occurred."

In his best form, Bellingham turned back to the juried men. "That is not the worst of it," he said. "The mother was a witch as well."

Glory lunged to her feet. "You are a liar! 'Tis all a lie!" she shouted, and would have flung herself on the minister had not the constables wrestled her back to her chair and held her there.

Bellingham charged on. "Take heed of my words," he said. "In death Goody Warren lay upon the floor in a saintly pose." He folded his hands to emphasize the point. "But she was a witch! God smote the mother for her sins." A sweep of his hands encompassed the assembly. "Let us do no less to this wicked child of a sorceress."

"Liar! You defile my mother's name!" Glory cried, the flashing eyes now as bright and dazzling as they were reputed to be. "You—" Her throat closed up and her heart turned over in her chest. Bellingham had not seen her mother at the foot of the stairs. He had not come until later, long after Maudie Lair Warren had been moved. "You were there." She spoke in a low murmur only to herself, but then her voice rose loud and accusing. "You were there when my mother died!"

Bellingham displayed but a flicker of alarm. He was too caught up in his travesty to be undone by the allegations of a witch. His head rocked slowly from side to side as if he pitied the poor possessed creature who spoke out against him.

"She would see me to her purpose yet," he petitioned the crowd.

To silence her cries the magistrate ordered a gag tied over Glory's mouth. Elated, Bellingham left the stand, convinced he had done his duty and absolved his soul of all sins.

With a flourish added to the last word of Bellingham's statement, Jones put aside his pen. The magistrates conferred but briefly before Dickenson charged the jury with finding a verdict. That small body no sooner left the courtroom than they returned.

"Guilty!" The magistrate's voice bounded off every wall and echoed from every pair of lips.

Dickenson silenced the assembly with a rap on the table. His duty as he saw it was to rid Sealy Grove of the convicted witch as quickly as possible. He ordered the gag removed from the girl, then rose to give the sentence.

"Glory Warren," began his solemn pronouncement, "for your sins of witchcraft and for your hardheartedness in refusing to recant those sins, you are hereby sentenced to hang on Gallows Hill. Let the hour be dawn that your blighted soul not plague us another day."

Glory stood slowly. The clatter of the crowd stopped when she gained her feet. Everyone wanted to hear the last words of a witch. Would she repent now at this late hour? She did not.

"My soul belongs to God," she said. "My blood is on your hands. As for those who have belied me, God will give them their reward in misery." A trick of the light made her eyes appear as a flash of silver, an impression long to be remembered. "Whose conscience will forgive the shedding of innocent blood?" she asked.

* * *

She was not afraid to die.

She told that to Rachel. Oddly, she felt no hatred for those who had judged and condemned her, not even for Josiah Bellingham. His sins would torment him. She had seen evidence of his self-inflicted anguish. He would have far less peace than she anticipated. He feared living. She was not afraid to die.

But life, she found, mattered enough that she refused to yield the last few precious hours left to sleep. She would use them to remember the happy events in her life: times with her father, his face, his laugh, his love; cooking meals with her mother, her mother's compassion, her spirit which never flagged; Tansy chasing her skirts; Paddy nibbling corn from her hand; and Quade holding her, teasing her, loving her, teaching her all the ways a man and woman could care for one another.

She had been a child, a maid, a woman. She had been loved, steeped in love every day she lived. Even if her life was to be short, she had missed but one experience, that of bearing a child to the man she loved. Even for that loss she refused to be sad. She had enough memories to fill a lifetime. From somewhere she found the courage to smile. How could she get through them in only one night?

She could not. But those memories she savored and relived were enough to instill her with the strength and serenity needed to face death. If she faltered once, it was when Rachel touched her hand as she was led from the jail in the blackness and chill before dawn.

The crowd was quiet, subdued by the darkness, perhaps by the burden of what they had begun. Glory was glad they had not found their voices as the constable loaded her into a cart. Pulled by a dappled horse the cart led the ascent up

Gallows Hill. The witch Glory Warren stood at the rail, her eyes casting back the light of the torches held by those who ventured for a close look at her.

At the crest of the hill the sheriff halted the battered cart beneath a spreading limb and bestowed on Constable Gerrish the chore of keeping the horse steady as he fastened a length of rope around the girl's neck. The dappled gelding was an old hand at hangings and far less nervous than the constable who held his reins. The dappled animal would stand like a statue unless a whip flicked. At that signal he knew to surge forward until the weight was lifted from the bed of the cart. It was not the gelding's fault that today one wheel lodged between two rocks and, as the sun inched above the horizon, the cart held fast when the signal came.

"'Tis the devil's work," Gerrish reflected, looking nervously about as he urged the horse to move. "He tries to save his disciple."

That was the sentiment of the crowd, who, though not close enough to distinguish the jammed wheel, saw the whip raised over the gelding's back. The horse strained, the cart rocked, but the wheel held fast. What could it be but the devil's work?

In a fine state of fright at having Satan so defiantly at hand, the throng parted quickly before a pair of galloping horses racing up the hill.

"Hurry, man!" shouted one of the riders.

His words were heard only by his companion. Such shrieking and bellowing started from the crowd that no one else could hear above it. Here they had come out to witness the hanging of a witch and were beset by two grizzled beasts of hell.

Monstrous creatures astride wild-eyed horses reached the top of Gallows Hill. One of them gave out such a hideous roar that those who had not fallen to the ground and covered their faces flew down the slope raising such a ruckus that the dappled gelding lunged in fear and jolted the cart wheel free of the rocks hindering it. Without driver or passenger, the horse bolted on, and with the empty cart rattling after him sped down the embankment toward the safety of town.

The sheriff and constable followed not far behind. Their duty to hang the witch did not include facing demons who rode and spoke like men.

Glory felt the cart lurch from beneath her feet and fully expected the next sound she heard to be the snapping of her neck. It was not to be. Some beast mounted on a snorting horse caught her before the slack gave out. Lifted as if on wings, she was settled across the beast's lap while the strange creature produced a flashing blade and cut the choking coils from her throat.

Glory, her fabled eyes wide with disbelief, looped her bound hands over the creature's neck and gasped in mouthfuls of refreshing air.

"You have got yourself in quite a fix, Glory Warren," the furry beast whispered.

A second later the horse was in a run, though none of those persons still on the hillside had the presence of mind to give chase. Soon the second beastly rider followed the first, presenting a sight that those who had witnessed it would not forget all the days of their lives. Most swore the horses' hooves struck fire as they rode off; all claimed the witch Glory Warren had survived a hanging they beheld with their own eyes, and then, yet alive, rode off in the arms of a dreadful beast.

Miles from Gallows Hill the horse slowed to a walk. Glory Warren pushed back a long bear's snout and revealed the lean, handsome face of Quade Wylde.

"I thought you dead," she whispered. "I was told you were shot."

"Aye, so I was," Quade acknowledged. "A shoulder wound not yet fully healed. But dead, nay. That I will prove to you later," he promised.

"But the blood on the saddle," Glory persisted. "Rachel heard . . ."

"A trick, love," he explained. "A trapper's ruse. I killed a deer and marked the horse so they would not look for me. John was not fooled," Quade went on. "When it was safe to search he found me and took me back to his camp." He cocked his head and gave her a bemused look. "Do you think a bungling constable could best me in the forest? Or John?"

"Nay. Nor anywhere else. I saw John in the courtroom. I thought he had come because of Johnnie. I thought he blamed me. How is the boy?"

"As ever. He's as wily as his father."

Glory smiled, at last understanding it all. "You sent John to look out for me, did you not?"

"Aye," he said. "I could not show my face near Sealy Grove and I did not know how you would plead, though I guessed right. You are a stubborn wench, Glory Warren."

"When I am right."

"If you should come to a like fate again, please remember I have a claim on that neck as well as you." He ran his fingers along the reddish lines marring the silky skin at her throat. "I prefer it the length it is."

"Then I will endeavor to keep it so."

"See that you do. John and I did not think they would send you to the gallows so soon. He scarcely had time to ride for me. I dare not think what would have happened had we been a minute later."

Glory shuddered, recalling the feel of the hemp around her neck.

"I love you, Quade Wylde," she whispered, touching his shoulder gently, recalling she was not the only one who had suffered. "How is your wound? I can make an ointment that will heal—"

"A witch's potion?" he teased.

Glory gave him a warning glance. "Do not use that word of me or I will show you worse than a witch's spell."

The dark brows lifted high. "That I sincerely hope," he said.

"'Tis a promise then." Her arms went around his furry back. She kissed him a long, deep, drugging kiss that might have gone on indefinitely had not the beast suddenly beside them roared.

"Give a man a hand," he cried. "Clemmie has sewn me into this skin so tightly I will become a bear in truth if I am not cut free this minute."

"John!" Glory cried as Quade flicked his knife through the sinewy threads holding the bearskin bound together across Bayard's broad chest. He shoved the hoary, long-fanged snout aside and, with the cut begun, ripped the remaining stitches apart. After divesting himself of the suffocating skin, Bayard took Glory on his lap while Quade shed his beastly costume.

"Well, girl," said the burly trapper, giving Glory a strong and affectionate hug, "you are the first witch to fly from the gallows."

"I am not a witch," Glory said softly, having endured much to prove the point.

Bayard shook his red head. "Ahh, girl." He handed her back to Quade. "I'm sorry to say that after today you are a witch for all time. You will not be forgot in this lifetime or

the next. The grandchildren of those who watched on Gallows
Hill will speak of the witch Glory Warren.''

"Let them," Glory professed, wrapping her arms tightly
around Quade's waist. "Only let me be a woman and let me
have the man I love.''

Quade's arms held her in a tender, loving embrace. His
mouth came down to cover her lips. Bayard discreetly rode
a ways ahead.

"Let me have the woman I love," he whispered, nuzzling
her soft cheek. "And I swear by all that is holy that when
she is snowy-haired as a high mountain peak, I will still not
let her out of my sight.''

EPILOGUE

1697

Her eyes dark-circled, her hands cracked and sore from scrubbing clothes, Sarah Bellingham decreed she would not leave her house on August thirtieth. The day was an anniversary of sorts, the day a witch was to be hanged in Sealy Grove. For Sarah the talk in the streets would be too painful to endure. She did not wish to hear her name bantered about with that of Glory Warren. But talk there would be until every detail of that day had been repeated and embellished for those few who had not been present. Five years following the date of the event, the townspeople were evenly divided as to whether God or the devil had delivered Glory Warren from the gallows.

Sarah no longer cared. Only a few weeks after Glory Warren's disappearance, the last witch had been hung in Massachusetts and then the jails were opened and those awaiting trial released to return to their families. The gale of irrationality concerning witchcraft had ended, but not without leaving a rent in the hearts of the people that was not yet healed. Whether the episode had been a true purging of evil or a horrendous misapplication of mad logic, Sarah could not say. Either way she had been cursed for her part in the proceedings.

She looked about her. On a dusty shelf lay her husband's ever-growing stack of unpublished tracts. Near the door a bulging basket of soiled laundry awaited her attention. It would have to wait. Her husband's needs came before all else. He never failed to make that clear.

Sarah pulled a stool near the fire that she might watch the simmering stew as she worked at other tasks. With her sewing basket at hand she picked up the garment awaiting her needle and shortly put a stitch in the frayed seam of her husband's threadbare doublet.

"Sarah!" Josiah Bellingham roared as he came in and snapped the door shut behind him. "Get up and attend to this." He jerked off his doublet and tossed it to her. The garment reeked with the smell of a rotted tomato. "That brat of Wharton's clouted me with a piece of spoiled fruit. Me! I'll have him strapped in the square. Where is my other doublet?"

"Do you dare complain against one of Wharton's brood? 'Tis said he has the governor's ear since that fur-trading business of his has made him the wealthiest man in the colony."

Bellingham's face reddened as he considered what his wife said. "How a man such as Wharton has excelled is beyond reasonable comprehension. He finds markets no other thinks of."

"He has a partner in London, I have heard."

"Then that is the cause. Wharton has not the brains to fill his pipe."

"Still he has gained wealth," Sarah said meekly.

"What is wealth against a good mind?" Bellingham demanded as he paced about the room. "I would not trade a fortune for what I know above other men. Suffering is what builds up treasures in heaven, Sarah."

"Then we shall have a palace there," Sarah said under her breath.

Bellingham would not have heard had she spoken at a normal level. Having slipped on his best doublet and taken a look at it, he went into a rage. "Can you do no better than this? Where is your famed skill with a needle? I am no better than a beggar in this rag! Do you think I can present myself for a new charge in a tattered doublet?"

"Nay," Sarah said. "Still it is the best I can do until I weave new cloth and I cannot begin that until I have done the washing that waits." This year the congregation had neglected to pay Bellingham's salary; was it not for the little she earned taking in laundry she wondered how they would eat.

Bellingham was much maligned in Sealy Grove. Among the elders only her father still supported his ministry. Those who yet believed in witches thought him weak in spirit to have been afflicted. Those who believed as the authorities had come to—that many innocent persons had been accused and condemned—held Reverend Bellingham in no better light for his part in the proceedings against Glory Warren.

Bellingham kicked the laundry-laden basket, spilling some of the contents on the floor. "I detest that you are washing for Thomas Leonard's family. Can you not find another to serve?"

Sarah scooped up the linens and shirts and replaced them in the basket. "She is the only goodwife who does not do her own or have servants to do it, excepting Goody Wharton, and you would be no more pleased with that. 'Tis strange,"

Sarah mused as she removed the basket from the path of her husband's pacing. "Like the Whartons the Leonard family has prospered in past years."

"Who would not prosper owning the Warren farm? How Leonard came to get it bears looking into." Sarah's face clouded and Bellingham realized he had spoken the name both had sworn would never pass their lips. "I'm going out!" he roared. "Do not be late with supper."

Sarah went back to her stool. The children were waking from their naps. From the cottage window she could see the big house Isaac Hawkins had built on the hill. He had wanted to marry her but she had put him off to have Josiah. He was another who had done well. Who would have thought it? Sarah wondered, as she did in such moments, what her life might have been like in a big house full of servants instead of a cramped cottage full of children. Well, there was that to be grateful for. At least now that two of the babies shared their bed, Josiah did not abuse her so much.

One of the three little ones playing at her knee—those surviving of the five born to her—tugged at her skirts. "Listen, Mama," she said, turning her hazel eyes upward and reciting a line she had heard from a neighbor's child. "Oo's the one with witch's eyes?"

"Hush, Charity," Sarah said crossly as she stirred the pot of stew. But she could not help wondering as did most in Sealy Grove if Glory Warren was still alive.

Beneath a gilded canopy in an English country house and amid a tangle of silk sheets Quade Wylde parted a pair of satiny thighs and slid his questing manhood into the soft woman's well of his wife's body.

"'Tis better than ever with you, Glory, love," he whispered as his kisses fell upon her mouth with warm hunger, his tongue darting inside the soft, sweet interior. "And the babe has but made you more beautiful than before."

Glory gave a cry of breathless joy as his lips plied her ear with loving words. "Aye, my lusty love. 'Tis better than can be believed with us." She moaned softly as he made a slow move within her. "Could any other pair feel as we do?"

"Nay," he said, his slow thrusts gaining speed. "This pleasure is ours alone."

She could well believe it. The fire in her eyes blazed back at her from his dark pupils. She felt him surge within her and then it was as if he had turned to flame, devouring her within and without, the joy of it almost unbearable. She whispered his name, feeling his heart beat savagely against her naked breasts as she lifted her hips to meet each drumming thrust.

Sated, Glory lay back against the pillows, counting all the joys in her life, recalling she had done the same on a night five years ago. She had been grateful then; she was more so now. She had wanted so little; she had so much. Her husband's uncle had died a few years after sending his nephew to the colonies. Most of the years Quade had spent trapping in the wilderness his estate had awaited him. Managed by Eden's guardians, it had grown in wealth and holdings until the immensity of it staggered Quade and went beyond all Glory could imagine belonging to one man.

If he had not looked like a duke when he arrived on England's docks, it had taken but a few months for him to learn the part. He wore silks as well as he had worn buckskins and to Glory's eye looked as fine in the one as he had in the other.

Nor had she had any trouble exchanging her drab garb for

the lush, soft gowns her husband chose for her. She was blessed, and she never failed to be thankful on the anniversary of her hanging.

"I would do it all again," she whispered to Quade. "But for losing my mother, I would do it all again to have you."

"Aye, my lovely," Quade agreed, nuzzling her soft shoulders. "Not one thing would I leave out since it led me to you. Not even Fisk's rod—well, perhaps that."

Glory laughed. "At least you did not have a noose around your neck."

Quade placed his finger on her lips. "We have better things to talk of. A letter came from Thomas Leonard yesterday. He reports the crops were bountiful this year. And that William Cook has taken a wife."

"William? That is splendid. He has proved a great help to Thomas, has he not?"

"Aye. So the man says."

"And what of Wharton? How fares he?"

"He boasts that our trading company is but second to the Bay Company. But soon you may ask of his welfare yourself. He sails to England in two months' time. What say you? Shall we invite him to the London house or would you rather have him here?"

Glory tapped her finger against her chin. "The London house. He will have had enough of the country."

"One thing is sure," Quade said, his voice teasingly solemn. "I have not had enough of you."

Pushing the silk sheets aside he rolled atop her, losing himself in the sensual feel of her body, kissing her inviting lips, loving her, until a raucous knock sounded at the door.

"Open up," came a girlish voice. "Do you think being lord and lady of the manor gives you leave to sleep until noon? The babe is hungry and I cannot oblige her."

"Eden." Glory laughed, nudging her chagrined husband aside as she pulled the sheets modestly over the two of them. "Bring her in."

Eden Wylde was a beauty, as fair-haired as Glory was dark. Glory took the babe she carried and placed it at her breast, gently stroking the head full of tousled black curls. The babe cooed delightedly and opened a pair of dazzling blue eyes on the three who loved her.

GET
LOVESTRUCK!
AND GET STRIKING ROMANCES FROM POPULAR LIBRARY'S BELOVED AUTHORS

Watch for these exciting romances in the months to come:

POPULAR LIBRARY